Young Haudo crept along the back of the ridge, remembering everything his father had told him about tracking game. Even before he slipped his head above the ridge, he smelled the acrid stench of the minotaurs. He caught, also, the greasy fish smell of the thanoi, the walrus men. And Haudo smelled something else—a nasty odor of garbage and rancid meat. Then he peered at his village, barely keeping from coughing in the smoky haze, and his breath caught in his throat. "Two-headed beasts!" he whispered.

He wanted to jump back, to avoid seeing the image he knew would never vanish from his mind. His kinsmen, his friends, lay sprawled in death on the blood-soaked snow. Minotaurs, walrus men, and the two-headed monsters brought body after body forth from iceblock huts and skin tents. A few bodies were still twitching. An old man moaned, and one of the two-headed brutes hurried over, waving a spiked club over its head.

Overseeing it all was the robed figure of a man, silhouetted against the southern sky. . . .

The DRAGONLANCE® Saga

Chronicles Trilogy
Dragons of Autumn Twilight
Dragons of Winter Night
Dragons of Spring Dawning

Tales Trilogy
The Magic of Krynn
Kender, Gully Dwarves, and Gnomes
Love and War

Heroes Trilogy
The Legend of Huma
Stormblade
Weasel's Luck

Preludes Trilogy
Darkness and Light
Kendermore
Brothers Majere

Meetings Sextet
Kindred Spirits
Wanderlust
Dark Heart
The Oath and the Measure
Steel and Stone
The Companions (January 1993)

Legends Trilogy
Time of the Twins
War of the Twins
Test of the Twins

Tales II Trilogy
The Reign of Istar
The Cataclysm
The War of the Lance (Nov. 1992)

Heroes II Trilogy
Kaz, the Minotaur
The Gates of Thorbardin
Galen Beknighted

Preludes II Trilogy
Riverwind, the Plainsman
Flint, the King
Tanis, the Shadow Years

Elven Nations Trilogy
Firstborn
The Kinslayer Wars
The Qualinesti

The Art of the DRAGONLANCE Saga
The Atlas of the DRAGONLANCE World

The Meetings Sextet
Volume Five

STEEL and STONE

Ellen Porath

DRAGONLANCE® Saga Meetings

Volume Five

STEEL AND STONE

Copyright ©1992 TSR, Inc.
All Rights Reserved.

First Printing: September 1992
Printed in the United States of America.
Library of Congress Catalog Card Number: 91-66497

9 8 7 6 5 4 3 2 1

ISBN: 1-56076-339-6

TSR, Inc.	TSR Ltd.
P.O. Box 756	120 Church End, Cherry Hinton
Lake Geneva, WI	Cambridge CB1 3LB
53147 U.S.A.	United Kingdom

**To all who have dared to enter Darken Wood,
this book is dedicated**

With thanks to the following: Mary Kirchoff, for taking a chance on me; Pat McGilligan, for his blunt criticism; J. Eric Severson, for the book title and many nifty ideas; Bill Larson, for his careful editing; and B. Wolfgang Hoffman, for the author photo.

————

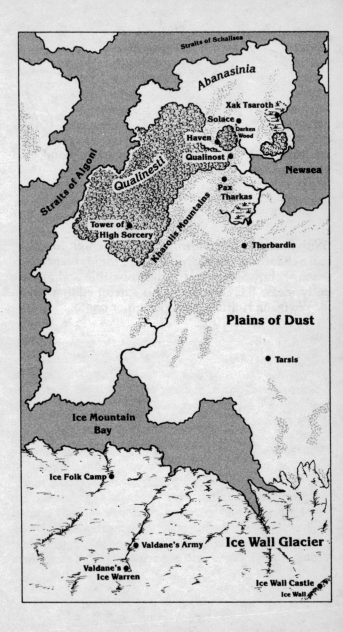

PROLOGUE

FOG HUNG LOW OVER THE DAMP GROUND, CLINGING
to scattered crusts of dirty snow as night eased into
predawn gray. A black-haired woman, mist curling
around her knee-high ebony boots, slapped canvas
tents with an ungloved hand as she wove through a
nearly silent camp. A few dozen soldiers were already
awake; they looked up and smiled as she passed.

"It's time to earn your pay, you lazy meadow slugs,"
she snapped at the slumbering men. "Get moving!" In
her wake, curses resounded. Soldiers verbally abused
the woman's ancestors as the men groped for weapons, boots, and helmets. One by one they opened tent
flaps and emerged into the winter chill. The soldiers

fastened woolen cloaks at their necks and swore at the
weather's bite.

"By the gods, couldn't the crazy Valdane and his accursed mage have waited until summer?" a bearded
man complained, glaring over a red nose and sandy
mustache toward two large tents erected uphill from
the main camp, a hundred paces away.

"Quiet, Lloiden!" his companion cautioned. An
elderly-looking man had appeared suddenly in the
opening of the smaller of the two tents and now fastened a dark gaze directly on the pair of complainers.
The old man's black robe was tied at the waist with a
silken rope, from which hung a dozen gathered
pouches. Gaunt fingers toyed with one pouch, and
Lloiden's companion went pale. He again gestured to
his tentmate to remain silent.

The woman halted her progress and turned back toward the bearded soldier. She spoke quietly. "The
head of the last man who questioned the Valdane's
judgment, or that of his mage, lies south of here, at
the last mountain pass. Some say it possesses an un-
canny resemblance to a toad's. The Valdane has the
wealth to pay his mercenaries well. That's our only
concern, Lloiden."

The first man set his chin obstinately. He waved
one hand, as if to leave the subject behind, and waited
until the mage wheeled and stalked back into his tent.
Then Lloiden continued his complaint.

"Surely the pay's one issue, but isn't strategy another?" he pressed, dew clinging to his beard. "What
are we doing attacking after a siege of only two
weeks? Why, I was at the siege of Festwild, north of
Neraka, years ago. That one lasted eighteen months,
and even then at the final surge the enemy held us
back for another three days of battle!"

Other soldiers paused in their preparations to cast curious glances at the curly-haired woman and her quarrelsome subordinate.

The woman's air of command seemed at variance with her years. She could be no older than her early twenties, they guessed. Black leather covered her body from neck to ankle, the accompanying chain mail doing little to spoil the youthful litheness of her form. Snow-marten fur warmed the neck of her woolen cloak and trimmed the tough leather that protected her arms from palm to elbow. The hilt of her sword glittered.

Lloiden's tentmate edged away. Another man whispered loudly, "Cap'n Kitiara'll have Lloiden's 'ead now fer doubtin' her ladyship's authority. This'll be good." The soldiers poked each other and grinned.

But Kitiara merely shook her head with a resignation that suggested she'd been over the subject too often. "Insane impatience," she said, agreeing. "Two weeks have barely touched the Meir's supplies. Even though the Meir has been slain, the time has done little to dishearten the castle's defenders."

"Then I repeat, why attack?" demanded Lloiden. "Why not starve them out?"

Kitiara opened her mouth, then snapped it shut again. She swept a hand through her damp, black hair, which flattened and then sprang back into curls. But there was no hint of her customary crooked grin as she glanced up at the mage's tent. "The Valdane wants a quick end to it."

Another soldier spoke, his voice just above a whisper. "Some say the Valdane fears his daughter would be able to muster Meiri forces against him."

"Especially now," a comrade agreed. "With her husband dead, the Meiri see Dreena as their only hope against her father."

Kitiara stopped and spoke again. "At any rate, the generals have gone along with the Valdane's haste, and they're not about to listen to the protests of a mere captain." She paused, her contempt for the commanders clear. "Especially with the mage backing up the Valdane's every command. Now *leave it*, Lloiden." There was no brooking her tone; Lloiden shook his head and continued his preparations.

The captain paused at her own tent and raised her voice. "Get up, Mackid! You can't be that tired. You certainly didn't keep *me* awake long last night."

The other mercenaries guffawed in appreciation, and several offered to take Caven Mackid's place in Kitiara's tent, but no answer sounded through the canvas.

"Caven?" Kitiara pulled the flap aside. The quick way she let it fall showed the onlookers that Caven Mackid was elsewhere. The half-exasperated, half-admiring glance she cast downhill toward the makeshift corral showed where she suspected Mackid might be. "Blast Maleficent," she muttered. "Would that the man paid as much attention to practicing his swordplay as he does to tending that stallion." She resumed exhorting her troops. They were gnawing a cold breakfast of cheese and dried venison as they prepared for battle.

Kitiara reached the western edge of the hillside camp and stopped to gaze toward a bank of mountains to the east. Dawn lightened the sky to gray. Far to the west, the crags of another mountain range still slept in the darkness, tree-shrouded and silent. The two ranges continued in a ragged **V** to the south, where they cradled the city of Kernen, home of the Valdane—who now crouched like a lynx at the door of his neighbor.

It was common knowledge that the Valdane had betrothed his only child to the Meir in the hope of persuading the younger man to annex the Meir's kingdom to the Valdane's. The marriage had not had the intended effect, and the Valdane had sworn vengeance.

Now Kitiara listened to the muffled clinks and oaths of a mercenary army planning to overrun the thin but loyal Meiri forces. She continued to pick her way over the slanted ground through fog and felled branches, seeking an overview of the intended battlefield. Of course, she'd been over the terrain often during the two weeks they'd camped here, but ground conditions could change quickly and treacherously in winter.

Shouts from the camp drew Kitiara's attention now. She saw mercenaries turn to face the Meir's castle, nestled in a treeless hollow below the camp. Kitiara had already noted the figure of a woman on the battlements, but she hadn't guessed who it was. Now she realized. The woman, blond hair shining nearly white, was dressed brilliantly in royal blue and blood red, the colors of the Meiri.

"Dreena ten Valdane," Kitiara whispered.

Although mist hid the bottom ten feet of the castle, the woman's slim figure made a splendid target atop the battlements, several hundred yards from her father's camp in the trees. Dreena ten Valdane stood some sixty feet above the soldiers. But that was within range of the Valdane's hired archers.

"Precisely where her husband stood last week when he took the arrow," Kitiara said softly to herself. "Perhaps she hopes to join him now." She snorted.

As Kitiara watched, Dreena ten Valdane waved

boldly at the largest tent in Kitiara's camp, the one that flew the black and purple standard of the Valdane of Kern. Then the young woman stepped back and was gone.

"She's a fool," said a black-haired, black-bearded man as he emerged from the mist near Kitiara. "Why antagonize her father like that? Her forces are bound to lose. Dreena ten Valdane will need whatever goodwill she can muster just to keep her head once this is over. The Valdane considers her an enemy as much as her late husband."

Kitiara squinted into the fog. "It's no treachery to defend your own country, Mackid."

"She's betraying her father."

"But not her husband."

Caven Mackid's tone was amused. "Is Captain Uth Matar going soft? By the gods, Kitiara, *you* defending romance?"

"Hardly. But I can appreciate her courage in standing up for someone she loves."

Caven grunted.

The sky continued to lighten, but the haze thickened and spread until it lay like a puffy blanket just above the ground. The vapor seemed to cut off Caven's and Kitiara's legs at the knees. The colorlessness of the day accentuated a certain resemblance between the man and woman—black hair, dark eyes, pale skin. But a close look at their expressions showed the similarities to be superficial. Whereas Kitiara's athletic skill made her body wiry and lithe, Caven's body bloomed with muscle. Even now, Kitiara's sidelong look showed appreciation.

"It will be difficult for the men to pick their way over uneven ground in this fog," Caven said, musing. "Perhaps the generals will decide to wait."

"Are the horses ready?" Kitiara interjected.

Her tone told Caven that bantering and chitchat were at an end. The time of battle was near.

"Maleficent and Obsidian are saddled and loaded," he said. "Wode is tending them."

"At least your squire is good for something."

"Still, he's my nephew."

Kitiara cast a brown-eyed glance at him. "Now who's turning soft?" She didn't wait for an answer. "Tell Wode to give Obsidian an extra measure of oats and to wait with the mare at the head of the western trail." She hesitated before continuing. "I don't like the feel of this battle, Caven," she admitted. "I'm not persuaded the Valdane's generals can lead us through this. They've already botched the siege, as far as I'm concerned."

Caven Mackid waited until he was sure Kitiara had finished speaking. "You expect a rout?"

Kitiara didn't answer directly. Instead, she stroked the hilt of her sword. "Go talk to Wode," she said. "And luck, friend. I fear we'll need it today."

It took only seconds for Caven to disappear into the fog and the trees. Dawn grew steadily nearer. "By the gods, why don't they sound the attack?" Kitiara whispered irritably. "We've already lost the best timing. What are they waiting for?" She took a few steps toward camp.

Voices arrested her movement. She paused and looked back downhill into the mist. Voices? Her brow furrowed, and her hand slipped again to her sword. The fog had gathered around the base of the Meir's granite castle, creeping up the walls more than a man's height. It made it appear as though the castle were floating—which Kitiara had to admit would be quite a tactical advantage. Was the fog magic-born?

Did the Meir's widow have some tricks at her disposal? Dreena was well known to be a spell-caster, although of only moderate ability. The Valdane's mage, Janusz, had taught her himself, from her girlhood on.

Dreena must know she can't match the mage, Kitiara thought to herself. He knows everything she could attempt.

Voices again. And again they came from the base of the castle. Whispers. Were the castle's occupants mounting their own attack? Kitiara looked back uphill toward her own camp. There was no time to go back for Caven or other reinforcements, and no sense in sounding an unnecessary alarm. Perhaps she was hearing the whispering of her own soldiers, reflected eerily off the stone castle.

"This infernal mist," Kitiara whispered. Drawing her sword, she used the fog and shrubbery as a cover and crept toward the sound. She could see almost nothing, could barely see her own feet, but she continued to edge forward.

The voices seemed to be coming from the left now. Suddenly the gray granite of the castle loomed before Kitiara like the huge tombstone of some prehistoric god. Despite herself, a startled sound burst from Kitiara's throat. She saw the silhouette of a bush growing out of the castle base and threw herself behind it.

"Who's there?" It was a woman's voice, an imperious voice accustomed to giving orders. Kitiara drew farther behind the bush and peered through the foliage. A woman appeared out of the vapor, only twenty feet distant but facing away from Kitiara. "Who is it?" the woman repeated into the mist. She waited, then swiveled to face the castle again. "Lida?" Her voice was fraught with sudden fear.

Kitiara caught her breath again, but silently this time, as the woman turned and the mercenary saw her cheek, then the side of her nose, then those unmistakable turquoise eyes. Dreena ten Valdane, outside the castle? Kitiara's thoughts raced as she tried to decide what to do.

It was clear that Dreena was disoriented by the fog. Why didn't she use her magic to probe the mist? The answer came to Kit instantly: Because if Dreena did, Janusz would sense where she was.

Dreena no longer sported the red and blue that she'd worn atop the battlements. Instead, her body was covered with shapeless homespun cloth in earth tones. A finger of fog curled around the woman. When the mist dissipated, Dreena was gone.

Kitiara gasped and rose from her half-crouch. She forced herself to be silent, to listen; she caught the sound of slippered feet hurrying down a damp footpath. Then—nothing. Kitiara stood erect, sword still ready. She shook her head. There was no point in remaining. Dreena was gone, and Kitiara had lost the chance to capture her. The woman could be anywhere under cover of this fog.

With an oath, Kitiara sheathed her sword and dashed through the mist toward the mercenary camp. With every step she took away from the castle, the fog lost a handspan in height, until it was again hugging only her knees as her slim figure flashed through the trees, past the tents, and up the incline to the mage's and Valdane's quarters. Soldiers gaped as she passed. She could see that Lloiden was again holding forth on the stupidity of the current campaign.

No guard waited at either tent. Pausing to take a deep breath and recover her air of assurance, Kitiara entered the largest tent, the one with the black and

9

purple pennant dangling above it.

It was as warm within the tent as it was bone-chilling and damp without, and the occupants of the shelter glared at the intruder. The Valdane, a red-haired man of middle age, was hissing something at the mage. Janusz looked decades older than the Valdane but was, according to rumor, actually a year or so younger. Kitiara pointedly ignored the two generals, and they ignored her, busy as they were quailing under a tirade of the Valdane.

"I will *not* attack until we are sure where Dreena is!" the Valdane was saying. "Janusz has tried his magical skills several times since she left the battlements, but he cannot find her. We know only that she's alive. I *must* know where she waits before we risk an attack." He pounded the main tent pole for emphasis. The generals swallowed as the pole creaked and the canvas swayed. Janusz barked a single word, and the poplar pole became still. The generals glanced uneasily at each other.

Cowards, Kitiara thought. With a younger brother who was a mage, she was more at ease with spellcasting than were the often superstitious denizens of the region northeast of Neraka.

The men continued to ignore her. Kitiara raised her voice and interrupted. "Dreena ten Valdane has escaped."

The men pivoted back toward her. Kitiara felt the right corner of her mouth quirk. It was funny, really—frightened little generals swiveling back and forth like puppets jerked by strings. The Valdane squinted at her; she squelched a smile.

"My daughter has left the castle?" he demanded.

Kitiara kept her gaze steady, her voice clear. "Moments ago. I saw her myself."

"You are sure?" the mage pressed. "I have been scrying . . ." A look from the Valdane silenced him.

One of the generals, the self-important one, spoke up. "We must be certain," he said ponderously, narrowing his eyes and rubbing his chin. "It is better if she has fled. If Dreena ten Valdane were to be killed in combat, it could arouse the Meiri peasants to our disadvantage."

The second general chimed in. "The Meiri peasants were fond of the Meir, but they adore his wife. We'd best be sure the captain is correct." His stare indicated that he, at least, didn't think Kitiara was reliable. "I suggest we wait," he concluded.

Kitiara ignored the two and spoke to the Valdane. "I am as sure that Dreena has left the Meir's castle as I am that I stand before you now." Her gaze never wavered.

The leader nodded to Janusz. "Mount the attack."

Janusz bowed and left, and the generals scattered. Kitiara waited at the Valdane's tent until the mage, his thin white hair fluttering above the collar of his black robe, disappeared into his own tent before she followed. When she reached the mage's tent, she stationed herself by the tent flap, eased it open a finger's width, and watched. Knowledge was power, her mercenary father had often reminded her. It wouldn't hurt to know more about the mysterious mage.

Janusz looked neither right nor left as he moved directly to his cot and pulled out a trunk that lay beneath it. He released a pinch of gray dust into the air and whispered, *"Rrachelan,"* releasing a magical lock. Then he slung up the heavy lid, reached inside, and drew out a sandalwood box carved with silhouettes of minotaurs and seal-like creatures with huge tusks.

He repeated the incantation, with a slight difference

in intonation, then opened the box. A look of relief spread across his face. "The power of ten lifetimes for the man who unlocks it," he whispered. Kitiara felt the hair rise on the back of her neck.

Janusz's fingers disappeared into the box and emerged with two—two what? "Gems" was the obvious word, but the stones were more than gems. They glowed with unearthly light. Once, traveling south of the Khurman Sea, two hundred miles to the south, Kitiara had seen a necklace of amethysts that had gleamed violet in lamplight but, outside, had deepened to the purple-blue of the darkest ocean. Those Khurman stones, however, were mere pebbles compared to these. These radiated the heat of light and the cold of winter.

Ice, Kitiara thought; they looked like glowing, purple ovals of ice, the size of robins' eggs. She'd never seen anything so beautiful. Her breath quickened.

The mage had said they held power. Kitiara knew he spoke the truth.

"Mage!" The Valdane was shouting from his own tent. The spell-caster looked up and caught Kitiara spying on him at the opening of his tent. He hurriedly slipped the two stones into a pocket of his robe, and the weird purple light went out as completely as if the gems had never existed. Shaking with anger, Janusz could barely speak. "Return to your post, Captain," he choked out. "And forget what you've seen here, lest you suddenly find yourself with the head of an eel."

Kitiara made a show of moving away from the tent flap, but seconds later, she peered back in. The mage was taking the deep breath that Kitiara had seen her brother, Raistlin, use to cleanse his thoughts and focus his attention on spell-casting. Then Janusz turned and swept from the tent, scant seconds after Kitiara had dodged around the corner of the mage's lodging.

The mage moved to a clearing in the trees downhill from the tents. He was in clear view of the castle. His hands twitched. It was as if Janusz's fingers had lives of their own as they danced through the complex movements that accompanied the spell.

"Ecanaba ladston, zhurack!" the mage intoned.

Kitiara felt her face tingle, and she looked away. She heard Janusz continue his chanting. Was he turning her into an eel after all? She looked around, seeking something shiny, a mirror or pool of melted snow that might tell her if she was still Kitiara Uth Matar. Even as she looked, however, a voice in her brain reminded her that the mage hadn't locked the box. Sudden thunder distracted her. She looked up.

Now clouds coalesced in columns above the Meir's castle, forming a thunderhead as high as a dozen castles. The sky above the mercenary camp was suddenly clear. The soldiers abandoned their duties. Frozen, mouths agape, they watched as the mage on the hillside drew the forces of nature into his grasp and commanded them against his enemy. On the parapets, the castle's occupants were nearly as still. They gazed upward with dawning horror.

The cloud throbbed above them. Lightning bolts of yellow, blue, and red burst from the churning mist. Thunder reverberated inside Kitiara's head. She forced herself to remember to breathe. Her knees felt watery, and she leaned against a tree. If she'd had to defend herself now, she would have been felled as easily as a young sapling. But no attacker advanced against the mercenaries.

Then suddenly the cloud opened, and fire poured down upon the defenders of the castle.

Soldiers, peasants, and nobles screamed and sought frantically, futilely, to escape the liquid flame. Some managed to remove their clothing, only to discover that the brimstone adhered to their skin. Many, to avoid lingering deaths, dove to quick ones off the castle walls. Others tried in vain to protect the castle, shooting arrows toward the surrounding army as it waited safely out of reach of danger.

Impotent against the brimstone, the Meir's supporters burned to death where they stood. The wooden gate of the castle exploded. The top floor of the castle collapsed. A section of the castle wall cracked open. Through it, Kitiara saw the contents of water troughs boil and bubble. Then the troughs, too, exploded.

So great was Janusz's control that the mercenaries felt none of the fire, felt only a comfortable warmth beneath their feet. A hot wind streamed through the camp, and that, too, was almost pleasant, given the dampness they'd grown accustomed to. But the wind also carried ashes, and the eyes of the mercenaries streamed with tears.

The wise ones held the wool of their cloaks before their mouths and noses. Lloiden did not. He collapsed, choking, to the ground before his tent, and Kitiara wondered if Janusz was avenging the insolence of a few hours earlier.

And then it was over. The fiery rain stopped as suddenly as it had begun. The cloud hissed into nothingness. The mercenaries released their breath. What once had been an imposing castle was nothing but steaming wreckage. The opening still gaped at the front of the castle, but still no one dared enter. The air was thick with ashes and the horrible smell of charred flesh.

One quavering voice rose out of the camp. "So why'd he bother to hire *us?*" the soldier asked.

Then the Valdane appeared around the back of Janusz's tent. He pointed his sword at Kitiara where she still leaned against the tree. "Attack!" he screamed, his face red with anger. "I hired you to annihilate my enemy! Now do it!"

"Valdane," Kitiara said wearily, forcing herself to stand upright, "there *is* no enemy. Your mage has killed them all."

But the leader waved his sword like a child tilting at an imaginary monster. "You will make sure, Captain! I want to be certain they're all dead."

Kitiara tried again. "Valdane, no one could possibly sur—"

"Find them!"

There was no defying him. Janusz, looking half-dead with the effort that the fiery rain had cost him, dragged himself up the hill. His voice was barely audible, his face streaked with ash and sweat. "Valdane, it's too hot in the wreckage for our soldiers to venture inside."

"Then send rain!"

Janusz took a long look at the Valdane, then turned soundlessly and stumbled back down the incline. Kitiara heard more chanting.

"It's raining!" a soldier shouted.

It was true. There were no clouds, yet the mage had created a gentle shower, warmed by the heat of the smoldering, hissing castle. One of the generals, the self-important one, ordered troops to advance into the Meir's castle. Kitiara's troops, the general commanded, were to stand guard around the stricken building's perimeter.

The soldiers had no sooner marched between the

smoldering columns that once had flanked the main gate when a cry went up from the advance guard of Kitiara's men. The cry passed from man to man and finally became audible. "We are attacked!"

"*What?*" the Valdane shrieked. His blue eyes bulged; he swept his sword back and forth more wildly. "Mage!"

Kitiara drew her sword from its scabbard and ran a few paces downhill to join her troops, but the Valdane called her back. "Get the mage and meet me in my tent!" he ordered.

"But my men . . ." Kitiara looked down at them. Already she could see them falling before hundreds of mounted nobles dressed in scarlet and royal blue, followed by swarms of peasants armed with hoes, axes, and plow blades mounted on staffs. Inefficient weapons, perhaps, but not in the hands of men and women defending their homes and lives.

The smell of smoke and mud thick in her nostrils, Kitiara ran down the hill and approached the mage. Janusz sat upon a boulder, face ashen, eyes closed, hands lying limp on his lap, palms upward. "The Valdane wants to see you, mage," Kitiara said.

His eyes opened. Kitiara had to lean toward him to catch his words. "I . . . have nothing left," Janusz whispered. "No strength." He coughed and closed his eyes again.

"We've been attacked by a large force of Meiri," Kitiara insisted.

"I know."

"Perhaps more fire—?"

The mage cast her a withering look and shook his head contemptuously. Kitiara remembered, from her brother, the rules of magic; once used, a spell vanished from the spell-caster's head until he could study it again. Great magic took a great physical toll. Asking more of Janusz now could kill him.

"But the Valdane—" she tried again.

"I will come. Give me your arm."

Kitiara helped the mage up the hill into the Valdane's tent and eased him onto a bench before the leader's small desk. She retreated to a spot by the door, but she didn't leave. One of the generals, streaked with blood, shoved her aside and entered the tent. "Valdane, we are losing!" he blurted.

The Valdane stood, eyes snapping blue below his carrot-red hair. "How can that be?"

"They outnumber us seven to one."

"But I hired you to defeat the Meiri!" The Valdane advanced upon the mercenary leader, his hand upon his sword hilt.

The general looked desperate. "We must retreat. Perhaps we can gather in the mountains and regroup. . . ." He stepped backward.

"No!" Quickly the Valdane drew his short sword and thrust it into the general's abdomen, jerking the weapon abruptly to one side to deepen the gash. The general collapsed, dead, in a puddle of his own blood.

The Valdane leaned over and yanked the badge of office from the corpse. He handed the blood-daubed crest to Kitiara. "General Uth Matar," the Valdane said soberly, "take command."

Kitiara swallowed. The mage, in the background, was smiling with ill-concealed contempt. She'd been named general of a losing army, answering to an insane leader who executed his defeated generals. No wonder Janusz was gleeful. Kitiara wouldn't survive the day, and the mage's purple jewels would remain his secret.

The Valdane's face showed that he thought he was

doing Kitiara an honor. "Thank you, sir," she said, barely keeping the irony out of her voice. She stepped over the corpse of her predecessor and resumed her position by the door. As soon as the Valdane's attention was focused on the mage, she slipped through the flap and sped toward her own tent. On the way, she hurled the general's crest into the mud.

Kitiara slowed as she passed the mage's quarters. Janusz was occupied in the Valdane's tent, and he was severely weakened now. Kitiara was practically certain that he hadn't set the wards that protected the sandalwood box. She hesitated. It was a safe bet the Valdane wouldn't be hunting down his defeated mercenaries to pay them the wages owed them. If she was going to flee the battlefield, she might as well take her pay with her, in the form of a purple jewel or two.

Kitiara looked around and slipped into the tent. In a second, she was on her knees before the trunk. She took a deep breath and, hoping the mage hadn't left a magical snake within to guard his wealth, she lifted the heavy lid. Nothing happened. She pulled out the sandalwood box. If the mage had set wards anywhere, it would be here. She lifted the box's lid. Again nothing.

She forgot her worries as the glow of nine purple stones streamed up from the sandalwood box. "The power of ten lifetimes," the mage had said. Perhaps she could unlock that power. She'd need a mage to help her. And what better mage than her own brother, Raistlin, back in the city of Solace? He'd been studying at a school for mages since he was a boy. She knew he was gifted; certainly he was loyal.

This would require some thought.

At the moment, however, the situation required action more than thought. Cursing her reverie, she scooped the nine stones into a pocket and dashed from the room.

She met Wode, Caven's squire, at the appointed place. The lanky youngster was holding Obsidian's bridle and staying out of range of a stamping black stallion tied to an oak. Saying nothing, Kitiara wrenched the reins from Wode and mounted the mare. She was pulling the horse around when a voice hailed her.

Kitiara pulled up. "Caven, I'm leaving."

He vaulted onto Maleficent, his stallion. Caven was the only one who could handle the beast, whom he'd acquired in a game of bones with a minotaur on Mithas. "I'm going with you."

"But—" Kitiara began.

"I'm going," he interrupted doggedly. He gestured to Wode, and the teen-ager dashed away.

Kitiara decided she might need him. Especially now. "Let's go." She could always ditch Caven later, she thought.

In moments, the two ebony horses with their black-haired riders vanished into the trees. Within minutes, Wode, mounted on a rangy brown nag, clattered after them.

Behind them, the battle neared a bloody end. The mage, leaning heavily on a staff, and the Valdane strode into Janusz's tent. "Use the stones," the leader ordered.

"Not yet," Janusz said, dropping onto his cot.

"You said they were powerful."

"They require much study," the mage protested. "I don't know their secrets yet."

"Use them!"

Wearily rising to his feet, the mage stepped to the sandalwood box, began the spell to unlock the box, then stopped in midincantation. Hands shaking, he reached out. The lid came up easily. The mage looked up, horror and anger warring on his gray face, then stared back into the sandalwood box. "They're gone!" he whispered. "That bitch!" Janusz, his lips thin, reached into his pocket and pulled out two glowing stones. "She has nine, while only one may be enough to rule Krynn, for all I know."

A shout sounded outside. The self-important general entered, nervousness apparent in every twitch of his hands. "We have found the body of your son-in-law, Valdane," he said, adding unnecessarily, "the Meir."

"So?" snapped the leader. "We knew he died days ago, in the first attack. Go away or get to the point. I have greater problems."

The general looked deflated. "The corpse of a woman lies at the coffin's foot."

"Do I care? Who is it?"

"It . . . it appears to be the body of the Meir's wife."

The Valdane grew deadly quiet, then spoke. "Kitiara swore Dreena escaped."

"It appears Captain Uth Matar was wrong, Valdane," the general said, his words thick with spite. "The body wears the wedding jewelry of Dreena ten Valdane—the malachite owl on a chain of silver thread. The chain is melted, but the stone is identifiable."

The Valdane's voice remained quiet. "Dreena would never part with that."

"By the dark god Morgion," Janusz said brokenly at last. His words rasped. "Dreena died in the magefire. And I . . ." He swayed and leaned heavily against the trunk that once held the sandalwood box. His voice trailed off. Dazed, he watched as the general met the same fate as his colleague only minutes before.

As the general choked out his last, the Valdane swung back to the mage. His face was colorless; his fists were clenched.

"As you value your life, mage, find Kitiara Uth Matar. Bring her to me. I will see her die."

Chapter I

Meeting in the Dark

The scream shredded the night like a broad-axe cleaves the head of an ogre.

Wayfarers in the woods learned to awaken in a hurry, or they didn't awaken at all. In an eyeblink, Tanis Half-Elven leaped into awareness and, with a smoothness born of many nights spent in lonely camps, pulled his longsword from his pallet. He swept sand over the campfire embers with one kick of a bare foot and froze, sword extended diagonally before him. Tanis pivoted slowly and waited, his elven night-vision probing deep into the surrounding underbrush.

Nothing. The breeze barely disturbed the spring leaves of the maple saplings that crowded around him. The wind wafted the scent of mud and decayed plants from the White-rage River to the north but carried no sound beyond the stream's gurgle and the creaking of the ageless oaks overhead. Both moons, silver Solinari and scarlet Lunitari, were waning, and the clearing's darkness would have been nearly impenetrable to anyone but a night-seeing elf.

Then, twanging against Tanis's nerves like fingers on a mistuned lyre, the scream came again. From the north, he realized.

The half-elf caught up bow and quiver and raced through the night, the fringe of his leather shirt snapping with his speed. The night creatures of the inland forest—skunks, opossums, and raccoons—flattened against the ground as the half-elf pounded past. His steps were lighter than those of his human kin, but far heavier than those of the elven brethren he'd left behind weeks earlier in Qualinost.

Tanis paused at a cleft in the path, waiting for a clue to send him down either left or right. The left wandered generally north and west, ending several days' journey away in Haven. The right path eventually ended at the White-rage gorge, pointing, across the river, toward Darken Wood. Rumors were rife of creatures, both alive and not quite alive, that made the forbidding wood their home. There was little in the way of firsthand knowledge about Darken Wood; people who ventured in rarely came out.

At that moment, another scream sent the half-elf sprinting along the left fork. Tanis dashed into a clearing in the oaks and maples in time to see a human, with a shout of satisfaction, plunge a longsword into a hairy behemoth. The victim, wearing blood-red armor, fell with a scream. The creature's weapon, a type of spiked cudgel called a morning star, rolled into the undergrowth.

"Hobgoblins!" the half-elf breathed. He slid to a halt in the decaying litter of the clearing.

Three monsters lay motionless. Three other snarling creatures, a head taller than Tanis, loomed over the slender human. They jabbed spears, twitched whips, and swung morning stars. All boasted the bluish noses of the hobgoblin warriors. One beast leaped forward, the watery moonlight of waning Solinari painting its red-orange skin with a silvery patina.

The hobgoblin waved a cudgel over the human's helmed head. The human deftly sidestepped, and the hobgoblin's eyes glowed yellow under its headpiece. The air reeked of blood, flattened plants, mud, and unwashed hobgoblin. The creatures stank of carrion and a hundred battles. The human, a lithe figure, decapitated the attacking hobgoblin with a slash and an oath, but the creature's fist struck the human a glancing blow as the monster fell, snapping the strap that held the helmet. The helm fell back, revealing a pallid face topped with curly dark hair.

"A woman?" Tanis demanded loudly. The new sound attracted the two remaining hobgoblins, who swung around to look toward Tanis.

The woman cast the half-elf a furious look and switched her sword from her right hand to her left. She straightened the helm on her head, mindless of the broken strap, and flicked the tip of her weapon, slicing an arc across the brawny arm of a monster. "Don't get cocky," she snapped in Common at the hobgoblin. "I could finish you at any time."

The creature grunted and retreated, but its companion continued to peer at the new intruder in the shadows. It abandoned its fight with the human, thundering toward the half-elf. "*Turash koblani!* Kill!"

Tanis dropped into a fighting stance as the hobgoblin, dogged by its partner, raced across the clearing. The woman stormed a few paces behind.

"*Turash koblani!*" The hobgoblin raised a sword streaked with what Tanis guessed was blood—and probably human blood; a dark streak smeared one bare leg of the woman, who had leaped onto a stump with another cry. The movement brought her eye level with the monsters.

Tanis swung up his bow and swept an arrow from his quiver with the smooth motion that was second nature to Qualinesti elves.

The human raised her sword and aimed a deadly stroke at one hobgoblin. "Prepare to die, son of a gully dwarf!" she called mockingly, but the hobgoblins, who hated everything elven, remained focused on the half-elf. With their swords, the hobgoblins swatted halfheartedly at the woman. They moved to keep this annoying, deadly female human in their side vision while concentrating on the half-elf.

"Run, girl!" Tanis shouted. "Save yourself!"

She cast him a withering look, one dark brow cocked above a sardonic eye. Then she laughed and slashed the hamstrings of one hobgoblin as Tanis sent an arrow into the breast of the other. The two monsters fell bellowing, and Tanis dropped his bow and finished off the hamstrung hobgoblin with a thrust of his sword. Then he turned to the woman.

Tanis was prepared for any reaction but the one he got. The woman unleashed a string of epithets that would have shriveled the soul of a Caergoth dockworker. Hatred blazed from her eyes. Tanis had never heard such invective—not, at least, from the mouth of a woman. He froze, hazel eyes wide, and she slammed him with the flat of her sword, sending him tumbling to the damp earth. His longsword flew out of reach with the unexpectedness of her assault. The half-elf lay immobile atop his quiver, broken arrows strewn around him, as she stood straddling him, laying to the right and left with her sword, chopping plants and snapping sticks with angry motions. Of average height for a human woman, she looked seven feet tall from this angle. And as strong as a minotaur.

While he was but half elf, Tanis was still Qualinesti enough to avoid mortal combat with a woman—even one whose swordplay would put the average man to shame. Although the Qualinesti women were trained in the use of bow and sword, the practice was more ceremonial than practical, and no Qualinesti male really expected to cross weapons with a female of the race. Looking up at the battle-hardened body of his human tormentor, however, Tanis felt his palms grow slick with apprehension. A trickle of perspiration trailed back from his brow and dripped through his rust-red hair. The smell of rotting leaves was thick.

"Idiot! Interferer!" she fumed, decapitating a currant bush. Leaf fragments rained on Tanis. "I had the situation well under control, half-elf!"

"But . . ." Tanis's right hand cast through the slippery leaves and closed on an arrow; any weapon at all would help if this crazed woman lost her tenuous grip on her temper.

Her blade, dripping hobgoblin blood, swept to the right of Tanis's head and whacked off a trista blossom; the blade found its way unerringly to the bare inch of stem below the ground-hugging white blossom. Tanis marveled at her control.

"How *dare* you spoil my fun?" she spat out.

Tanis tried again. "Fun? It was six against . . ."

The sword blade halted above him, and the half-elf

had the notion that the woman was moments away from plunging the weapon into his ribs. He bit off his protest and tensed, ready to fling himself aside if an attack came.

Tanis probed the darkness for anything he could use to vanquish her. His elvensight, sensitive to heat released from objects, showed little but a half-dozen rapidly cooling hobgoblin corpses, two of which were only a few feet away.

"Eight," the woman corrected at last. "It was eight hobgoblins to one. Near-even odds for me. You missed the two by the river." She paused. "Although I'm sure you heard them." A crooked smile creased her face for the first time, and Tanis felt the deadly moment pass.

"Eight hobgoblins," he echoed, swallowing.

"I'm no amateur, half-elf. I've been a mercenary for over half a decade," she said.

How many enemies, Tanis wondered, had heard those silken tones as their life's blood drained away?

But the voice continued, warming again as to an old injury. "And when the day comes," she ranted, "that I can't trounce eight hobgoblins without help from a half-dressed half-man, half-elf, I'll gladly retire!"

She raised her sword in a mock salute to Tanis, wiped the bloody blade on a leg of his fringed breeches, then slid the weapon into a battle-scarred scabbard. Insolently she let her gaze flicker over the supine half-elf. His pointed ears, his most obvious elven heritage, showed through his shoulder-length hair. Her dark eyes also took in the broad shoulders and muscled chest that broadcast his human blood, and her smile grew wider. Tanis felt a flame ripple through him; then he shivered as the dampness of the ground permeated the back of his shirt.

27

Above him, the woman thrust out a hand. "Kitiara Uth Matar," she proclaimed. "Originally of Solace, most recently of wider horizons. Including the employ of numerous lords who are my business only." She raised a mocking eyebrow and stood back, arm stretched toward him. "Come on, half-elf. Get up!" She gestured impatiently. "Afraid of a woman?" Her smile curved lopsidedly again.

After some hesitation, Tanis met her handclasp, but she dipped forward at the last instant, clenching his forearm with a strong right hand. He, in turn, ended up grasping her arm at the elbow. Then the woman stepped back and began to haul upward, raising the half-elf despite his greater weight. "My name is Tanthalas," he said, letting himself be drawn to a half-seated position. "Also most recently of Solace."

"Tanthalas," she repeated. "A Qualinesti name."

"I was raised there. Most humans call me Tanis."

"Tanis, then."

He returned her smile in what he hoped was a disingenuous manner. Suddenly he tightened his grip on her arm and pulled her toward him. Kitiara's eyes widened in surprise. She began falling forward, and Tanis braced for the impact of her body on his. He would flip her; she deserved it—he'd tip her over and sit on her like a big brother until she cried uncle. He relished the thought.

But Kitiara, after her initial surprise, caught herself. Obviously guessing her opponent's intent, she used her momentum against him. Her right arm still caught in Tanis's grasp, she dove over him into the beginnings of a somersault.

Tanis refused to loosen his grip on Kitiara's arm. Her somersault halted in midflip, and she landed, with an exhalation of breath, on her back.

Tanis released his hold, then rolled onto his left side and leaped to his feet. He scrambled toward the woman and lunged, his body slamming down perpendicular over hers. But she foresaw his movement and balled up a fist before her, bracing her elbow against the earth. She waited, her gaze calm.

Tanis twisted aside and took the fist high, in the gut. He lay on the ground, frozen, struggling to regain his breath as Kitiara shoved him off her, rolled gracefully to her hip, and rose to her feet. Irritably she removed her helm and examined the broken strap. She brushed fragments of slimy leaves off her legs and arms.

She raised a hand in farewell, her expression mocking. "Don't think me ungrateful, Tanthalas. Maybe the next damsel you rush to save will actually *need* your help."

She watched him a moment, pivoted, and stalked away. The word "weakling" drifted back to him, with a bark of laughter. As soon as her back was turned, however, the half-elf ceased his feigned collapse and rose to his feet, using techniques of stealth perfected through years of living with the forest-wise Qualinesti. He moved carefully through the damp leaves, nearly soundlessly—to a human's ears, at least. Then he dove toward Kitiara, crashing into her shoulder, clasping his arms around her waist, and entwining his leg with hers. He yanked to one side.

One moment he was locked around Kitiara, breathing her odor of sweat and a deeper, musky scent. The next second, Tanis was sailing through the air over her head, flipping like a cat struggling to land on its feet. He hit the ground with a grunt, ripping his leather shirt down the front. Kitiara glanced at his bare chest and nodded appreciatively even as she dropped into a half-crouch. Tanis matched her stance. They circled in the dark, two shadows facing each other, each waiting for an opening. Neither drew a sword.

"Tanis, you begin to annoy me," Kitiara said. Her words were laconic, but her lithe body was tense.

What a magnificent woman, Tanis found himself thinking, but his mind tallied the corpses of hobgoblins. Even as he admired Kitiara, he wondered if anyone could tame her.

"Are you so weak that you descend to attacking someone from the back?" Kitiara taunted. "Wouldn't a *brave* man have met me face-to-face?" She darted toward him, and the half-elf leaped backward. They resumed their slow circling. Tanis could hear her consciously slowing her breath, seeking equilibrium, finding balance. His nightvision gave him an edge in the dimness, but she didn't appear bothered by the dark. Kitiara's eyes were luminous. Tanis couldn't take his gaze from her oval face. He traded her taunt for taunt. Half-elf and woman continued to circle. Kitiara's foot twisted on a stick, but she caught herself. Her words betrayed no trace of weariness. "I must tell you, Tanis, that I am *very* used to getting what—or whom—I want." Her gaze was direct.

At that moment, Kitiara stepped directly in front of one of the hobgoblin corpses. Tanis feinted, and Kitiara attempted to counter, but she stumbled against the hobgoblin's outstretched arm and, this time, recovered too slowly. With a lightning move, Tanis tripped her with his heel and let himself fall on top of her.

Her body took the brunt of the impact. Kitiara winced as she struck the packed earth of the clearing, but she didn't cry out. She reached for her sword, but Tanis wrenched her hands away, pinning her wrists to the ground at shoulder level, her elbows bent. He intertwined his legs with hers, immobilizing the proud woman who hurled curses into his face.

Then Tanis stopped, staring at Kitiara. Suddenly he became aware of the curves and hollows of the body beneath his. As she glared up at him, her look of fury gradually changed to amusement.

"Well?" she said, and raised an eyebrow.

"Well," he replied. He pulled himself back a bit.

Her crooked smile snared him. "Here we are."

Tanis breathed musk deep into his lungs. Kitiara raised both brows mockingly and stared pointedly at the muscles gaping through Tanis's torn shirt. Her look dared him. Tanis muttered an old elven oath; Kitiara's smile grew wider. He held himself motionless. No good could come from a union between human and elf, he knew only too well.

Tanis suddenly wished he'd checked this Kitiara Uth Matar for a hidden dagger. But there was no going back now.

* * * * *

Later that night, as Tanis slept on Kitiara's pallet in her camp, the swordswoman eased away from the half-elf and reached for her pack, between pallet and fire. Checking once more to make sure the half-elf was sleeping, Kitiara slipped a hand into the pack, shoving aside spare clothing and provisions as she groped for the catch of the pack's false bottom. Barely breathing, she eased the piece of stiff canvas to one side and peered into the pack. Violet light streamed into the clearing. She let her fingers dance over the source of the glow. ". . . eight, nine," she murmured. "All there." She sighed and smiled, as with sweet contentment, but her eyes glittered.

Chapter 2

Danger Shared

"And so when my half-brothers were born, I took care of Raistlin and Caramon. My mother . . . couldn't," Kitiara concluded. That one word masked so much—her mother's frequent trances and illness, and those weeks on end that the woman spent in bed while Kitiara, with some help from her stepfather, tended the twins.

"When they were six and Raistlin had been admitted to the mage school, I left Solace. That was a long time ago—seven, ten years." She kept her tone off-hand.

"This is your first trip back to Solace?" Tanis asked, guiding his heavy-boned gelding, Dauntless, around an outcropping of rocks. He kept the chestnut horse on the easier path of beaten earth. One hand pulled the leather headband from his forehead; the other wiped the sweat from his face. Then he replaced the band. The summer heat was oppressive, even on the shaded path.

"I come back now and then." Kitiara shrugged. "I was there when my mother died, and a few other times. I bring the twins presents and money when I have any."

"You don't seem . . ." Tanis bit off the words.

Kitiara surveyed him. "What, half-elf?" When he failed to go on, she reached over toward him and, smiling, prodded the half-elf with a fist until he grimaced.

"For someone who hasn't seen her brothers in a year, you don't seem to be in much of a hurry to get back," Tanis finally said. "We've been on the road more than a month, and you haven't pushed the pace at all. In fact," he added, warming to the topic, "you were the one who insisted on taking off after the horax."

The six-foot-long, insectlike monster had burst into camp one morning more than two weeks ago, rampaging through their belongings and making off with Kitiara's pack. The creature, built low to the ground, with armorlike plates protecting it from its mandible to its rearmost pair of legs, had twelve legs and possessed frightening quickness and ferocity.

Kitiara's first suspicion had been that the Valdane's mage had sent the horax after her to recover the pack and the ice jewels. But she dispelled that notion when the carnivorous creature, after some wandering, finally had simply returned to its subterranean colony. She and the half-elf had taken advantage of an early-morning cold snap, which slowed the cold-blooded creature and several of its mates.

The campaign against the horax had drawn them back south and west into the forests of Qualinesti, Tanis's turf, but still far off their planned route to Solace. The expedition had taken up half of the one month that had elapsed since Tanis and Kitiara's initial skirmish with the hobgoblins. Now the travelers, the pack restored to its spot behind Kitiara's saddle, were several miles south of Haven.

"I still think it would have been easier for you to get a new pack," Tanis persisted. "That one looks like it's been through a civil war."

"Well, it has," Kitiara muttered defensively.

"So why were you so determined to get it back?" He gazed at her inquisitively, but his expression was mild.

She bristled. "I told you it's none of your business."

Tanis brushed aside her protest like one of the flies that circled in the heat. "I risked my life for it, Kit."

Kitiara slapped the saddle's pommel. "I have a business arrangement to discuss with Raistlin," she said heatedly. "Some of the . . . background information . . . is in the pack."

"That explains why you were bent on pursuing the horax," he said doggedly. "It doesn't explain why you're in no hurry to meet with your brother now."

By the gods, the half-elf was nosy! "I'm still working on the plan," she said hotly. "You could have gone on without me, half-elf. It wasn't your fight. You could have gone on to meet your dwarf friend in Solace."

"As though I'd abandon a woman and let her take on a carnivorous monster alone."

Kitiara whipped a dagger from a sheath. Before Tanis could draw another breath, he was gazing at the point of the wicked weapon. He didn't seem terribly impressed with her lightning speed, however, which enraged the swordswoman all the more. Kitiara finally spoke, spitting out each word. "Half-elf, I do *not* need a man to protect me!"

Astoundingly, Tanis smiled. Then he threw his head back and laughed. "Of course, Kit. Of course."

Kitiara sheathed the dagger, still fuming. They rode on for a mile without speaking. Finally Tanis, with an apologetic look, broke the silence. "Can I help you? With your plan, I mean?"

The mercenary snorted. "As if you could."

"I handle Flint Fireforge's metalsmithing dealings, and no one is more disorganized than that dwarf when it comes to business. I might be able to make some suggestions for you and your brother."

Kitiara looked at Tanis. "Thanks, but no thanks," was all she said.

Tanis didn't seem bothered by Kitiara's rejection of his offer of help. The two rode companionably, side by side, for nearly an hour through the late afternoon calm. When Kitiara finally spoke again, however, it was as though only a short time had elapsed.

"You don't seem in any great hurry to get back to Solace yourself," she commented. "What about this dwarf friend of yours? Won't he be wondering where you are?"

The half-elf shook his head. "Flint knows I went to Qualinost to visit my relatives. He knows I'll be back whenever I get back."

Kitiara reached out, pulled a leaf from an overhanging sycamore tree, and casually began to shred it. "Relatives? Your parents?"

Tanis hesitated before answering. "My mother's dead. My mother's husband's brother raised me."

"Mother's husband's . . ." Kitiara looked in confusion at Tanis. "Not your father?" She tried to sort out what he'd already told her in light of this new information. "But you said you were raised in the court of the Speaker of the Sun." She couldn't hide that she was impressed; everybody knew the Speaker of the Sun was the leader of the Qualinesti nation. "Did the Speaker's brother marry a human? I thought humans haven't been in Qualinost in centuries."

"If ever," Tanis said tersely. "My mother was an elf. My father was human."

Kitiara jerked on Obsidian's reins. The well-trained mare halted in midstride. "All right, now I'm lost," the swordswoman confessed. "The elven Speaker's brother is human?"

Tanis looked away. "Can't we just leave this be?"

"Fine." Kitiara kicked Obsidian into a canter. "Your parentage makes no difference to me, half-elf." Her back was stiff as she rode off.

Tanis sat motionless on Dauntless for a few moments, deep in thought, while Kitiara rode on ahead without a glance back. At last, as she was disappearing around a curve, the half-elf hailed her. She waited atop the black mare as the gelding pounded up.

The half-elf didn't look at Kitiara. "My mother was married to the Speaker's brother—who, yes, was an elf," he said tonelessly. "They were waylaid on the road by a gang of humans—thugs and thieves. They murdered my mother's husband. My mother was raped by a human; after I was born, she died. The Speaker raised me with his own children."

"Ah." Kitiara thought it wise to say nothing else. But Tanis wasn't finished. He seemed driven to say it all and get it over with. His jaw was set, his hazel eyes hard; the hands that clenched Dauntless's reins were white at the knuckles.

"The one behind the attack was not a human," he said. "It was the Speaker's *other* brother."

Kitiara's eyes widened. "I thought elves were above all that," she murmured. "Elven honor and all."

Tanis pierced her with a stare. "It's not a joke, Kitiara. Honor is important to me. My mother and the man who *should have been* my father lost their lives because of dishonor." He paused, a sudden flush coloring his cheekbones.

Kitiara nodded soothingly. But to herself, she thought, No, Tanis wouldn't be a good one to help her with the purple gems.

* * * * *

The village had all the charm of stale beer.

Tanis and Kitiara pulled up their horses. The community boasted two short lanes and several faded grayboard houses, some no more than one large room with a thatched roof and a greased-parchment window. One house, larger than the rest, stood out; its owner had stained the exterior planks rich brown. The gray buildings looked dead next to the warmth of the brown one. A picket fence and double row of tall rachel flowers circled the place, the globes of bright pink and purple brightening an otherwise dismal scene. The companions saw no residents.

Kitiara sniffed and pointed at the open front door of the brown home. "Spices and yeast," she said. "Can you smell them?"

Tanis had dismounted and was on his way to the dwelling. "The owner may sell us some bread," he called back. Kitiara's empty stomach growled an affirmative.

Kitiara remained mounted on Obsidian while Tanis hopped onto the porch of the brown house, knocked at the doorjamb, waited a moment, then entered despite the lack of a hail from within. The town had no stable, no public house where a traveler could lift a tankard of ale, but it wasn't that different from dozens of other villages where Kitiara had stopped over the years. Someone in such towns usually was willing to provide refreshment to strangers for the right price.

Yet this community appeared deserted. Doors and shutters had been closed fast. "Anybody home?" Kitiara called. She waited. Obsidian, accustomed to the siege as well as the charge, stood quietly, her only sign of life the switching of her black tail. The place was rife with flies.

Finally a plank creaked. "Why are you in Meddow?" came a woman's strident call from behind a cracked door. "What is your friend doing in Jarlburg's confectionery? We have many men here, all armed with swords and maces. We can defend ourselves. Go away."

Kitiara hid a smile. Defend themselves indeed! They were as frightened as rabbits. She removed her helmet. "We are travelers bound for Haven. We desire food and drink, nothing more. And"—she paused significantly—"I can pay."

Another pause, then a middle-aged woman dressed in the gathered skirt, scarf, and leather slippers of a peasant stepped hesitantly onto the porch of the shack next to the brown building. Her chapped hands held a large wooden crochet hook attached by a strand of green yarn to what looked to be the back portion of a child's sweater. Her hands never stopped moving, looping the handspun yarn; the hook's end bobbed like a chickadee. Kitiara traced the yarn to a bulging pocket in the front of the peasant's skirt. Every few stitches, the woman gave a yank on the yarn, which made the pocket jump and released a few more circles of yarn from a ball in the pocket.

"I can give you water, but I have no food to spare," the woman said edgily. She kept flicking her gaze from Kitiara to the floor of the porch.

"No bread?" Kitiara demanded. "But I can smell the yeast."

"We get . . . got . . ." The woman took a deep breath and started again. "Jarlburg . . ." Her courage fled; she pressed the crochet hook against her quivering lips, then pointed with the implement to the open front door of the brown building. "There." Her eyes filled with tears. "Jarlburg's dead, too. I just know it. One by one, we're all dying."

"Dead, *too?*" Kitiara repeated and pulled Obsidian back a pace. "What is it—a plague?" Her skin crawled. Kitiara would gladly take on any living foe, but a plague? No one on Krynn knew what caused disease, although some people said that clerics and healers who had followed the old gods, years ago before the Cataclysm, could cure such illnesses. These days, seekers of the new religions said the sick invited their own fate by straying from moral purity.

The woman shook her head. "No, no plague. People just . . . disappear. I think they go into the swamp." She pointed to the east with a thin hand that, all at once, could barely hold the crochet hook.

"Any signs of a struggle?" Kitiara asked.

The peasant, shaking her head in reply, seemed suddenly convinced that the strangers were not the force behind whatever preyed on Meddow. She ventured from her front door. The woman didn't look at her crocheting; her nervous chatter kept pace with the frenetic movements of the wooden yarn hook.

"We find their doors open in the morning and they're gone," she said tearfully. "I just know they're all dead—Berk, Duster, Brown, Johon, Maron, and Keat so far. And now Jarlburg! We've only three men left, and half a dozen women, and more than a dozen children. What will our babies do if all the parents are taken?" She began to wail, wiping her tears with the crocheting. She gazed at Kitiara through wet eyes. "You appear to be a soldier, ma'am. Can you and your friend help us?"

Kitiara considered. "What can you pay?"

The woman took a step back. "Pay?" she quavered. "We have no money."

"Sorry, then," Kitiara announced curtly. "My companion and I have urgent business in Solace. We cannot delay." She turned Obsidian's head toward Jarlburg's confectionery. The woman burst into fresh tears behind her.

"Wait!" It was the woman again. "I can give you this." She waved the sweater piece at Kitiara. "It will be finished soon. Perhaps you have a daughter or son it would fit?"

"Gods forbid," Kitiara said with a short laugh. "That's all I need!" She refused the peasant again. "I must meet my companion and be moving on. We hope to be in Haven by dark."

The woman's hands ceased their crocheting, fluttered to her apron, and entangled themselves there. As Kitiara turned away, the beseeching look in the peasant's eyes faded. "There's a shortcut," the peasant called to Kitiara. "Follow the path behind Jarlburg's; take it to the east. You will quickly reach a fork at the rose quartz boulder. The left fork winds a bit, but it will take you to Haven."

"And the right fork?" Kitiara turned as she stepped up on Jarlburg's porch.

"It goes straight into the swamp. Be careful."

Kitiara thanked her and entered the brown dwelling.

The peasant turned back toward her shack. "Or maybe it's the other way around," the woman muttered with a humorless smile. "I forget."

* * * * *

Despite the open door, Jarlburg's confectionery was stuffy. A trickle of sweat curved down Kitiara's back. She could detect the odors of cinnamon, ginger, cloves, and something sweet, like flower petals. She heard Tanis moving about in the back room, a huge kitchen, she now saw, with a brick oven at one end and a wooden slab of a table that dominated the center of the room. A sack and a half of wheat flour lay under the table.

Tanis stood near the split door into the alley. The bottom half was closed, but the top was open. "You can smell the swamp from here," he said, adding, "The place is deserted, yet obviously someone was here baking recently."

"Something's been preying on the village. It happens at night, a peasant woman told me." Kitiara related the peasant woman's story, leaving out her futile request for help. "We should take some provisions and get moving." Bleached flour sacks protected a few trays, including one on a shelf near her elbow. Kitiara peered under the towel and saw a dozen frosted buns. She pierced one with the point of her dagger and bit into the morsel.

"Mmmmm," she said, talking before she swallowed. "Persimmon filling. Want some?"

Tanis was digging out a coin—payment for the provisions, no doubt—from a pouch at his waist. He looked around, then placed it on a knife-scarred counter. "Someone will find it there. Anyway, how can you eat in this place?" he demanded. "The owner is probably lying dead somewhere out in the swamp."

She finished the confection in three bites, licked her fingers elaborately, and took another bun. "If I went off my feed when circumstances were less than perfect, half-elf, I'd starve. And I'm no good as a swordswoman if I'm weak with hunger." She brushed her hands on her short leather skirt. "Do you see any bread? Check under that towel by the door."

Tanis didn't move. He didn't say anything.

"Squeamish?" Kitiara snapped. "I doubt old Jarlburg will mind if we sample his stock. What good are a few biscuits to him now?"

Tanis still didn't say anything. Kitiara slipped her dagger into its sheath. She emptied a tray of buns into a towel and tied it in a knot. "These will come in handy later," she commented.

"Aren't you even a little curious about what has happened to everyone?" Tanis asked.

Kitiara shook her head. "As long as it isn't me that's in danger, I have no curiosity." Tanis watched dispassionately, his expression unreadable. "What?" she demanded.

"I'm trying to decide something," the half-elf said mildly, turning toward the alley.

"What?" she asked.

"Whether you're inhuman or typically human."

Tanis stepped into the alley, leaving Kitiara standing motionless in the middle of the kitchen, one hand clenching a loaf of rye bread, the other holding the towel full of biscuits. Kitiara watched him leave, her blood pounding with anger.

Damn the man. And damn his arrogant elven blood.

* * * * *

Tanis didn't say anything to Kitiara as they left Meddow. She pointed out a shortcut she said she'd learned about, and when they reached a fork after a few minutes of riding, she motioned wordlessly down the left path. They kicked their horses into a trot as dusk descended around them.

Soon the path grew spongy, and the horses's feet began to make sucking noises as they pulled their hooves from the sodden peat.

"This can't be the right trail," Tanis said, looking back from his position in the lead.

"The woman said the left fork curved a bit," Kitiara snapped. "This is the left fork, damn it. Hurry up. It's getting dark."

Tanis nodded. "I'd hate to see the right fork," he murmured.

The vegetation changed as they continued along the trail. The trees now sagged under festoons of gray-green moss that resembled tresses of a desiccated corpse. Strange grasses, red, shoulder-high, with clouds of tiny insects around their tips, poked up beside the path. Kitiara touched one and snatched her hand away with a cry. "I've been bitten!"

Tanis reined in Dauntless and leaned over to examine her hand. "By the insects or by the plant?" he asked. Blood oozed from a pair of cuts at the base of her thumb. "They look like teeth marks," he mused.

Kitiara's temper snapped again. "Don't be ridiculous. Whoever heard of plants that bite?"

The half-elf's expression was thoughtful. "I've heard of stranger things," he said.

She jerked her hand away. "You're trying to spook me, half-elf. Let's get moving." She shoved Obsidian past the chestnut gelding into the lead. Tanis followed slowly.

The path narrowed; red grasses pushed in from the sides until Tanis and Kitiara could barely see to the right or the left. There was only room for the horses to pass in single file. The smell of muck increased, as did the whine of insects. Once something purple, the size of a horse's hoof, scampered across the path right in front of Obsidian, dragging a small, fluttering bird. So startled was the mare that it was all Kitiara could do to restrain her rearing mount. When Obsidian had settled down at last, Kitiara shouted back, "What in the shadowless Abyss was *that*?"

"Bog spider," Tanis said tersely. "Poisonous."

As evening darkened, mosquitoes descended in hordes upon the travelers. Tanis unrolled a blanket from his bedroll and wrapped it over his head to discourage the biting insects. Kitiara followed suit. "Don't brush against the plants," he warned. Kitiara grunted in reply but kept Obsidian in the center of the trail.

Tanis suddenly dismounted, picked up a stone from the trail, and tossed it into the reddish grasses. A splash followed. "The left fork led to Haven?" he repeated.

Kitiara stopped and looked around. "So she said." Her gaze flicked from moss to grass to the narrow path. "So she said."

Grasses pressed in on each side. As dusk deepened,

they heard something large splash into the water off to their left. Bats swooped and circled overhead, feasting on nighttime insects. A humming, like the sound of a thousand insects, thrummed through the marsh.

"Have you ever done battle in a bog?" Tanis asked quietly. Ignoring the mosquitoes, he let the blanket fall from his head and felt for his sword.

Kitiara shook her head. "You?"

Tanis nodded. "Once. With Flint."

By some unspoken decision, they kept their tone offhand. "What lives here?" Kitiara asked.

"Ever heard of the Jarak-Sinn?"

Again she shook her head.

"They're a race of lizard people. Their venom is deadly," Tanis said. With the night growing more dense around them, it seemed more appropriate to whisper. "And of course, there are ogres; you find them everywhere," he continued. "And shambling mounds. They look like piles of rotting leaves—until they rise and envelop you. Swamp alligators; I fought gators with Flint. They carry venom in a spine at the ends of their tails. They try to paralyze you and pull you into the water and drown you." He didn't mention that the feisty dwarf had almost lost his life in such an encounter, surviving only after liberal doses of Qualinesti herbs to offset the poison.

Kitiara pushed the blanket back from her head and drew her sword. Tanis's was already out.

"So we're in the swamp. Should we retreat or go on?" the swordswoman asked.

Tanis looked at the scarlet grasses. "We couldn't turn the horses on this narrow path if we wanted to. Push on, but be ready, Kit."

They moved on more slowly, their ears pricking

with every new splash and bubble from the swamp. The stench of rotting plants and animals grew worse. Solinari had risen and was bathing the travelers in platinum moonlight.

Then, all at once, what looked like *two* silver moons hung in the sky. Kitiara pointed and shouted. "Look, half-elf! A light! It's Haven after all!" Ignoring the half-elf's cry of dismay, she kicked Obsidian in the sides and clattered confidently ahead. The half-elf had no choice but to force Dauntless into a gallop.

"Kitiara, wait!" he shouted. "It's a will-o'-the-wisp!" The swordswoman raced on as though she hadn't heard him.

The path widened and curved to the right of a black pool. Solinari shone above them, its light giving an otherwordly glow to the sphagnum moss in the trees that ringed the travelers. Tanis drew up behind the mounted swordswoman and lunged for Obsidian's reins. Kitiara turned toward him. For a moment, confusion flickered across her face. Then her countenance cleared. "A will-o'-the-wisp?" she asked.

The second orb hung lower, behind the pond. It was an arm's length in diameter. Its pulsating color shifted from white to pale green to violet to blue.

"A will-o'-the-wisp is intelligent," Tanis explained, his sword still at the ready. "It lures its victims, masquerading as lanterns and confusing people until they stray into quicksand."

"Quicksand?" Kitiara looked about her.

Tanis pointed to the black pool at their feet. "Quicksand."

Her voice was hushed. She glanced at the hovering globe of twinkling lights. "Will it attack?"

"It may. Don't let it so much as touch you. You'll receive a shock that could kill you outright."

Kitiara dismounted, sword in her right hand, dagger in her left. "That must be the creature that killed Jarlburg and the others," she said. "It probably came to the edge of the swamp near Meddow and coaxed them in." Tanis nodded his agreement. "What does a will-o'-the-wisp eat?" the swordswoman persisted.

"Fear."

Kitiara's glance showed that she thought Tanis was making fun of her, but the half-elf continued. "I've heard that a frightened person emits an aura. Some creatures can sense it. Instead of killing its victims immediately—by brushing against them, for example—the will-o'-the-wisp prefers slow death for its victims because the creature can absorb fear and store it as food."

At that moment, the pulsating ball brightened, slowly but steadily, until its glow allowed the half-elf and swordswoman to make out the litter around the pool of black quicksand. In the eerie glow, they spotted skulls, swords, and pouches of money. Kitiara pointed. "Treasure?"

"Probably thrown to the will-o'-the-wisp by victims hoping to buy mercy," Tanis said.

The lower branches of trees that overhung the pool were bare of leaves, evidence of desperate hands groping for anything that could resist the black sand's pull.

Kitiara's face was shiny with perspiration—as was Tanis's own, no doubt, the half-elf realized. The will-o'-the-wisp glowed ever brighter, its color transformations coming more swiftly now. "Kit," he said, "it's feeding on our fear! Think about something else."

She closed her eyes. "Solace."

"That's good," Tanis said soothingly. "The vallenwood trees . . . think about them."

"Everywhere I've gone," she said, "people have asked me what it was like to live in houses in the great Solace vallenwood trees."

"With the rope bridges from tree to tree."

"You could live your entire life without putting a foot on the ground."

"Which is not the way for a dwarf," Tanis commented. "Flint Fireforge has one of the few houses at the base of the trees. He rarely leaves the ground except to visit Otik's tavern."

The light dimmed, then brightened, then dimmed again.

Then darkness.

Suddenly, the only source of illumination was the faint light of Solinari. Tanis leaped from Dauntless, slinging his bow across one shoulder. "It's going to attack!" He slapped the gelding on the flank while Kitiara followed suit with Obsidian. The two horses galloped down the path in opposite directions. The half-elf and swordswoman placed themselves back to back, waiting. Tanis heard Kitiara whispering to herself, "Solace, Solace."

"Vallenwood trees," he replied. "Remember the vallenwoods."

Then the night burst around them. There was an explosion so bright that it momentarily blinded the half-elf. When his vision cleared, he saw a ball of blue flame streaking toward them. Grabbing Kitiara by the arm, he dragged her down on the path, and the cometlike creature, lightening to pale green, whisked overhead. The ends of Tanis's hair crackled as the will-o'-the-wisp rushed by. Kitiara swore.

"Huuu-mannnzzz!" The ghostly voice seemed to surround them, ebbing and strengthening and insinuating itself into every pore of their bodies. Yet the will-

o'-the-wisp itself had returned to its position above the quicksand. The creature oscillated, its swirling colors shifting many times with each breath the companions drew.

"By Takhisis!" Kitiara ejaculated. "You didn't tell me the thing could speak!"

"I didn't know myself."

"Youuu havvve no chanccce, huuumanzzz." The will-o'-the-wisp flickered from green to blue to violet to glaring white.

Tanis swallowed and gripped his sword more tightly. "It's vibrating faster. It must make sounds that way."

"I willlll . . . killllll youuu . . . slowwwllly."

Kitiara whispered, "How can we slay it?"

"It can die by the sword, but we have to kill it without letting it touch us."

The thing drew closer. *"You willllll feel much painnn, huuu-manzzz."*

Tanis and Kitiara held their swords before them. Both had their daggers drawn as well.

"Would an arrow kill it?"

Tanis nodded.

"Imagine the fearrr, humanzzz. Think about yourrr deathsss."

"You're the bowman, half-elf," Kitiara said. "The sword's my weapon. I'll cover you."

"Youuu willlll strugglllle . . . for airrr, huuu-manzzz. Youuu willlll pannnic." The thing floated still closer. *"Halfff-elfff. Youuu willll die firrrrst, I thinnnk."*

"It's trying to unsettle you, Tanis. Remember, you have Kitiara Uth Matar at your back."

Tanis whispered, "Keep it distracted. When I shoot, hit the ground."

Kitiara was silent, motionless for a brief time. Then

she pivoted to face the will-o'-the-wisp. She set her boots in the soggy peat.

"All right, beast," she snapped.

"*Yessssss?*" The sibilance echoed in the dangling moss, reverberating off the quicksand's surface. Out of the corner of Tanis's eye, he saw a bog spider creep from the shadows onto the flattened peat.

Kitiara's voice was haughty. "We hold no fear for you, beast!"

Something like sibilant laughter throbbed around them. "*My sssensssess telllll mmmee otherwisssse, huuu-mannn. Indeeeed, I'mmmm feeeeeding quite wellll on yourrr terror. I will ssavvvorr yourrr ttasty deathsss.*"

At that moment, Tanis slipped an arrow from his quiver and, in the same motion, dove for his bow. He rolled away from Kitiara and the will-o'-the-wisp, sending the spider scrambling back into the grass. Then he nocked the arrow and let it fly. Kitiara was already down on one knee, her sword outstretched. Her dagger carved circles in the air.

The arrow arced through the night and nicked the edge of the pulsating ball of light. The thing disappeared in a small white explosion.

There was silence.

Then more silence. Tanis and Kitiara looked at each other. "That was it?" Kitiara asked disbelievingly.

"I don't know," the half-elf said, rising. "I've never fought one of these things before." He nocked another arrow and moved toward Kitiara. She kept her battle stance. Her gaze flicked from side to side.

Suddenly another explosion rocked the clearing. Purple, blue, and green lightning fizzled in the grass.

"*Halfff-elfff!*"

Standing next to the quicksand, Tanis swung to

meet the new threat and fired off another arrow. The shot went wild, and the will-o'-the-wisp bore down on him, flashing deep blue lightning bolts into the air. Tanis heard Kitiara shout, "Don't let it touch you!" and then he leaped out of the way. The thing whooshed past as he jumped.

The instant his body hit the cold, black surface of the quicksand, the half-elf knew he'd done exactly what the will-o'-the-wisp wanted. He started to thrash in the sticky muck until he realized that his struggling was only drawing him deeper into the deadly sand. Already he was submerged to the waist, out of arm's reach of the edge of the pit.

Kitiara shouted a battle cry, and Tanis saw her slash at the will-o'-the-wisp. He struggled again but only succeeded in sinking farther.

He lay back against the muck. Above him and off to his right, the battle raged on. The will-o'-the-wisp, sparking green and purple, attacked and withdrew, obviously hoping to push Kitiara toward the quicksand, but the swordswoman refused to comply. She maintained her position amid the scattered bones, weapons, and coin pouches on the wide path. Tanis shouted encouragement; Kitiara smiled grimly and fought on.

The half-elf caught sight of a branch overhead, silhouetted by Solinari. If he could just reach it. . . . Tanis stretched. His fingers brushed a few twigs. He tried not to think of previous victims who'd tried the same escape. He stretched again. His right hand clenched a twig and pulled; the twig broke off in his hand. His left hand managed to catch a slightly larger twig, and he pulled the branch toward him; this time it held.

Finally Tanis hung by both arms from a branch the

thickness of his thumb, which, while not enough to stop his sinking, did slow it. That might buy enough time. Stouter branches, ones that still had leaves, bobbed a foot above the small one, but that short distance might as well have been a mile.

The will-o'-the-wisp still battled with tenacity. The swordswoman fought back with dagger and sword, darting, feinting, slashing at the bobbing ball of light. "Come on, you insignificant firefly!" she taunted. "I've seen bigger sparks from steel and stone!"

"By the gods," Tanis whispered in awe, "she's *not* afraid of it!"

The will-o'-the-wisp flared at Kitiara's taunt. When it subsided, it had diminished in size. Tanis realized Kitiara's stratagem. If the will-o'-the-wisp fed on fear, maybe it could be weakened by experiencing the opposite emotions. As Kitiara continued her taunts, Tanis shifted his grip on the branch.

His left hand brushed against something furry.

Tanis looked up, and his breath caught in his throat. A poisonous bog spider, larger than his fist, crouched on the branch right next to his hand. He tried to shift to the right. His movement pulled him a hand's span deeper into the quicksand, and the purplish creature followed him along the branch.

"Kit!" he shouted.

The swordswoman looked over, grimaced, and doubled her efforts against the will-o'-the-wisp. But the bobbing creature swooped away and halted just above the branch where the half-elf hung.

"The will-o'-the-wisp is growing larger on your fear, Tanis!" Kitiara yelled. "Don't feed it!"

The purple spider reached out a leg and caressed Tanis's little finger. "Vallenwoods," the half-elf murmured to himself.

"Solace," Kitiara added. "Rope bridges. Spiced potatoes and ale at the Inn of the Last Home."

The will-o'-the-wisp hovered lower; the poisonous spider placed another leg, then another, on Tanis's hand. The tiny claws at the end of the legs pricked the skin on the half-elf's hand. He dared not move; he tried not to think of the spider's venomous fangs, but the will-o'-the-wisp's color deepened and flared.

"Flint Fireforge," Tanis muttered desperately. "Spiced potatoes."

Kitiara shifted her handhold on her dagger; her strong fingers now gripped the blade instead of the hilt. The will-o'-the-wisp was still, only a foot from Tanis, apparently concentrating on the half-elf. Kitiara squinted, aiming. Then, with one fluid movement, she flung the dagger, shouting, "Tanis! Let go!" at the same time. Tanis plummeted into the quicksand, followed by the spider.

Kitiara's dagger flipped end over end through the air, through the place where Tanis had hung, and caught the will-o'-the-wisp in the exact center.

The air was filled with the force of the explosion. This time the creature was gone for good.

Chapter 3

A Complication

"Amazing how a bath and clean clothes can improve a man," Kitiara remarked the next day while she and the half-elf inspected the teeming Haven market. "You little resemble the slimy creature I pulled from the quicksand, half-elf. Dauntless barely knew you—once we caught up with him, that is."

Tanis smiled. "The horses are enjoying oats and mash at the livery and could use a day's rest. We have the will-o'-the-wisp's treasure to spend, a sunny day, and time to enjoy it." He inclined his head. "May I buy you breakfast, Kitiara Uth Matar?"

Kitiara assented with an elaborate nod. They'd eaten once, in their room at the Seven Centaurs Inn, but now, at midday, their stomachs rumbled again. "It must be the result of weeks of those infernal elven battle rations," she commented, pausing to admire a vendor's wares—metal trays of fragrant venison sizzling with onions and eggs. "I'll eat anything but more elven quith-pa. Dried fruit, pah!" She was about to order a plate of the fried meat when her gaze was attracted by a display of flaky pastry filled with custard and drizzled with strawberry icing. She halted as if mesmerized. "Oh, the decisions," she murmured happily.

"We'll have a plate of the venison and two of those frosted pastries," Tanis told the vendor as Kitiara vacillated. "Lest you drool all over the man's wares," he told the swordswoman, who took the teasing with good humor.

Conversation took second place to eating for a time as the half-elf and swordswoman strolled down an avenue of the teeming market. Dressed in a short, split skirt of black leather and an overblouse of eggshell-colored linen, Kitiara drew many admiring looks from passersby, which she accepted with insouciance. Tanis, on the other hand, wore a pair of floppy, gathered pants in dark blue, plus a matching cotton shirt, both borrowed from the portly innkeeper at the Seven Centaurs. The shirt rippled with the slender half-elf's movements.

Kitiara eyed him again. "We need to find you new clothes to replace your ruined leathers, half-elf. I'm used to you in Plainsman garb; it suits you better than the dress of an overfed city-dweller."

Taller than Kitiara, Tanis had a better vantage, and in response he slipped a hand through her arm and drew her through the crowd. "I see just the place," he said.

The half-elf stopped before a large wagon, uncovered at the back but with a shell-like contraption over the driver's seat. Kitiara could see from the wagon's design that it took four mules to pull the top-heavy thing. Standing atop the ribbon-festooned vehicle was a hill dwarf with a rust-colored beard that curled down to his belt buckle. He wore homespun dyed forest green, plus brown leather boots scuffed with what was probably decades of use.

Tanis and Kitiara waited while the dwarf finished with a customer, a loud woman who couldn't decide between a pearl-and-platinum hair ornament and a seashell comb. "How old would you say this dwarf is?" Kitiara asked casually.

Tanis considered. "Flint's nearly one hundred and fifty, and this dwarf certainly looks younger than Flint. I'd say this fellow's been around about a century. About ten years older than me."

Kitiara protested, "I'm spending time with someone who was an old man when I was born?"

When Tanis nodded and murmured, "In human years, yes," she snorted.

"Do you care?" he asked.

Kitiara laughed. "No," she admitted. "It's not as though we're going to get married or anything."

The woman finally left with the comb and the hair bauble, and the dwarf who owned the wagon ambled over to Tanis and Kitiara. The vendor remained on the back of the wagon, glaring down at the crowd and picking his way among his wares with delicacy. "What do *you* want?" he muttered to the half-elf and swordswoman.

Kitiara looked annoyed by the dwarf's brusqueness, but Tanis, accustomed to Flint's blunt ways, only smiled. Crustiness wasn't exactly uncommon among hill dwarves. "We're looking for clothes for me, and a dagger for the lady," the half-elf said.

The dwarf looked pointedly at Tanis's ill-fitting garb. "Thinking of leaving the traveling minstrel revue, then, are you?"

Kitiara bristled; Tanis put a restraining hand on her arm and signaled her to overlook the jibe. The surest way to annoy hill dwarves—or Flint Fireforge, at least—was to pretend to ignore their griping.

"Do you trade with Plainsmen?" the half-elf asked.

"I trade with everybody," the dwarf said grumpily, "and they all try to take advantage of me. Plainsmen, gnomes, even other dwarves. You'd think I was an infernal nabob, the way they try to cheat me."

"I'm looking for a pair of leather breeches and a leather shirt," Tanis interjected.

"With fringe, I suppose," the dwarf complained. "Everybody wants fringe. Damned frippery. What use on Ansalon is fringe, I ask you?"

Tanis smiled gently while Kitiara steamed, her brows knit over smoldering eyes. "Fringe would be fine," Tanis said, "but it's not necessary"—the half-elf paused significantly—"*if* you don't have it."

The dwarf rose to the bait. " 'Course I have it! What kind o' cheap outfit you think I'm runnin' here, half-elf?"

Kitiara pulled her arm away from the half-elf and pointed at the dwarf. Her voice crackled. "Listen, old dwarf, do you want us to spend our steel elsewhere?"

The dwarf slowly swiveled to glare down at Kitiara from the back of the wagon. His eyes were the same green as his breeches and shirt. "The name's Sonnus Ironmill, not 'old dwarf,' young lady. You the hoyden lookin' for a dagger?"

Looking over Kitiara's head, the dwarf addressed

the crowd in general. "A sword ain't enough for this minx; noooo, she needs a dagger, too. How about a mace and pike as well?" He looked down at his fuming customer. "What kind o' folks you hang around with, anyway? Or"—he leaned over and whispered— "do things get a mite touchy at the ladies' quilting parties now and then?"

Tanis bent toward Kitiara. "He's enjoying this," he whispered.

Kitiara looked from Tanis to Sonnus Ironmill and frowned. "I'm looking for a dagger," she finally said. "I lost my old one in some quicksand."

The dwarf did a double take. "Eh? Quicksand?" Then he caught himself and recovered his grousing tone. "You'll want lots of jewels and pearl inlay and the like, no doubt. Damned unnecessary. Decoration can throw off the entire balance of a weapon."

"Listen," she snapped, "do you have a dagger to sell me or not?"

" 'Course I have a dagger!" the dwarf said, stomping over to a trunk, opening it, and tossing a folded bundle of leather at the half-elf. "Got scabbards, too, but I can see by the sheath showing from under that short skirt of yours that you don't need one of those."

Tanis caught the bundle of leather; it was a full suit in the style of the Plainsmen—fawn-soft deerhide the color of polished oak, fringed along the back yoke. Someone had embroidered the hem with beads. "May I try it on in your shack?" the half-elf asked, pointing at the turtlelike contraption at the front of the wagon.

" 'Course. Were you planning to take your clothes off right here in publ . . . Hey! Did you say 'shack'?" The dwarf pulled up short. As Tanis leaped onto the wagon, the half-elf took the full force of a vile stare from Sonnus Ironmill. Tanis merely shrugged and headed for the dwarf's quarters. The dwarf snatched a tray of daggers, plucked off a nest of silk scarves that had fallen over on the tray, and turned back toward Kitiara. " 'Shack,' he calls it," Ironmill groused under his breath. "Price o' leathers just doubled for that."

As Tanis changed into the garb in the dimness of the cramped interior, he heard a new, piping voice mingle with Sonnus Ironmill's complaining tones.

"Nice daggers, Sonnus! I found a jeweled sword once, which was a lucky thing because the owner showed up when I was trying to figure out who to return it to, and he was really upset that he'd lost it. I knew he was glad I'd found it, even though he was too upset to be glad, really. I guess he'd been plenty worried. I—"

"Get out of here, you wretched kender!" the dwarf shouted. "And if you steal just *one more* thing from this wagon, I'll . . . I'll sell you to the minotaurs for goat food!"

"Steal?" The little voice dripped with hurt feelings. "I wouldn't steal, Sonnus. I can't help it that everyone loses things and that I'm lucky enough to f—"

"Enough!" the dwarf boomed. "Out!"

Tanis heard a thump that might have been a kender hitting the side of a wagon. As the half-elf pulled Sonnus Ironmill's shirt over his head, Kitiara's cool voice was the next sound he heard. "How much for this dagger, dwarf?"

The dwarf named a price. Kitiara haggled him down, and they had just struck a deal as Tanis emerged from Ironmill's hut. "I'll take it," he told the dwarf, admiring the fit, "if the price is right."

"Well . . ." The dwarf stroked his luxuriant beard. "It seems to me that suit may well be the only one of its kind west of Que-Shu, which is where I got it, and didn't it cost me a pretty pile of coins. . . . Its rarity increases its value, I'd think."

"Except no one west of Que-Shu but the half-elf would want it," Kitiara said as she fingered the gathered pouch into which they'd put the coins they'd found at the will-o'-the-wisp's lair. "You're lucky to be getting rid of it, dwarf. Maybe we should look somewhere else, Tanis." Tanis nodded.

Sonnus Ironmill frowned at them both. "Five steel," he pronounced.

"Three," Kitiara and Tanis said at the same time.

"Four."

"Done!"

Kitiara paid Sonnus Ironmill and slipped her new dagger, with its hilt inlaid with tiger's-eyes, into her sheath. As she and Tanis plunged back into the milling crowd, they heard the dwarven vendor greet a customer with, "Well, what do *you* want?"

Kitiara brushed past a female kender, a waist-high creature with the race's characteristic long brown hair gathered in a topknot. "That's the creature who tried to rob the dwarf," the swordswoman commented to Tanis.

"Rob!" the kender exclaimed. "I never steal. I do have incredible luck finding things. Do you think some people are just born with luck? I do. My sisters and I all have it. But I . . ." Brown eyes doelike with innocence, she was still chattering when a trio of teenaged boys shoved between Kitiara and the kender. The childlike creature was lost to view, her lilting voice swallowed by the cacophony of the late-morning marketplace.

Tanis and Kitiara slipped among the marketgoers. The din was practically deafening. A seller of tapestries argued with a vendor of leather footware; each accused the other of letting his wares spill into the other's territory. Dozens of vendors tried to outdo each other in shouting their products' superiority to the crowd.

An illusionist charmed the crowd. A juggler balanced a bottle on his head while twirling flaming batons. A veil-draped seeress offered to look into the future of those with money enough—and gullibility enough—to pay for the service. A gnome sold cymbals and Aeolian harps, flat boxes with strings, played, not by fingers, but by the wind. Two humans, a man and a woman, sat on a grassy hummock overlooking the market, tuning a pair of three-stringed, triangular guitars.

Sellers hawked scarves, perfumes, and fine clothing, all of which Kitiara ignored, and swords, armor, and saddlery, which she stopped to admire.

"I'd like to find something for my brothers," Kitiara said. "A weapon for Caramon—he's athletic, like me. And a set of silk scarves for Raistlin, I think. They'd come in handy for certain magic spells."

"I may pick up a gift for Flint," Tanis rejoined. "His first choice would be ale, I'm sure, but I'm not sure I want to haul a keg of Haven ale from here to Solace."

"Isn't it lunchtime?" Kitiara asked, her attention arrested by the calls of a man stirring a caldron of soup, which scented the air with sage, basil, and bay leaves.

Tanis followed her obligingly to an open bench near the soup vendor. "You guard the seat," he told her. "I'll pay; I've got a few coins."

"We ought to divide up the booty from the will-o'-the-wisp," Kitiara murmured.

Tanis nodded. "After lunch."

He returned a few moments later, bearing a wooden tray upon which sat two steaming bowls of soup and

thick slices of white bread sprinkled with toasted sesame seeds. They ate in silence for a while, savoring the
chewy bread and peppery soup. Tanis carefully
brushed sesame seeds from the beading on his new
shirt, which prompted Kitiara to drop her hand to her
thigh, where the sheath held—nothing.

"Tanis! My dagger's gone! The kender!"

The half-elf leaped up. So did Kitiara. Then they
were off in different directions.

Tanis pushed through the packed lanes as quickly
as he could, gazing right and left, but he saw no sign
of the brown-eyed kender. He made his way back to
Sonnus Ironmill's wagon. The dwarf was perched at
the back of the vehicle, his short legs dangling off the
back. Studiously ignoring several prospective customers, Ironmill clutched a tankard and munched a
sandwich. Tanis smelled fish, garlic, and ale as he
drew near and asked about the kender. He had to
shout his question three times, each time louder, before the dwarf deigned to look down and reply.

"The last time I saw the thieving sneak, she was
headin' that way." Ironmill pointed. "Guard your
money pouch, half-elf. Drizzleneff Gatehop's a quick
one." He paused, then resumed grumbling. "But
Drizzleneff's no worse than most of the scalawags I
have to deal with. At least a kender doesn't *intend* to
be a scalawag."

Ironmill looked away; clearly he considered the
conversation over. He was obviously startled a moment later when Tanis swung himself up onto the
wagon next to Ironmill and stood on tiptoe, scanning
the crowd for signs of the kender.

The view wasn't much better from the wagon than
it was from the ground. Tents and banners gave the
half-elf mere glimpses of what lay beyond the imme-

diate row. Tanis's quick eyes did catch sight of Kiti-ara, who strode through the marketgoers, shoving and glowering at anyone who got in her way. He found himself hoping, for the kender's sake, that the half-elf caught up with Drizzleneff Gatehop before the swordswoman did.

He didn't get his wish. An outcry at the end of Iron-mill's lane and ripples in the crowd as marketgoers turned to watch the fracas alerted Tanis. He leaped down and shoved through to the middle of the com-motion.

Kitiara had her dagger back. In fact, its glittering blade danced near Drizzleneff's neck. Kitiara's left arm was around the creature's chest; her right hand held the blade. "I should end your miserable existence right here, and no one could stop me, kender!" Kitiara shouted. A few of the vendors cheered.

"I was *looking* for you!" Drizzleneff squawked. "I found your dagger . . ."

". . . in its sheath on my leg, you sneak!"

Drizzleneff Gatehop, breath rasping, stopped to consider Kitiara's words. Then she shrugged and went on. "Well, it *did* seem to be a dangerous place for you to carry it, if you ask me. What if there were pickpock—" Her sentence ended in a choking sound as Kitiara clamped down tighter with her left arm.

"Listen to me, kender."

Drizzleneff barely nodded. Her face grew pink.

"*Never* come near me again." Kitiara's voice was al-most a whisper. The fascinated passersby had to lean close to catch her words. "*Never*. Understand?" The kender's eyes grew glassy as she struggled to break free.

Tanis moved to intervene. "Kit?"

Kitiara looked up and winked at the half-elf. Then

she spoke again to Drizzleneff. "In fact, I think you should leave Haven—right now. Understand?"

"Kit!" Tanis interrupted. "She can barely breathe!"

Kitiara loosened her hold slightly and moved the dagger away a bit. "Understand?" she repeated.

Drizzleneff Gatehop nodded. "Tomorrow morning," she croaked. "Right after breakf—"

"Today! This very afternoon."

"But . . ."

Kitiara waved the dagger. The kender nodded. "Well, okay. I was planning on heading out anyway because . . ."

The swordswoman released the kender, and Drizzleneff Gatehop, topknot bouncing, vanished into the crowd. The throng dissipated as soon as people realized the entertainment was over.

"Don't you think you were a little rough?" Tanis asked.

"She'll think twice before she steals again."

"No, she won't," the half-elf commented. "Kender don't steal, not from their point of view. They have no fear and no real sense of private property—just the curiosity of a five-year-old."

The swordswoman didn't reply. She was polishing her new dagger with the edge of her shirt.

* * * * *

"How did you meet this Flint Fireforge fellow?" Kitiara asked that evening.

They'd dined at the Seven Centaurs and were sitting in rows of near-empty benches that marked the circumference of the courtyard of the Masked Dragon, one of Haven's largest inns. Before them, minstrels were setting up a low stage. Ignoring the clouds

64

gathering overhead, servants of the innkeeper lighted torches set into brackets at intervals on the walls. People were just beginning to wander in.

"Flint came to Qualinost when I was a child," Tanis said. "We became friends, and when he left, I did, too. We've been in Solace for years."

It wasn't the whole story, of course. The dwarf, an outsider in the elven kingdom, had befriended the lonely half-elf, had eased him through one scrape after another, and in fact had often seemed to be Tanis's only friend in Qualinost. Later, when Flint decided to leave the Qualinesti city for good, Tanis, nearly full-grown, went with him with few regrets. Unlike the dwarf, however, the half-elf had continued to visit the elven city now and then.

Kitiara seemed disinclined to inquire into details, however. Her attention had turned to a pair of minstrels. The woman, a wispy creature with shoulder-length blonde hair and large blue eyes, positioned herself in the center front of the stage while her companion, an equally slender man with dark hair and a ready smile, set torches in freestanding holders at the right and left front corners of the platform.

The man stepped back and looked critically at the woman. "Light's too dim," he said to her. He moved the torches closer, stepped back again, and approached the stage.

"Better?" she asked.

He nodded and replied, "Perfect. The lighting, and the singer, too." Then he hopped up on the platform and kissed her. The couple's three children, an older girl and her young sister and brother, sat cross-legged on the back of the stage. They groaned as their parents embraced. The couple broke apart and grinned unabashedly at the youngsters.

Kitiara rolled her eyes. "How sweet," she commented acidly.

Tanis realized that this was the same couple that
had been rehearsing in the Haven market earlier in the
day. Trailed by the children, they disappeared under a
wooden arch that must have led to a back room. The
next moments saw the five come and go, bearing instruments of every type and laying them gently on the
stage. Tanis recognized one as a dulcimer, a stringed
instrument played on the lap, popular among ladies
of the Qualinesti court. The man came out holding
two triangular guitars. There was a clavichord, an oblong box with a keyboard, which the man set up on a
stand in front of a bench. The woman placed a cylin-
der drum at the back of the stage; her husband helped
her maneuver a slit drum, made from cutting a narrow opening in a polished, hollow log, next to it. The
couple's older daughter set a gong in a stand next to
the drums. The couple's younger daughter plopped
down and practiced trills on a flute while her brother
warbled on a recorder. Tanis watched raptly.

"You're looking at the stage as though you'd like to
be up there with them," Kitiara teased, breaking into
the half-elf's reverie.

Tanis indicated the family with a jerk of his head.
"Music. That's one difference between elves and
humans."

When Kitiara raised her eyebrows, the half-elf went
on. "In Qualinost, it's assumed that every child will
study an instrument. Often, at sunset, elves gather at
the Hall of the Sky and hold impromptu concerts."

"So?" Kitiara demanded. "Humans like music, too."

Tanis frowned. "But humans see it as something
only musicians do. I don't know many humans who
play their own music. They come to places like this."

He gestured. The courtyard was filling up. They'd taken spots on the ends of the benches—Kitiara disliked being trapped in the middle of a crowd—and onlookers kept shoving past them for the few seats remaining.

"What do you play, half-elf?" Kitiara asked.

"Psaltery, gittern . . ."

"Which are what?"

"The psaltery's a type of dulcimer," Tanis explained. "The gittern is like a guitar. I've tried other instruments, but I'm more enthusiastic than I am accomplished. Flint makes me practice outdoors." He looked at Kitiara. "Do you play an instrument, Kit?"

Kitiara's upper lip curved. "The sword's my instrument. But I can make it sing like nothing that pathetic crew can play." She gestured at the stage, where the family was lightly chanting a lilting but apparently endless melody designed to warm up their voices. "And my sword's a lot more effective against hobgoblins."

Kitiara's discourse was interrupted by the woman, who stepped to the front of the platform and welcomed the crowd. Her voice was dusky and low. She looked back at her husband, positioned by the drums and gong, and at her children, ready with flute, recorder, and clavichord. Then she faced the audience again, opened her mouth, and sang,

"There was a fair lady of old Daltigoth,
Was scorned by her lover, alone left to weep . . ."

Her voice was as rich as spring earth, and the portly man next to Tanis shivered. " 'The Fair Lady of Daltigoth,' " the man said in an undertone. "I love that song."

The crowd settled down to listen. Dusk had given way to evening. Solinari was high in the sky above the courtyard, and Lunitari, the red moon, was beginning to rise. The torches focused attention on the stage, but the half-elf could see spectators leaving through arched doors to the inn's tavern, then returning with foaming mugs of beer. Kitiara had also noticed, he saw. "Would you like some ale?" she asked.

Tanis had barely nodded when the swordswoman was on her feet, moving toward the adjoining tavern. Suddenly her way was blocked by a muscular man with black hair, black eyes, and a set expression. He wore ebony breeches and boots, white shirt, and a scarlet cape, and he stood before Kitiara with an air of self-assurance. "Kitiara Uth Matar!" the man said quietly.

"Caven Mackid." Her tone was chilly. She didn't introduce the man to Tanis, who'd risen silently from the bench and approached the two. A slender teenager with emerald green eyes sidled next to the half-elf, gazing on with interest.

Caven looked neither to the right nor left. "You don't take many straight lines in your travels, woman," he said. "It took me a week to pick up your trail, and more than a month to track you here." Caven seemed to notice Tanis for the first time. "Fortunately," he said to the half-elf, raising his voice, "Kitiara is the kind of woman that people pay heed to as she passes through. As I'm sure you've noticed." Caven looked back at Kitiara. "A suspicious man might think you'd been avoiding him, my love," he said.

Kitiara pulled herself up straight, but she was still came up only to Caven Mackid's shoulder. "I'm still your superior officer, soldier. Watch yourself." Her tone was bantering, but her eyes showed no warmth.

The minstrels' tune continued, but several onlookers, sensing a possibly greater show in the making, gaped instead at Kitiara and Caven.

At Kitiara's words, Caven's hands dropped to his sides, and the friendliness faded from his face. The big man gazed at Kitiara with a strange light in his eyes—anger mixed with something else. Something was afoot that the half-elf wasn't privy to, but he was experienced enough with women to realize that Kitiara at one time had been much more than a commanding officer to this man.

"I believe you have something of mine, Captain Uth Matar," Mackid said silkily. "A money pouch, perhaps? No doubt an oversight on your part; our personal belongings did get a bit *mingled* there for a while, as I recall."

The slim teen-ager snickered. "I'll say," he said with a leer at Tanis.

"And as I recall," Caven Mackid went on, disregarding the youth, "you left in quite a hurry, my dear—too hasty even to leave a message. Pursued by ogres, no doubt. But I trust you've kept my money safe and have it now."

The teen-aged boy leaned toward Tanis. "Took off while he was out hunting, she did, and nipped most of his savings," he whispered. "If she'd just took off, I don't think he would've minded much. But it was the filching that stuck in Caven's craw."

"Wode!" Caven gently reprimanded the boy. "Good squires keep their mouths shut around strangers."

Behind Kitiara, the minstrels finished the ballad and launched into a reel. The swordswoman finally noticed the half-elf. "Tanis, this is Caven Mackid, one of my *subordinates* in my last campaign."

Caven smiled in an almost friendly fashion at

Tanis, but he addressed his words to Kitiara. "A half-elf, Kitiara? Lowered your standards a bit, haven't you?" His squire snickered again, but the man quelled the outburst with a look. Instead, Caven gazed directly at Kitiara. His next words were an order. "My money. Now."

* * * * *

Off to one side, unnoticed by any of the four, a woman with skin the umber of burnished oak pulled back warily into a shadowed portal. A soft woolen robe, the color of a dove, set off her dark features. Her gaze was direct, her eyes azure around pupils of surprising darkness. Her straight, blue-black hair poured over her shoulders, over the crumpled hood of her robe, and down her back.

"Kitiara Uth Matar," she murmured softly to herself. "And that dark-haired soldier . . . I know him, too."

Eyes narrow, slim fingers fondling the silk pouches that dangled from her waist, she continued to watch wordlessly from the shadows.

Chapter 4

Double Trouble

The whining of a thousand mosquitoes couldn't mask the thud of the monster's footsteps or the complaints of the beast's two heads in the darkness.

"Res hot!"

"Lacua hungry."

"Dumb bugs. Want snow. Why hot?"

"Spring. You stupid."

Pause. "Res go home now."

"No!"

In a small prairie south of Haven, the thirteen-foot ettin faced off with itself—no mean feat for a creature with such short, fat necks. The ettin's watery eyes were tiny, like a pig's, and at the moment, bloodshot with anger. Each hamlike hand, controlled by the head on that side of the body, waved a spiked club. The argument came in a mishmash of orcish, goblin, and giant tongues.

"Quit time," Res, the right head, roared. "Res go home now!"

"Mage say not! Find soldier lady," Lacua, the left head, insisted.

"On trail long. Too much long. No soldier lady. Gone, gone." It might have been the longest speech Res had ever made. He stopped for breath, then, brow furrowing, struggled to remember where he'd started. "What Res say?" he asked Lacua.

The left head thought hard. Lacua's piglike snout curved in concentration. "Think, think," he mused. The heads of the carnivore were balding at the top, but each sported a ponytail of stringy hair, which swung greasily now as Lacua searched his brain. No use. Res-Lacua shrugged and continued walking. Neither Res nor Lacua could keep the subject of a new discussion in mind long enough to get into a major battle.

Janusz had taken the precaution of equipping Lacua with a magical device that allowed the spell-caster to keep tabs on the beast from Janusz's new home in the Icereach, half a continent south of Haven. The ettin had been successful in the past for the mage—proof more of his loyalty and stubbornness than his thinking ability. The ettin's left head, Lacua, while barely beyond a rabbit in raw intelligence, was leagues ahead of the right head, Res. Thus Janusz, anticipating frequent ettin tiffs on a mission so far from home, had appointed Lacua the leader of the expedition and the final arbiter of all disputes.

This would have annoyed Res, had he been able to concentrate on it.

Suddenly a skunk darted from a hollow log, and the ettin's right hand flashed through the darkness and slammed the animal senseless with its club. Ignoring the cloud of stinging spray, the right head devoured the skunk in three bites while Lacua watched, salivating.

Skunk musk, added to the coat of filth that clung to the hide of the ettin, did little to change the intensity of Res-Lacua's stench. "Cleanliness," like most words of more than two syllables, was not in the ettin vocabulary. An ice bear skin, untanned, covered the creature's ample midsection. A constellation of fleas inhabited the fur.

Between the heat and the bugs, the ettin scratched a lot. The spiked clubs came in handy for that.

"Hot," Res muttered again. "No snow."

"Spring, stupid," Lacua repeated.

"Snow," Res moaned. Lacua looked over irritably. Mosquito bites peppered both heads like pox. Res had scratched his until they bled.

"Snow?" Lacua repeated. "Where?"

"*Want* snow."

"No snow here. Nope."

"Go home?"

"Soon."

"Now?"

"No. Later. Maybe."

Res-Lacua shoved north through the purple hestaflowers and other prairie plants. Weed seeds clung to the beast like lint. Before the ettin, plant stalks stood up from the ground like exclamation points. Behind the creature, vegetation lay flattened in a swath as wide as a human man was tall.

Infravision helped the ettin see up to ninety feet in the dark, but Res-Lacua's nightvision had done little so far to help ease the creature's prodigious appetite. The two-headed troll had managed a small snack of two goats and a cow at sunset, but that had been hours ago.

Lacua suddenly stopped, dropped his club, and thrust his left hand into his tunic.

"Flea?" asked Res, face creased with sympathy.

Lacua didn't reply. He pulled two items from a pocket that Janusz had had sewn into the ice bear hide—a jewel that cast an amethyst glow on the twin faces above it, and a second stone, which looked like an ordinary flat, gray pebble. But Lacua handled them both with the ettin version of reverence.

"Not lose talk stone," he chanted. "Not lose purple rock."

"Not, not, not," Res chimed in.

"Dead ettin, if."

Both heads nodded sagely.

The sound of sheep came now to the ettin, who shoved both stones back into his tunic. He scanned the darkness. Then, from behind a rise in the terrain, his four ears caught the sounds of barking and a shouted command. And more sheep sounds.

"Baaa?" asked Res. "Baaaaaa?"

"Baa food," Lacua answered knowingly.

"Ah."

The ettin eagerly moved toward shepherd and flock.

Chapter 5

The Triangle

"Well? Did you steal his money, Kit?" Tanis demanded.

"No," she replied with a glare at Caven Mackid. "I won it from him fair and square. And it's too late now, anyway. I spent it."

"Fair?" Caven spat on the courtyard floor. The minstrels were playing loudly, but the arguing voices sounded over the music. "Ten steel she takes from me," he shouted. "She wins the money from me at faro. Then I catch her cheating and take it back."

"At knifepoint," Kitiara insisted.

Caven and Kitiara were nose to nose with each other, hands clenched, but they addressed their remarks to Tanis. Wode grinned from earlobe to earlobe at the building tension.

"I didn't give it back to him willingly," Kitiara said. "I conceded no guilt; thus the money was still mine."

Caven's face grew redder. "And then, when my back is turned, she goes through my things, steals the money back, and sneaks off like the lying cheat she is!"

Tanis put a rough hand on Kitiara's shoulder. "Did you cheat the man at faro?"

"I never cheat, at faro or any other card game," she said loftily. "I don't have to." When Tanis continued to gaze doubtfully at her, the swordswoman flushed and glared at the two men.

The half-elf turned to Caven Mackid. "You've been tracking her for more than a month for only *ten steel?*"

The swordsman was silent for a moment. "It's the principle of the thing," he said finally.

In the quiet that followed, Tanis realized the minstrels had stopped playing. Four of the innkeeper's servants, dressed in sandals, breechcloths, and a mountain range of rippling muscles, were heading toward the quartet with disapproving faces.

"We're leaving," Tanis called, and hauled a protesting Kitiara into the street. Wode slipped through the door just ahead of them. Caven looked as though he were considering making a stand, then he took stock of his reinforcements, found himself alone, and dogged the half-elf and Kitiara into the night. The inn's door guards stopped at the portal and folded their arms across their considerable chests.

Solinari and Lunitari had vanished behind a blanket of clouds. Tanis glowered like a thundercloud himself as he faced Kitiara. "Pay him, Kit."

"The money was mine."

"Pay him!"

"No!"

Tanis's scowl grew deeper. "Then I will—just to get rid of him. Give me my half of the will-o'-the-wisp money." He put out his palm. Kitiara in turn placed a hand on her belt, where she'd hung the pouch with the captured money. At first surprised and then increasingly frantic, she checked around her.

"Tanis! The pouch is gone! Why didn't we divide the money when we said we would?"

Caven laughed. "She stole it, half-elf. Kitiara nicked you, too."

"Drizzleneff Gatehop!" Kitiara exclaimed. "It was the kender. I know it!" She moaned. "And she's probably far from Haven by now, thanks to me. By the shadowless Abyss, we'll never catch her."

Caven's smooth voice continued. "Take care, half-elf. Kitiara was probably going to run off with your money tonight anyway. No one turns his back on Kitiara Uth Matar."

Suddenly Kitiara cried out. Even in the yellow light of the torches around the inn door, her face looked white. "By the gods, my pack! If that kender . . ." She twisted around to drop to the cobblestones the pack she'd insisted on carrying with her all day. Kitiara dug into the worn baggage, shoved something aside, then sighed. "Thank the gods."

"Our money?" Tanis asked, throwing a triumphant look at Caven Mackid as Kitiara replaced the items in her pack.

But Kitiara shook her head. "Something more valuable. The . . . things for Raistlin."

"Ha!" Caven snickered. "She's got your money in there, half-elf. Let me check." He bustled toward Kitiara, reached for her pack—and found himself backpedaling away from her new dagger.

"You can't value your life much, Mackid," she drawled, "to try something like that."

"She has your money, half-elf," Caven protested. "And mine, too, probably. Go ahead and look."

Tanis put out a resolute hand. "Let me see, Kit."

Kitiara gazed at Tanis for a long time, her expression unreadable. Caven whispered, "Don't let her snooker you, half-elf. She's lying."

The swordswoman, still looking at Tanis, came to some decision. "I'll show you, half-elf." She told Caven over her shoulder, "But you can go to the Abyss, Mackid." Kitiara opened the top of the canvas pack and held the opening wide toward the half-elf. "Look inside," she urged.

After some hesitation, Tanis placed a hand within the pack. His fingers touched clothes, crumbs of provisions left over from weeks on the road, and a small-bladed knife in a wooden case. No money pouch. He pulled his hand back. "Nothing," he said to Caven.

"I told you," Kitiara said. She gathered up the pack and slung it over a shoulder.

For a moment, Caven looked as though he thought Kitiara and Tanis might be in consort against him, but a glance at the half-elf seemed to change his mind. He kicked a booted toe against a cobblestone. "Ten steel," he muttered. "I follow the woman for a month for ten lousy steel, and she doesn't have the money anymore. And I have one steel left to my name." He looked up. His tone was suddenly hopeful. "How much money do you two have?"

Tanis and Kitiara looked at each other. Kitiara seemed unperturbed by her fellow mercenary's mercurial change of mood. "I'm broke, Mackid. Give it up."

"I have a few coins," the half-elf said. "Enough for supper and drink for Kitiara and me." He emphasized the latter words.

"And I have one steel coin," Caven finished. "Let's find another tavern and discuss our situation over some ale."

Tanis felt the lines of his face settle into hardness—what Flint Fireforge called his "infernal mulish elven look." "*Our* situation?" he repeated.

Caven nodded. "The situation," he explained, "in which the two of you are going to find ten steel to replace the ones Kitiara stole or risk having me go to the Haven city guards, who will take you in custody for thievery."

With a cry, Kitiara, dagger drawn, flung herself across the cobblestones at Caven. She narrowly missed impaling the big man before Tanis dragged her off. Wode's look of fascination had changed to one of utter glee. "Half-elf, let me go!" Kitiara shrieked. "I'll disembowel him and his scrawny squire both, I swear it! Mackid have *me* thrown in prison? It was *my* money, I tell you!"

"It might take some time to prove that, Kit," Caven said, smiling gently. "Weeks, maybe months—if you can do it at all. How will you prove it from a Haven dungeon, my dear?"

Kitiara stopped struggling to consider his words. The anger seemed to seep from her body into the stones at their feet. After a slight hesitation, Tanis released her. The swordswoman straightened her clothing and headed down the street away from the Masked Dragon. "Come on then, you two," she called back irritably.

"Come on?" Caven repeated. He looked from Kitiara to the half-elf.

"To an alehouse," she shouted. "To talk. You invited us for a drink, Caven, after all."

Caven Mackid stood motionless, but Tanis, smiling despite himself, hastened to catch up with the swordswoman. Finally, after a short hike, Kitiara paused before a smoky den from which torchlight spilled. A hand-lettered sign, exuberantly misspelled, had been nailed above the door. It read "The Happee Ohgr" and was decorated with a drawing of an obviously drunken ogre. "This place looks appropriate for this type of discussion," Kitiara said and pushed down the steps into the crowded tavern. Tanis, shrugging, followed with Wode, and Caven brought up the rear.

They found a table by evicting three torpid traders who were too drunk to protest. The barkeep didn't argue; clearly these new customers had more room for ale than did the sodden trio that now sat propped, forgotten and snoring, against a wall.

Wode said nothing, but Tanis, Caven, and Kitiara had to shout over the din of arguments and occasional fistfights.

"Where'd you get the money the kender stole?" Caven yelled, taking one swig of ale and then another. He now seemed inclined to believe Kitiara's tale about Drizzleneff Gatehop. The swordswoman, using gestures almost as much as shouted phrases, sketched out the details of the previous night's battle with the will-o'-the-wisp. Then Caven launched into ideas for the three of them to band together and make some real money. Grandiose ideas, Tanis thought with a yawn. But he listened politely, realizing that Kitiara took Caven more seriously.

Both of them were getting drunk at a record pace, the half-elf realized. Wordless, Tanis considered his untouched tankard, then the pair of mercenaries.

They made a formidable duo. Kitiara was slender but muscular, her dark hair especially curly in the unseasonable humidity, her eyes luminous with—what? The alcohol? Caven, with the massive, toned body of one who devotes much time to his body's care, dwarfed her and the half-elf. The two humans shared black hair, dark eyes, pale faces—and at the moment, a greedy look of eking whatever they could from their pathetically short human lives, at whatever cost.

Caven waved to summon the barmaid, a plump, blonde teen-ager with pink skin and a bovine look. Wode, who must have been a year or two younger than the girl, sat up a little straighter, thrust out his thin chest, and gave her a leer. She appeared unimpressed. "Yah?" she asked Caven.

"Another pitcher of ale."

"Ya kin pay?"

Caven glared at her. "Of course we can pay."

"Show me th' money."

When Caven bridled, the girl said, "Place like 'is, ya got yer travelers what guzzle but don' pay, yah? I never seed ya before. Y' dress nice, sure, but ya mighta stole yer duds. So ya show me th' money now, all righ'?"

Caven slammed his last coin on the table. The girl, expressionless, picked up the money with a dirty hand and studied the coin. "Looks good," she said, pocketing it, picking up the pitcher, and turning away. Moments later, she returned and placed the filled pitcher before the four with a thump that slopped liquor onto the table. Wode rose and followed her back to the bar.

"This place reminds me of the Sandy Viper in Kernen," Kitiara commented. "Smoke, sticky tables, and drunks in the corner."

Caven snickered and refilled Kitiara's glass. "Remember the night Lloiden threw the pitcher of beer into the fire?"

The swordswoman chortled in response. "He thought he could prove they were watering the beer. He said watered beer would put the fire out," she explained to Tanis. "Instead, he practically burned the place down." When the half-elf failed to smile, Kitiara spoke instead to Caven. "Tanis isn't in a mood to be amused tonight, Mackid," she said with mock gravity.

Abruptly Tanis got up. He joined Wode, who was now lounging at the bar, his lustful gaze following the barmaid, who studiously ignored him. "Ah, what a woman!" the lad said wistfully. He stuck a skinny hand toward Tanis. "Name's Wode. Caven's my uncle. My mum's his big sis. I'm 'is squire—have been for a year now." Tanis shook the proffered hand.

The teen-ager pointed at Kitiara and Mackid, who were roaring with laughter and pounding each other's shoulders. "Might as well give up on 'em tonight, half-elf. I've seen 'em like this before. Once they get going on the ol' stories, they're set for the night, drinkin' and talkin'. . . . At least they don't have much in the way of money, or they'd still be sitting there in the mornin'."

"But Mackid threatened her with prison. Didn't he mean it?"

Wode nodded with a wise air. "Oh, he meant it, all right. Maybe he don' remember it right now, 'course, bein' as he's been swilling ale like a pig. But he'll remember in the mornin'. And my guess is that she'll remember, too—in the mornin'. But that's the way the paid soldiers is, half-elf. Kinda changeable, like the breezes. Everythin's forgiven while they're in their cups. Least, Caven's that way. Captain Kitiara can get a bit snappish with more'n a couple under her belt."

The barmaid swept by them without a word. Wode sniffed the scent of fried onions, spilled beer, and grilled beef that hovered in her wake. "Wonderful," he sighed.

"She's not your type," Tanis advised him.

"Eh?" Wode turned a bright green gaze full on the half-elf. Then he frowned as the barmaid swept by again, nose high in the air. "I suppose you're right." He sighed again.

"How long have those two known each other?" Tanis indicated Kitiara and Caven.

Wode mused. "There was two weeks for the siege, a month to get ready for it, plus another bunch of months of gadding about after the rout. Then Kitiara lit out on Caven, and Caven lit out after 'er. Ah, you shoulda seen him when he found out she'd nipped his coins!"

Tanis tried to divert the lad into more fertile areas of information. "The rout?" Kitiara had let drop the information that she had been up in Kern—"soldiers for hire," as she put it. But she had been reticent on the subject of the campaign. This might be a chance to learn something.

The boy sighed. "It was awful. Magefire burnin' from the sky, and people screamin' and dyin'. Then Kitiara comes runnin' up and grabs her horse from me and tries to take off, but Caven catches her and makes her wait for him, and the two of 'em head west outa Kern, and I follow, of course."

"So Kitiara tried to leave him behind?" Tanis was glad of that news, at least.

The youth assented. "But Caven's a stubborn one. He was set on goin' with her, 'specially as the Valdane is known for treating losin' troops sort of bad, if you catch my meanin'." He looked at Tanis, who raised his eyebrows questioningly. "Kills 'em. Or rather, has the mage do it. But, gads, he pays well when he does win, so the paid soldiers, being gamblin' types anyhow, are willin' to chance it." The lad sketched in what little he knew about Kern and the Valdane and his mage, Janusz. "Some say they've got a—" The boy paused and looked around—"a bloodlink." He winked and nodded significantly.

If Wode was expecting a certain reaction from Tanis, however, he didn't get it. "A bloodlink?" the half-elf asked, not bothering to lower his voice.

Wode shushed him with a panic-stricken look to each side. "Quiet, y' idiot! Don't they have 'em around here?" Tanis shook his head. " 'Course," the lad continued, "they're not supposed to have 'em at home, either. They've been illegal in Kern since my great-great-grandpa was a cub. But rumor has it the Valdane's father, the old Valdane, had a rogue mage who was willin' an' not afraid of what the Conclave of Wizards would do to 'im, so he went ahead and set one up with the Valdane—the current Valdane, that is; the one who was a boy then—and another boy who turned out to be Janusz, the current mage."

Tanis's head was starting to spin, but he urged the boy on. "There was rumors all over Kern," Wode said, " 'specially when the Valdane's parents—that is, the parents of the current Valdane, who was a boy then— died right after the bloodlink—the one we think was set up—was set up. But it's death to talk about it in Kern, so don't repeat anythin' I said if you ever go there." He stopped for air.

Tanis nodded, so thoroughly bewildered that he couldn't have repeated a word of what he had just heard. He sorted through the youth's jumbled sentences. "What's a bloodlink?" the half-elf managed to ask, remembering to lower his voice.

Wode managed to look self-important and surprised at the same time. "Where you been living, half-elf?" he finally choked out.

"I grew up in Qualinesti," Tanis replied.

Wode pursed his lips and nodded, as though that explained everything. "Ah. A rustic. Well, a bloodlink—which may or may not exist, now, y'understand, except everybody in Kern believes it does because—"

Tanis interrupted. *"What is it?"*

Wode cast him a reproachful look but, swelled with importance, went on. "They link two people, usually one of 'em a mage and the other one someone from the nobility. The lower one—usually the mage—takes the knocks for the highfalutin one." Wode nodded haughtily, then continued irritably when it became apparent that the half-elf still didn't comprehend. "All right, say you and I got a bloodlink—if there is such a thing, but I bet there is . . ."

"All right," Tanis said a little dispiritedly, "say we have such a link."

"Well, if I'm the one with the power, then anything bad that's supposed to happen to me happens to you."

Tanis lifted one brow. Wode released a heavy sigh. "All right. Say a hobgoblin belts me in the gut with his mornin' star." The half-elf waited. "I ought to be practically dead, right? But you suffer the injury instead, and I get off without a scratch. Or so the story goes. There's some that says it's just a myth, but I think . . ."

He continued to rattle on. No longer heeding the youth, Tanis leaned back against the bar. If Wode's blather was to be credited, a bloodlink with a mage would give a nobleman quite a powerful edge in the world, to say nothing of a considerable hold over the wizard. No wonder the Conclave of Wizards had banned such practices. Wode said this Janusz had been a boy when the bloodlink was set up. Assuming, of course, that the bloodlink even existed . . .

Tanis shook his head; he was starting to think like Wode. The half-elf focused again on Kitiara and Caven. They were leaning confidentially on the table, starting their third pitcher of ale, talking furiously at each other. Neither appeared to be doing much in the way of listening.

Tanis was in no mood to stay up all night listening to stories of camaraderie between Kitiara and Caven. Tanis and Kitiara's room at the Seven Centaurs, thankfully paid for in advance, seemed more inviting than a smoky tavern in the bowels of Haven. Kitiara knew how to get back to the inn on her own.

He left the Happee Ohgr without saying good night.

*   *   *   *   *

Three hours later, Kitiara pushed herself away from the table and rose unsteadily, making sure to grasp the pack that, even after her ninth tankard of ale, she'd kept safely under her feet. Caven raised a bleary head from its resting place on the sticky table. "Whazzup?" he murmured. "Wanna refill?" He reached for the pitcher, found it empty, on its side, and grimaced. Then, blinking slowly, he groped about on the table. Kitiara guessed his intent.

"There's no money left," she said softly. As his hand continued to search through the detritus on the table, she added, "We've drunk our quota, and the barkeep is giving us the eye. I always could outdrink you, Mackid."

Caven grunted. "Tell 'im to put it on a bill. I'm good for it."

Kitiara laughed too loudly, then watched with a lopsided grin as Caven winced. "You tell him, Mac-kid. It's time for me to leave." She stepped over a sprawled dwarf and headed for the door, avoiding the nastiest spots on the floor.

"Where're you stayin'?" Caven shouted back, his face red. "You're not getting away without paying me, y' cheat!"

At this time of night, in such a place, such epithets were routine terms of endearment. The few patrons still conscious paid little attention to what no doubt seemed to be a typical lovers' quarrel.

"The Masked Dragon," she lied. "I'll see you there in the morning."

"I'm going with you. It'll be a lot better than sleeping in the stable with Maleficent." While Kitiara wondered whether such a remark was worth a challenge, Caven leaned on his arms and straightened. When his focus returned, he gazed slowly over the room. "Where's Wode?" he snapped. "That lazy—"

"Wode left an hour ago with the barmaid. Or rather, the blonde cow left and the boy followed."

"Hot on her trail," Caven said, satisfied. "Good lad. Which reminds me . . ." He maneuvered carefully over the dwarf, nearly falling headlong when the sodden creature hiccuped and rolled over. The room stank of stale things—food, beer, and breath. "I'm going with you," he repeated. "To the Masked Dragon."

"Tanis is already there. I doubt there's room for three."

"Then tell 'im to leave," Mackid said mulishly. "I can flatten any elf any day."

"Half-elf," Kitiara corrected. "And don't count on it."

Caven gestured magnanimously, which threw him off balance. "Tell him to get lost, then go along with me." He winked. "I'll generously forgive your debt." He caught his balance against the doorjamb.

Kitiara looked up, eyes skeptical but clearer than most others in the room. Caven Mackid was a splendid physical specimen of a man, but not exactly irresistible in his current state. And she wasn't tired of the half-elf yet.

"I'm leaving, Mackid." She turned away and walked up the three steps to the street.

It was raining. The cobblestones, slippery even in dry weather, were oily slick. Kitiara put one hand on the wall of the Happee Ohgr and moved quickly down the street, paying attention to her footing and trying to ignore the growing damp of her clothing. Behind her, she heard Caven's muffled oath as he emerged on the street into the wet weather. "Kitiara!" he bellowed. But she went on without stopping, rain trickling through her curls onto her face.

At this time of night, practically no one was left on the streets of Haven but a few drunks and an occasional bored town guard. Kitiara took a sharp left turn and found herself in a side alley devoid of life and light; it led in the general direction of the Seven Centaurs and was made of packed ground rather than slippery cobbles.

Caven appeared some distance behind her. "Kitiara?" He peered into the gloom.

"Leave it, Mackid," she snapped, and doubled her pace. At that moment, however, thunder crashed and the drizzle turned into a downpour. She leaped into a doorway with an exclamation. Caven joined her moments later.

The doorway was wide, protected, and dry. Locked

double doors led into what was a warehouse of sorts. Caven stood motionless between Kitiara and the street, an air of expectation about him. She shivered, realizing that her short skirt and light blouse, while okay for freedom of movement and for attracting admiring stares in the Haven market, were less than adequate for a chilly downpour.

She was soaked to the skin. Caven, on the other hand, was protected by his tightly woven wool cloak.

She pointed. "You wear that cape even in the warm weather, Mackid?"

Caven smiled. "It comes in handy."

Suddenly Caven Mackid didn't look so drunk to her. What he did look was *warm*, and Kitiara found herself coveting his body heat as much as admiring his physique. She shivered again. "Lend me your cape, soldier," she ordered.

"Cold?" He grinned again. Caven loomed over her, not quite touching her. She could feel his heat. "I can do more to warm you than lend you my cape, Kit," he murmured. His eyes were dark in his pale face.

Kitiara leaned back against the rough stone wall of the doorway. Chill emanated from the rock. Out in the street, rain streaked down in needles.

She drew a shivery breath. Then she nodded. Caven reached for her.

Chapter 6

Mage and Friend

Smoldering blue eyes peered at Kitiara and Caven's refuge from a doorway across the street. The hood of a voluminous woolen robe, charcoal gray in the gloom, hid the woman's other features.

Kai-lid Entenaka had been trailing Kitiara Uth Matar unseen since the swordswoman and the three men had left the minstrel show earlier in the evening. But Kai-lid was mindless of the chill and the damp; her robe, magically augmented, warded off discomfort. Her fingers traced the silken cord at her waist. She could cast a light spell, of course, to see what the couple in the entryway across the alley were up to, but Kai-lid didn't need such illumination. Memories of similar moments in her own marriage washed over her. Since the end of the marriage, she'd sought to keep those recollections away, but they returned at times unbidden, usually at night.

She shook her head slightly to cast off the unwelcome thoughts. "What about the half-elf, Captain Uth Matar?" she whispered to herself.

Kai-lid waited patiently until the rain eased and the two figures, adjusting their clothing and combing their rain-soaked hair with their fingers, finally moved out of the doorway. Huddled under the man's cape, they headed off together into the night. The mage waited until they were gone, then crossed the lane. Her fingers searched through the pebbles and dirt on the doorway's floor. Warmth still clung to the brick paving, but she discovered no other vestiges of the couple's presence. She was about to give up when something small and hard skittered away from her moving hand. Now she did intone a light spell, and a pale green glow illuminated the doorway, revealing her delicate features, the color of warm oak. She searched again and found a dark button wedged in a corner against a finger of broken brick. It was probably of tortoiseshell; polishing had failed to eliminate the whorls of the creature's carapace.

The button was a small thing, but if it had belonged to Kitiara Uth Matar or that man, it would be enough for the mage's purposes. She held it in a clenched hand and slipped away through the dark streets. She kept to the shadows and met no one.

The inkiness of the night might have slowed an ordinary woman, but Kai-lid's magic helped light her way as she left the town behind her and paced along a path that led northeast out of Haven. She didn't bother to probe the underbrush around her. Although Kai-lid was not a powerful mage, she had tricks to keep her safe if the need arose. The rain failed to bother her; the forest canopy, far above her head, was a thick shield.

The path grew rockier, narrower, less packed by constant footfalls as she sped along. It led to Darken Wood, and it was the rare man or woman who ventured far in that direction.

The closeness of Darken Wood and its fearsome reputation made her hermitage perfect from Kai-lid Entenaka's viewpoint. She made the two-mile trek from her cave to Haven once a week, often enough to trade the herbs she foraged for money or items she needed. She didn't require much.

Kai-lid lived comfortably near the woods. She was no threat to its varied occupants, and that innocence, she believed, ensured her safety. When she'd arrived in the area, the dark forest's inhabitants had kept their distance. She'd sensed they were there, but they had not shown themselves.

Naturally stories came to her from well-meaning— or just plain nosy—Haven residents with whom she did business.

"There are souls of knights who fought and died centuries before the Cataclysm in those woods!" exclaimed a leatherworker when he found out where Kai-lid lived. "And creatures, neither dead nor alive, whose howling can drive a person mad. Move into town, woman!"

His fingers moved agitatedly over one of Kai's sandals, repairing a strap, but his voice rattled on. The man had gone on and on about the denizens of the Darken Wood. Kai-lid had no doubt that much of what he said was true. At times when she entered the woods in search of herbs and other things useful for magic, it seemed to her the trees were not quite where they'd been on earlier forays. Occasional strands of wild songs—like Plainsmen's death cries—came to her on the wind. And some nights, hoofbeats clattered to a halt just out of sight of Kai-lid's home.

"I have no fear of the dead. I've seen worse behavior from the living," she had said to the leatherworker. Her blue eyes had deepened to purple, and the questioner had had the common sense to change the subject.

Kai-lid knew the man would have been aghast to learn that she hadn't even bothered to fashion a door to her home, a cave whose gray granite matched the hue of her woolen robe. Only a curtain of Qualinesti-woven silk covered the opening, and that covering was usually tied back. Kai-lid loved the feel of open air around her. Even in those few instances when hail or snow pounded the area, she let the wildness enter without restriction.

Now, however, an unusual sound came to Kai-lid's ears. She halted and gazed around her in the dark. Nothing. She took a few steps, then heard it again—a clicking, as of a mandible opening and closing. A giant ant? It was difficult to know what was fact and what was fiction in the tales of Darken Wood. For example, spectral minions were rumored to prevent intruders. Yet Kai-lid came and went without molestation.

With one hand on her spell-casting materials, she expanded her light spell and looked around her more closely. Kai-lid saw nothing noteworthy. A sycamore, common around here and five times the height of the tallest building in Haven, stood off to one side, casting a craggy shadow in the green magelight. An opening at the very bottom of the wide tree showed it to be hollow, and Kai-lid knew that a family of raccoons had taken up residence there. Bracken ferns stood up from the damp earth, fleshy fronds swaying in a breeze that Kai-lid felt now for the first time. The area was rich with the scents of fertile soil and dampness and plants, and Kai-lid could detect no hint of danger.

Then she heard another sound—a thrumming, as of a huge heart, beating quickly but with each beat distinct. And a whooshing, as of deep breathing. Whatever caused those sounds was relaxed, that was clear from the pattern: inhale, exhale, pause . . . inhale, exhale, pause. She detected an odor—a dusty smell, like straw, not unpleasant. Kai-lid sensed a rustling, as of something shifting, something massive. Then the clicking again.

Suddenly a voice came to her, making no sound but entering her mind directly, and Kai-lid knew who lurked in the trees.

I am a fierce, evil monster come to eat you alive.

"Stop it, Xanthar," Kai-lid answered wearily. "I'm too tired for games. I need to think, and I need to do it alone." All clicking, whooshing, and rustling stopped; the being was still. "And please don't sulk."

The mage resumed walking and followed a curve in the path until she saw the mouth of her cave, its blue curtain still tied back, in a clearing before her. The shadow of a huge bird was hulked over at the top of another dead sycamore, rejection apparent in every drooping feather. The mage paused and surveyed the bird affectionately.

Finally, as she knew it would, the soundless voice resonated in her brain again. *It's time for your mind-speaking lesson, Kai-lid Entenaka. You're late. I've been worried.*

Kai-lid dipped her head and apologized. "I was in

Haven, Xanthar."

The voice in her mind carped, *You know I don't like it when you go into Haven alone. I should accompany you.*

"We've had this discussion before, Xanthar," Kai-lid said calmly as she moved across the clearing and paused under the sycamore. "Your magic will diminish if you go too far from Darken Wood. Besides, giant owls sleep during the day, remember?" Her voice held suppressed laughter.

But the other voice hadn't finished yet. *And you should remember that I can go that far from the woods, at least. A few hours' lost sleep won't kill me. From what you've told me, no city is safe for you. You might meet someone from Kernen.*

"I did."

The owl clearly was unprepared for this reply. After a shocked delay, it rose to its utmost height and flapped great wings, with a span twenty feet wide, against the night air. The dead sycamore creaked and groaned, and gouts of wind sent the mage's hood flying back and her hair whipping about her face. A screech rent the clearing, and Kai-lid, cringing, expanded her light spell until she could see the owl.

"Xanthar, they didn't see me," she hastened to say. "I was careful." Despite her exhaustion, Kai-lid smiled at the giant owl.

Xanthar finally folded his wings against his sides. He nestled his golden beak, the length of Kai-lid's arm, into the beige fluff at his neck. His face was speckled brown and gray and black, with a patch of white over his left eye, which gave him an endearingly rakish air, Kai-lid thought. Black and brown feathers were scattered across his creamy breast. His legs were feathered, too, right down to the mahogany scales on his strong feet, each toe tipped with a deadly claw. Xanthar's wings were mahogany-hued, verging into dark gray toward the tail. The wing tips were beige. He turned his plate-size eyes, each with a huge pupil of depthless ebony, toward the spell-caster and surveyed her with mingled concern and annoyance. His feet clenched and unclenched on the sycamore branch, betraying his agitation.

Why are you smiling? This is serious. They could be seeking you.

"I'm smiling because you are the most beautiful bird I've ever seen, not to mention the most beautiful I've ever talked to."

You make me sound like a pet parakeet. Anyway, you should be practicing your mind-speaking.

The creature's mind-voice was pettish, but Kai-lid knew he preened at her compliment; his lids drooped lazily across orange eyes and he arched his neck, affording Kai-lid a better view of his beaky silhouette. Suddenly exhaustion pulled at her. She sat on a broken limb near the bottom of the sycamore.

You are tired.

Kai-lid nodded.

Whom did you see? Tell me in mind-talk; this is an opportunity for you to practice.

Kai-lid leaned against the trunk and groaned. "You never give up, do you, Xanthar? One species wasn't meant to communicate telepathically with another species."

I can. At least, he amended, *I can with you.*

"You have special magic, Xanthar, powers I've not heard of in any others of your race." She paused. "Speaking aloud is so much easier for me."

Typical human. The giant owl, still grumbling, stepped carefully from the top limb to a lower one, and then to another still lower, until he was only ten feet away, although still above her. He leaned over and examined her with softly glowing eyes. *Whom did you see in Haven?*

"A captain in the Valdane's mercenary forces— Kitiara Uth Matar. And another soldier. I don't know his name, but I saw him often with the captain at the siege. They were with a half-elf tonight. Him I didn't recognize."

Xanthar whetted his beak against his perch in annoyance. *I should have gone with you.*

"You know that's not wise." Giant owls fetched great prices in the marketplace. Xanthar had lost his mate and their last clutch of nestlings to poachers years ago. The great birds mated for life, and Xanthar had remained solitary, in and near Darken Wood, ever since.

What will you do now? When Kai-lid looked up questioningly, the giant owl continued. *Will you go back to Haven to watch this Matar person and the other two?*

"I won't have to." Kai-lid felt a question quiver in her mind, but no words. In reply, she held up the button. "I can watch them magically."

Chapter 7

A Gnome and a Jewel

Tanis awakened before dawn the next morning to find Kitiara on her knees in the dark, retching into the empty chamber pot. He rolled over in bed and watched her wordlessly.

"Either offer some help or stop staring, half-elf," Kitiara said. She sat up on the braided rag rug next to the bed. The movement sent her clutching her temples. "By the gods, I ache all over."

"Too much ale." Tanis's lips curved.

"Don't be a prude. I can drink any man under the table and wake up to fight a hundred hobgoblins the next morning." She moaned suddenly and leaned over the chamber pot again. Her skin was clammy and ashen.

Tanis took his time swinging his legs out of bed. "You came in rather late." He kept his voice deliberately neutral.

Kitiara, still kneeling with her head down, surveyed him with bloodshot eyes. "I thought you were asleep. Anyway, I had to put Caven Mackid off our trail."

"Oh?"

"Get me a blanket, will you? I'm freezing."

Tanis didn't move. "Perhaps you should have worn something to bed," he said laconically instead.

"And perhaps *you* should—"

"Mmmm?"

Kitiara didn't finish the sentence. Instead, she crawled over to the bed and, when Tanis shifted aside, hoisted herself back in. "By the chasms of the Abyss, I've never felt like this. Maybe I've caught something." She collapsed with a groan, facedown on the feather mattress.

"And maybe you're getting too old to drink like that."

"That's fine advice from someone who's over ninety." She reached back, still facedown, and pulled the down comforter up over her head. The bedding muffled her voice. "I spent the time telling Caven all sorts of lies to put him off our track. We can sneak out of town and never see him again. He thinks we're staying at the Masked Dragon, the gullible idiot."

"Mmm-hmmm." Tanis padded over to a chair near the door and pulled on his breeches.

Kitiara rolled over with an effort.

Tanis slipped on his fringed leather shirt.

"Which means . . . ?" She tried to sit up but fell back against the pillow with a mild oath.

Tanis groped under the chair for his moccasins. "Which means I think the results of that faro game may not have been left entirely to chance. Which means I think Captain Kitiara Uth Matar, under certain circumstances, is entirely capable of 'acquiring' a man's savings and disappearing."

Kitiara changed the subject. "Where are you going, half-elf?"

"To have the kitchen boy bring you some weak tea and something to eat, and to walk about Haven thinking up ways we can earn ten steel to pay back Caven Mackid."

Shock registered on Kitiara's features. "Pay him back?"

"One thing I've learned in my ninety-odd years," he said smoothly, "is that it's a bad idea to leave debts unpaid. They always come back to haunt you."

"You damned moralist." Kitiara was smiling, however, her arms crossed against her bare chest.

"Besides," he continued, "if we repay Mackid, then we're rid of him for good, and you and I can be on our way to Solace."

Then he was out the door.

*　*　*　*　*

Stopping in the kitchen on his way out, Tanis found the scullery boy dozing on the hearth. The lad leaped to his feet when the half-elf entered the room. "Kin I help y', sir?" His sandy blond hair was tousled, his hazel eyes crusty with sleep.

"Have you made tea yet this morning?"

The lad nodded and gestured toward a pot steeping atop the mantel. A slice of bread leaned against the pot. "One. For the missus—the innkeeper's wife. Herself is w' child and can't start the day w'out her tea and dry toast. And," he added, as if warming to an old grievance, "it's gotta be winterberry tea with rosehips and peppermint. Herself says some herbalist told her it'll help the unborn babe, but I think it's just 'cause she likes the taste of it and it causes more work for everybody. But to tell the truth, once she drinks it she don't upchuck no more, so maybe . . ."

Tanis, visions of Wode dancing in his head, interrupted the lad's monologue. "Send some of that up to my room, will you? With more toast."

The boy got busy pouring hot water from a kettle, which was setting on an iron spider placed over the fire, into a second pot, next to the steeping one on the mantel. "Y' have a lady w' you, true? One mug or two?"

"Just one. I'm going out." Tanis handed the boy one of the few coins he had left. "Oh, and one more thing."

"Eh?"

"Make sure the lady knows the tea is especially good for pregnant women, but don't tell her that until she's drunk a good bit."

"Ah! The lady's w' child, then?" The youth looked wise.

"No," Tanis replied.

The boy grinned. "A joke, then. I see."

Tanis smiled down at the lad and nodded. "Just make sure you're standing near the door when you tell her."

"Ah," the lad repeated. "A temper?"

The half-elf laughed.

The lad winked. "I'll be careful."

*   *   *   *   *   *

Wode looked on as Tanis paused in the Seven Centaurs' doorway, filled his lungs with soft morning air, then strode toward the center of town. Wode had been watching the front door of the inn since Caven had trailed Kitiara there after she pretended to enter the Masked Dragon. The mercenary had a pallet behind Maleficent's stall, back at the livery stable. Wode looked about, momentarily uncertain. Should he follow the half-elf? No, Caven had said Kitiara, not Tanis, was the one to watch, and she had not left the Seven Centaurs. The lad settled back on the bench, pulled Caven's cloak up around his shoulders, and waited.

*　*　*　*　*

"Great Reorx at the forge!"

Heading down the main street of Haven toward the marketplace, Tanis heard the oath, one of Flint's favorites, before the half-elf actually saw the creature responsible for the racket. The voice was too high, too nasal to be dwarven. That left one possibility. Early-morning vendors and traders were giving a wide berth to an abandoned stable from which lantern light spilled. Tanis waited. Soon a small explosion cracked, seeming to surprise no one, and a short, round figure, trailed by rolling gears and a great deal of smoke, tumbled end-over-end through the building's open door. "Hydrodynamics!" cried the figure in midroll.

No one but Tanis moved to help him. Instead, three Haven men ran to put out the small fire that licked a corner of the building. Tanis squatted, which put him on eye level with the figure, and dusted off the gnome. "Are you hurt?" the half-elf asked gently.

The creature, sitting on the sandstone that made up this stretch of Haven road, looked dolefully up at Tanis through violet eyes. Soft white hair, dusted with bits of ash, festooned the gnome's head and chin and upper lip. His skin was rich brown, his nose lumpy—no doubt the result of earlier experiments—and his ears were rounded. He was dressed in typical mismatched gnome fashion—baggy silk pants in purplish pink, teal-colored linen top, brown leather boots, and a gold scarf shot with silver threads. "Are you hurt?" the half-elf repeated.

"ItmusthavebeenthehydroencephalatorbecauseI'dalreadygoneoverthedrive—" the gnome replied. "Thechaininhibitorandthegearratiowereexactlywhatmycomputationssaidtheyshouldbeexceptofcoursethesunhasn'trisenyetandperhapsthere'saluminaryquotienttherethathasn'tbeeninvestigatedyet. . . . Yes! Aluminaryquotient!"

Then the gnome jumped up and, ignoring the half-elf, dashed back into the building, paying no heed to the humans, now numbering nearly a dozen, who were dashing in with buckets of water. The half-elf followed. "Shouldn't you stay out until the fire's extinguished?" he asked the gnome. The fellow clambered onto a tall stool placed before a contraption that stretched from wall to wall and from the floor two stories up to the rafters.

The gnome glanced back at the opposite corner. Flames no longer flickered, but smoke streamed from blackened boards that occasionally glowed orange and red. "Perhaps," the gnome said, "afireinhibitorymechanismwhichIcanseewouldhavetohave—"

Tanis interrupted. "Speak more slowly."

The gnome looked up from the computations he was already scrawling on a slip of parchment. "Eh?"

"Slowly," the half-elf repeated.

Light dawned in the gnome's face. With a visible effort, he interjected a half-breath between every word. "I'm . . . sorry. . . . I . . . forget . . . I'm . . . not . . . among . . . my fellows." He inhaled deeply. Obviously it took more energy for him to speak slowly than to blurt out the unending sentences that marked the speech of the gnomes. Gnomes, who could talk and listen at the same time, believed continuous speech by all conversants was more efficient than the balky give-and-take chatting of the other races.

Tanis introduced himself. "What's your name?" he added, then saw his error too late. "Wait!" "Speaker-SungearsonofBeamcatcherSungearillustrious-inventoroftheperiluminohighspeedelevatorand-grandsonof . . ."

The rest of the name—gnomish names, which included genealogical history stretching back dozens of generations, could go on for hours—was muffled by Tanis's hand, clapped over the gnome's mouth. The piping tones trailed off, and the creature glared up at Tanis. Behind them, the last bucket of water extinguished the last of the blaze with a splash and a hiss, and the grumbling fire fighters left.

"What do *humans* call you?" the half-elf asked in the sudden silence, releasing his hand gingerly.

"Speaker . . . Sungear," came the reply. "Of the Communications Guild."

Gnomish workers were divided into various guilds—agricultural, philosophical, education, and many others. "I haven't heard of the Gnomish Communications Guild," Tanis observed.

"You will, once I'm through here," Speaker said, turning back to his project. Speaking slowly seemed to come easier now that the excitement of the fire was past. "I'm going to form it as soon as I perfect this mechanism."

Tanis looked up at the contraption, fashioned of gears of all sizes, wire in three colors, and a gigantic horn shaped like a morning glory blossom. The horn's tip fit into a small box the size of the half-elf's thumb. "It seems a bit large to call it a mere mechanism," the half-elf observed.

"Oh, it has a much longer name, of course. It's actually a . . ."

"No!" Tanis shouted, just in time. "Mechanism is fine."

Speaker looked disappointed. But he shrugged and continued adjusting dozens of knobs and toggle switches on the machine. Finally he stood atop the stool to reach one knob, which he called "an adjustatory demarcation facilitator."

"What does it do?" Tanis finally asked.

"Do?" Speaker repeated. Standing on the stool, his exasperated face was mere inches from Tanis's. "It facilitates the adjustatory demarcation option. Isn't it obvious, half-elf?"

Tanis gazed again at the shiny but ash-spotted apparatus. Then he looked back at Speaker Sungear. The gnome sighed heavily and sat down on the stool. "This apparatus will revolutionize life on Ansalon," the gnome said.

Tanis looked from Speaker to the machine. "Really."

The gnome nodded vigorously. "It will allow all races to speak to one another *without being anywhere near each other.*"

"Really." Tanis wondered if Speaker Sungear had received a knock to his noggin when he tumbled through the door.

"Really," the half-elf reiterated, gazing at the machine.

"Why?" the gnome demanded. "What does it look like it would do?"

Tanis strolled before the contraption. "It looks like its chief purpose is to make noise." The gnome looked askance. The half-elf reached out to touch a toggle switch, only to bring Speaker Sungear tumbling from his stool in frantic haste.

"This is a carefully adjusted mechanism! Not for *amateurs* to fool with."

Speaker's expression told the half-elf that the gnome thought his visitor had the intelligence of a gully dwarf. "This"—he pointed to the flower-shaped horn—"collects sunlight, focuses it through my special illuminatory derivation device"—he pointed to the small box at the base of the horn—"and picks up the auditory emanations of ordinary speech"—he indicated a series of small gears ribboned with copper wire—"and translates the auditory ululations into illuminatory permutational vectors"—he showed Tanis a spool wrapped with more wire and a paper covered with figures—"which can be perceived and retranslated back into auditory emanations suitable for comprehension by the ordinary ear!" He stood back and folded his arms across his small chest. It was apparent that he expected an outburst of applause.

"You don't say," Tanis said. He cast about for something else to say. "Why?"

The gnome's violet eyes bugged. "Why? Why!" A pinkish streak was forming across his cheeks and nose. Tanis hoped it wasn't a sign that the gnome was having an apoplectic seizure.

Speaker Sungear inclined his head. The blush faded from his face. "How do you find out about events now?" he asked in an almost fatherly tone, as if explaining dewdrops to a child.

Tanis thought. "From friends. At alehouses. Overhearing things on the road."

"And in larger towns?"

Tanis felt his brow furrow. "Larger alehouses?" he guessed.

Speaker rolled his eyes. "Town criers!" he crowed triumphantly.

"Oh. Town criers."

"Think about it—some human standing on a street corner, yelling the day's events to passersby. It's not efficient!" That seemed to be the worst condemnation the gnome could devise. "Think of the improvements in communication if we could get machines to do it!" Speaker Sungear was enthralled with his notion.

"Machines?"

"Specifically my machine here. It will translate sound into sunlight and back into sound. We could send messages with this apparatus, learn about events in far-off corners of Ansalon almost as they happened!" Speaker, tears in his eyes, caressed the contraption with one hand, then cocked his head. "In fact, as a test, I will use this very machine to transmit some important news to all the inhabitants of Haven." Speaker's mustache drooped. "Of course there are a few wrinkles to smooth out."

"I should say." Tanis decided the creature was harmless, and certainly entertaining. He pulled up a wooden barrel and seated himself. "Tell me more."

"Well, the technological aspect I was working on when . . . when . . ." Speaker floundered.

". . . when the bugger exploded?" Tanis supplied helpfully.

Speaker cast him a dirty look. ". . . when I experienced a momentary scientific setback was the illuminatory collection function." He explained how fully half the machine's workings were devoted to collecting the rays of the sun and concentrating them in the tiny box at the tip of the horn. "But I need to create an egress to the outdoors through which the illuminatory emanations will be transmortified. I've tried yards of tubing"—coils of which looped up to a hole in the roof—"but the light evaporates before it ever drains into the device."

"Why not move the contraption outside?" Tanis suggested. "There's plenty of sun out there."

"Unscientific," the gnome said. "Anyway, the device will rust if it gets rained on."

Tanis pointed across the room to the eastern wall. The rising sun made coronas around cracks in the wooden shutter that blocked the window opening. "Why not just open the shutters?"

Speaker looked from him to the window. He murmured and stroked his bearded chin. "It just might work," he agreed. "I'll need an automated illuminatory facilitation coordinator, using wire and a trip switch and . . ." He set to work, turning his back on the half-elf.

Tanis watched the busy gnome for a short time, then walked across the stable and threw open the shutters. He folded back the two halves and fastened them in place. "There."

Speaker jumped. "How did you do that?" he shouted. When Tanis showed him, the gnome's face crinkled in revulsion. "Crude. What if no one's around to open the window?"

Tanis was saved from replying, however, by the gnome's burst of activity. The small creature bustled from switch to gear to lever, adjusting the sunbeam collection horn into alignment with the window and traipsing from machine to window and back innumerable times.

"What's in the little box?" Tanis pointed to the tiny box at the tip of the horn. The gnome had fondled it with particular awe.

"My beam-conducting concentration device."

"Which is?"

"A wondrous piece of rock. See!"

The gnome flipped down a little door in the side of the box. Violet light poured into the shadowy stable. Tanis felt his eyes grow wide. "Where did you get that?"

The gnome looked away. "I acquired it—andelevenothersImightadd—fromaQualinestielfwhohad-retrievedthemfromakenderwhoborrowedthemfroma-hilldwarfwhoboughtthemfromahumanwhowon-themfromagamblingsailorwhogottheminsomefrozen-southernportthenameofwhichIneverlearned-althoughnowIwishIhad."

"In other words, you stole them," Tanis observed. Gnomes were not above outright theft—acceptable in the name of technology and science, of course.

"This could revolutionize . . ." The gnome stopped at the frown on the half-elf's face. "Ah, what would a half-elf know of science? Elves know only magic, magic, magic." He turned his back and resumed work on his machine. After a while, Tanis realized he'd been dismissed, and he moved toward the open double doors. But he turned back when he heard the gnome crow, "And now the test!"

Speaker Sungear threw the main switch just as the sun rose above the low building to the east. Its beams poured into the window, over the floor, and into the huge metal horn.

"By the gods," Tanis said in awe. Unbelievably, the contraption began to percolate. It spluttered and creaked and groaned, and Tanis remembered Flint reciting a proverb about gnomes: *Everything gnomish makes five times the noise it needs to.* The air around the horn began to glow. Speaker Sungear leaned forward and hummed a gnomish folk tune into a mesh of wire. Sparks of purple and magenta erupted around the box that held the violet stone. Then the machine gave a hum—the same notes the gnome had hummed. Speaker froze, wordless, before the apparatus; tears streamed down his cheeks. "It works! By the great god Reorx, father of gnomes and dwarves, it works!"

The machine continued to hum—the same tune, over and over, faster and faster. Metal rasped against metal. The violet glow around the stone's box became an angry, plum-colored haze.

Tanis took a step toward the gnome. "Speaker . . ." The gnome didn't seem to hear him. More sparks spat from the base of the horn. The creaking turned to shuddering, which in turn became convulsions. Bits of metal were being shaken off the contraption. Light and smoke spewed from widening gaps between parts. Tanis leaped to close the shutters. Darkness closed around them, but the machine continued to heave and shudder. "Shut it off!" he shouted to the gnome.

"I . . ." Speaker faltered. ". . . can't."

Tanis grabbed the gnome around his thick middle and catapulted toward the open door. Speaker struggled, protesting all the way. "Half-elf, I've got to see what hap—"

Tanis dove into the street just as the contraption, and then the building, shattered into a thousand flaming pieces. Bits of wood and metal rained upon fleeing onlookers. Tanis flung Speaker Sungear under a wagon and dove after him. They caught their breath as dozens of people, in various stages of undress, dashed from surrounding buildings to form a bucket brigade between the conflagration and the town well. A quick check by the half-elf revealed nothing but minor bumps and bruises on either of them.

"It must have been the tangential hydroencephalator, now that I think about it," Speaker said. "Inadequate water filtration to prevent ancillary overheating."

Tanis had nothing to say.

"I've no time to build another device today. Or money, for that matter." For the first time, the gnome seemed deflated. Then he brightened. "Of course, there might be pieces of the device left. Oh!" He dimmed again. "The beam-conducting concentration device!"

"What?" Tanis had about had it with gnomes. "The what?"

"The purple stone. It's destroyed. I saw it explode as you hauled me away." His face crinkled with thought. "This will take some engineering." He seemed delighted at the prospect.

"Didn't you say you'd 'acquired' eleven others?" Tanis asked.

"Yes, but I sold them to buy wire. Nearly a year ago. To a mage. Before I knew what technological promise they held." The gnome mused, "Perhaps I could buy them back . . . but I have no money."

"You could always *steal* them back," Tanis said spitefully, and he began to back out from under the wagon. Speaker Sungear looked reproachfully at him, and the half-elf relented. "Why don't you just *tell* people your important news? Wouldn't that be just as efficient under the circumstances?" he added tactfully.

"Yes, but . . ."

"So stand on the street corner and holler."

The gnome looked aghast. "Do it *myself*?"

Tanis nodded.

"Me, a town crier," Speaker muttered. "If my mother could see me. So unscientific. So inefficient."

"So necessary."

With another reproachful glance, Speaker Sungear crawled out from under the wagon. Ignoring the throngs of people who'd gathered to watch the fire burn itself out and without so much as a glance back at the smoldering heap of wreckage that used to be his laboratory, the gnome started toward the busiest corner of the market. Tanis trailed behind. Speaker took up a stance. "Hear ye, hear ye!" the gnome bellowed. No one listened.

Tanis sidled up to Speaker. "You need a platform of some kind," he advised.

The gnome looked about. "I could build one," he conceded. "An automatic gnome-lifting trans—"

In reply, the half-elf scooped up the gnome and set him on one wide shoulder. "Now, town crier, spread your news."

"Oh, this is so . . . manual," Speaker murmured, clutching the half-elf's auburn hair to keep his balance. Then he waved the other hand and bellowed "Hear ye, hear ye!" again. This time several people turned to listen. "I have news . . ."

He recited his litany of news—only three items, it turned out, but one drew Tanis's attention. "The heads of the Haven agricultural consortium, meeting in an emergency session, have offered a reward of fifteen steel to the person or persons who kill the ettin that's been slaying farm stock south of Haven," Speaker trumpeted.

"What's an ettin?" a man shouted from the back of the throng.

"An ettin is a creature, twelve or thirteen feet tall, with two heads, usually native to cold, mountainous climates. It is related to the trolls, and in fact is sometimes called a two-headed troll."

The crowd murmured. The man in question shook his head and moved away, followed by several others. Speaker continued, "The ettin eats only meat. In fact, this one has slaughtered and devoured fully a half-dozen cows, several dogs, numerous chickens, and a dozen sheep. Last night it came upon and attacked a shepherd south of Haven. The man assayed to stop the beast from raiding his flock and paid with his life."

The remaining listeners blanched and hurried away. Speaker said a few more words, then halted. His audience was gone. "Was it my delivery?" he asked the half-elf.

"No, my friend. It was the ettin," Tanis said good-naturedly.

Tanis bid the confused gnome good-bye and minutes later was taking the steps of the Seven Centaurs two at a time. He didn't see Wode sit up suddenly on a bench across the street.

"How would you feel about hunting down a monster for pay?" Tanis said without preamble as he entered his and Kitiara's room.

The swordswoman was dressed but pale. The empty tankard of tea, with crumbs of toast next to it, stood on a tray on the chair by the door. "Pregnancy tea, my foot, half-elf," Kitiara said with a growl. Then she caught what he'd said. "Kill a monster? For how much?"

"Fifteen steel."

She whistled.

"Ever hear of an ettin?" he asked.

Kitiara stood stock-still. "A two-headed troll?" Two lines appeared between her eyes; she seemed to look deep within. "No, it's impossible," she murmured to herself. Aloud, ignoring Tanis's quizzical look, she said, "My last employer had an ettin slave. I know something about them. They're dangerous but stupid and, like most stupid things, very, very loyal."

"Feel like trying to slay one?"

Kitiara didn't react with the immediate enthusiasm Tanis had expected, but the half-elf put that down to her probable hangover. "We'd take care of your debt to Mackid, send him on his way, and have five steel left over," he said.

Kitiara gazed at him. "Why are you doing this, Tanis?" she asked softly. "You don't owe Caven Mackid anything. An ettin is a dangerous beast."

Tanis began folding his few belongings into his pack. He didn't speak for a few moments, and when he finally did, his face was averted. "You saved my life back there with the will-o'-the-wisp," he said.

Kitiara's expression was a study in suspicion.

"We worked well together then," the half-elf continued at last. "We could do so again."

He said no more. After standing for some time in apparent indecision, Kitiara shook her head and also began to pack. "It's your skin, half-elf. At any rate," she said quietly, seemingly to herself, "I'd rather take on the ettin here than in Solace. I don't want to draw the creature near home."

Tanis looked up from his pack, surprise on his face. "Why would we draw it toward Solace? What are you thinking of, Kit?"

But Kitiara would say no more. Moments later they were astride Dauntless and Obsidian, heading for the trail that led south out of Haven.

* * * * *

"What is it?" Tanis asked an hour later. He heard nothing but rustling foliage.

"Someone is following us." Kitiara bit her lip and moved her hand to her sword.

In response, Tanis clicked his tongue at Dauntless; the big gelding, used to the ways of the road, was already heading for cover along the path. Kitiara and Obsidian melted into the vegetation at the other side.

Soon two horsemen hove into view, galloping with a fever that left their horses lathered. Kitiara and Tanis, recognizing the followers, moved back onto the trail. Caven pulled up his black stallion with such abruptness that the horse reared, showering Tanis and Dauntless with sweat and towering so high that Mackid's black hair brushed against the pine and maple branches. Behind him, Wode eased a wheezing nag to a halt and remained several paces back, out of reach of the stallion.

Caven's steed was a raw-boned hulk, coal-black except for the whites of his eyes, a star on his forehead, and the gleaming teeth that snapped even with a bit in his mouth. Dauntless was large, but the stallion dwarfed him.

"I knew you'd try to slink away, Kitiara!" Caven shouted.

Kitiara didn't reply at first. Then she drawled, "Posted a spy, did you, Mackid?"

"With good reason, it seems. Where are you going?

This isn't the way to Solace. Trying to throw me off the trail, aren't you?"

Tanis spoke up. "We're off to win your money back, Mackid."

Caven's face reflected disbelief. "How?" was all he said.

"To catch an ettin. For the reward money."

"An ettin?" Caven's black horse danced back and forth, apparently as impatient as its rider. The other three horses stamped, too, responding to the big stallion's agitation. "Then why not tell me so?"

Tanis looked at Kitiara, an unspoken question in his eyes. The swordswoman sighed and shrugged. "I told the half-elf I would leave you a message."

"That . . . ?" Mackid snapped.

"That we'd be back in Haven in a week with your money."

Mackid gazed at Kitiara. "Doubtless you forgot," he said, irony oozing from each word. Then he smiled at Tanis. "I warned you. Don't trust her, half-elf."

Tanis only grunted and frowned at the swordswoman.

"Anyway," Mackid added, "the message is unnecessary. I'm going with you."

"We don't need your help," the half-elf said.

Caven Mackid laughed. "Do you think I'd let Kitiara get away again? What's to stop her from collecting the reward money and slipping away from us both?" He reined in the stallion, then guided the horse between Dauntless and Obsidian, who edged away. Wode, looking bored, took up a position at the rear. "Let's go," Mackid said.

There seemed to be no recourse. The four rode on in silence, speaking only when Caven's stallion nipped at the other horses when they drew too close.

"Where did you get such a beast?" Tanis finally asked.

"On Mithas." Mithas, on the far side of the Blood Sea of Istar, was the home of the minotaurs, the half-man, half-bull creatures noted for their ferocity in warfare and their willingness to fight for pay.

Caven grinned and answered the unspoken question. "I won Maleficent in a game of bones. From his minotaur master." Mackid threw back his head and laughed. "As if anyone could be master to Maleficent! The creature barely tolerates me, and that's only because he knows I'm as stubborn and black-hearted as he."

Minotaurs were notorious for slaying outsiders. The man had taken the ultimate risk in challenging a minotaur, even in something as seemingly harmless as a game of bones.

Caven nodded at Dauntless. "Where'd you get that . . . carnival pony, half-elf?" Tanis felt annoyance rise like a boil. Dauntless had taken the half-elf through dozens of encounters, facing all manner of dangers, from highwaymen to goblins. If he also was gentle enough to trust with children, what of it?

But the four would have to keep some peace if they were to bring back the ettin. Thus Tanis didn't respond to Caven's jibe; he merely nudged Dauntless into the ragged gait that passed for the gelding's canter and moved into the lead.

It was time to find an ettin.

Chapter 8

The Portent

"Dreena."

Kai-lid struggled in the web between sleeping and waking. The voice that spoke was ghostly, as if it could belong to either world.

"Dreena."

She knew the voice, or one just like it. She'd heard it as a large-eyed child learning simple spell-casting at her mother's knee. But Kai-lid's mother was dead.

Still the voice persisted. Kai-lid opened her eyes to total darkness. Sitting up partway on her cot in the cave and striving to see through the blackness, Kai-lid could smell something large and warm-blooded moving near her, sensing but not touching her. The being was magical, but incompletely so. Kai-lid moved her lips to begin a light spell, but the voice sounded first. "*Shirak.*"

Silver light streamed over Kai-lid and over the tall creature whose head brushed against the ceiling of the cave. The spell-caster gasped.

It was a unicorn.

White light bathed the platinum hide of the imposing creature. The unicorn was tall, its muscles well defined, its intelligent eyes the liquid blue-white of ice. But the voice was gentle. "Hello, my Dreena." That whispering sibilance. Surely Kai-lid had heard it before.

"Mama?" The question came in the quavering voice of the five-year-old Dreena ten Valdane, not the husky tones of the grown-up who'd fled from her father and renamed herself Kai-lid.

Kai-lid/Dreena remembered fleetingly the sad woman who had reared her through infancy, then disappeared—died after giving birth to a stillborn baby brother, her father's aides had said. For a long time before her death, that woman had cried in pain and sadness.

Rumor had it that the Valdane had ordered his mage to ease his wife out of life with some post-pregnancy complication. The Valdane had convened a state funeral with a closed casket—which sparked more rumors. But the common folk believed Dreena's mother had fled one night, that a fleet-footed silver horse had met her at the edge of the wood outside the castle.

"Mama?" Kai-lid repeated now.

The unicorn dipped its head and touched the tip of its horn to the ground before Kai-lid. "If it helps you to think of me as your mother, let it be so, Dreena."

"But are you?"

The unicorn didn't answer, and when Kai-lid asked again, the creature said simply, "We have no time. There is trouble, Dreena."

"I came here because my mother grew up near here," Kai-lid persisted. "My father married here during his travels as a young man."

"I know. You cannot hide—here or anywhere—any longer," the unicorn said. "Your father has fled to the Icereach. There he is amassing an army."

"Surely he cannot be a threat to me all the way from the Icereach," Kai-lid protested.

The whisper continued, almost hypnotic in its effect upon the young woman. "He and the mage have a powerful artifact."

Kai-lid shivered. She pulled her robe tighter around her. "Janusz believes I'm dead. He'll never think to scry for me. Here I am safe. I don't want to leave."

"I know." The unicorn dipped her horn once more and began to back out of the cave. "But there is no time."

"Wait! What should I do?" Kai-lid cried.

Instead of answering directly, the silvery creature stood in the cave's mouth. "Remember this, Dreena. It will help you."

"But . . ."

The unicorn began to chant:

> "The lovers three, the spell-cast maid,
> The winged one of loyal soul,
> The foul undead of Darken Wood,
> The vision seen in scrying bowl.
>   Evil loosed with diamond's flight.

"*Vengeance savored, ice-clenched heart
Seeks its image to enthrone
Matched by sword and fire's heat,
Embers born of steel and stone.
      Evil cast with jewel's light.*

"*The lovers three, the spell-cast maid,
The tie of filial love abased,
Foul legions turned, the blood flows free,
Frozen deaths in snow-locked waste.
      Evil vanquished, gemstone's might.*"

As the last line resonated in the night air, the light around the unicorn began to fade. The creature pivoted toward Darken Wood. "Wait!" Kai-lid called again, lunging from her cot and racing barefoot over the stone floor. When she reached the opening, the unicorn was gone.

The night was silent. Kai-lid heard no stamp of hooves, saw no gray shadow slip into the woods. A mist enveloped the scene.

Then suddenly she was back in her cot, her blanket on the floor, and she was shivering in the predawn chill.

* * * * *

"It was a dream," Xanthar insisted moments later, when she'd finished relating what had happened.

"No," she insisted. "It was real."

They were in their favorite spot for talking—two branches, one above the other, jutting out of a dead sycamore. "If you flew very high," Kai-lid said sullenly, "you might still spot her. But you're too stubborn."

121

"Legend says that if a unicorn wants to be seen, it will be. If not, no amount of searching or wishing will help. Anyway, I've never heard of a unicorn venturing out of Darken Wood."

"My cave is very close to the woods." Her voice rose. "You're so obstinate. It was my mother, I tell you."

Xanthar fluffed his feathers and shifted on his perch. "Since when is your mother a unicorn? Anyway, you told me your mother is dead."

"When I was little, she told me she came from north of Haven. That could mean Darken Wood."

The owl snorted and muttered, "Hardly," but Kai-lid went on, carried away by her story.

"I used to think she was a unicorn in human form, that she fell in love with my father and married him and went away to Kern with him. When life grew unbearable, she resumed her unicorn form and returned home. I never told anybody. But she would know what is in my heart."

"It's romantic nonsense, Kai-lid, a dream born of eating something you shouldn't have in Haven yesterday."

"I saw my mother."

The discussion circled on itself until both owl and mage grew weary. Each sat wordless, stubbornly silent at first and then merely lost in thought. Finally, as the sky was growing light in the east, Xanthar spoke again as though no time had passed. "And you believe it, that your father will attack from the south?"

Kai-lid hesitated. Then she nodded. The owl nodded, too. "Then we must act," he said softly.

"We?" she asked, sitting up. Her hood fell back. "You can't go far from Darken Wood. You'll lose your magic."

"We don't know that for a certainty. The rules of Darken Wood may vary. They say that travelers who enter much of Darken Wood find their weapons have disappeared—but not here. They say ghosts prevent travelers from entering—but not here. I may be able to go farther away than we have thought."

"You've said . . ."

"We must stop the Valdane."

"We're safe here."

The giant owl was silent for a time. Then he said, "No one is safe anywhere." Kai-lid remembered Xanthar's dead mate and nestlings.

"You are his daughter. You can't hide from him if he is determined to find you."

Kai-lid turned her back on the owl. Her voice was tight. "He forced me into a marriage I didn't want, hoping to gain control of the Meir's kingdom. Then, when the Meir and I fell in love and barred him from our land, he attacked. He killed my husband. Should I forgive that?"

"I'm not telling you to forgive anything. I'm telling you that you have to stop him. You alone may be able to."

Kai-lid slid from her branch to a lower one, then to the ground. She glared up at the owl. "I won't do it."

"You escaped because your lady's maid went back, you said."

Kai-lid's face went white. "Stop it."

But Xanthar continued. "Lida went back," he said. "You told me this yourself, Kai-lid. Lida went back; she dressed in your clothes, realizing your father would destroy the castle, and knowing that only if they found a body they believed to be Dreena ten Valdane's would they stop from coming after you."

123

The owl's voice was relentless. Kai-lid put her hands over her ears. The bird switched to mind-speak.

She was your friend. You grew up together; her mother reared you both. And she died for you. Whether you are Dreena ten Valdane or Kai-lid Entenaka, can you be selfish now?

The spell-caster began to cry.

Recall that morning, Kai-lid. Recall it, Dreena.

Against her will, the spell-caster remembered fleeing the castle with Lida. The servingwoman balked halfway down the escape tunnel, saying she had to go back for something and asking if Dreena wanted to leave her wedding pendant with the Meir in his coffin as a final gesture of love.

Memories from that hasty predawn exchange still haunted Kai-lid. Lida's shadowed face, resolution and fright alternating in her features. The damp of the stones that walled the corridor. The musty smell of the earthen floor. The sound of water dripping. And over it all, the booming of the enemy's drums, mimicking Dreena's heart. She'd removed the pendant, kissed the broad green stone, and placed it in Lida's hand. She half-guessed what her faithful friend had in mind, but she made no protest. Dreena told Lida to meet her in a cave beneath a copse of trees west of the castle. Then the servingwoman threw her arms around Dreena, kissed her, and whispered "My sister" before hurrying back through the corridor.

How many others will you let die to keep you safe, Dreena?

Kai-lid cried out, ran back into the cave, hid in the shadows, and sobbed. Finally, rustling and the scraping of clawed feet on stone told her Xanthar was just outside. His mind-speak was gentler.

I believe this dream you had, Kai-lid. But I believe it is a sign that only you can stop your father. He paused. When Kai-lid didn't answer, he added, *I will go with you.*

"You can't," Kai-lid whispered.

I won't let you go alone.

"And someone else will die for me, Xanthar?" she demanded bitterly.

I am sorry. I should not have said that. People make their own choices. Lida chose to stay at the castle. I choose to leave here with you. A hint of humor found its way into the owl's mind-speak. *I should add that I also choose to come back here, hale and hearty, to continue to inflict my curmudgeonly presence on my grandnestlings.*

Kai-lid sat on her cot until her shivering stopped. She drew on her sandals, then rose and closed the curtain to the cave, shutting out the owl.

What are you doing? Xanthar asked.

"I have an idea."

She sensed the owl's question and replied before it quivered in her head. "The mercenaries. Perhaps I can persuade them to go with me. They're trained."

The owl hesitated before speaking. *It is a thought. You can find them by scrying?*

"Perhaps. I'll need quiet, Xanthar."

She felt rather than heard the bird's assent. A shadow fell across the curtain as Xanthar took up the guard there.

The bowl that the spell-caster reached for looked like an ordinary tureen on the outside—maple wood, polished until it gleamed. But the inside glittered with hammered gold. At the very center, another mark broke up the pattern of the hammering—the image of an edelweiss plant etched in the metal.

Now she leaned over, retrieved a purple silk shawl from a leather bag beneath the table, and pulled a cloisonné pitcher from a niche in the stone cave wall. The fluid that Kai-lid poured from it appeared to be ordinary water, but the liquid came from a nearby stream, a tributary that entered the White-rage River west of Haven. "A stream born at the periphery of Darken Wood itself," Kai-lid murmured reverently.

She poured water into the tureen and watched the edelweiss motif waver, then return to sharpness when the water stilled. "With stillness comes clarity," she intoned, ritual words that Janusz himself had taught her years ago. She motioned in the air with slender fingers and draped the shawl, the color of red grapes, over her head and the bowl. Her thumbs held down the edges of the shawl; her fingers continued to twitch as she wove the spell. She closed her eyes, concentrating.

"*Klarwalder kerben. Annwalder kerben,*" she murmured. "*Katyroze warn, Emlryroze sersen.* Reveal, reveal."

She opened her eyes, waiting. At first nothing happened. Then the water dimmed and stirred and changed, as if reflecting a bank of storm clouds; the same gray-blue shone in her eyes. She released the shawl; the sides collapsed around her head but formed a tent over the bowl. Her left hand retrieved from her pocket the tortoiseshell button she'd found in the doorway in Haven. "I seek the owner of this artifact," she whispered. "*Wilcrag-meddow, jonthinandru.* Reveal."

At the command, the water in the bowl cleared, showing no evidence of the golden edelweiss beneath its surface. It depicted a woodland scene. Kai-lid suppressed a cry of joy. There was the half-elf, leading a chestnut gelding through the early-morning grayness, and behind him, Kitiara Uth Matar and the other mercenary on black horses. A yawning lad trailed, gnawing at a large roll. The small band was deep in conversation, although her scrying spell allowed Kai-lid only to see, not to overhear. She could see a frown crease the half-elf's face as he pushed plants aside, poked at the soil, and, balanced on his haunches, elbows resting on his bent knees, hands dangling between, scrutinized the ground.

Kai-lid watched for some time, hoping to tell from the group's surroundings exactly where they were. Not Darken Wood, of course, but definitely some temperate woodland. She saw maples, oaks, sycamores, and pines, and an undergrowth of maple saplings. Thick, low shrubbery told Kai-lid the travelers were near the edge of a forest, where sunlight had more of a chance of nourishing the plants near the ground.

Suddenly she saw the half-elf stiffen and lean over, his gaze fixed on something on the ground. His whole attitude changed from watchfulness to action. He moved from the trail to a place just off to the right. He poked at something on the ground—a footprint?— while the two other mercenaries waited on their horses and the squire chewed and swallowed. Then the half-elf pointed to his right, virtually in the opposite direction, back the way they'd come. The mercenaries sat up in their saddles, impatience apparent in their stance as the half-elf returned to his horse. The group wheeled around.

"They're following something," Kai-lid said. She watched a few moments longer, then nodded. "*Mortmegh, mortrhyan, merhet*. End it."

The water once more was water, the bowl just a

bowl; the edelweiss shone as before at the bottom. She pushed the purple shawl back and felt its folds at the back of her neck. Kai-lid rested her temples on suddenly weak hands. Her black hair slipped forward like silk, and elation vied with weariness. Xanthar remained silent at the cave's opening. He must know from the sounds that she had finished, but he also knew that scrying always exhausted her.

Finally she lifted her head from her arms and moved to open the curtain. A pair of worried orange eyes peered at her. "I found them," she said quietly.

"I've been thinking. Perhaps we should let this be," the owl interjected. He whetted his beak twice against the granite of the cave mouth. "After all, it *was* only a dream."

"It was real," Kai-lid began anew. "I saw the two mercenaries, the half-elf, and a boy. They're tracking something."

"Where?"

Kai-lid shrugged. "Near Haven, I'd guess. But north, south? . . . I'll have to watch them, look for landmarks." She was silent for a time, frowning. Then she spoke again, more tentatively now. "Do you think I can . . . persuade the four of them to take on such a quest?"

The owl cocked his head. "They are mercenaries, after all. You have no money. What can you offer them?"

"I don't know . . . yet." Kai-lid leaned against the doorway and gazed around the clearing—her clearing. For a few short months, it had afforded her a safety she hadn't known before. Now she must leave it.

"They may recognize me," she mused.

"As Dreena? You are disguised."

"No, not as Dreena. When I realized what Lida had done, I took on most of her appearance to . . . to honor her memory and to leave Dreena behind forever. They may recognize Lida."

The owl touched her shoulder gently with his beak, and Kai-lid intertwined the fingers of one hand in the soft feathers of his cream-colored breast. His voice came lightly to her mind. *You can adopt a new guise, of course.*

They moved apart, the mage shaking her head. "No. It may not be such a bad idea if they recognize Lida. I'll think about it. First of all, I must discover where they are and where they're going." She turned back toward the cave, but the owl's movement arrested her.

"Scrying tires you. Perhaps I can find them," Xanthar said aloud, switching once more to regular human speech. The owl flexed his wings. Kai-lid closed her eyes against the grit and dust that suddenly swirled around the clearing before her cave. Then the owl settled down again. "Hop aboard," he invited, spreading low one huge wing.

"I'll get my things," she said.

Chapter 9

On the Ettin's Trail

"Morning. Time for bed."

"No. Lady soldier follows. Master says so."

"Too bad. Res sleep days."

"Not now!"

"Hunger. Food soon?"

"Maybe."

"Soldiers follow?"

"Yes, yes."

"Good," Res announced. "Eat them."

"No!" The ettin's left head struggled to recall the word the Master had used. A long word, and so long ago—nearly an hour. The Master had forced the left head to repeat the word, and the warning, many times. "Capture!" Lacua finally crowed now, remembering. "Not eat. Not, not, not." Its watery eyes, shaped like a pig's, squinted. The ettin's left hand brandished a spiked club with each "not."

The right head spat. Then Res brightened. "Are four," he pressed. "Capture one, eat—" he hesitated over the impossible arithmetic—"eat rest?"

"Capture," Lacua repeated. "Not eat. Not, not, not."

"One? Only?"

Lacua argued the proposition with himself. The Master, whom he had spoken to through the Talking Stone just before dawn, had said to lure the lady soldier to the appointed mountain in Darken Wood, capture her, and wait. But Janusz had omitted rules about her companions. The lady was for capture, the mage had said. That meant . . . what? The others weren't for capture? Or were?

Lacua pondered. The range of choices gave him a headache. But he finally decided. "Capture girl, eat one not-girl." The two heads smiled, revealing rotten teeth. The ettin, its four beady eyes open for small game, continued north, careful to leave plenty of footprints as the Master had ordered.

* * * * *

Hours later, just as the sun passed its zenith, Tanis and his companions stood on the same spot, staring at the footprints—nearly three fingers deep, the right foot larger than the left—and then at the forbidding environs into which the prints were headed.

"Darken Wood," Caven whispered. Tanis nodded, his gaze probing the underbrush.

There was no gentle transformation from one type

of forest to another here. Instead, it was as though the icy finger of an angered god had drawn a line among the trees. Those on one side remained normal in appearance, while the rest withered or twisted. A dank breeze flowed from the woods, prickling the hair at the back of the two men's necks. Although a light wind moved the tattered leaves in the woods, no sound came to their ears.

Wode was fidgeting with his horse's mane. "It's the silence of the Abyss," he said softly. Kitiara slugged him on the arm to silence him.

"Half-elf," Mackid said, just above a whisper. "I'll concede you this: I've never seen such an evil landscape in all my days on Ansalon." Tanis nodded again, deep in thought.

Without another word, the companions dismounted and drew their swords; even Wode carried a small knife, which he seemed to draw some slight comfort from. Suddenly the teen-ager spoke again, his voice cracking. "The trees bleed!" He pointed a quivering hand at one of the pines.

The other three looked where the squire gestured. A strange look crossed Caven's features. "By the gods, Wode, this is no time for jokes!" he exploded. He clenched his hands and started toward the teen-ager.

With one hand, the half-elf pulled Caven back. "You see blood, Wode?" he asked quietly.

The boy's voice was shrill. Hands trembling, knife shaking, he pulled himself up on his nag, nearly cutting the reins in the process. "Are you all blind? Don't you see it?" Wode cried. "Blood, half-scabbed over, oozing down the bark in great gouts." He yanked at his horse's reins, but by then Kitiara had reached the youth's side, pulled the knife from his hand, and held the horse steady.

Tanis took one more look at the tree in question, which appeared unmarked to him except for a smear of what looked like sap—pinkish, it was true, but definitely sap, not blood. He used the same tone he adopted with a jittery horse. "On that tree only, Wode? Or more than one?"

The cords stood out in Caven's neck. "You believe the cowardly—?"

"He sees *something*," Tanis interrupted. "It may be that we can't count on our senses. Darken Wood may appear different to different eyes."

"Darken Wood," Caven repeated. His temper evaporated as quickly as it had flamed. He worried his lower lip with his teeth. "Perhaps we should wait until morning to enter," he suggested. "It's only a few more hours until nightfall. I don't care if they're offering ten times fifteen steel for that ettin back in Haven, it's not worth traipsing through Darken Wood at night. We should be sensible and wait for morning."

Tanis said nothing. Indeed, he'd been about to suggest a similar tactic. But Kitiara snorted. She'd been shifting from foot to foot as the two men examined the ettin prints and marked the monster's progression into the woods. "You three can hide out and waste three-quarters of a day, but I, for one, am not afraid of the unknown!" she cried. "Besides, the spoor is fresh. The beast can't be that far ahead. We can capture it and be on our way back to Haven by nightfall."

She released Wode's horse, leaped onto Obsidian, and turned the mare's head toward the woods, not heeding whether anyone followed. Wode began backing his mount away from the forest perimeter.

The other two men remained where they were. "We can't let her go in there alone, half-elf," Caven said almost plaintively.

"I never intended to," Tanis said shortly, and he stepped toward the gelding. "You are free to go back, of course."

Caven reddened. Then he shouted for Wode to get moving—in the proper direction—mounted Maleficent, and pushed the stallion past Dauntless. Scrambling not to be left behind so close to the fearsome place, Wode followed as they entered Darken Wood.

The tracking continued to be easy—ridiculously so, the half-elf thought. Either the creature was remarkably stupid to leave such obvious signs or it had great faith in its ability to defeat all comers. Tanis didn't even have to dismount to see the five-toed prints, each as long as his hand and forearm.

Broken branches, as well as pine needles scuffed by heavy feet, marked the way. Although the path wended among the bent-trunked pines, the way was occasionally rocky. Pines crowded around them, the trunks just far enough apart at times to admit the horses. It was almost, Tanis thought, as though the trees were reaching for whatever brushed against them. He dispelled the thought with an oath and looked around him warily. Far above their heads, the evergreens expanded into a thick canopy. A haze seemed to hang over the woods—at least to the half-elf's eyes. The late afternoon air hung yellow-gray and humid, and Tanis found that he could not see more than several yards ahead.

They rode in silence for a while, with Tanis in the lead, followed by a thoughtful Caven, an elaborately nonchalant Kitiara, and, close upon Obsidian's hooves, the reluctant Wode. Every so often, the squire would glance at a tree trunk with revulsion and guide his horse in a wide circle around it. Caven looked jumpier by the moment. So far, the half-elf had spied nothing stranger than the clinging haze. Nonetheless, he felt as though every living thing about him—and he tried not to think about the rumors of dead ones—were glaring at the spot where his pulse throbbed in his throat. He tried unsuccessfully to pierce the haze with his nightvision. "Does night fall earlier in Darken Wood?" he whispered to himself.

Tanis heard an exclamation as Caven pulled Maleficent to a walk and Obsidian practically collided with the feisty stallion. Maleficent struck out at Kitiara and her horse. Staying solidly in the saddle as Obsidian leaped aside, Kitiara drew up her whip and lashed Caven's stallion across the flank. With a snort, Maleficent sidestepped away, halting as Caven sawed at the reins. Wode, long tormented by the Mithas stallion, giggled nervously. Blood welled from a jagged cut in the stallion's glossy hide, and Caven opened his mouth to remonstrate with Kitiara.

The swordswoman hissed at him, cutting off his protest. "If you travel with me, Mackid, you will keep that horse in line, or I will kill it—with my bare hands, if necessary. Understand, soldier?"

Mackid shut his mouth, nodding dumbly. Kitiara took a deep breath, no doubt preparing to go on berating the man, but the half-elf interrupted.

"Until now I thought you were impervious to fear, Kit," Tanis said. "I can see now that you merely hide it better than the rest of us."

"I—" she began, glaring daggers.

"Temper, temper," the half-elf muttered. Then, as Kitiara sat astride Obsidian, almost speechless with rage, Tanis turned to Wode. "Are the trees still bleeding, Wode?" The squire bit his lip, looked sidelong at a nearby maple sapling, and nodded. The half-elf persisted, turning to Caven. "And what do you see,

Mackid?" When the Kernish mercenary only shook his head, Tanis said, "I'll tell you what I see. I see a haze, like dusk in the tropics, closing around us."

"Like a shroud," Wode added, the words seeming to jerk from him unwillingly.

"So Wode sees it. Do either of you?"

Kitiara snapped something about "traveling with a bunch of superstitious weaklings." Caven raised an eyebrow at her, then addressed Tanis in a low voice. "I see men lined up at the very farthest distance I can see in these damned woods."

"Men?" Tanis looked where Caven indicated, but the half-elf saw nothing but haze.

"I *know* these men." Tanis waited patiently until Caven took a deep breath. "They are men I've killed in battle. They are all there, each one represented over and over. Their wounds still bleed. They carry severed limbs, hold their entrails to keep them from spilling out. Their eyes—" he stumbled over the words—"their eyes are scarlet, and they've been here waiting for me ever since we ventured into this unholy woods."

A groan and a crash sent them all jumping. It was Wode, sprawled in a faint next to his bug-eyed horse.

Kitiara ribbed Wode ceaselessly once they revived him. Even Tanis began to look annoyed at the swordswoman, and Caven finally assigned Kitiara a new position as rear guard. "The easier to ignore your complaints," he commented when she protested. Kitiara would have snapped back, but another wave of dizziness and nausea passed over her just then, angering her as much as it sickened her, and she let the others pass ahead without a word.

Certainly, she thought when the other three were ahead of her, she wasn't still hung over from last night's binge. She'd been fighting exhaustion all day, and once she had even found herself sliding from her horse when she fell asleep in the saddle. She'd caught herself with a jerk and shaken back her curls to mask the near fall. But this new wave of queasiness, this sudden vertigo, was harder to hide. That was all she needed now, to mimic Wode's swoon after all the guff she'd given him.

She pulled up her mount and let the other three move farther ahead. They were utterly silent, with none of the jovial horseplay that Kitiara remembered from other forays with comrades. There was only the sound of the horses' hooves, the squeak of Tanis's saddle when he leaned over to catch sight of the ettin's prints, and her own forced breathing. When they were far enough away, Kitiara leaned carefully away from the saddle and vomited into a bush at the side of the path. Then, blinking rapidly to clear her vision, she spurred Obsidian into a trot.

Night was falling. It was as though something, watching them, had decided that it was time to pull the noose tight. They'd resheathed their swords but their hands never drifted far from the hilts.

"Half-elf," Kitiara called. "Can you use your night-vision now?"

"I've been trying," Tanis replied. "I see nothing but the trees. Nothing else—no small game, no birds. Nothing but the haze."

Kitiara grunted. She twisted back in the saddle at a sudden noise behind her, unsheathing her sword with the soft sound of metal against tanned leather. "Half-elf," she repeated. "Look back."

Tanis and Caven followed her directive. Caven swore. "The path," Tanis murmured.

"Gone!" Caven added needlessly.

Wode moaned. It was true. The trees had closed behind them like a phalanx of soldiers. Both men drew their swords. Wode clutched his knife nervously.

At that moment, afternoon turned to night in the space of an eyeblink. One moment they could see each other and the tormented trees, and the next, all they could see was pitch blackness.

Wode's voice quavered out of the dark. "Uncle Caven?"

"Right here." Mackid had not budged, Kitiara could tell.

"At least we can hear each other." It was Tanis's voice.

"We're not alone," Kitiara said suddenly.

The air began to glow, and Kitiara saw the faces of her companions in the reflected light. The glowing light coalesced into a pair of eyeballs. Just below the eyes, two skeletal hands formed, edged with green flame. "Tanis," Kit repeated. Her mouth was dry, but her hand was steady.

"I see it, Kit." Tanis dismounted, moving slowly toward her.

"What *is* it?" Caven asked.

Kitiara answered. "A wichtlin."

"What's that?"

Tanis looked at Kitiara. She'd donned her helm. Although Obsidian was shifting restlessly, nearly at the point of panic, Kitiara sat straight and tall on the mare. She held the reins with one hand and gripped her sword with the other. Her face was pale, but flashes of pink lurked just below the surface, high on her cheekbones. Kitiara was in her element now, Tanis knew.

The fire-limned wichtlin made no motion toward the swordswoman, but its gaze never wavered from her. Hers was as steady.

"Wichtlins," Tanis whispered to Caven, "are elven undead."

"By the gods!" Caven exclaimed. "And it's just the eyes and hands, no more? How do we fight it?"

"There's more there—the rest of the decayed skeleton," Tanis said. "Be thankful you can't see it." Wode's teeth were chattering.

"And it used to be Qualinesti?"

"Silvanesti," Tanis corrected. "Some Silvanesti elves who follow the path of evil during life are claimed by Chemosh when they die."

"The lord of the undead!"

"And they become wichtlins."

Caven took a moment to absorb that. "What do these wichtlins do?" he asked at last.

As Caven spoke, the creature began to move. It edged closer to Kitiara, who calmly backed Obsidian an equal distance away. Kitiara answered Caven's query. "A wichtlin wanders the world searching for souls to claim for Chemosh. It can kill with its touch." She moved Obsidian back another pace.

"Will swords kill it?"

"We'll just see," she answered softly. Even as she spoke, she struck with a lightning-fast movement. Her weapon flashed through the air, slashing between the creature's hands and its eyes. Obsidian whinnied and leaped back from the trail. The wichtlin, unharmed, swooped toward Kitiara, who continued to flail at it with her sword. "Half-elf!" she cried. "By the gods, tell me how I can kill it!"

Tanis felt horror clutch at him as the wichtlin feinted again and again at Kitiara Uth Matar, driving her farther off the trail and farther from her companions. "Magic, I've heard," he called. "Only magic."

"I have no magic, but it'll be a strong beast that can withstand this!" Caven shouted. He spurred Maleficent forward. The giant horse reared, then charged toward the wichtlin, pebbles spraying behind the huge animal's hooves.

The evil creature vanished just before the horse and rider reached it.

Confused, Caven pulled up the stallion and wheeled about on the trail. "Where—?"

"Caven! Behind you!" It was Kitiara.

Caven turned to find himself inches from the wichtlin. Its left hand, green flame visible at each joint of a digit, reached out toward him. "Caven!" Kitiara shouted again. "Don't let it—"

But it was too late. The creature grazed Caven's arm, and the soldier froze, a look of dawning terror etched on his bearded face.

As soon as the paralysis felled Caven, the wichtlin seemed to lose interest in its victim. It turned toward Tanis, who held his sword ready even though it was clear now that the weapon was as useless as a feather against this monster. The wichtlin fastened its unblinking gaze on the half-elf, moved nearer, and attacked. In moments, Tanis, too, stood immobile. Wode tried to flee, but the being vanished, only to appear directly before the squire, who, with his nag, ran into the creature and froze instantly.

That left Kitiara alone against the wichtlin. She pulled her dagger and prepared to vault from Obsidian, who now stood hock-deep in a tangle of ground-hugging plants.

Then the horse screamed, and Kitiara halted her dismount, twisting in midair, only one foot in a stirrup, as she looked down.

Skeletal hands, dozens of them, were reaching up

through the plants, up through the ground. They held the struggling mare, who continued to whinny with fright until Kitiara thought she'd go mad. Her gaze darted around. The wichtlin bore down slowly upon her. The skeletal hands reached out to grab her if she fell from Obsidian's back. The mare gave a shudder, a paroxysm of death, and Kitiara kept her seat only by dropping the dagger and holding on to the dying mare with both hands.

Then a voice sliced through the night. *"Idiandin melisi don! Idiandin melisi don!* Dispel!"

Kitiara fell into the waiting hands.

But they vanished as her body crashed into the damp soil next to her horse. The swordswoman lay still for a moment, casting about her for the wichtlin. It, too, was gone. "Obsidian!" She sat up slowly, reached out a hand, and stroked the animal's lifeless shoulder. As she caressed her longtime animal companion, the horse turned to dust beneath her fingers. A moment later, even that last trace of Obsidian evaporated. Kit leaped to her feet, spied her dagger in the weeds, and retrieved it. Slowly she circled, ready for anything that challenged her. Where was the possessor of the voice? The words shouted were undeniably magical, but was the one who shouted them her savior or a new attacker?

She heard nothing. Caven and Maleficent, arrested in midstride, stood like a statue in a village square. Wode and his nag were likewise frozen in a tangled mimicry of Caven's stance. Tanis, on foot, had been caught in the middle of a lunge, his sword pointing straight toward . . . nothing. Dauntless stood stolidly near the half-elf. To all appearances, the horse was the only other living thing within view. There was no sign of whatever had uttered that cry of magic in the night.

Chapter 10

Janusz, the Mage

Janusz took a deep breath to halt his tremors as he leaned away from his scrying bowl. Kitiara's face faded from the surface of the water.

She'd be safe for a time; he'd seen to that. The groping hands had returned to their owners in the Abyss. The wichtlin was now crawling harmlessly along the bottom of Ice Mountain Bay. It would have to search some time to find living souls to claim in those frigid depths.

The explosion of magic that allowed the mage to both scry and speak left his ears ringing and his hands trembling. For a moment, he feared he might faint. But it had been necessary. The mage had come within a heartbeat of losing Kitiara Uth Matar.

And Kitiara Uth-Matar was the only person who could tell him where the nine ice jewels were.

He had only two of the ice jewels, one of which the ettin carried, and he thanked Morgion for the luck that had prompted him to hold back two of the eleven purple gemstones in the encampment at the Meir's castle.

Janusz eyed the iridescent jewel that lay atop an alabaster pedestal on the table. The purple crystal, the size of a small egg, glowed as if it contained all the knowledge of Krynn burning within it. The doltish gnome who'd sold him the jewels had launched into a tiresome litany of the stones' history. The mage had ignored much of the creature's prattling, but one thing lingered in Janusz's memory—that the gnome believed the jewels had hailed ultimately from the Icereach. Staring into the amethyst-colored orb now, the mage didn't doubt that its glittering coldness had been formed in the snowy reaches. That was why he'd persuaded the Valdane to flee to the southernmost point of Ansalon. They'd come to the Icereach in search of more jewels. And under the spell of the ice jewel, the Valdane's dream had expanded, grown from a yen to overrun a neighboring fiefdom to a hunger to command the entire world.

Janusz forced himself to look away from the stone, but the movement seared his eyes. The jewel held his gaze like a spell. The mage had commanded dozens of ettin slaves to search ceaselessly for the spot that just might offer up more ice jewels—because, he told the Valdane, the jewels could hold the secret to the Valdane's ultimate power over all of Ansalon. In truth, Janusz hoped that the charismatic stones would do far more for the mage himself than for the

Valdane—that, in short, they would show Janusz how to dispel the bloodlink that bound him to the ruler's will. But that would occur, if ever, only far in the future, after exhausting years of study, he knew.

The mage quaked inwardly at the risk he was taking in letting Res-Lacua carry one of the precious artifacts, but it was necessary if Janusz were to use the stones to teleport the ettin and Kitiara to the Icereach. That was one mystery of the stones that the mage, through months of study, had been able to discover. Handled correctly and cautiously, the stones allowed him to teleport objects, both living and nonliving, from the site of one jewel to the whereabouts of another.

When Kitiara arrived at the top of Fever Mountain in Darken Wood, the mage would use the ettin's ice jewel to bring them both to the ice warren. Then, he vowed, he would interrogate her himself and discover the hiding place of the other nine precious stones.

Janusz forced himself upright, rolled back the sleeves of his robe, and glanced at the entrance to his chamber. The mage sat atop a stool. Obviously made from the same magical ice from which the mage had fashioned the ice warren, the stool was festooned with a brocaded version of the canvas that protected the walls and floor. Off to the right, a curl of steam rose from a ceramic beaker set over a flame. Dozens of stoppered containers littered the worktable.

A window broke the monotony of the room's walls. The opening showed a panorama of the Icereach. Snow swirled around an outcropping of ice. Janusz glanced at the window and swore. He muttered an incantation, traced a figure in the air, and the scene in the window shifted to one showing a castle, flying black and purple pennants at every spire. Golden sunlight poured over the scene, and the mage's face looked wistful for a moment.

The walls of Janusz's Icereach quarters, of course, were of solid ice. But the door was equally solid oak, banded with iron, teleported by the ice jewel to this accursed frozen wasteland months ago.

"Not that time matters in this place," Janusz muttered. "Forsaken by the gods. A fraction of a year, a fraction of a lifetime. What's the difference?"

There were no seasons now, no shy blooming as of a spring maiden after winter's crone had eased her dying clutch upon the land. He smiled at his fancifulness. Habits died hard. He'd been a romantic soul long ago.

Once time had mattered. Once he'd felt himself bloom with the seasons, had felt his heart expand and thaw with the warming of the soil and the unfolding of new leaves. His romanticism may have been laughable, given the grayness of his hair and the wrinkles that creased his cheeks from nose to mouth. But he'd known true love—he'd known Dreena—and the world had seemed young and new.

"Pah!" he muttered, and pushed the useless past from his mind. "My heart is as frozen as the Icereach."

The walls, floor, and ceiling, were solid slabs of ice, slicked to a mirrorlike smoothness. Much of the icy surface was covered with thin canvas to protect the warren's occupants from sticking to the ice in the same way that warm flesh adheres to frigid metal on an especially cold day.

"An especially cold day," he repeated now. Janusz laughed soundlessly. "There are no days here that don't fit that description."

There was no fuel for a real fire, nor was there a fireplace. A fireplace of ice? No, and magical blazes drained too much of his strength. It took nearly all his power these days to keep track of Kitiara and Res-Lacua, a continent to the north. Even now, he'd had to expend still more energy to give Res-Lacua the power to speak in Common rather than in the orcish gibberish the ettins used. The beast might need to speak to Kitiara in order to lure her to Fever Mountain.

Janusz swore an oath to Morgion and crashed a fist against the frozen tabletop, sending the water slopping over the edge of the scrying bowl and cascading down the front of his robe.

He cursed again and dabbed at the black wool with a linen cloth. Once he'd aspired to the white robes of good magic. But now there were only snow and ice and evil in Janusz's life. Even now, within the ice warren, winds insinuated themselves through chink and crack to swirl around his wool-enshrouded ankles. The castle should have been warmer. After all, he'd supervised the building, overseen the crews of thick-backed and thicker-headed ettins. They'd performed the labor that his magic couldn't manage.

Janusz's robe, double-woven of the rarest wool, served him ill as a barrier against the needle-sharp winds of this cursed land. Everything in the room was bluish, bathed in the light that gleamed from Janusz's magical ice. There was no need for lanterns; the walls themselves lit the castle. But the mage longed for a warm lamp with orange-yellow flame. He longed for Kern.

These days he had only his memories to keep him warm. The banality of that thought, as well as its futility, brought a grim smile to his lips, for he did have something else to warm him—his hunger for revenge. He'd had plenty of time to devise ingenious methods of torturing Kitiara.

Suddenly the oak door shuddered beneath a great blow and crashed open. "Janusz!"

The mage leaped up. His mortar and pestle tipped, rolled, and dropped with a clatter, spilling half-ground herbs over the table and floor. His shock quickly passed. The Valdane often thundered into a room like a god of war. Janusz tried to pull together a semblance of dignity before the tall man who came to a halt before him. "By the god Morgion, Valdane," the mage said laconically, "what demon keeps you warm?"

The leader still dressed as he had in the warmest months back in Kern—black hose, white gathered shirt of watered silk, sleeveless purple doublet with gold braid, purple cape, black steel-tipped boots with steel rivets in the soles. The fashionable outfit, Janusz knew, had played well with the ladies back in Kern. Today, however, the Valdane's eyes were bloodshot against the carrot-orange of his lashes, brows, and hair. His complexion was nearly bloodless; the sun-enhanced freckles that had given him such a ludicrously boyish cast in Kern had faded in the long nights of the Icereach. His eyes, while still blue in the brightest light of what passed for spring here, now tended more toward gray.

"Hatred keeps me warm, mage," the Valdane replied. "That, and my plans for my future."

The Valdane, who never seemed to be cold, also seemed never to sleep. Often late at night, as Janusz pored over his spellbooks and replenished his spell components, he heard the leader's metal-soled tread in the ice-girded hallway outside the mage's quarters.

The mage uprighted the mortar, swept spilled powder into his hand, and returned it to the bowl. "You sought me for a reason, Valdane? Or merely to chat?" he asked mildly.

147

A flutter of the man's eyelashes suggested the ruler wasn't fooled by Janusz's nonchalance. "When will you bring Kitiara here?" he demanded.

The mage sighed. "I've told you that. As soon as the ettin can lure her to the top of the mountain."

"You can see her by scrying. Use your accursed jewel to bring her here now."

"She must be near the other ice jewel for the teleportation to work," said the mage. "Even then it is dangerous. How often must I explain this?"

"And if the ettin fails?"

"He won't."

"Kitiara has the morals of an alley cat. You say she's picked up another lover? What if this new lover and the old one together are able to slay the ettin?"

Janusz didn't lower his gaze. "I have faith in the ettin."

"I believe you are losing control, mage."

Janusz felt blood rush to his face. "My powers are considerable, Valdane, but they, like all magical powers, have their limits." He spat out each word. "Spells weaken me physically, as with all mages. And also as with all mages, I lose a spell from my mind when I use it, and I must study it again. That takes me late into each night." He gestured toward a shelf of parchment-leaved books with deep blue leather covers. "You ordered that I transport hundreds of ettins and minotaurs to the Icereach—which, of course, required me also to create living quarters for them. I must maintain and enlarge this warren, provide what little heat I can spare to keep it warm, and do my best to control the ettins, minotaurs, and thanoi."

"The walrus men," the ruler said, "are native to the Icereach. The thanoi sleep out in the open, so you didn't have to provide them shelter."

"It's little relief. I must scry the ettin and Kitiara, expending vast bursts of energy to communicate with Res-Lacua over the vast distances. You're taxing the limits of my powers already, Valdane, and there's not a mage on Krynn who could serve you better."

"Certainly none with better motivation," the Valdane murmured.

Unheeding, Janusz went on. "I must produce or teleport the food and supplies we need. I must scry for you, oversee the mercenaries and slaves, and do countless other tasks. I must do all this on but three hours of sleep each night."

The Valdane leaned against a brocade-covered stool, twin to the one the mage occupied. He waited until the mage's outburst had burned itself out. "Yet think of the prize that awaits, Janusz. The man who has the ice jewels and knows their secret can rule Krynn. Think of the armies that could be teleported around Ansalon! The tactical advantage!" He licked his lips with a red tongue, and Janusz averted his eyes in revulsion.

"Think of the power," the Valdane said, smiling. He studied the mage. Then he reached to his belt and withdrew an ornate dagger. Pointedly ignoring Janusz, he tested the point by using it to stroke the thin skin over the pulse at his wrist. It was like pricking the vein of a dead man. The wound remained clean and bloodless, then, in an eyeblink, closed smoothly, leaving no scar. "Should we test the bloodlink further, mage?" Valdane teased. "Or are you loyal to me?"

"Don't!" The cry was wrenched from the mage.

The Valdane laughed and slipped the weapon back into its sheath. He was still chortling as he reached the doorway. Once there, he commented without turning

to face Janusz, "Remember your family, mage. Your
brothers and sisters would have been grown by now,
wouldn't they?"

Remember his family? As if he could ever forget.
The door slammed behind the red-haired man. As if
he could forget.

As a child, Janusz had had the easy good looks of
many children. He'd shown magical ability early, but
his family had been as poor as the rest of the farm
workers in the fiefdom north of the city of Kernen.
The only relief in their pressing poverty came each
midwinter, when the peasants gathered at the castle of
the Valdane's father to seek their yearly boon—a special gift, determined by the Valdane himself.

Janusz's parents, burdened with too many children
and seeking to provide training for at least one of their
offspring, had brought him to the Valdane's castle in
his tenth year. Bowing low, they'd asked that Valdane
to take the boy into court and see to his training in
magic. The boy would repay him amply in service
and fealty, they were sure.

Janusz saw that midwinter festival now as clearly as
though it were yesterday. He recalled the worried blue
eyes of the then-Valdane and the sharper, more eager
look of the boy, Janusz's age, who sat on a small
throne next to his father and mimicked his sovereign's
every move.

The Valdane drew Janusz and his parents out of earshot of the rest of the court. Yes, the Valdane told the
couple, he would agree to their plan, but with one
codicil—that the lad agree to a blood bond, sealed
with magic, with the Valdane's own young son.

The Valdane then took the young Janusz aside. "I
know of you," the old Valdane had said, his lined face
close to Janusz's young one. He smelled of sickness;

his hands were desiccated claws. "I have heard of your early promise in magic. My aides tell me you will have great power when you are grown." He coughed, reached for the lad, and leaned heavily on the boy's shoulder. "It speaks well of your parents to want the court to have the advantage of your considerable gifts."

Janusz had looked at the marble floor, not knowing what to say. He knew why he and his parents, Sabrina and Godan, were here. They were expecting another child; the hut in the valley was already bursting with children. The man and woman needed strong offspring, children who could work from first light to the last in the fields. This slender, easily fatigued boy had brought them but little income for performing sleight-of-hand tricks at fairs.

"Lad?" the Valdane whispered. Young Janusz had looked up into the man's eyes, marked at the edges with wrinkles of pain. Then the youngster glanced at his parents. His mother clutched her patched robe before her, her pregnancy showing.

"I will do it," he said resolutely.

"A blood bond is not an easy life," the older man cautioned. "You will be trained in magic, true, but you will have to use that magic as my son commands."

The warning brought the boy up short. "What if he orders something I believe is wrong?"

The Valdane smiled. "It's been a long time since anyone questioned a Valdane about the morality of any decision. It's refreshing to hear someone consider it." He looked back toward the group clustered around the large empty throne and the small one that was occupied by his son, Janusz's age. The youngster, hair gleaming orange in the torchlight, was gesturing imperiously, giving orders to the Valdane's top aides, who hesitated, obviously hoping the ruler would return and countermand the dictums.

"Janusz," the Valdane had asked urgently, "are you a good person? And do you intend to become a good man, to eschew all forms of evil?"

"I hope to wear the white robes of good, sir."

The Valdane's forehead furrowed. "But are you strong of will?" He gripped Janusz's arms above the elbows and squeezed painfully. Beads of sweat appeared on the leader's upper lip.

"My mother says I am egregiously stubborn, sir," Janusz replied.

At that, he found himself looking deep into the ruler's eyes. The Valdane had smiled again faintly. "Mothers are wont to say that to boys of your age, lad," he whispered. "My own wife, also." The ruler's smile died. Then he pierced Janusz with a stare. His hands were hot with fever.

"I wouldn't do this if I had any choice," he said to the boy. "Blood bonds haven't been chanced here for many generations. But . . . I will try to provide for you. You are sure about your decision? You make it freely, without pressure from your family? You must provide a steadying influence on my only son. He is prone to be selfish. I'm afraid I've been a poor father to him, especially these last months."

Janusz had let his gaze wander over the sumptuous hall, stifling with the heat from three fireplaces. The remains of a great repast were still on the table. The picked-over roasts, pocked with congealed fat, made him salivate with hunger. He hadn't had meat or milk in over a month. Then he caught his parents' anxious gaze. His mother was sagging against his father's arm.

"I'll do it, sir," Janusz said. "You can count on me."

The Valdane, his reluctance obvious, summoned his wizard and his son for the secret, illegal ceremony.

Not long after, the Valdane and his wife died suddenly. It hadn't taken long to discover the true tenor of the new Valdane's young soul. Janusz gave up hope of wearing the white robes someday.

A few years after that, as mage and the new Valdane were entering manhood, Janusz had added a hefty dose of poison to the Valdane's ale and watched carefully as his blood twin quaffed the drink. But it had been Janusz, not the Valdane, who had grabbed at his throat and collapsed to the floor, writhing on the flagstones.

The young Valdane watched from his chair at the dining table. "Someone see to my mage, please," he announced dispassionately. "He appears to have drunk something that disagrees with him."

Then he leaned toward Janusz, his eyes chips of flint, and whispered, "Or maybe *I* did, eh, Janusz?" At that time, Janusz had known the bloodlink had cursed him forever. The mage would suffer what the Valdane deserved. Gasping, Janusz ordered the antidote to the poison, but he came close to death. Thus had begun Janusz's deterioration, even as the Valdane continued to boast the health of a young man.

"I cannot kill him," the mage had whispered in agony that night, "for *I* will die instead." And the Valdane would be left to torment, unchecked, all who opposed him.

Janusz's family died only two weeks after his failed attempt on the Valdane's life.

The fire that killed Janusz's family had been an accident, according to the Kernish reeve who investigated the tragedy. Janusz's parents hadn't cleaned the flue in ages; the deposits from years of wood fires had ignited, showering sparks on the tinder-dry roof. Or so the reeve, who owed his job and life to the Valdane, had informed Janusz.

Janusz hadn't seen the point in pressing the man for further explanation. He didn't ask the reeve how the door of the hut had come to be barricaded the night the family died. The neighbors who had rushed to his family's aid told him they couldn't pry the entrance open. They could only cover their ears as the trapped family screamed from within, engulfed by the inferno.

The message wasn't lost on the mage. Over the next decades, Janusz wore himself ragged protecting his leader—and thus himself. Three times the Valdane's enemies had attempted to kill the ruler, twice by poison and once by knife. Each time it was the mage who had cried out and collapsed. Each time the Valdane had emerged unscathed, able to slay the attacker. Stories were whispered throughout Kern that the Valdane was immortal, that the rumor of a bloodlink was true. The peasants watched the mage, and hate burned in their worn faces, but none dared attack a spell-caster of Janusz's repute. The Valdane was remorseless in his pursuit of those who opposed him. One by one his enemies died of strange illnesses or simply disappeared in the night. Eventually no one was left in the region who would stand against him—until the Valdane turned his eyes toward the lands of the Meir.

Chapter 11

The Owl and Kitiara

Twigs and brambles caught at Kitiara's gathered blouse and scratched the leather of her leggings. The air around her shivered with oaths. She was well aware that out in the darkness, shadowless forms watched and waited, but so far they had done no more than mark her every move. Her saddle pack, slung across her back, hampered her movements, but she slashed undaunted at the clinging tentacles of plants with her sword and dagger.

The darkness had eased a bit, as though Solinari were rising behind the clouds. The moon, even weakened as it was, provided enough light for Kitiara to see a few feet, at least, to each side. Trees bent like crones before and behind her. The ominous sound of breathing came to her, sighing like the wind.

Caven Mackid would have said she was mad, attempting this alone. Tanis would have advised her to wait until morning. Wode would have grinned in glee at her present discomfiture.

But they were all dead. And Kitiara was journeying through Darken Wood—looking for the way out—at night.

Motionless, she gazed at the rocky ridge close on her left, then toward what she sensed was a valley off to her right. It was too dark to see much detail, but she pushed on, following what looked like a path, even though the trail that had brought her and the other three into Darken Wood had vanished. Branches and vines pressed around her once more. Reflexively, Kitiara brushed the tendril of a vine away from her face.

Another spasm of dizziness left her drenched with sweat. "By the gods," she murmured, "what ailment have I picked up? Or have I been bewitched?" She waited for the moment of weakness to pass. She was covered with scratches; her back itched from sweat and dust. Thorns had pulled threads from her blouse, ripping holes into it. Blood oozed from a long scratch on her right cheek, skirting her eye.

Suddenly something stood in front of her on the path. She nudged it with her sword. It looked like a gigantic tumbleweed. Surely a good push would send it cascading into the valley below. She nudged the tangled ball with one hand, then, when it seemed unaccountably fixed in place, put one shoulder to it and pushed. Instantly she realized her error. Hundreds of tiny hooks fastened onto the front of her shirt. Tendrils twitched at her ankles, at her wrists. One tenta-

tive, quivering tendril tickled the base of her throat.
She tried to pull back from the brambles. The tendril
at her neck nevertheless moved along her jugular
vein.

With an oath, Kitiara slashed into the brambles—
were they thicker than before?—with her sword, and
the vegetation fell back. "Ah," she murmured. "So
you can be defeated." She stepped again toward the
brambles and smiled to see the tangle move away
from her.

Then Kitiara took another step, and the bramble,
the path, the ridge, and the valley all vanished. The
night, in the same instant, became darker, as though
Solinari had been a candle, suddenly snuffed out. She
reached her left hand forward and moved her dagger
carefully back and forth. The point clinked against
something hard, something tall—too smooth for
rock. Holding her sword ready, Kitiara sheathed the
dagger and reached out again with a bare hand. Her
fingers touched something smooth and hard, traced a
curve, found a wavy ridge, and followed it—to what
was unmistakably a boot.

It was the stone statue that Caven and Maleficent
had become.

Kitiara was back in the clearing with her companions.

Undaunted, Kitiara set off again for Haven, on a
different path this time. An hour later, the swordswoman encountered the same tangle of burrs and
weeds and landed back in the clearing again.

Then Kitiara, her jaw set with anger, sat down,
sword across her knees, her back to a tree, to wait for
dawn. Within moments, despite her vow of vigilance,
she was fast asleep.

Perhaps a sixth sense warned her. Perhaps she

awakened because of the intense emotions brought on by her dream, in which her dead mother stood in the middle of a bridge calling to her. At any rate, opening her eyes to slits, Kitiara tried to pierce the darkness around her, but she lacked the half-elf's nightvision. The darkness was opaque to her all-too-human eyes.

Inwardly she cursed her unfounded weakness. Kitiara Uth Matar did not fall asleep on watch. She had no way of knowing how much time had passed. Moving as though she were still asleep and merely finding a more comfortable position, she shifted a bit against the oak, letting her right hand drop to the earth, as near her sword's hilt as she could manage. She studied her surroundings surreptitiously.

Pairs of greenish lights glowed from the underbrush. Lightning bugs, she thought, even as she realized that the beetles didn't travel in pairs. She peered closely at one set of lights. Another wichtlin? The lights blinked. The wichtlin that had killed her companions certainly had not blinked.

Other pairs of eyes joined the first, and then more, until dozens of fiery orbs watched, fixed on her. Hearing no new sound, Kitiara finally rose cautiously to her feet, catching up her sword and shaking her head to clear it of the cloud of exhaustion that had seemed, in the last few days, to descend on her all too often. Was she ill again? Or had the wichtlin poisoned her after all?

Hundreds of lights now peered from the darkness around her. Teardrop-shaped green eyes. Round gold ones, with pupils shaped like diamonds. Horribly, a few single eyes. The shining orbs pressed toward her. Again she heard indistinct breathing. Were the woods themselves inhaling and exhaling? She cast the thought away.

Yet the creatures seemed to come only so close, and no more. Kitiara detected an odor—the sharp scent of sweat, which in anyone else she would have called the scent of fear. Her own fear? But Kitiara never admitted to fear.

Why in the Abyss did the things hold back? Why didn't they attack? They'd lost the element of surprise, but clearly they outnumbered her.

They fear me. With good reason, I might add.

The words came into Kitiara's head unbidden. The magic that had dispelled the wichtlin, the ettin's presence, the ice jewels in her pack—all pointed in one direction. Her voice hissed. "Janusz? If it is you, show yourself, you coward."

There was no answer, merely a muffled gasp—from where, Kitiara couldn't tell. The Valdane's mage, who certainly had more reason than anyone to plot revenge against her, would not have answered thusly. Therefore the presence was someone else.

Kitiara gazed around her at the pinpoints of eyes.

No. Up here, Captain Uth Matar.

Keeping her sword ready, Kitiara pivoted and peered into the branches of the aged oak above her. At first she saw nothing in the darkness. But then two horizontal slits appeared in the murk high above her. They opened, curved, and curved still more until she was gazing at two circular orange shapes the size of saucers. Within each flaming circle floated a smaller orb, as black as the night around her. As she watched, the orange circles narrowed to thin bands, and the black orbs within—the creature's pupils, she realized—dilated. The thing was studying her, by the gods! But what was it?

You'll see me better with your eyes closed, my dear captain. Look into your heart, Kitiara Uth Matar. Its message is plain, even when the eyes play tricks.

"What idiocy is this?" Kitiara cried. "Show yourself, vermin!"

Vermin? I?

At that moment, she heard a faint buzzing. "Are you a giant hornet? A venomous bee?" she demanded. Yet those creatures would hardly be about at night, and certainly they wouldn't be hovering in a tree making conversation with a human. She pulled her dagger with her left hand. Her right already held her sword. Kitiara backpedaled into the clearing, away from the danger.

Put away your puny weapons, Kitiara Uth Matar.

"Don't be ridiculous, creature."

We are no threat—to you, at least.

"I'll decide that. Show yourself. Now."

A long silence, and more buzzing. Finally Kitiara sensed a whooshing, like an otherworldly sigh.

You are rude, human. I should abandon you here with the undead and your pathetic, ensorcelled friends. But that might hasten your own death, which I have promised to prevent—for the time being, at least. But do try to stay on my good side, Captain.

Kitiara had stopped listening halfway through. "Ensorcelled? Tanis . . . ? So they're not dead?"

You are so easily fooled, human. I said you trust your eyes too much.

"Show yourself, monster."

There was a sudden ruffling noise above her, as though something large had fluffed out its feathers in a sudden huff. Then the air warped around her and wind buffeted her—the beating of wings, she realized. A screech like a banshee's rent the darkness. "Oh, by the gods," Kitiara said dismissively, letting the point of her sword drop. "You're just a big, dumb bird."

There was more buzzing from above. The creature screeched again. The tree creaked as the thing shifted from clawed foot to clawed foot. Then silence reigned, broken only by that strong buzzing that seemed trapped inside Kit's head. Finally a new voice sounded, a woman's voice, threaded with warmth and humor. "I fear you've alienated my companion, Kitiara Uth Matar."

"I've heard this voice before. Show yourself."

A pause. *Shirak.* A glow emanated through the clearing. A huge owl, as tall as two men from ear tufts to stubby tail and obviously piqued, glared down at the swordswoman. "A giant owl," Kitiara said softly. "I've heard of your kind. Yet you speak Common and have some magical ability, which I'd not thought possible."

A dark human face with delicate features peered over the side of the bird's wing. "You are in Darken Wood. And my friend Xanthar is extraordinary in many ways," the woman said softly. Even in the greenish magelight, Kitiara could see that her eyes were startlingly blue.

"I know you," the swordswoman said slowly. "You were a maid to Dreena ten Valdane. And a magic-user, if I recall. But I do not recall blue eyes."

"Lida Tenaka," the woman whispered. Kitiara could barely hear her next words. "I have come looking for you, Kitiara Uth Matar."

The owl sprang into the air, spread his wings, and landed, astonishingly softly for one so large, between the frozen forms of Tanis and Caven. Then the owl extended a wing, and Lida Tenaka glided gracefully down its feathered surface to the ground. For all her delicacy, she seemed comfortable being in Darken Wood at night. Kitiara studied her but didn't sheath her sword. This Lida Tenaka might be an apparition, a manifestation of some evil that had tunneled into Kitiara's consciousness as she slept. There was no proof that this slim, robed woman was the real Lida Tenaka. Kitiara observed her carefully.

Over her shoulder she carried a large drawstring bag, heavy from the looks of it, the leather thongs that kept it closed gathered into a knot. The sack showed the outline of a large circular object, appearing to be flat on one side, and, when the woman's movements caused the contents to shift, convex on the other side. The woman's face was expressionless, her lively eyes the only sign of humanity in her somber face. But her voice was kind. "Xanthar and I have flown long hours looking for you, Captain Uth Matar. I am glad to have finally found you."

Kitiara barked her questions. "You have magic? The owl has magic?"

Lida Tenaka nodded toward the bird, hair rippling against her robe. "Xanthar controls certain powers. He can use telepathy, within a certain range and with certain types of creatures—mainly humans and other giant owls. And as you can attest, he can communicate his thoughts to other sentient creatures."

"Sentient creatures," Kitiara repeated. It sounded like an insult.

"Thinking creatures."

"Can he read minds?"

Lida shrugged. "To a very limited extent, he can tell what others are thinking."

"The skill comes slowly, with long, long practice," the bird interrupted gruffly.

"Can he revive my friends? Can you?" Quickly she told them about the wichtlin and her friends' fates.

The owl and the mage exchanged looks; Kitiara

sensed that they weren't being completely frank with her. "Can you or not?" she demanded.

"They are dreaming, I believe," Xanthar said, his voice a husky whisper. Lida cast him a startled look, but neither explained.

Lida spoke slowly. "Whether I can help them depends on how they were put under the spell of magic and by whom. It's difficult for one mage to offset the spells of another."

"But you will try."

"Will you help me in turn?" the mage asked.

Kitiara looked away. Her gaze fell on the ensorcelled Tanis, his body frozen in midaction. Lida's green magelight made him seem almost alive. For a moment, she thought the half-elf's almond-shaped eyes flickered her way. A warning? "I'll consider helping you," Kitiara finally said. "That is all I care to promise."

The owl finally spoke, its voice thick with sarcasm. "An interesting attitude, Captain, considering that it is you, not us, trapped alone in Darken Wood," he drawled.

"Xanthar," Lida said warningly. The owl snorted and turned his back on them both.

Moving around the owl, caressing his feathered shoulder, Lida stepped over to Caven. She placed slender hands on Maleficent's withers and closed her eyes. After a time, she opened them again and began to speak. "I cannot—"

"Yes, you can, Lida." The owl interrupted suddenly, urgently. "Use a dispel ensorcellment incantation."

"A . . . But there's no . . ." The owl's warning look stopped Lida. She frowned. The owl gazed directly at her, and as the silence lengthened and Lida's eyes widened in sudden shock, Kitiara realized that Xanthar was speaking telepathically to the dark-skinned woman. Finally Lida nodded. "All right, Xanthar. I'm glad you suggested that. It might work."

"Can't hurt, at any rate," the owl muttered with a nasty glance at Kitiara. "After all, they're practically dead now. How much worse can it get? Although I suppose being *undead* . . ."

"Wait!" Kitiara burst out. "Don't!"

The owl inserted himself between her and Lida. Kitiara considered running him through, but instead she found herself gazing directly into his eyes. *Don't even consider it, human.* The edges of his huge beak, she noticed, were as sharp as any sword's tip. Kitiara stepped back warily, peering around the bird.

Lida was standing before Maleficent. She stroked the animal's flank, murmuring strange syllables and scattering pinches of gray powder from a pouch. Then she moved to Wode and his mount and did the same. Finally she turned her attention to the half-elf. At last she stepped back and stood beside Xanthar.

"Stand back," Lida warned Kitiara. "The three have lost no time. They will believe they're still fighting the wichtlin." She raised her arms dramatically, threw her head back, and chanted. Kitiara frowned again.

"Barkanian softine, omalon tui." Lida repeated the phrase three times, pausing after each utterance. With the first chant, the figures in the clearing lost their statuelike luster. With the second, the pink glow of life returned to the humans' faces. And with the third chant, they burst into action, finishing the movements they'd begun hours before while dueling the wichtlin.

Tanis dove to the ground and rolled. He halted in bewilderment, then spotted Kitiara. "Kit! You're all right?"

Kitiara scoffed. "I'm always all right."

Caven, meanwhile, was struggling to control a rearing, bucking, biting Maleficent. Wode and his horse scampered to one side to avoid the hooves. The Kernish mercenary finally brought the animal to a stop before Kitiara, Lida, and Xanthar. "By the gods! A giant owl! I thought they were legends," he exclaimed. "What a dream I had. My mother came to me with a fantastic story about the Val—" When he noticed Lida Tenaka, the words died on his lips. "You're Dreena's maid," Caven said with surprise.

Tanis approached. "You dreamed about your mother, too?" Wode moaned, and the swordswoman turned to him. "And you?"

"All of you dreamed of a portent," said Lida reassuringly. The spell-caster began to recite. With every word, the faces of the four travelers grew more sober and tense. By the end, Caven was reciting the lines with her.

> "The lovers three, the spell-cast maid,
> The winged one of loyal soul,
> The foul undead of Darken Wood,
> The vision seen in scrying bowl.
>> Evil loosed with diamond's flight.
>
> "Vengeance savored, ice-clenched heart
> Seeks its image to enthrone
> Matched by sword and fire's heat,
> Embers born of steel and stone.
>> Evil cast with jewel's light.
>
> "The lovers three, the spell-cast maid,
> The tie of filial love abased,
> Foul legions turned, the blood flows free,

> *Frozen deaths in snow-locked waste.*
> *Evil vanquished, gemstone's might."*

For a heartbeat, no one spoke. Then all began talking at once.

"It was my mother, I tell you."

"But mine died when I was born."

"As did mine."

"But mine is alive."

"What does this mean?"

Through it all, Wode whined, "I want to go back to Kern." Vainly Kitiara tried to persuade the other three to stop worrying about the portent and resume the hunt for the ettin.

"To the Abyss with the ettin," Caven yelled from atop Maleficent. "The beast must be long gone by now."

"You were seeking an ettin?" Xanthar suddenly asked.

Kitiara nodded. "You saw it? Where? Tell me!"

The owl stepped back a pace, swaying its big head from side to side, the white patch gleaming over the bird's left eye. "No, no. I merely wondered why you were seeking an ettin here in the woods. They're not normally found in this part of the world."

"No." The voice was Lida's. She stepped in front of the owl. "But there is an ettin here, and it's not far ahead. I saw it from the air as we flew here. You could catch up with it if you made haste."

Silence greeted her. Then Kitiara spoke deliberately to her friends. "Don't trust her. I would remind you that we are in Darken Wood."

"As if we could forget," Caven murmured, glancing nervously at the surrounding darkness. Kitiara glared him into silence, then she went on. "This owl, who can do what no giant owl I've heard of can do, and this woman, who purports to be Lida Tenaka, could be evil manifestations of the woods or the illusions of the wichtlin. And I would remind you, Caven, that the mage Janusz may be capable of ensorcelling us all, even from the distance of Kern."

"Janusz is in Kern no longer," Lida interrupted.

The four faced her. "Who is this Janusz? What do you know about this, Kitiara?" Tanis demanded.

Briefly Kitiara sketched in the details about the end of the Kernish-Meiri campaign, omitting any mention of the ice jewels.

"The mage Janusz and the Valdane no doubt hold me responsible for the death of Dreena ten Valdane," she concluded. "The Valdane refused to unleash the mage until he was certain his daughter was gone. The peasants had been in disarray, left unsure what to do in the face of the Meir's death; the Valdane, I'm guessing, didn't care whether his daughter lived or died." Lida moaned softly, but Kitiara went on. "The Valdane did know that the Meir's subjects had grown to love Dreena. He feared that slaying her would be enough to prompt the peasants to revolt against the Valdane rather than submit quietly to a new ruler."

Kitiara looked from Tanis to Caven and back to Tanis, whose expression was growing increasingly dark. "It was on my word that they dared attack the castle," Kitiara said. "I saw Dreena leave it, and I told the Valdane it was safe to attack."

Tanis spoke slowly, his rage barely under control. "This mage Janusz has an ettin slave, and you failed to mention that when we set off after another ettin that *just happened* to show up in this vicinity? By the gods, Kitiara, have you no sense? You've no right to put us in that kind of danger! Mackid, didn't you wonder about the ettin?"

"I did, yes," came the stolid answer. "But all I was thinking about was my money."

Tanis fell back, disgusted. The half-elf swept the clearing with his gaze. Finally he gave a bark of laughter. "My guess is that we have ridden straight into a trap set by Janusz."

Lida broke in. "You could stop Janusz, the four of you. You could stop the Valdane. At first it was enough for him to capture the Meir's fiefdom, but now he wants to lay claim to all of Ansalon. Kitiara, you know him well; you were his mercenary, and you are used to leading troops. I can see that you, half-elf, are a wise man and an honorable one. And you, Caven, are an accomplished soldier and a brave man." Caven smiled tightly. Lida said nothing about Wode, but she included him in her next sweeping gesture. "You four could stop the Valdane. You could be heroes. No one else is in a position to stop him. Even now the Valdane is amassing an army to ride north out of the Icereach."

"The Icereach?" Kitiara and Caven demanded together. They gave each other unintentionally comical looks of disbelief, then Kitiara went on. "We left him in Kern, five hundred miles northeast of Darken Wood, and now you tell us he's three hundred miles south of here? And you say we're in a position to stop him? How gullible do you think we are, mage? What do you really want?"

"How do you know this?" Caven demanded.

Lida looked flustered. "My dream," she finally said.

Caven slapped his saddle, startling Maleficent. When he had calmed the stallion, the soldier said, "The dream could be a trick as well. Sent by Janusz."

"Can you help us get out of Darken Wood?" Tanis

asked Lida, who shook her head. "Xanthar can carry me, but no more."

Kitiara spoke next. "Why do you care what Janusz and the Valdane do, mage? Surely you are safe this far away."

The maid paused and seemed to be gathering her thoughts. "Dreena was my friend, and they are responsible for her death."

"You're lying," Kitiara snapped. "You and the owl are both lying. You want something from us. I say that if you want us to do something, offer us something. Wealth."

"I have no money."

"Power, then. After all, you are a mage."

"I follow the course of good. I do not barter power."

Tanis's voice interrupted. "You would accompany us to the Icereach, of course."

Kitiara turned on him. "Half-elf! You're not thinking of going to the Icereach, are you? She may not even be who she says she is!"

"I haven't decided whether I'm going or not." Tanis eyed Lida thoughtfully. "I've seen the effects of magic, too, Kit. And I would say that this mage, while she may not be telling us everything she knows, has an honorable intent. I believe she really does wish to avenge the death of her friend."

Kitiara spat in disgust and turned her back on the half-elf. With the movement, she caught the wide smile on Caven's face. "And what's *your* problem, soldier?" she demanded.

"Ah, Captain, it's so refreshing to see you lose an argument now and then," the Kernan said.

"Lose?" Kitiara was nearly apoplectic with rage. She waved her hands. "I have no intention of taking a jaunt down to the frigid depths of Ansalon so that this servant can avenge the death of someone who was the enemy of the man I served. Capturing an ettin for the bounty was one thing. Gadding off—unpaid, to boot—to save the great unwashed populace of Krynn . . . well, forget it!" She began to stomp off, continuing to rail over her shoulder. "Although you two men are welcome to try. I've no use for either of you anymore. Idiots. Gullible sots!" She kicked a tree trunk, then, gripped by nausea, grabbed the bark with steadying hands. In a moment, the spell passed and she shoved herself away from the tree.

Tanis took a step after her. "Kit . . ." The swordswoman ignored him.

Caven stopped the half-elf with a hand on his forearm. "Let her work it off, Tanis. Kit'll rave for a bit, but she'll calm down. Talking to her when she's in this state will do nothing but goad her on." Tanis paused, then nodded. Kitiara glared back at them, still spitting threats and curses.

Tanis and Caven continued speaking in low voices, and Lida and Xanthar withdrew to one side.

A dispel ensorcellment incantation indeed, Xanthar.

It is not I who held back the beings in the woods, Kai-lid. They don't fear giant owls. Someone has cast a protection spell about Kitiara—the same person, I would guess, who released the spell on the three travelers while you went through that splendid bit of mummery. We are within the protective circle; I can feel it. We are being watched, Kai-lid.

Kai-lid thought for a moment, her heart pounding. *It must be Janusz, Xanthar. It has to be. He has seen them, and he has seen me. Now we are trapped.*

Don't forget that the mage sees Lida, not Dreena.

He could see with his magic who I really am if he chose. Kai-lid's lips were trembling.

He has no reason to try, my dear. He believes Dreena to be dead.

Why did he dispel the ensorcellment of the half-elf and the others?

Xanthar was silent for a time. *I don't know. It must fit his plan. Surely he sent the ettin to fetch them.*

And they, in turn, followed it into a trap. Do you believe the dream now, Xanthar?

I do.

At that moment, Tanis broke away from the group and approached the owl and the mage. He spoke without preamble. "I want to know why you want to help us."

Lida exchanged a glance with Xanthar, but the owl offered no assistance. "We have no choice," she finally continued. "We must pursue this ettin."

"Why?"

Lida swallowed. "I believe the ettin will lead us to the Valdane. Res-Lacua is Janusz's ettin and his slave. The ettin must return to him."

Tanis spoke slowly, never taking his gaze from her. "It feels like a trap to me, Lida. We follow the ettin, and the mage gets the chance to take revenge on Kitiara. How will we take on an entire army?"

Lida found herself stammering under Tanis's steady hazel gaze. "Half-elf," she said at last, "it's too late to back away from this. Kitiara is far from helpless, and she will have us to protect her. I believe she knows far more than she is telling any of us." When Tanis said nothing, she swallowed again and went on, inwardly berating Xanthar for forcing her to carry the argument alone. "I will go with you, half-elf. My magic is far from strong, but I will do what I can. Perhaps this is a trap, but I'm not the one who set it. I believe we're the only ones standing between the Valdane's greed and the deaths of many, many people. It's a question of honor, Tanis."

"A question of honor," Tanis repeated softly.

She reached out a hand toward him and rested it on his sleeve. "Half-elf, in turn I have a question for you. What is Kitiara to you?"

Tanis stared at the magic-user. Her straight black hair poured over her shoulders. Her voice was low and vibrant. "She is important to you, this swordswoman?" the mage prodded when he did not reply.

"She is—" Tanis faltered under the intensity of her blue gaze, so startling against that dark skin—"an acquaintance. We are traveling together."

The black pupils widened, and the edges of the magic-user's lips curved. "Ah. An acquaintance."

"Yes." He looked away.

The woman's words carried an undertone of amusement. "This is Kitiara's battle, not yours, Tanthalas Half-Elven. How fortunate for Kitiara that she has an 'acquaintance' with the strength and courage not to abandon her at such a dangerous time. One wonders what you would do for a wife or child if you would go to such lengths for a mere acquaintance."

Tanis flushed. "You are bound to fight against this Valdane, then?" he said hurriedly.

She nodded. The half-elf, after hesitating, returned to the group.

You have no intention of accompanying them. Xanthar's voice carried a note of reproach.

I am afraid, Xanthar, and I am not a very powerful mage. They don't need me. They'll do fine alone. But they may not follow through on the task if they think I intend to leave them behind.

Xanthar reached over and plucked a twig from a tree with his beak. Then he peeled the bark from it, rotating it with his tongue while removing the bark with the edge of his beak. *And you believe the ettin is leading them to the Icereach? I must point out, Kai-lid, that the ettin seems to be heading north, whereas the Icereach, the last time I checked, was in the southernmost reaches of Ansalon.*

Kai-lid didn't answer. Xanthar mused, *I have heard that there is a sla-mori in Darken Wood, one that leads far to the south. It might be rumor, or it might not.*

A sla-mori?

A secret passage. A magical tunnel that whisks occupants far, far away, if they can fathom its mystery. Rumor has it the elves built the sla-moris long ago.

And this sla-mori is to the north?

The owl nodded. *A short distance—in a valley next to Fever Mountain. Perhaps that is where the ettin is going.* Then Xanthar changed the subject once more. *You have looked closely at Kitiara, I assume.*

Yes.

And you have seen? Not with your two eyes, but with your inner eye?

I have seen, Xanthar. I wonder what she plans to do.

Xanthar laughed out loud. *You believe she knows, then, Kai-lid? Truly you give humans more credit for self-awareness than I do.*

But how could a woman be with child and not know it?

Never underestimate humans' deafness to their inner voices, Kai-lid. Never.

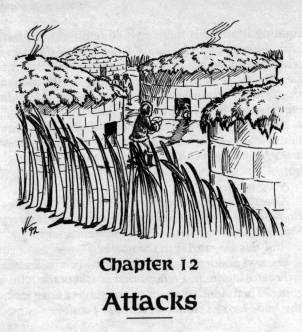

Chapter 12

Attacks

The girl's face, like that of her older brother, was dirty with soot and walrus grease, rubbed in by their mother early that day to ease the bite of the cold wind that swept across the Icereach.

"Haudo," she whispered to her brother, her black eyes bright with the delight of her idea. "I am an ice bear." She stretched her fur-mittened hands far above her head, warm in its sealskin hood with seabird-feather trim. She emitted an approximation of the polar bear's roar. Then she giggled.

But Haudo frowned. "We must never mimic the ice bear, Terve," he reminded her with the pedantic tone that was second nature to older brothers. "He is the

---

174

grandfather of this land, and we must honor him."

Terve sulked. "You are a spoilsport, Haudo. I wish I'd stayed home."

Haudo sighed. "You pestered me to come along until Father ordered me to take you. I told him you were too little. I told Father you'd get tired, that you'd be no help at all. But they wanted you out of the way so that they could braid sealskin into ropes in peace for once, so I—"

"That's not true! I can too help find the frostreaver ice!"

"Then do it," Haudo grumbled. "And for once in your eight winters, Little Sister, be silent while you do something."

"You have only four winters more than me, Brother," Terve complained, but she held her tongue for a short time after that. The boy and girl poked through the litter around Reaver's Rock, an outcropping of densely frozen ice an hour's ride from their camp by iceboat. Their boat lay on its side a short distance away, its large sail flat against the ice and its long, wooden runners shiny. The packed ice of the Icereach was slick enough here to permit the use of the Ice Folk's traditional form of transport, although buckling of the snow and ice and occasional crevasses that had filled with drifting snow made the way treacherous. From here, the Icereach seemed to undulate in gentle hills; Haudo could barely see the smoke from the peat fires of his home village.

The Ice Folk boy probed at the base of the gigantic outcropping, looking for slivers of reaver ice dislodged by frost heaving. The steel-hard material could be fashioned into hide scrapers, small knives, even into sewing and knitting needles, although only the Revered Cleric could supervise the gathering of the large chunks suitable to become The People's traditional weapon, the battle-ax known as a frostreaver. Terve wrapped even the tiniest shards in tanned seabird skins and laid them reverently in the basket she'd woven from strips of walrus gut.

Inevitably Terve piped up again. "Why do The People call it Reaver's Rock, Haudo? Who was Reaver? And this is ice, not rock."

Haudo grinned at the shortness of his sister's self-imposed silence, but he answered gently. Haudo was of the Storyteller Clan; it was his role in life to memorize the thousands of tales that made up the oral history of the Ice Folk. This telling of the Reaver's tale would be good practice, even though little Terve had surely heard the story dozens of times. And a tale would help pass the time.

He puffed out his chest, took a deep breath, mimicked the storytelling stance of his father, and began, following the ritual of his clan. "The elders say The People can see the edges of the world from the top of Reaver's Rock. And that all they can see is theirs, as it always has been and always will be, to be shared only with the ice bear. So say the elders."

"Let's go, then, Haudo!" Terve squealed. "Let's climb to the top!"

Haudo glared at her. "It is unseemly for someone to interrupt the telling of a Tale of Origin," he reminded her loftily. Terve grew silent. "Anyway," he added in ill-humor, "no one's been to the top of Reaver's Rock. It's too slippery."

Terve opened her mouth to speak, then shut it again after a nasty look from her brother. Feigning nonchalance, she pulled a snack of fresh raw fish from a packet and munched it. Haudo resumed his tale.

"Many, many winters past, the great polar bear that

shaped the lands of The People placed here, at this very spot, a holy gift, a fruitful place." Haudo repeated that last phrase. It sounded so grown-up. "A holy gift, a fruitful place. A place that would hold the polar bear's gift of reaver ice, the dense ice from which The People would fashion, with much prayer and singing, the frostreaver. The frostreaver, weapon feared by the enemies of The People, is the gift of the polar bear."

"You said that, Haudo." Two frown lines broke the smoothness of the smudged skin between Terve's eyes.

Haudo closed his eyes and inhaled slowly. When he finished exhaling, he was outwardly calm. "For centuries, The People have gone to the secret places along Icewall Glacier to harvest the ice, to bring to their tribes the material that only the tribes' Revered Cleric can fashion into the frostreavers. Such is the intricacy of these weapons that each one takes a month to fashion."

"I know that, Brother," Terve muttered.

"The frostreaver is the gift of the polar bear," he reiterated, just to annoy her. "The frostreaver is the only weapon that will stave off the bull men and thanoi, foes of The People."

Terve looked around her and shivered. The mention of the walrus men and the minotaurs, who made periodic forays into the Icereach to steal slaves and sealskins, sent her edging a little closer to her big brother. Haudo pretended not to notice. He continued his tale of the ice bear, the reavers, and the debt that The People owed to the polar bears. No Ice Folk man or woman would slay a polar bear; the one who did, even accidentally, owed the bear's spirit seven days of fasting and prayer and many gifts.

"Haudo." Terve spoke quietly for once.

"Terve," he complained, "I'm trying—"

"Haudo, The People don't need great fires to make the skin ropes, do they?"

"What?" Without moving, Haudo absorbed the growing fear in his sister's eyes. Then he turned around and faced the wind, to where the fires of his people had sent thin spires of smoke into the southern air only a short time before.

Now the air was black with smoke. Even this far away, Haudo could smell burning fur and skins. He could have sworn, too, that he heard screams, but of course that was impossible.

"Haudo?" Terve was suddenly standing, pressed against him. He placed an arm around his little sister's shoulders. She's too little to be motherless, he thought. "We must go to the iceboat, Terve."

"What has happened?" Terve was on the verge of tears, but a child of The People does not cry easily. She still clutched her basket of reaver shards.

"We will see, Little Sister." He righted the boat, helped Terve into it, and set the sail. Soon he was running alongside, guiding it onto the packed snow, then leaping into the iceboat when the sail caught the wind. They sped silently toward the smoking village.

Haudo pulled up the iceboat and hid it behind a ridge of mounded snow. The village was a short distance away, behind the ridge. "Stay here," he ordered Terve.

The twelve-year-old boy crept along the back of the ridge, remembering everything his father had told him about tracking game: Heed your nose and heed your ears. They will tell you as much as your eyes. Even before he slipped his head above the ridge, he smelled the acrid stench of the minotaurs. He caught, also, the greasy fish smell of the thanoi, the walrus men, who contended, against the proof of thousands of years of legend, that the Icereach was theirs, not The People's. And Haudo smelled something else—a nasty odor of garbage and rancid meat. Then he peered at his village, barely keeping from coughing in the smoky haze, and his breath caught in his throat. "Two-headed beasts!" he whispered.

He wanted to jump back, to avoid seeing the image he knew would never vanish from his mind. His kinsmen, his friends, lay sprawled in death on the blood-soaked snow. Minotaurs, walrus men, and the two-headed monsters brought body after body forth from iceblock huts and skin tents. A few bodies twitched. An old man moaned, and one of the two-headed brutes hurried over, waving a spiked club over its head.

Overseeing it all was the robed figure of a man, silhouetted against the southern sky.

As quietly as he'd ever moved in hunting seal or walrus, Haudo raced through the shadow of the snow ridge to the iceboat and Terve. The little girl, for once, had followed orders. She sat huddled in the boat. Haudo said only, "We must leave, little sister." She nodded mutely.

Soon the iceboat was speeding across the snow to their kinsmen's village, several days' journey to the northwest.

* * * * *

Kai-lid awakened with a start and sat up. The half-elf, keeping guard, looked over at her but said nothing. Caven and Kitiara and Wode lay wrapped in blankets around the fire. Xanthar perched above them, watchful. The eyes of the undead, as always, gazed at them from the darkness.

179

The mage sent her thoughts forth. *Xanthar?*

I saw it, too, Kai-lid. The devastation of the Ice Folk village.

It was no dream, then?

No more than the other. The village has been crushed by your father's armies. The Valdane is testing his strength, Kai-lid.

Xanthar, we have no time to linger. We have to lead these four to the sla-mori and get them to the Icereach.

I have an idea. As Kai-lid watched, the owl launched himself from the tree and soared off over Darken Wood. Within moments, he was lost to sight.

"What were you two discussing?" Tanis asked quietly from his post. "Kitiara told me of your telepathy."

Kai-lid answered slowly. "I think Xanthar is going to search for the ettin."

Tanis nodded, although his eyes seemed doubtful. "You believe we should still continue to try to capture it, then? Even though it seems to have been sent by this evil mage, Janusz?"

She hesitated. This half-elf appeared to be a decent sort; perhaps she could be more honest with him. Perhaps Tanis would volunteer to come to the aid of thousands of people who, she felt sure, would die at the hands of her father if the Valdane were not defeated. Kai-lid opened her mouth hesitantly.

But Caven Mackid broke in. "We should capture the damned ettin, go back to Haven immediately, and get our reward, Tanis. Let the lady fight her own battles." He gestured rudely toward Kai-lid. "I don't understand why Dreena's maid is involved in this ettin business, anyway." He clearly had not slept at all. His voice was snappish and his eyes shadowed.

"I agree with Caven," Kitiara said, renewing the debate. "Slay the ettin. That's what we set out to do."

"And then?" Kai-lid asked.

"Then?" Kitiara repeated.

"Then you can go home safely with your fifteen steel while the Valdane destroys everything in his path to power," Kai-lid said bitterly.

"So you say, mage. I'm not convinced." The swordswoman stretched elaborately. "Anyway, it's not my problem. I don't work for the Valdane anymore."

Caven nodded. "That's two votes in favor of fifteen steel," he said pointedly.

Kitiara nodded, but Tanis looked unconvinced. He gazed at Kai-lid. "I think you're holding something back, mage," he said softly. "I only wish I knew what it is. Why should we trust you, Lida Tenaka?"

Kai-lid started to say something, then turned away.

* * * * *

"Big chicken!" Res shouted. He rose first, hoisting Lacua's side upright. "Food! Food!"

The ettin's left head protested. "Not chicken, stupid. Too big. Maybe goose."

"But supper?"

"Yes."

Xanthar sighed from his perch high above the ettin. "I am a giant owl, you dunderpated chuckleheads."

The two heads looked at each other. "Chicken talk?" They turned suspicious faces toward Xanthar. "Dunder—What say?

"It's a great compliment," Xanthar said, deadpan. "Trust me."

"Ah," Lacua said, nodding. "A compliment."

"Supper use big words," Res observed.

"I have information for you," Xanthar said.

"Inform—" Lacua stumbled over the word.

Xanthar amended himself. "I have a fact for you."

"Ah!"

"About Kitiara Uth Matar."

"Who?" Res muttered.

Lacua poked him. "Lady soldier, stupid," the left head said. Then, to Xanthar, "Say fact now."

"She's about to leave Darken Wood."

Res protested. "Can't. Must follow Res-Lacua to Fever Mountain. Master said—"

"Quiet!" Lacua slammed Res over the head with his club. Res rubbed his pate and sulked.

"They will not follow you any longer, ettin," the owl said smoothly, twisting his head back to preen a wing feather with a doting beak. "They are going to leave." He pulled his head upright, watching the worried-looking monster.

"Good. Res go home, too," the right head caroled.

"No!" Lacua interrupted. "Must get lady soldier."

"You could kidnap her now," the owl suggested.

The ettin looked up again. "Kidnap?"

"Capture."

"Capture! Res know capture!" The right head grinned. Lacua looked thoughtful, then repeated, "Capture now."

"I brought you an important fact," Xanthar said. "Don't you think I deserve some sort of favor as a reward?"

Twin looks of suspicion fell over the ettin's countenances. "Favor? What favor?"

"You must not injure anyone. Take Kitiara, the lady soldier, the two men, and the boy if you wish." Xanthar stared at the ettin until Res-Lacua's feet shuffled uneasily. "But not the other woman."

A crafty smile came over Lacua's face. "What if

Res-Lacua not give this favor to giant chicken?"

Xanthar narrowed his eyes at him. "Then I'll take my fact back."

"Wait! No! Need fact!"

"Well, then . . ."

"Not hurt nobody. Not, not, not. Capture lady soldier, men guys. Yes, yes. Keep fact now?" Lacua stopped for a deep breath.

"Yes," Xanthar replied. "Keep fact."

The giant owl flew away.

As soon as Xanthar was out of sight, Lacua exclaimed and clapped his hand to his chest. He drew out the Talking Stone. "Master talk?"

The voice came from the small, flat rock, filling the forest around the ettin. The eyes of the undead, which hovered around the monster as they did around the travelers, drew back as the leaves of the twisted trees quivered with the vibrations. The voice sounded weary. "Do as the owl says. Attack Kitiara and the others."

"Yes," both heads whispered.

"As soon as possible."

"Yes."

"Take them to Fever Mountain."

They nodded.

There was a pause, as though the voice were pondering. "As for the other woman . . ."

"Master?"

"Capture her, too. I'm curious about her."

"What about nice favor?"

"Forget the favor. We have the fact."

"Ah. Capture."

Janusz made the ettin repeat the instructions three more times. "Any questions?" he finally asked.

"No supper here. Rotten woods empty. Res-Lacua don't like dead food. Hungry."

Janusz decided to be generous with the ettin. "Slay one of the others if you like. Just don't hurt the two women. Bring them to me."

"Eat?"

"Fine."

* * * * *

Kai-lid. I have told the ettin where we are. The ettin will kidnap them.

Xanthar! What have you done?

These four will debate forever while innocents die. I've merely speeded up the process. Don't worry; you will be safe. The ettin promised. But it appears I was right, Kai-lid. They will be taken to Fever Mountain, and from there to the sla-mori, in the valley just south of the mountain.

And?

When the ettin captures them, we will follow and make sure they find the sla-mori. Once in the Icereach, they will fight the Valdane. What other choice will they have? If the magic of Darken Wood holds true, they will soon forget they were ever here. And you, my dear, will not be suspected.

Kai-lid was speechless.

You could thank me.

But she said nothing.

* * * * *

When the attack came a short time later, Tanis and Kitiara whirled as one, swords flashing, to meet the challenge.

A hulk of a monster, stinking of rancid meat and dead skunk, roared out at them, slinging a club in each hand. At first sight of the fearsome creature, Wode's nag reared in fright and galloped off into the woods. The monster's two clubs dwarfed the steel swords that thudded against the petrified wood. Kitiara recoiled despite herself. Beside her, she felt Tanis's horror, too.

The giant owl dove overhead, screeching, but the mage seemed unable to react. Through it all, the eyes watched from the surrounding woods.

Across the clearing, Caven struggled to mount Maleficent, but the horse reared. Caven turned to Tanis's gelding. Dauntless submitted docilely to Caven's weight.

Tanis and Kitiara leaped to meet the ettin's second charge, then just as quickly dove aside as the ettin's weapons whizzed toward them. Both clubs sported a half-dozen iron spikes, each as long as a man's hand. The spikes bore the scrapes and dents of years of use.

Tanis feinted, then slashed at the beast with his longsword. Kitiara followed suit. But the monster's reach exceeded Tanis's and Kitiara's so greatly that the two could only pounce and jab before leaping back. Only Tanis could see well enough in the dimness. Kitiara had to rely on an intuitive sense of where the beast moved; until it came within a few feet of her, it was less than a blur in the blackness.

Tanis maneuvered until the thick trunk of an oak stood between him and the monster. Kitiara followed, squinting into the dark. Xanthar continued screeching, hooting overhead until Kitiara thought she would scream, too. The half-elf seemed oblivious to the owl's commotion.

"You'll never get near it, half-elf," Caven shouted from atop Dauntless, trying to angle the horse closer. "This requires a mounted swordsman."

"Do something besides talk, Mackid!" Tanis shouted back. The half-elf turned to Kitiara. "The ettin has brains of granite, yet, by the gods, the strength of granite, too!" He frowned. "Caven's right, for once. We've no chance with swords."

Suddenly Tanis picked up a fist-sized stone. "Stay here! Cover me!" he hissed.

"What? How? Half-elf, I can barely see!" Kitiara protested. She lunged for his arm. "What are you—?"

Her question went unanswered as the half-elf lobbed the rock at the ettin. The creature's heads snapped backward, its confusion mirrored in its watery eyes. At the same time, Caven spurred the gelding forward.

Tanis nocked and released an arrow. It hurtled toward the ettin as Caven and Dauntless came tearing at the creature. The arrow sliced along the tough hide of the ettin's shoulder. The beast's left head swung around, looking more surprised than pained, and the left arm arched toward Dauntless. Caven was knocked off the mount, and suddenly the gelding hung by the neck in the grasp of the thirteen-foot beast. The horse pawed uselessly at the air.

The ettin shook the gelding's neck. "Food!" the right head crowed. Lacua, the left head, echoed Res, and the ettin slammed the horse into a tree. Tanis cried out as he heard the animal's front legs break. Res-Lacua released his grasp, and Dauntless went down.

Kitiara dove for the ettin. The monster's left hand dropped its club, reached out, and backhanded Kitiara. Then it grabbed her and shook her fiercely, sending her weapon flying. Caven, on foot now and wielding his sword, struggled to close with the beast. Tanis joined Caven; he dared not loose an arrow at the ettin now for fear of hitting Kitiara. The ettin shook her one last time and dropped her unconscious body over one shoulder.

Then Res-Lacua halted and looked around him. "Lady mage!" he hollered. He stormed across the clearing toward Kai-lid. Tanis saw her freeze. Her fingers moved frantically, fumbling with the pouches of spell components at her belt. "Xanthar!" she shouted. "My magic! I can't . . ." The giant owl dove toward the ettin, but Xanthar's wingtip caught against a branch, and he careened into the ground.

"Xanthar!" Lida screamed again. The owl lay there, unmoving.

Then the ettin was striding out of the clearing, with Kitiara draped over one shoulder and dragging Lida by one arm. Res-Lacua shoved past Tanis and Caven as though they were reeds. Just as the ettin reached the edge of the clearing, a new figure stepped in front of the monster.

Of all things, it was Wode.

Clearly terrified, the young squire brandished Kitiara's dropped sword. "Halt!" Wode cried in a cracked, piping voice. Bravely he pointed the weapon at the ettin.

The ettin slowed only temporarily. As though Kitiara were no heavier than a sack of onions, the two-headed beast shifted her body and wedged it in the space between his heads. That freed one hand—a hand that held a spiked club.

Wode screamed Caven's name. The bearded man searched around desperately, spied a boulder, and, muscles bulging, hefted it above his head. He plunged across the clearing with Tanis close behind.

Wode screamed one more time; then the ettin's club connected. The youth crumpled to the ground, and the beast leaped over him and raced out of the clearing.

Chapter 13

The Chase

CAVEN KNELT BESIDE WODE, HIS SQUIRE AND HIS
nephew. Tanis stood uncertainly next to the grieving
mercenary until the wild neighing of the half-elf's
gelding drew his attention and brought him to the
edge of the clearing. Dauntless was struggling vainly
to rise. His eyes were glassy. The faithful horse grew
quiet as the half-elf stroked his beautiful neck with a
broad, gentle hand.

"I don't need telepathy to know what you're asking, old friend," Tanis whispered. He drew his sword,
uttered a silent prayer, and slit the horse's throat.
Dauntless's life bubbled into the soil of Darken Wood.
Tanis stayed with the horse until his breathing ceased.

Using Kitiara's sword to fashion a grave, Caven was making little headway in the hard ground.

"It will take you hours at that rate," Tanis said quietly. "We must hurry after Kitiara and Lida."

"I'm going to bury him." Caven's voice was toneless.

"We could pile stones over the lad. It's the usual way for those who die where burying is difficult. And it's faster."

"He's my sister's child. I will bury him as she would have, back in Kern."

"But Kitiara . . ."

Caven's voice rose in determination. "Kitiara got herself into trouble; she can wait. I will bury Wode. You can help or not, as you choose. You owe me nothing, half-elf."

Tanis knew he would need Caven Mackid in the hours and days ahead, so he put aside his sword and began to dig with his bare hands. There came a rustling behind them, and Tanis wheeled quickly, expecting another onslaught. Instead it was Xanthar, pulling himself weakly to his feet. "Kai-lid," he said faintly. "We must find . . ."

"Who?" Tanis asked. The giant owl looked straight at him.

"Lida," Xanthar corrected himself. "We must go after Lida and Kitiara. To save them."

Tanis gestured mutely to indicate Caven, who hadn't bothered to look up. The swordsman was working steadily, scraping at the ground with his blade and picking rocks out of the hollow with his fingers. He had wrapped Wode's body in his own scarlet cape.

The owl nodded. "He will not leave him?" Tanis nodded his head. The owl hesitated. He looked toward the north. Then Xanthar gave a near-human approximation of a shrug. "Caven Mackid is right," Xanthar said. "It is best, in Darken Wood, to leave no funeral rite unobserved. We would not want to encounter this Wode in the ranks of the undead." The owl surveyed Caven a moment longer, then said briskly, "Nevertheless, there's not a moment to lose, and you are making little headway, human."

At this, Xanthar edged forward. "Allow me," the bird whispered. He opened his great, saw-edged beak and began to dig. Soon the depression grew into a shallow oblong trench.

Finally Xanthar drew back. "It is deep enough," he said. He spat and cleaned his beak of soil by running it through his wing feathers.

Caven started to object to the shallowness of the grave, then gave in. "All right," he said wearily.

They gently moved Wode's body into the hollow and covered it with twigs and leaves, dirt and rocks. "Kernish observances are silent," Caven said, and the half-elf and owl followed his lead as he stood beside the grave and bowed his head for several long minutes. When at last he looked up, his eyes were wet, but his face was resolute. He whistled for Maleficent. The horse stood uneasily as Caven and Tanis loaded Kitiara's pack and necessary belongings. After searching Wode's pack and finding nothing of consequence save a small amulet from his name-giving day, they hung the pack on a stick atop the teen's grave as a remembrance.

Then both men mounted Maleficent. "I'm not accustomed to cozying with any but women, half-elf," Caven complained. Tanis snorted and settled behind the Kernan on the stallion's broad back. With Xanthar circling overhead, they set off after Kitiara and Kailid.

The path seemed to head into mountainous terrain, but this time the ettin's footprints were nearly impossible to spot. Time and again the half-elf slid off Maleficent to search under plants and debris for the huge print. "He's being more cagey now," the half-elf mused.

Dawn seemed imminent, and Tanis realized he'd long since lost track of what time of day it was outside Darken Wood. The woods were lightening, losing some of their fearsome quality. One by one the eyes of the undead blinked and went out.

"This is *your* fault, half-elf," Caven said almost bitterly. When the half-elf, mounted behind Caven, drew back in surprise, the swordsman continued, "*Your* horse. *Your* useless gelding failed me."

"Your stallion was poorly trained. It would not even let you mount it."

"Yours was a coward."

"Dauntless carried me safely through many dangers, Mackid. You caused his death yourself with that melodramatic stab at a rescue."

"No great loss, losing a nag like that." Caven was silent for a time." Tanis was doing his best to keep his temper. "Anyway, you were the one who brought Kitiara the news of the ettin, half-elf."

"And you knew there might be a connection between the ettin and the Valdane and Janusz, but you didn't speak up!"

They continued in this vein, growing increasingly heated and acrimonious, until Xanthar dropped out of the sky and landed ahead of them on a branch overhanging the trail. Maleficent neighed and halted.

You two tire me.

"The same to you, owl!" Caven exploded, twisting to face the giant bird. "Why don't you just lead us to Kitiara and the mage, and spare us your babble?"

"Surely you speak telepathically with the mage," Tanis observed. "That at least would save us hunting for that damned creature's prints."

I have tried to mind-speak to her. She is too far distant. My ability has its limits.

"Then what good are you? You're as useless as the half-elf!" Caven kicked Maleficent into a trot.

Xanthar spoke offhandedly, but with the bright eyes that gauged the men's every emotion. *Kitiara is with child, you know.*

The two slammed to a halt.

"Pregnant!" The two men spoke at the same time. "I'm going to be a father?"

Horrified, they looked at each other. Caven's expression changed to one of mere annoyance, but Tanis was speechless.

The owl chuckled. *Both of you, is it? Something else for the two of you to argue over. I refuse to listen.* With a flick of his stubby tail and a thrum of his wings, Xanthar resumed circling. Maleficent moved into a canter without a signal from Caven. The black-bearded soldier spoke harshly to the half-elf.

"It's me, you know, half-elf. I'm the father."

Tanis snorted.

"She's known me longer than she knew you."

"As if that matters, Mackid." The revelation explained Kitiara's queasiness and ill temper, at any rate.

"It must be me," Caven persisted angrily. "It's me she loves. She lied to you that night at Haven. She stayed with me. Oh, Kitiara may rob me and run away, but she can't resist me when I turn up!" He laughed.

Enraged, Tanis slugged Caven. The two rolled off the stallion, hit the ground without loosing their holds

on each other, and writhed and wrestled in the dirt.
Dust and plant stems flew in the air as they pummeled
each other. Xanthar coasted down again and landed
nearby, watching with amusement.

Tanis was outweighed by the larger human, and
soon the slighter half-elf was prone on the ground,
fighting for breath under Caven's bulk. Tanis spat out
dirt and fumed with the humiliation. The half-elf
flailed ineffectually, but with Caven sitting on his
back, there was little Tanis could do. Finally he gathered enough air to speak just above a whisper. Caven
couldn't hear him and leaned closer.

"What is it, half-elf?"

"I said it should be interesting being the husband of
Kitiara Uth Matar. Imagine marrying your own commanding officer. What a marriage that will be!"

Caven stood up hurriedly, disconcerted, allowing
Tanis to roll over and get up.

"Marry?" Caven asked. "Who said anything about
marrying? You know Kitiara. There's probably a half-
dozen men between here and Kernen who could vie
for the title of papa of Kitiara's byblow."

"And one half-elf—you forget."

Sarcasm oozed from the swordsman's words. "I
suppose the honorable Tanis Half-Elven would marry
his lady, set her up in a cozy cottage, and live happily
ever after." Tanis felt his face grow red; it was embar-
rassingly close to what he *had* been thinking. Caven
roared and slapped the half-elf on the back. "Half-elf,
this is real life, not a fairy tale! You couldn't contain
Kitiara in anything less than a prison cell."

"Are you saying you're not the father?"

Caven stopped short on his way back to Maleficent. "I'm saying I'm the most obvious choice"—he
preened—"but there's no way Captain Kitiara could

prove it."

A huge branch suddenly fell out of the sky, narrowly missing them. Both men leaped back with oaths and looked up, swords drawn. Xanthar was poised in the act of sending a second broken branch after the first.

You disgust me. Each man wants the credit, but not the blame.

"I would marry her," Tanis said mulishly, with a glare at Caven, who rolled his eyes and sheathed his sword.

That's laudable, half-elf. Perhaps you might consider asking Kitiara—if the opportunity arises, that is. But first, don't the two of you overgrown bullbears think we should rescue her from the ettin? It's either that or lose her—and Lida—in the recesses of the sla-mori.

"The sla-mori?" Tanis asked. "Then you know where the ettin's taking them?"

I can guess.

"Now, wait a minute," Caven said. "What's a sla-mori?"

"A sla-mori is a secret passage—a magical way of getting from one place to another," Tanis explained.

When Caven still looked perplexed, the owl took over. *There is a rumor of a sla-mori somewhere in Darken Wood, although rumor places it in several locations. One of them is not too far from here, in the valley near Fever Mountain. This one, some say, will take its user far to the south—perhaps all the way to the Icereach, although some say the sla-mori's destination is elsewhere.*

"Rumor?" Caven asked weakly. "We're plunging deeper into Darken Wood on the strength of a rumor?"

"Following advice given us in a dream," Tanis added. A half-smile lit his face, then vanished.

The owl pressed on. *The sla-mori is the most logical solution. The ettin mentioned that Fever Mountain is near the sla-mori—or at least where it's rumored to be.*

"Wait," Caven interjected again. He was livid; the only sign of color in his face was a scarlet streak high on each cheekbone, framed by his black hair and beard. "You knew all along that the ettin wanted to capture Kitiara? If you'd shared the information with us, Wode might be alive now!"

Xanthar had the grace to look ashamed, but he hid the expression by whetting his beak against a branch. *I didn't know the real danger. I believed he'd take the swordswoman and the rest of you, but I didn't think any harm would befall anyone.*

"But you were willing to let us take the risk!" Tanis cried.

Xanthar glowered down at them. *We're on the same side now, half-elf. You have no choice but to trust me on the subject. And I'm not saying any more.* The owl took off with a screech.

Caven and Tanis looked confusedly at each other, at the giant owl soaring above, and at Maleficent, foraging under a nearby bush.

"Well, half-elf?" Caven asked. "What do we do now?"

Tanis frowned. "Whatever the owl has been plotting, the fact remains that the ettin has Kitiara and the lady mage and intends to spirit them far away unless we stop them."

"And this is our problem, half-elf? Yours and mine?"

"Possibly. There's the lady mage's poem, after all.

'Lovers three, spell-cast maid.' It doesn't take the brightness of a will-o'-the-wisp to suspect that might refer to us."

"So what?" Caven muttered. "Who's paying us to get involved? Or are we supposed to risk our lives out of the goodness of our hearts?"

"It's worth keeping an open mind." Tanis glanced back in the direction from which they'd traveled. "The path has disappeared," he reminded Caven. "Unless you know Darken Wood well enough to guide us out, I'm guessing that going forward is our best choice."

Caven thought a moment, then shook his head as if he were in pain. "I've lost my nephew. I'm stuck looking for a woman who has double-crossed me at least once and who may—or may not—be carrying my child. To make matters worse, I'm traveling with a romantic half-elf who believes that only he could be the father. By the gods!"

The half-elf smiled. "That's right," Tanis said, and started toward Maleficent with a look that said that he'd brook no nonsense from the stallion.

"Eh?" Caven dogged the half-elf's steps and caught up with him just as he reached for the black horse.

"You're stuck," Tanis said, mounting the stallion. He extended a hand to Caven Mackid, indicating that the Kernan should swing up behind him on the horse. "As am I. So let's go."

*　　*　　*　　*　　*

"Look!" Kitiara cried suddenly. "Did you see that, mage?"

The spell-caster looked where Kitiara was pointing. "I don't see anything," the mage said. "Nothing but the eyes of the und—" Kitiara poked her in the ribs, and the mage broke off.

The ettin followed Kitiara's pointing finger, too. Until now, he'd walked behind them with both clubs ready to help keep them on the path, which opened before them and then closed just as suddenly as soon as the two-headed creature passed. "The hand of Janusz," Kitiara had muttered when she'd first observed the phenomenon.

"What see?" Res-Lacua cried now. "What see?"

"A pig!" Kitiara pretended to spy it off to the right. "There—a tender piglet!"

"Yes!" Kai-lid chimed in. "I see it now."

"Food!" The ettin rejoiced. He darted toward the underbrush, where Kitiara knew nothing waited but the hungry undead. The ettin paused and looked back at the women. He gestured and shouted, "You stay here!" Kitiara and Kai-lid nodded as he plunged out of sight.

"The undead should finish him off in no time," Kitiara said quietly to Kai-lid. "Then you can call your owl to come get us."

The mage looked dubious. Several times since the ettin had dragged them off, Kitiara had whispered to Kai-lid to unleash her magic and free them from the ettin's influence, but Kai-lid had only shaken her head. "I can't," she finally said. "I already tried a spell. Nothing happened."

"Why not?" Kitiara demanded. "Is it the woods?" But the mage only shrugged. Worry lines wrinkled her forehead.

Now Kitiara, having taken matters into her own hands, waited for the screaming that would tell her that the undead were pressing around the ettin, feeding off his fear, heightening his terror, slaying him—

and freeing the women.

Then she, with this useless mage in tow, would go back to the clearing. She'd go back for her pack. She'd retrieve the ice jewels that had caused all this. She wondered if Tanis and Caven would still be at the clearing. If they'd left, would they have had the sense to take her belongings with them? Or would they have left the irreplaceable pack behind for the undead? Kitiara listened to the ettin crashing through the underbrush and waited for Res-Lacua's lingering death.

But there were no sounds other than those of the ettin uprooting saplings in his search for a pork dinner. The two women exchanged grim looks. "Well?" Kai-lid asked. Kitiara lifted her shoulders and let them drop.

The ettin appeared before them on the trail. Both of his faces were long. The right head appeared near tears; the left head looked merely baffled. "Pig got away," Lacua complained. He motioned them on with one club.

"I don't get it," Kitiara whispered as they resumed walking. "If you can't count on the undead to kill something, who can you count on?"

Kai-lid blinked, seeming to hide a smile. "The undead feed off fear?" she asked. Kitiara nodded, and Kai-lid ventured, "Perhaps Res-Lacua is too stupid to know he's supposed to be afraid of them."

Kitiara stopped in her tracks and swore until Res-Lacua poked her with the club. Kai-lid grabbed the swordswoman's arm and hauled her along, but the mercenary continued spewing oaths for several minutes before she finally ran down.

"It's all right," the mage said. "Women in your condition are often emotional."

"What are you talking about?" Kitiara snapped. "I'm in fine condition!" She even picked up the pace, hiking along at a speed that ate up the distance. While the ettin merely lengthened his strides, Kai-lid practically had to run to keep up with her. Thus Kitiara was moving at rapid speed when the mage calmly mentioned her pregnancy.

This time Kai-lid found herself staring at Kitiara's fist. "Not funny, mage," the swordswoman hissed.

Kai-lid's hood slipped back from her face. "You mean you don't know?"

"And how would you know if I *were* with child, which I assure you I am not?"

"Are you so certain?"

Kitiara's hand wobbled as she reviewed the past few days and weeks. "By Takhisis!" she finally breathed, horror flickering across her face. Then reason reasserted itself, and she glared at the mage. "You say you're a mage, not a healer, and every so-called healer I've met has been a charlatan, anyway. So I repeat: How would you know?"

Kitiara pointed behind an oak. "I just saw that young pig again, ettin!" Kai-lid nodded vigorously at the creature, who scrambled toward the tree. "How would you know?" Kitiara reiterated to Kai-lid, grabbing her by the shoulders and shaking her.

Kai-lid shrugged out of Kit's grasp. "I can look within people sometimes. I cannot heal, and I cannot diagnose, but I can sense things. Xanthar showed me how. He cannot do magic, but he has other powers, some of which you've seen. He sensed your condition as well, back at the clearing."

"Damn!" Kitiara said, then looked hopefully at the mage. "Can you do anything about it?"

"Do?"

"Get rid of it."

The mage's dark face flushed. "I said I am a mage, and a mage only. That is beyond my talents—and my inclinations."

Kitiara had endured trials in her life—the desertion of her adored soldier father when she was young, the remarriage of her mother, the birth of her half-brothers, the death of her mother and stepfather, and her decision to leave home and become a mercenary at an age when other girls in Solace were occupied chiefly with dreaming of marriage. But this . . .

All thought that the mage might be lying had flown from her mind. Her own body told her Lida must be speaking the truth. "Blast it to the Abyss!" Kitiara breathed softly. "Now what?"

The ettin returned to the path. "Dumb pig fast," he complained.

* * * * *

"What is it, Lida?" Kitiara finally snapped.

"Fever Mountain," the mage said, pointing to the near-treeless escarpment. "Xanthar said the sla-mori is in its shadow."

"So?" Kitiara had heard of sla-moris, but the significance of this particular secret passage eluded her.

"He'll meet us there, I know. Xanthar says those of Darken Wood believe a sla-mori near Fever Mountain leads far to the south, perhaps to the Icereach. He believed the ettin might try to take us there in order to transport us to the Valdane."

"And Xanthar knows where this sla-mori is?" Kitiara asked, brightening. "That's perfect! He'll bring Tanis and Caven and Wode, we'll all kill the ettin, and we'll be on our way back to Haven."

They gazed up the side of the mountain, Kitiara smiling with satisfaction, Kai-lid frowning. Large chunks of shale and granite were strewn over the escarpment. Huge rocks had slid down the incline, leaving the ground littered with boulders, some the height of a human. Finally the swordswoman noticed that the mage didn't share her exultation. "What's the problem?" Kitiara asked. "We're where the owl expects us to be, aren't we?"

Kai-lid shook her head. "No, we're not. The valley is back there." She pointed south, where a patch of green could barely be seen at the edge of the towering mountain. As Res-Lacua prodded them up a path that would have strained a highland goat, the mage said, "We're not going to the valley of the sla-mori at all. And I'm too far away to mind-speak to Xanthar to let him know."

Kitiara stared at the woman, her head beginning to swim again. She'd felt this way often enough lately to know that she was about to be sick—whether it was from Lida's revelation, Darken Wood pressing in around her, or the blows to the head she had suffered, she didn't know. From a long distance away, she heard Lida cry out and reach for her.

Kitiara fainted.

* * * * *

Janusz poured water into a wooden trencher. Melted snow—that's what he was forced to use now. It was nothing like the artesian waters he'd had in Kern. He cast the special powders upon the surface and said the words. The liquid reflected his lined face; the undissolved powder floating in the water looked like mold upon his image.

Then the scene began to shimmer in the water. Janusz saw a rose-gray granite slab carved with the leaves, flowers, and animals Dreena had loved. The mage forced himself to look at the inscription. Despite his fatigue, the sight stirred his strength and anger.

Dreena ten Valdane
Lagrimat
Ei Avenganit

"Dreena, daughter of Valdane," Janusz translated from Old Kernish. "We mourn. And we will avenge."

Janusz ended the scrying with a shiver. He hadn't been truly warm for months. He longed for the comforting embrace of the stone fireplaces of the Valdane's castle back in the woodlands of Kern. He recalled the earthy smell of woodsmoke, the tang of warm drinks, the infectious music of lyre and flute that formed a backdrop for the movements of serving girls bearing trays of fruit and cheese. That had been a splendid time.

It was before the war, of course. And long before Dreena's marriage. He'd worn the red robe of neutral magic then, having discarded the white garb of the mages who followed the path of good. Not yet had he donned the black robe he wore now.

Janusz shook off the image of the gravestone. The two fiefdoms, Kern and Meir, were now one, he knew—ruled, to worsen the insult to the Valdane, by a committee of minor nobles who'd served under the Valdane and the Meir. They'd even hinted at giving peasants limited governance over aspects of their lives—aspects that wouldn't inconvenience the ruling families too greatly, of course.

Soon Res-Lacua would bear Kitiara Uth Matar and Lida Tenaka to the pinnacle of Fever Mountain. Soon Janusz would draw out his remaining ice jewel and command the ettin, through the Talking Stone, to bring out the ice jewel that the monster held in its possession. Then Janusz would speak the words, engender the magic that would teleport the women and the ettin across the continent of Ansalon. He would torture Kitiara until he discovered the whereabouts of the other ice jewels, and he would also satisfy his curiosity about Lida's mysterious connection with the swordswoman.

He was being indulgent in abducting the serving-woman, too, he knew. It was difficult enough to harness the power of the ice jewels to teleport one, much less two or three beings. He'd spent long hours coaching the ettin, practicing with the jewels; once he had teleported a bewildered gully dwarf who, upon arriving at the snowy Icereach, had taken one look around and passed out cold. The next instant, thanks to the mage's powers, the nasty little creature had been sent back to a knoll north of Que-kiri. Upon awakening, the gully dwarf had instantly proclaimed that the long-dead rat he carried around with him had given him inestimable powers to travel through time and space.

Janusz smiled. He'd gained better control since the gully dwarf incident. He was actually looking forward to using the ice jewels again.

*　*　*　*　*

The first thing Kitiara noticed was that she seemed to be outside her own body, observing herself dispassionately. This is absurd, Kit thought hazily. I'm dreaming.

The Kitiara she saw wasn't wearing chain mail.
This woman crouched over a fire in a hearth, dressed
in—of all the ridiculous costumes—a flower-print
dress and an apron, both festooned with lace. The
dress was pink, the apron white, and as the dream-
Kitiara moved to check the cornbread and lamb stew
that bubbled in a pot above the embers, the lace of her
dress kept tearing against the bricks of the hearth. It
was steaming in the kitchen. Sweat poured down her
neck; the brocade of the impossible dress clung to her
arms and back. Yet this dream-Kitiara hummed as she
slaved over the hearth, apparently mindless of the
torturous heat, even as the real Kitiara—who would
rather be caught dead than in a dress or a kitchen—
watched from a side corner, unable, in the way of
dreams, to protest.

When the domesticated dream-Kitiara rose from
the hearth, something else was apparent—she was
very pregnant. As she moved toward the worktable,
it was obvious that she must be under a physical
strain. Her ankles were swollen, her face puffy. Yet
she was singing, by the Abyss! Some witless song—a
nursery rhyme set to a simple tune.

A wail rose from a cradle in the corner, and the
pink-and-white Kitiara brushed floury hands against
her apron and raised a dimpled creature of about nine
months. The baby was as bald as a marble, but what
caught the real Kitiara's attention were the infant's
huge, pointed ears and its eyes so tilted that the baby
could barely open them. How could a quarter-elf baby look more elven than even its half-elf father?

As the dream-Kitiara settled into the rocker, pro-
ceeding to balance the infant over her pregnant abdomen and offer it a breast, a door slammed
somewhere, and the kitchen filled with screaming

children—all with ludicrously large and pointed ears. They were constantly in motion, like a school of fish; there seemed to be hundreds!

Kitiara had watched wounded comrades choke to death on their own blood without feeling much except annoyance that they'd gotten themselves killed. Now, however, she found herself dumb with horror at the thought of such an army of children clinging to her skirts. The real Kitiara would rather face a phalanx of goblins than this mob of urchins.

The dream-Kitiara got up and rested the still-nursing baby on the table as she opened a ceramic container and dispensed cookies to the jostling children like a cardsharp dealing from the bottom of a deck.

All the girls wore frothy confections of pink and white. Each cradled a fat elf doll; not one wielded a toy shield or battle-ax. The boys, on the other hand, pranced in tiny buckskin outfits and clutched minuscule bows in grubby hands.

Then the door slammed again, and a roar filled the dwelling. The children scattered like leaves before the wind, coalescing again behind their mother. Tanis appeared in the doorway. But this Tanis was overweight, flushed, and unwashed—a very drunken half-elf, who belched as he leaned against the doorframe. He surveyed the crowd of children with a repulsion that matched the real Kitiara's.

"Where's my supper?" he demanded. "I'm hungry."

"You haven't been home in months!" shrieked the dream-Kitiara. "Where have you been, sloth?"

"Nowhere in particular." The dream-Tanis did a double-take, leering at her. "What? With child again? Good gods, woman!"

From the corner, the real Kitiara tried to offer advice to the dream-Kitiara, who stood with tears dripping onto her frock. "Draw your sword!" Kitiara tried to shout. "Slice him through! Drop these hellions at the nearest orphanage and get out of there!" But no words issued forth.

The dream-Kitiara turned and, groaning with the effort, stretched for the unsheathed sword that decorated the wall over the hearth. The real Kitiara felt her heart leap. But her dream-twin merely used the blade, which had saved dozens of lives and stolen countless others, to slice a loaf of homemade bread. Then she herded her flock to the supper table. She hustled Tanis's inebriated frame from the doorway to the head of the table. "Stew again?" he complained.

Wordless and unseen, the real Kitiara shuddered. If this was what awaited her, she'd rather be tortured to death.

Although, truth to tell, what was the difference?

Chapter 14

Power of the Jewels

Kitiara awakened to find herself slung over the ettin and staring straight down the near-vertical drop of Fever Mountain. The valley floor spread out hundreds of feet below. From this distance, the valley looked like any ordinary woodland, not the fearsome Darken Wood. Kitiara closed her eyes to let a spell of vertigo pass.

When she opened them again, reason reasserted itself; she yelled and struggled against the grasp of the creature. Its bullish necks held her pinned between them. "You oaf!" the swordswoman shouted, pummeling the ettin's back. "Let go of me! I can't breathe!"

Res-Lacua dumped her on a narrow ledge. For a

moment, Kitiara clung to the side of the mountain and the world swirled beneath her. Then her vision cleared, and she saw the lady mage's anxious face behind the ettin. Kitiara filled the air with curses.

"Pretty noisy," the ettin observed. Kitiara closed her mouth. Res-Lacua pointed to the summit of the mountain, only a few paces away. "Up."

It was cold and windy at the top of Fever Mountain. Lida's hood fluttered in the gale, and her hair whipped nearly straight behind her. She clung to Kitiara for support. The ettin was fumbling inside the filthy skin that covered his body, and Kitiara whispered to her companion, "Now what's he doing?" Lida only shook her head.

There was no giant owl in sight. Was the ettin going to kill them? If so, he wouldn't succeed without a fight. Kitiara glanced around her, seeking a weapon, but all she saw was shale. As high up as they were, there was no sign of any vegetation.

The ettin was holding a smooth gray pebble and crooning to it. "Master, Master," he said reverently.

"What's that?" Kitiara demanded.

"Magic," Lida whispered.

Kitiara kneeled surreptitiously, picking up two jagged pieces of shale. The ettin was too rapt to notice. Kitiara handed one of the slivers to the mage. "Be ready," the swordswoman warned. Lida didn't answer.

The ettin reached again into his covering and pulled out another small object. Kitiara gasped as she recognized it. There was no mistaking the purple jewel, identical to the ones hidden in her pack—the ones she had stolen from Janusz. Bolts of violet lightning flashed from the crystal, and a loud humming drowned out the sound of the wind. The violet light encircled the ettin.

Then the ettin nodded as though he were responding to some unheard directive, turning toward the
women as he did. He held the gray pebble in one hand
and the ice-jewel, high above his head, in the other.
As he moved toward Kitiara and Lida, the air around
the trio began to expand and shimmer.

Particles of air swirled around them. "Snow?" Kitiara whispered. Lida, awed by the display, said
nothing.

The particles continued to swirl, glittering scarlet,
purple, deep green, golden, and white. Kitiara heard
the lady mage murmur something. The swirling thickened to a storm as the ettin edged toward them.

Kitiara couldn't move. Janusz's magic had already
entrapped her, and she stared in horror as Res-Lacua
and Lida—and she—began to disintegrate, dissolving
into the swirling magic tightening around them, spinning faster, until it was as if the three figures stood at
the center of a great vortex. The purple light and the
mystical humming intensified until Kitiara's eyes and
ears sensed nothing else.

Then, with a flash of amethyst, they were gone.

*　*　*　*　*

As Xanthar and the others neared the valley, the giant owl spotted the strange scene at the summit of Fever Mountain. Screeching futilely, he flapped his
wings and tried to fly straight toward the highest
ridge where only he, with his farseeing eyes, could see
what was happening. But he was too heavy to move
very quickly; his great wings strained against the
wind. Caven and Tanis watched in puzzlement, not
moving.

"What's with the bird?" Caven muttered. "We're

here, aren't we? At the valley? So where's Kitiara?"

"Can't you feel it?" Tanis interjected. "The charge in
the air?" He put a hand to his head and felt his hair
cling to his hand. He fought back panic, feeling suddenly as though he were helpless.

Caven had twisted around in the saddle and was
gazing at the half-elf with consternation. Then the
Kernan looked up at the owl, who was crying out as
he swooped upward. "Whatever it is, it's driven both
of you daft," the mercenary said.

But Tanis wasn't listening. "We're too late!" he cried
and pointed past Caven to the peak of the bald mountain to the north. A glittering miasma churned around
the mountaintop; it seemed to sap energy from the
very ground around them, from their own bodies.
Now Caven himself swayed in the saddle, and Tanis
had to reach to prop him up. At that moment, the
mountain pinnacle seemed to explode. But when the
explosion faded and the glitter evaporated, the escarpment was unchanged.

"It was them," Tanis said with great feeling.
"They're gone!"

"Gone?" Caven demanded. "Half-elf, this is Darken
Wood! That flash could have been anything."

"No," Tanis said stubbornly.

Minutes later, Xanthar landed atop a barren tree
nearby. He kept twisting, facing the mountain, then
to the south, then the mountain again. Suddenly the
bird opened its beak, displaying a gray, wormlike
tongue the size of Tanis's hand. And then Xanthar
cried out, his rage and loss and desolation echoing
through the valley. Even Caven shuddered.

After a while, the bird quieted down. Xanthar fastened a stare on the half-elf. Lida carried that same
look in her eyes, a riveting stare that sucked the vic-

tim in, picked him over, practically stole his thoughts. Caven had to glance away, but Tanis held the giant owl's stern gaze.

On the ground, the creature dwarfed the half-elf. But from his vantage point atop the spire, even with the two men mounted on the Mithas stallion, the bird still towered over them. Fury emanated from the bird. Then the giant owl blinked, and he was the sardonic Xanthar again.

We have erred.

Tanis nodded. Caven did, too, so the half-elf knew the mercenary also had heard the owl's mind-speak.

They are in the Icereach now.

"Why the Icereach?" Caven snapped. "Because some stupid dream said so? The Valdane lost the war in Kern; why go nearly a thousand miles south to a place like the Icereach if you want to conquer the world? Assuming, that is, you and the mage are correct in guessing that's what he wants. Why the Icereach, owl?"

Perhaps there is something there that he values . . . something he seeks.

"Like what? Snow?"

The portent mentions jewels.

Caven was having nothing of the owl's argument. "Jewels in the Icereach? That's a laugh."

Stranger things have happened, human.

But the Kernan merely sputtered. "I say we go back to Haven."

Do what you will, human. You will find it difficult to wend your way out of Darken Wood without the help of a guide.

Caven glared. "You'd abandon us?"

You are nothing to me. I am going to the Icereach.

Tanis finally spoke. "Lida said you couldn't leave

Darken Wood."

A pause. *She was wrong.*

Tanis thought for a moment, then slid down from Maleficent. He began to pull his own pack and Kitiara's from the tangle of equipage behind the saddle.

"Half-elf!" Caven demanded. "What are you doing?"

"I'm going with Xanthar."

Caven chortled. "You Qualinesti are more talented than I'd thought. You can fly, too, half-elf?"

"No, but he can."

Caven paled. He grasped the pommel of his saddle and leaned toward the half-elf. "You'd ride a giant owl?"

"If he'll let me." Tanis looked at the bird, who dipped his head in what Tanis took for assent.

Caven's voice hissed, drawing the half-elf's attention again. "But why? Kitiara isn't worth the risk. There are millions of other women in the world, half-elf. Besides, what guarantee do we have that she is there?"

Tanis snorted, pawing through his pack. He would have to lighten the load as much as possible. Tanis outweighed Lida. He selected what little food remained in his pack, his bow and quiver, and his sword. Then he picked up Kitiara's pack, thinking.

Caven's voice broke in. "Why not just give this up? We can find our way out of here together. To the Abyss with the crazy owl and his lady mage. And with Kitiara, too."

Tanis shook his head. He shoved aside clothing in Kitiara's pack, searching for anything that would aid him in his quest. "I'm not a mercenary like you, Mackid. That's the only explanation I can give you. I don't do things for money but for my own reasons."

Caven gestured broadly with his arms. "How will the two of you find them? The Icereach is practically a continent away."

The owl broke in. *I will attempt to mind-speak with Lida. I will reach her. She will lead me to them.*

"You lost contact with her in Darken Wood almost immediately," Caven replied irritatedly. "What are you going to do, search the entire Icereach? How much time do you think you have?"

My relatives have been there. They have described this place. I remember my grandfather's tales when I was a nestling. There is a likely area—a place, I was told, of vast warrens under the ice. Such a place, I believe, would attract a mage. I will search there first. I will find her, human.

At that moment, Tanis's fingers rubbed against something at the bottom of the swordswoman's pack. Puzzled, the half-elf kneeled, dumped the contents of the pack on the ground, and examined the canvas back. The pack, in the bright light of day, looked deeper from the outside than it was on the inside. "A false bottom," he murmured.

Caven dismounted, crouching beside the half-elf. Even Xanthar hopped to a nearby perch. Tanis prodded the bottom, searching for a catch. Then he uttered an exclamation and pulled up the stiffened canvas that hid the cache. The three gasped as purple light erupted from the travel-worn pack. Caven stepped back warily, but Tanis thrust his hand into the false bottom. He cradled three ice jewels in his palm as he withdrew his hand.

"By the gods! What are they?" Caven asked.

Tanis shook his head, but Xanthar murmured something the half-elf couldn't understand. "What is it?" Tanis asked.

Ice jewels. My grandfather mentioned them long ago, but he thought they were only legend. They were said to be ice compressed under great weight, until they turned to precious gems.

"Are they magic?" Tanis asked the giant owl. "There are more in there."

In the right hands, yes, they must be magic. But they frighten me. Tanis and Caven looked up again, startled. *Am I correct in assuming that the swordswoman wasn't the rightful owner of these jewels?*

Caven replied carefully. "After we left Kern, Kitiara said something that made me wonder. I was complaining that all of the Valdane's mercenaries had gone unpaid, and she said, 'All but one.' But she wouldn't explain further. Later I took that to mean she was planning to rob me. But now I think . . ." He gestured meaningfully at the glowing ice jewels.

Tanis was still gazing at the ice jewels when Xanthar's voice penetrated his mind. *Perhaps we can make use of these stones.*

The half-elf looked up, immediately comprehending the owl's drift. "Ransom?" he asked.

The bird nodded. *Or magic. If we can discover their secret. But I say we bring them along.*

Tanis thrust the jewels back in the pack, replaced the false bottom, and transferred his own things to Kitiara's pack. Then he stood and faced the owl. "I'm ready."

Caven sighed, rising as well. "As am I."

I cannot carry you both.

"I will ride Maleficent."

We will outdistance you quickly.

"Leave a trail for me to follow."

I have many relatives. I could mind-call to them. Perhaps you could ride . . .

"No!" Caven said, adding hastily, "I'll not leave my horse. Maleficent and I will go day and night if need be. He is a Mithas stallion; he can endure the strain. And so can I."

You fear heights, then, human?

"No!" Caven repeated stubbornly. He mounted Maleficent. "I fear nothing."

Xanthar hopped to the ground, hunkering down into a squat. The half-elf clambered aboard, pulling Kitiara's pack and his weapons behind him and securing them to the bird with a leather strap that Caven handed over from Maleficent's saddle. Xanthar made a soft, clucking noise. Tanis clamped his legs around Xanthar's body and held tight to the harness and the grip of the bird's wings. He dipped his head behind Xanthar's. Without any further ado, the giant owl sprang into the sky.

"Wait!" Caven shouted after them. "How will you mark your path?" Even as he spoke, his form shrank beneath them.

You will know it. Perhaps we will toss down some of these shining jewels for you to follow.

"Wait!" Caven hollered, a note of desperation making his voice thin. "They're too val—" Then he could no longer be heard.

The bird spiraled higher until it soared high above the mountain peaks. Tanis bit his lip to take his mind off the sight of the ground spinning slowly below him. Caven and Maleficent gradually faded to inconsequential dots. Vowing not to look straight down, Tanis ventured glances to the side. He gauged the direction by the sun.

"You're not serious about using the jewels to mark Caven's path, are you?" Tanis shouted at the back of Xanthar's head. The bird didn't reply, but the half-elf felt a quiver ripple through the creature; it might have been a chuckle.

Far to the west, Tanis saw four small, dark forms rise in the sky. He pointed them out to Xanthar. *They are my sons and daughters. They will guide Caven and protect him from the less honorable inhabitants of Darken Wood. Despite his foolhardy bravery, the swordsman deserves help.*

To the northeast, the half-elf could just about imagine that he could see the tops of the towering vallenwoods of Solace. No trees grew taller than those, so tall and strong that the city's residents built homes in the branches and constructed systems of walkways and bridges between them. Someone could journey from one end of Solace to the other without ever touching the ground.

Somewhere in Solace, Tanis thought with a pang, Flint Fireforge was at home now, probably preparing a pot of stew—Flint was not one for sophisticated cuisine—and looking forward to an evening of conviviality at the Inn of the Last Home. Tanis looked forward to seeing the dwarf again, but it would surely be a long while.

Xanthar came out of the last climbing curve turning toward the Icereach.

* * * * *

Wind buffeted the pair as they flew southward. Tanis lost his grip on the harness. For a dizzying moment, the half-elf felt unseated and imagined himself diving toward the ground. Then his hands found the strap again, and he managed to pull himself upright. The bird kept up the steady motions of long-distance flight.

Exhaustion and the soothing warmth from Xanthar's feathered body conspired to lull him to sleep, his arms entwined in his makeshift harness. When he awakened, the brassy blue and white skies told him it was early afternoon. He watched the sky turn orange-yellow as afternoon deepened. Finally the horizon grew pink, orange, and red as sunset eased toward twilight. Through it all, Xanthar never flagged. Tanis looked back over his shoulder but saw no sign of Caven Mackid.

Occasionally the great bird coasted to conserve his strength. When the owl turned his head, the half-elf could see that his eyes were orange slits in his brown-and gray-feathered face. Owls were night creatures, he knew, wondering how Xanthar had fared in the bright light of day.

For a long time, the giant owl flew as high as possible, but by evening, he had eased lower, and some details revealed themselves to the windblown half-elf clinging to his back. They were passing through the southern boundary of Qualinesti, the half-elf guessed, marveling at the strength and speed of the giant owl. All around them, rising especially steeply to the southeast, were the jagged peaks of the Kharolis Mountains. Xanthar drifted closer to the ground. The highest mountaintops were draped with snow; lower peaks showed crags of lichen-encrusted rock, unbroken by tree or bush until the tree line hundreds of feet below marked the sudden appearance of ground-hugging yews and scrub trees. Below that, starting up almost as abruptly as the tree line had, the real alpine vegetation started—spruce and fir and birch standing out in stark blue and green and white against the mottled gray of the rocky soil.

The giant owl swooped and glided to a perch atop a

knoll. He dipped to one side to help Tanis dismount and then flexed his wings, resembling a feathered Flint easing the kinks out of his shoulders after a hard stint at the forge. Tanis stretched, too.

"It feels good to be back on the ground," the half-elf commented.

Xanthar, for once, answered directly, not in mind-speak. "You ride well for a novice, half-elf. Now I must hunt for supper. And then I will rest, too. Although it surely will be strange to sleep during the dark of night. Usually, for me, it is the other way around."

"Do you think Kitiara and Lida are all right?" Tanis asked suddenly.

The owl considered before replying. "I think they are alive. I believe that if Kai-lid were dead, I would sense it."

"You mentioned that name before. Who is Kai-lid?"

The owl hesitated. "Kai-lid Entenaka. It's Lida's Darken Wood name," he finally explained. Tanis nodded, feeling uncertain as to whether he should pry further.

The half-elf offered the owl a bit of bread from his pack. The bird eyed the offering, then turned his head away. "I must hunt," was all he said before coasting off into the valley below. Tanis sat against a rock, munching the bread, enjoying the last display of the sunset and keeping an eye on the diminishing form of Xanthar. If it weren't for his concern about Kitiara, this would be almost pleasant. Xanthar was a crusty companion with a short temper and a sarcastic turn of wit, but so was Flint Fireforge, after all. Cradled against the rock, lazily following the movements of the owl as he swooped over the terrain, Tanis felt his eyelids drooping again.

He awakened with a start when something crashed into the ground before him. Instinctively he leaped to his feet, his sword in his hand, although he couldn't recall unsheathing it. But no goblin or slig crouched before him. In fact, Tanis could see no threat at all in the twilight. His gaze fell to the ground. The body of a small rabbit lay twisted on the rocks. He looked up, and his nightvision caught Xanthar far overhead.

Bread will not take you far, half-elf.

Tanis waved his thanks. Then he gathered dry grass and twigs and found a few branches at the bottom of a dead tree. He was on one of the few escarpments with foliage, and he realized that Xanthar had taken that into account before choosing a spot to land. Tanis scraped at the inner bark of the branches and added the resulting fluff to his pile of tinder, which he moved to the leeward side of the boulder against which he'd slept. Then Tanis struck steel against flint. Several times sparks fizzled, then one finally caught. Carefully, the half-elf fed dry grass and twigs to the spark until it grew into a flame. Then he poked larger twigs into the tiny blaze. Soon he was crouched before a respectable campfire, skinning and gutting the rabbit and sliding the meat onto a long, peeled stick. He propped the stick on two rocks and sniffed the aroma as fat from the rabbit dripped and sizzled.

Xanthar returned as Tanis removed the cooked rabbit from the fire. The bird landed on the ground but stayed well away from the flames. He shook his head at the half-elf's offer to share.

"Cooked flesh doesn't suit my pallet," the giant bird said. "Fire destroys the taste, to my mind."

As Tanis dined, the owl walked—although "waddled" might better describe his passage, the half-elf thought—to a bent pine and made himself comfortable on the stub of a broken branch. Xanthar closed his eyes and buried his golden beak deep in the pale fluff of his throat.

Tanis, his belly comfortably full, leaned against the warm boulder and gazed at Xanthar, who huddled next to the trunk of the tree. Once, as though sensing the half-elf's stare, the giant owl opened one eye a slit, then reversed his position on the branch, presenting a dark back to the half-elf. Tanis saw the horned feet lock around the branch stub. The bird seemed to sag, and Tanis knew his companion was asleep.

Chapter 15

The Icereach

It was the cold of death, Kitiara was sure. Her face, breasts, and hips were pressed against snow. The front of her shirt was sodden; the back seemed stiff, as though coated and frozen. Her feet felt like logs. She was dimly aware that her right hand still clutched a shard of shale from Fever Mountain. In the far distance, waves crashed. Nearer, she heard coughing.

If this was the Abyss, it was like no Abyss she'd been warned about. She must be dead, yet Kitiara sensed the cold, tasted the snow, felt hunger. Certainly she heard what sounded like the ettin, rejoicing about something. And over it all, the moan of the wind and the boom of the sea.

Kitiara raised her head. Her hair was nearly solid with sleet. She pressed nerve-impaired hands against her face and, ignoring the wind that drove into her exposed skin like needles, picked at the ice that coated one cheek. Her eyelids were nearly frozen shut. Finally she managed to open her eyes to slits.

She found herself staring straight into a pair of fleshless jaws, incisors hanging down like icy stalactites, other teeth jutting up like stalagmites. Kitiara drew back with a shout, fumbled for her sword and her dagger, and remembered that she no longer had either. The beast into whose mouth she now gazed had been dead for generations. What it originally had been, Kitiara couldn't tell, but she could have nestled comfortably in its gaping jaws. It was the skull of some long-dead beast; the rest of the skeleton was nowhere to be seen.

The ettin leaned against the thick joint that held the jaws together. Its right head was asleep, lolling against the left, a frozen dribble of drool down one side of its chin. The left head grinned at the swordswoman. There was no sneaking away when the ettin was asleep; the creature's heads slept in shifts.

"Where are we?" she shouted over the sound of the storm. She could barely see the ettin through the clouds of blowing snow.

Res-Lacua grinned wider. "Home," it said. "Home, home, home."

"The Icereach?" she demanded. Her tone awakened the right head, and now two ettin faces grinned at her. Cursing the wind, the snow, and particularly the ettin, the swordswoman managed to pull herself to her feet, but her muscles were too numb to respond easily. She lurched like a drunkard, catching herself against one long tooth of the monster. How long had she and

Lida been lying exposed in the snow?

"Kitiara! What . . . what is that thing?" It was Lida Tenaka, huddled in her robe, staring in horror at the jaws of the fleshless beast. Her lips were blue, but her hands were busy. When Kitiara shrugged, the mage shuddered. Lida returned to her task—tracing magical symbols in the air. She began to chant. Kitiara waited for a magical campfire to warm them, for a pair of mugs of steaming buttered rum to materialize before them, for anything that would ease the bitter cold that engulfed her.

But there was nothing—just a sputter and a tiny flame that wouldn't have lit the driest tinder. Lida's hands fluttered to her lap and her lips stopped moving. Her eyes looked stricken. "It's just like Darken Wood," she said, her words barely audible above the howl of the wind. "My magic won't work right, Kitiara. I can't reach Xanthar. It's as though I'm in the presence . . ."

". . . of a far greater power," finished Janusz, stepping into view from behind the skull. "A power who finds it easy to stop you, Lida. I taught you and Dreena, after all." Despite his thin robe, the ancient-looking mage seemed comfortable in the bitter weather, and Kitiara noticed that the air around him shimmered as he moved.

"You've cast a spell to protect you from the elements," Lida murmured. Her shivering was nearly out of control now. Kitiara had no feeling left in her extremities; when she tried to take a few steps toward the man—intending to do what, she wasn't sure—her limbs would not respond.

Janusz laughed harshly. At his gesture, the storm lessened. "Yes, I warrant the two of you are getting a bit chilly by now, as opposed to my two-headed friend, who seems quite content without any magical help." He gestured toward Res-Lacua. The ettin was capering in the snow and sleet like a lamb in a meadow.

"The jaws," explained Janusz, "are the remnants of long-gone races of creatures whose size and strength weren't enough to save them from the Cataclysm. The Ice Folk scavenge the bones of these creatures to build fences around their pitiful villages."

Neither woman spoke. Both were unbearably cold. After surveying them with barely veiled contempt, Janusz barked an order to Res-Lacua, who scampered behind the skull and came back with two mounds of thick white fur. Within seconds, the two women were wrapped in the skins. "The Ice Folk who once owned these garments no longer need them," Janusz said with a thin smile. Lida shivered at his words, but Kitiara glowered.

"I want to know where we are," Kit snapped.

Janusz pursed his lips. "So demanding, for a captive. Yet I'm inclined to be generous. After all, I'm about to get my stolen property back." He sneered at Kitiara, who narrowed her eyes but said nothing.

"You are correct, Captain," Janusz finally said. "You are on the Icereach—at the northern edge of the glacier, actually, just south of Ice Mountain Bay. That doesn't help? It doesn't matter. Neither of you will be going anyplace—unless, of course, you choose to cooperate with us."

"How did we get here?" Lida asked quietly. Her breath froze in the air as she spoke.

"I teleported you to this spot, then teleported myself to meet you here. I thought that the uninhabitable surroundings might dissuade you from any thoughts of escape."

"I don't understand," the lady mage said. "That's not how teleporting works. I thought you needed an artifact."

"The ettin had one."

"But—"

"That's all I intend to reveal."

"But—"

"Enough!" Janusz thundered. Fearfully Lida clutched the front of her fur coat. "Ask Kitiara about the ice jewels she stole from me. She can clarify why you are here."

Lida turned toward Kitiara. "You're responsible for this? Do you know what he and the Valdane are doing, the damage they're causing? The deaths, the heartbreak among the Ice Folk?"

Kitiara snorted. "Do I care?" she shot back. "Let the Ice Folk take care of themselves."

At that moment, Kitiara heard a howl from the south. "Wolves," the swordswoman said. "But like none I've ever heard before."

"Dire wolves," Janusz said.

That information offered no solace. Moments later, snow churning under their broad feet, a dozen huge wolves drew up, attached to an empty sledge by braided leather thongs.

Kitiara had seen wolves before, of course, but these were fearsome, snarling beasts, a sea of gray, white, and black fur on scraggly bodies. One gray beast, the largest of the pack, stood motionless at the fore, eyeing Kitiara through bloodshot eyes. Plumes of steam rose from its mouth, forming ice drops on its muzzle.

They didn't seem to be primed for attack. Kitiara looked questioningly at Janusz.

"They eat only meat, dead or alive. There's not much else to eat down here, of course. They're as stupid as ice floes and always hungry, so don't turn your back on them, Captain Uth Matar."

Kitiara raised her eyebrows. At a sign from Janusz, Res-Lacua brandished a whip and hustled the women on board the wooden sledge. The ettin cracked the whip and sent the wolves driving to the left, then to the right, breaking the runners free of the ice. The lurch sent the swordswoman crashing back into the lady mage. Soon the two women were kneeling as they rode with their hands braced on the wooden sides. The ettin raced behind.

Kitiara looked around for Janusz. Janusz was levitating a few inches above the ground, off to their right, his robe fluttering in the wind as he matched their speed across the Icereach, heading inland over the snow.

All of a sudden they stopped. The ettin pushed warily ahead, placing one foot in front of the other cautiously. Janusz watched but said nothing.

"What is it?" Lida whispered to Kitiara. "I sense nothing magical—nothing new, anyway."

The swordswoman shrugged. "Looks the same as the rest of the Icereach to me. Windswept, chunks of ice strewn all over. A few hill-sized blocks, but otherwise snow, snow, and more snow. Maybe a bit of a depression up ahead, but . . ."

At that moment, the ettin broke through the snow and disappeared with a shout into a gaping hole. Janusz chanted and traced figures in the air, and Res-Lacua floated back up through the hole, laughing as he landed back on solid ice. Kitiara slipped out of the sledge, dashed forward, and leaned over the edge of the crevasse.

The crevasse was a hundred feet deep. Kitiara hastily backed away from the edge. "It's a crack in the ice," she told Lida. "And it's practically invisible until you fall into it."

"Another barrier to an invading army," Janusz commented.

Soon they resumed, cutting to the west around the crevasse and then veering south again. Nearly as quickly, however, they drew to another stop. "Now what?" Kitiara muttered. Lida pointed to a dark patch in the snow. "A lake?" Kitiara asked. "In this climate?"

The ettin didn't move forward to investigate. It merely snapped the whip, forcing the dire wolves around the dark patch. Sun glinted off the surface, revealing the ice that formed a thin skin on the water. "An ice lake," explained Janusz. "Filled with fish. Everything that lives in the Icereach feeds from these ice lakes—except us, of course. I offer far better fare at the ice warren. Unless, of course," he amended, "you like raw fish. The Ice Folk certainly do, but they're not civilized. Raw fish, untreated skins, smoky peat fires, and the infernal stink of walrus grease. They use fish for everything from cooking to greasing the runners on their iceboats."

After a short time, Res-Lacua shouted to the dire wolves, who slowed as they curved around a line of huge blocks of ice. The captives had seen isolated outcroppings of the formations, but these blocks looked as though they'd been placed there by intent and design, not chance.

Lida pointed wordlessly to the silhouette of a figure at the top of one block, but Kitiara had already noticed the bulky form, the short horns that curved forward over the creature's forehead. "Minotaur," the swordswoman said.

The sledge swung around the end of the blocks, and suddenly they were in the middle of a shouting, gesturing mass of minotaurs and ettins. Res-Lacua barreled into the crowd with a cry of joy, greeting several ettins with undeniable affection. The ettins, nearly twice the height of the minotaurs, crashed their spiked clubs together, pounded each other on the shoulders, and roared in orcish. The minotaurs overlooked the display, seeming to think it beneath them, but a third group of creatures, half-men, half-walrus, watched with stupid expressions. "Thanoi," Kitiara said. "Walrus men."

One of the thanoi, a broad creature with long tusks growing from each side of its mouth, seemed especially irritable. It was unclothed, with the arms and legs of a human and the face, build, and dark gray hide of a walrus. Thick webs of skin joined its fingers and toes. Coarse bristles hung from its upper lip, masking the thanoi's broad mouth. One hand clenched a harpoon; the other hand reached for the women. It reeked of dead fish. Lida shrank back against Kitiara; the swordswoman thrust the mage to the floor of the sledge, leaped out onto the packed snow, and assumed a combat stance, even though she had no weapon. She lunged for the thanoi's harpoon just as a cry rent the air.

"Despack!"

The ettins and thanoi drew back. The minotaurs stood their ground, but made no move toward Kitiara or Lida.

Janusz spoke again, in a language Kitiara did not know. The minotaurs listened, however, and when the mage's speech was over, one of the bull men stepped forward, glanced down at the swordswoman as though she were no more worrisome than a flea, and used the butt end of its double-edged ax to prod the swordswoman toward the mass of walrus men and two-headed trolls. Kitiara shouted back at Janusz, "Remember, mage, if I am killed, you will never get the information you seek."

The mage only smiled; his self-assurance seemed limitless, and Kitiara, looking around her at the weapons of the hundreds of evil creatures that served him and the Valdane, thought for the first time that she might finally be up against an unbeatable foe. She marched in the direction that the minotaur had indicated. The crowd parted before her and the minotaur, and Janusz called after them. "Toj is pledged to protect you, Captain—unless, of course, he believes you are trying to spurn my hospitality. So do take care, Captain."

Kitiara didn't reply. Clearly she was outnumbered, and Lida Tenaka, her magic weakened, was only a hindrance. Toj drew up next to Kitiara. "You were a mercenary?" the minotaur said.

"Not were," Kitiara corrected. "*Are.*"

Toj laughed. "The mage said you were a stubborn one. I see he was right."

The creature had a curiously formal way of speaking, as though he were translating from some other language into Common. Kitiara didn't even come up to his shoulders, and she was unarmed but unafraid. For the moment, at least, the minotaur wouldn't harm her, and she might learn something if he proved talkative. "You are a soldier for hire?" she asked. "Like the ettins and the thanoi?"

The minotaur faced her. His eyes flashed and his bull nostrils widened. Toj wore a steel ring through his nose, and another through his right ear—insignia of rank among some minotaurs, Kitiara knew. She saw glimpses of broad teeth. His double-edged ax swung dangerously; the muscles of his upper arm bulged and flattened as he controlled the heavy weapon. When the minotaur finally spoke, his voice was thick with anger.

"I am a mercenary," he said. "I fight for hire. There are no fighters like the minotaurs. These fish men"—he gestured contemptuously toward a tusked thanoi—"have the brains of snowflakes. They believe the Valdane will turn the Icereach over to them when the battle is won and the Ice Folk are gone. The fish-eyed fools! The ettins are slaves. *Slaves.* And they, too, are stupid, so stupid they don't even understand they are slaves. Do not compare a minotaur with thanoi or ettin. We do not belong in the same breath with such vermin. We are the warriors. Our duty is to conquer the world. By Sargas, we are the chosen ones!"

Toj poked Kitiara with the ax. "Resume," he ordered, and she tramped on.

Their surroundings were like military camps everywhere: noisy, dirty, smelly. But after his speech, the minotaur seemed disinclined to talk. Kitiara stole sidelong glances at the creature as she strode along.

Minotaurs generally inhabited seacoast regions. They were known throughout Ansalon for their skill as shipbuilders and sailors and for their ferocity as warriors. Kitiara remembered the warning that one mercenary had offered her years ago: Never surrender to a minotaur, for that would be viewed as a sign of weakness and rewarded with execution. Males and females alike were trained in battle, and males and females alike went to war. Toj, with curving horns nearly two feet long, was an impressive specimen of his kind. Reddish-brown fuzz covered his bull face, the fuzz thickening to short fur on the rest of his massive body. Despite the cold, he wore only a leather harness and kilt; numerous loops along the former held a whip, a flail, and several daggers.

Finally they came to a stop on a ridge overlooking a shallow valley. Toj and Kitiara were at the very end of the line of ice blocks. A short distance in front of them, dozens of women, children, and men, dressed in rags and filthy parkas, groaned as they pulled at an ice block the height of three men. Thongs of what was probably sealskin bound them to the block. The formation moved only a scant inch or so at a time.

"Ice Folk?" Kitiara asked.

The minotaur nodded. "We have captured several villages," he commented.

The captives were rugged-looking, as one would expect from dwelling in such a harsh climate. Their skin was leathery, their hair long. Kitiara had heard of these nomadic people of the snowy reaches, with their special weapons made of dense ice, their fierce pride, and their iceboats. But these captives looked as though they hadn't eaten in days.

"The survivors make good slaves—while they last," said Toj. "But they wear out quickly."

Even as the minotaur spoke, one of the men slumped silently and was borne away triumphantly by an ettin. The remaining Ice Folk pulled with a burst of energy, edging the block into position in line with the others. Then, prodded by armed ettins and thanoi, they headed back into the vast spaces of the Icereach.

"What is the purpose of the wall of blocks?" Kitiara asked.

The minotaur laughed. The sound had an odd, mooing quality.

"The mage said you are not only stubborn," Toj said. "You are curious. It appears to be a wall, and that is all it is. There is another wall far to the south. It is a natural formation and much larger than this one, but of no strategic use to us. The Valdane wishes a second one built upon this spot to slow the enemy, should he come." He pointed. Although his legs ended in the hocks and hooves of a bull, his hands were like a man's. "The wall will nudge the enemy toward a crevasse. They will never see the opening. The mage has cast a spell around it, and some say that the crevasse even moves, although I suspect that's a tale to discourage the thanoi from wandering about. The enemy, to be sure, will not glimpse the danger until they are hurtling through the air to their deaths!"

"And who is the enemy?" she asked quickly.

"All of Krynn," the minotaur replied just as swiftly. "Everyone who would oppose us." He cast a sly look down at her. "You would do well to join us, Captain Uth Matar. I hear you have uncommon military skill. The Valdane could use you. I would not mind such an assistant."

Kitiara snorted. "Somehow I doubt I'll have the opportunity. The mage doesn't seem to like me."

"Ah, but mage Janusz is not running this campaign. It is the Valdane you must impress. Perhaps he will be forgiving."

Indeed, Kitiara was tempted. The Valdane certainly had might on his side. But the mage would never allow her to strike a separate deal with the Valdane. She shrugged her shoulders, and Toj didn't pursue the subject.

They returned through the camp. Lida and Janusz were waiting silently when Toj escorted her up to the sledge. Hostility was apparent between the mages, and they avoided even glancing at each other. Res-Lacua galloped up, belching and smelling of fish.

Wordlessly Kitiara and Lida entered the sledge, and this time Janusz joined them. The dire wolves leaped against the traces, and they left the camp behind.

"An impressive outpost, eh, Captain?" Janusz said at last.

"Adequate," Kitiara said. "It needs an able commander to whip the troops into shape, but it has potential—in the right hands." Lida cast her an amazed glance.

The mage threw his head back and laughed. "Ah, Kitiara, you have nerve. I'll grant you that."

The ettin ran behind the wolf-drawn sledge. Kitiara saw, in the shadows at the bottom of the sledge, the shard of shale that had been teleported with her from Darken Wood. She had dropped it earlier. Now she edged toward it, covering it with her booted foot.

Snow began to fall, turning quickly to sleet.

The ettin gloried in the feel of the sleet against his nearly bare body. Lida and Kitiara pulled their coats around them against the relentless wind.

"At least he stinks less in this cold," Kitiara muttered. Lida barely smiled.

They appeared to be climbing. Kitiara soon realized they were ascending another lip of the glacier.

The wind was fiercer here. Lida pulled the hood of her robe tighter around her head. Kitiara caught snatches of the ettin's humming.

The wolves skimmed over the deepening snow. Lida seemed to lapse into a reverie. Falling asleep, she awakened with a scream when she tumbled backward off the sledge. Kitiara dove off after her and hauled the lady mage to her feet, holding off the wolves with curses. The display amused the ettin and Janusz, but more important, all the commotion distracted them. When Lida was rescued, the piece of sharp slate was safe in the pocket of Kitiara's parka, and the swords-woman was certain neither foe knew of it. It wasn't much, but it might come in handy.

The trek continued. Silence overtook them all, unbroken by anything save the wolves' panting and the squeaking of the snow as it compacted beneath the sledge. The ettin had stopped humming.

Eventually the snow and sleet slacked off, and the grayness gave way to some of the brightest sunshine Kitiara had ever seen. The sun glared painfully off the whiteness, bringing tears to her eyes. The glare didn't seem to bother the ettin. Kitiara and Lida pulled the hoods of their fur coats forward, narrowing their eyes to slits, and restricted their gaze. It was at that point that Kitiara realized the conveyance had stopped.

"Get out," Janusz ordered.

"Here?" Kitiara lifted her head. For a moment, she saw nothing but snow. Then her teary eyes adjusted, and she saw a gash of gray-blue before her. She and Lida climbed out of the sledge, stretching to ease their stiffness.

Beyond the shadows, the curve of the glacier was steeper than anything they'd seen so far.

"Castle," said the ettin.

Kitiara and Lida looked around them and then at each other in wonderment. There was no habitation in sight, and certainly no castle.

"Magic?" Kitiara whispered. "Is it invisible?"

Lida looked around, then shook her head. "I see no sign of magic."

The ettin pointed to the promontory up ahead.

"Perhaps we'll be teleported again," Kitiara suggested. Her thoughts were occupied as she moved forward. Suddenly strong hands slammed into the small of her back. She pitched into the blue grayness. Into the snow shadow.

Into . . . nothing.

Kitiara heard Lida shout and saw the lady mage drop into the void with her. As Kitiara spun and fell, thrashing, she knew her mistake. She'd been pushed into a snow-filled chasm in the glacier, invisible in the glare of the setting sun. She caught swirling glimpses of sky, of smooth wall, of a distant V at the bottom, rushing toward her with terrifying speed. Twisting, she saw the Valdane's mage near her, floating down like a feather. Why would he kill her before he knew where the ice jewels were? It defied logic.

The swordswoman saw the jagged ice at the chasm's bottom. There was nothing Kitiara could do. The surface had shrunk to a dot of light far overhead. She heard Lida screaming again. Kitiara laced together a string of obscenities. At least the gods would see that Kitiara Uth Matar, unlike the lady mage, would not leave life mewling like a kitten.

The thought of her unborn child broke into her oaths. Kitiara would die without bearing this infant. Not, she assured herself, that she would have chosen to give birth anyway. There were certain mages who could be paid to take care of inconveniences like that.

Still . . .

She forced her thoughts away.

Would the baby have had her black curls? Caven's ebony eyes? Or Tanis's pointed ears and tilted hazel stare? Would it have inherited the half-elf's irritating, judgmental, always-do-the-right-thing attitude?

Was that another chasm opening below, within the glacial chasm through which she hurtled?

Kitiara would have been braver than her mother had been in the throes of childbirth, she knew.

Believing that death was near, Kitiara comforted

herself with the knowledge that she would not have whimpered during the birth pains. She would have astounded the midwife with her bravery. Not, Kit reminded herself again, that she would have had the baby. Or, she amended, if she had given birth, certainly she wouldn't have kept the baby.

She hadn't taken precautions against a pregnancy, not ever. The thought had never occurred to her. How could her woman's body have betrayed her like this?

Then Lida vanished—into a side channel.

Kitiara hurtled after her. As suddenly as if she'd passed from air to some thicker medium, her descent slowed. Below her, Lida floated, now feetfirst, to the bottom of a vertical tunnel. Kitiara landed next to her. She heard Janusz cough, and she whirled to see the mage standing thirty feet above in an opening along one wall. He raised a hand in a lazy parody of a welcome. Kitiara looked away.

They were in a dungeon, but it was unlike any dungeon that Kitiara had ever seen. This prison was built solely of ice, huge slabs of it. The walls extended, unbroken, hundreds of feet upward.

Around the periphery of the dungeon, hanging from the walls by no visible means, dangled a dozen corpses in various stages of decay. Kitiara heard Lida retch. The swordswoman recognized the clothing of the corpses—the white parkas of the Ice Folk. She looked back up at Janusz.

"The ice jewels originated in the Icereach," the withered mage said quietly. "I'm sure of it. As certain as I am that the Ice Folk know where to mine the stones." He gestured toward the decaying warriors. "So end the lives of those who refuse to yield the information I want. A point you might want to keep in mind, Captain."

The walls of the dungeon were slick, as though

they'd been melted and refrozen, Kitiara thought. The floor, on the other hand, was covered with something that looked like thick canvas. There was no other padding, yet she and Lida had landed unhurt. Lida seemed hypnotized by the sight of the corpses. Her face was an ashy blue in the cool light that filtered from the walls.

Now the swordswoman leaned over and brushed snow from her leggings and parka. She was finally warm enough for a change, despite the ice walls that stretched upward as far as she could see. Kitiara moved toward the nearest corpse and extended a hand up toward the dead man.

"What holds them in place, do you think?" she whispered to Lida. "What—"

"Don't touch it!" Lida called out. She thrust out a hand, too late and too far away to arrest the swordswoman's movement.

Kitiara had rested her fingertips against the ice wall. It was cold, but not too . . .

Then she frowned and tugged.

The fingertips of her right hand were frozen fast to the wall. Behind and above her, she heard Janusz erupt into laughter.

Lida was at her side in an instant. "Don't touch the wall with your other hand," she warned as she examined Kitiara's fingers. "Does it hurt?"

Kitiara shook her head. "What *is* this stuff?"

"Ice," Lida replied irritably. "Didn't you ever touch your tongue against frozen metal in the winter? The same principle is at work here. Anyway, I warned you. Don't you ever listen to anyone but Kitiara Uth Matar?"

The upstart! "I'm not going to stand around and be insulted by the likes of you," Kitiara snapped.

"No?" Lida asked. "And where are you going, Captain Uth Matar?" Faint steam curled from the frozen wall.

Kitiara glared at Lida. Then the swordswoman turned back toward the wall, wrapped her left hand around her right wrist and tugged. "I need some sort of dagger. I'll cut myself free."

She felt in her pocket for the sharp piece of rock she'd palmed in the wolf sledge. The angle at which she was forced to stand was difficult, but Kitiara began to chip clumsily at the ice around her trapped fingers with her left hand. The stuff seemed invulnerable. Janusz laughed again. Then the ancient mage stopped and barked a few words to Lida in another language. It sounded like Old Kernish. Kitiara had occasionally heard the Valdane's servants speak in that tongue when they didn't want the foreign mercenaries to understand them.

Lida looked wordlessly at her former tutor, who had not yet guessed her true identity. Then she turned to Kitiara. "Let me."

There was no doubt that Lida would be able to work better with two hands than Kitiara could with one. Kitiara handed over the sliver of rock.

"Close your eyes," Lida said. Kitiara, marveling at her sudden tractability, followed the orders of the lady mage.

Lida moved closer to Kitiara, speaking softly. She seemed to be offering entreaties to someone—some god. Kitiara heard rustling and knew that Lida was fishing in a pocket of her robe. A faint puff of warm air brushed against Kitiara's left cheek, contrasting with the cold that flowed from the wall. She felt something hard tap at each finger, but she didn't open her eyes.

Kitiara pulled on her hand, and the ice beneath her fingers moved. It was as though the ice had melted and refrozen in a heartbeat. But her fingers were still fastened to the wall.

"I thought your **magic** was impaired," Kit whispered.

"Janusz has released me," Lida replied in her normal voice. "He says I am no threat here, even with my normal powers." She swallowed, then took a deep breath and continued. "Stay still. When you feel the ice quiver, pull back suddenly. Make sure you don't touch the ice with your other hand, or with any bare skin. I think this will work. I've never done it before."

Lida whispered fresh words of magic.

Kitiara's eyes flew open. "You *think* . . . ?"

"Pull!"

Kitiara pulled. There was a brief jolt of pain. Then her hand was free. She looked at the wall. Five dimples showed in the ice. As she stared, the wetness turned again to ice. She examined her hand. Her fingertips were pale and blue but unharmed. "Nice work," Kit said grudgingly.

"Indeed," Janusz commented from above. "A minor trick suitable for a carnival sideshow. I could show you so much more, Lida."

Kitiara swung toward Lida. "That's what he asked you back at the minotaur camp, wasn't it?" Kitiara asked. "While I was gone. He asked you to join him. And you refused, didn't you?"

"I'm no traitor," Lida snapped. "I do not cooperate with the enemy."

Suddenly Janusz was shoved to one side, and a new face, distorted with anger, protruded into the open space above them.

"Kitiara Uth Matar!" the Valdane thundered. His

red hair stood up from his head like a crown. Lida's face convulsed, and she took an involuntary step backward.

"What are you afraid of, mage?" Kitiara asked Lida in a piercing whisper. "At the very worst, you'll end up the consort of a powerful wizard. You're not the one in real danger." Kitiara addressed her next words at the Valdane. "Are you so weak that you must hide behind the skirts of your mage, Valdane?"

The Valdane seemed to gain resolve at her taunt. "You make it so easy to hate you, Captain. Yet I brought you here for a specific reason."

"To regain the lost ice jewels," Kitiara rejoined. "I do not have them . . ."

"Kill her," the Valdane snapped to Janusz.

". . . but I know where they are."

Smiling, Kit locked gazes with the Valdane. Slowly, almost unwillingly, the ruler also cracked a smile. Cruelty gleamed in his stare, stubbornness in hers. "I know you well enough, Kitiara Uth Matar, to know that you will not respond to the best torture we have to offer. That's what made you such an outstanding mercenary."

"Whose error caused Dreena's death," the Valdane's mage injected hastily, but the ruler ignored him.

"Perhaps, Captain, we can negotiate a compromise," the leader said. "I can offer you almost limitless power."

"As soon as you have the ice jewels, you'll kill me," Kitiara said.

"We could torture your friend here, my daughter's former servant. Perhaps that would sway you."

Kitiara cast a cool look toward the younger mage. "We are not friends." Kitiara replied. "Do what you will with her."

The Valdane laughed. "Then how about torturing a few of your lovers? My mage tells me two of them already head south, accompanied by a black stallion and a giant owl. Is not one of the men the father of your child? Certainly that must mean something, even to you."

Lida spoke. "You were able to scry them? And the giant owl is with them?" She seemed near tears.

Janusz nodded. "Unfortunately for you, Kitiara and Caven left things of theirs when they fled from the Valdane's camp. That gave me the personal artifact I needed to scry them. I know more about your life in the past few months than you may think, Captain."

Kitiara thought fast. Clearly the mage believed she had hidden the ice jewels. That information gave her some leverage—for the time being. She needed time to scheme. And she needed reinforcements. If only she *had* hidden the ice jewels. As it stood now, they were either lying forgotten in the clearing in Darken Wood or Tanis and Caven were unwittingly delivering them to the Valdane's stronghold.

"My friends and I are working together. They carry valuable information about the ice jewels," she said smoothly. "You must allow them to arrive here safely if we are to strike a deal, Valdane."

The leader fastened his piercing gaze on her. "Perhaps," he said at last. "After all, if you are lying, I can always kill them later. And you, too. At the very least, a week or two in my dungeon may change your tune, Captain."

With that, he was gone. Kitiara heard two pairs of footsteps resounding down some upper corridor.

Chapter 16

The Dust Plains

"Xanthar, where are we?" When the giant bird didn't respond, Tanis leaned over the front of the owl's wing and shouted his question.

The owl drew up with a start. He blinked in the dazzling sunlight. The feathers around Xanthar's eyes were sticky with rheum. His night-seeing eyes hadn't stopped watering in the week they'd been flying south.

The two had long since left the Kharolis Mountains behind. They'd entered the vast wasteland, great expanses of nothing but bare rock, the day before. But now, far beneath the owl and half-elf, wheat-colored sand glittered in the harsh sunlight, appearing to undulate in the heat. The wind never seemed to let up.

Pillars of swirling dust occasionally rose upward, then collapsed under their own weight.

We are . . .

Tanis waited, but the bird didn't go on. "Where are we?" he finally shouted again.

South. Far south. The Plains of Dust, west of Tarsis, or maybe southwest of Tarsis. I don't know exactly, Kai-lid.

"I am Tanis."

Ah. Of course. Tanthalas. The half-elf.

Tanis let his gaze wander over the terrain. Sand and dust stretched far ahead.

"What did this wasteland used to be?" Tanis persisted.

An ocean, I believe—until the Cataclysm changed the face of the world. When the gods punished Krynn, some portions of Ansalon were flooded. Here the sea drained, leaving only sand and grit. Or so said my grandfather.

And where was Caven? At first the half-elf had caught occasional glimpses of the horseman, who seemed to be driving Maleficent as hard as Xanthar was pushing himself. But Tanis had not spied Caven Mackid in two days.

Tanis had lost his nervousness after soaring miles above the ground, attached to the giant owl only by the jury-rigged leather harness. Xanthar was a steady flier. Since leaving Darken Wood, the owl had allowed only short respites, in which the half-elf cooked small game, replenished his water supply, and relieved himself. Tanis could sleep on Xanthar's back as he flew, but as far as the half-elf could tell, the giant owl napped only during his brief time on the ground.

Kai-lid.

"This is Tanis," the half-elf repeated.

The owl shook his head dazedly. He opened his eyes to their fullest, and Tanis could see, when Xanthar turned his head, that the owl's irises had dulled to a flat terra-cotta color and that the pupils no longer reacted to variations in light and shadow.

"Xanthar, how are your eyes?"

Sometimes the light grows dim. It passes, however. I am not accustomed to such bright daylight. Another drop of thick yellow liquid oozed from the bird's eye.

"We should stop for a while to let you rest."

No.

"We should let Caven catch up."

Caven will find his way. My kin escorted him to the southernmost edge of Darken Wood. Beyond that, he knows how to navigate by stars and sun. He knows to head due south, as much as these shifting sands will let him.

"Can you send your thoughts to him?"

He is too far away, and untrained in telepathy. I cannot even reach Kai-lid, and she was well tutored— by a master.

"Do you think she and Kitiara are all right?" The owl didn't answer, but all his muscles tensed. "Xanthar?"

To the left. Do you see something? I sense a change, but I cannot see that far.

Tanis gazed in that direction. "It's only a small cloud, Xanthar."

No. More than that.

"What, then? Magic?"

No magic. A storm. We must find shelter.

"But . . ." The half-elf's words died as Xanthar, without warning, tucked his wings to his sides and arrowed toward the earth.

You must be my eyes now, half-elf. Tanis felt himself slip backward on the plummeting owl. When he reached the limit of the harness, his head snapped back with the force of the dive. The ground was rushing toward them at dizzying speed. "Xanthar! Pull up!" Immediately the giant owl leveled out, mere feet above the ground, and zigzagged over the terrain.

Watch for shelter.

With nearness came detail. This portion of the plain, seen up close, was a warren of sand and rocky juttings of fire-colored sandstone pocked with animal dens. The dens were too small to accommodate a half-elf and an owl nearly twice his size, however.

Keep looking.

Tanis no longer protested the wisdom of the bird's actions; the small cloud was burgeoning into a blanket of dark blue and pea green. Lightning crackled as the cloud sped toward them. Below the bank hung a curtain of swirling, vanilla-colored grit. Tanis dug a rag out of the packs on the bird's back and tied it over his mouth and nose. The first blast of grit hit them from the side. The grains stung like needles. Xanthar battled to keep flying. More than once, the tips of his wings brushed the ground, sending the half-elf sprawling first one way and then the other. Tanis squinted through the blowing dirt. Tears poured down his cheeks. Xanthar's eyes were shut tight, but he kept barreling through the air.

"There!" The half-elf lunged forward with both hands, grabbed the sides of the bird's head, and pointed toward a cave, now gone from view, now visible as a shadow through the driving sandstorm, now gone again. "Look!"

Where? I don't see . . .

The cave loomed again right before them. Tanis flung himself down into the feathers on the bird's back and shut his eyes. He sensed the bird pass from the blinding sandstorm into cool, silent darkness. The bird skidded to a crashing stop against a wall. Tanis released the harness and slid off Xanthar's back. He looked around him, his elven nightvision probing for signs of warmth. The den appeared to be devoid of all life, save half-elf and owl.

The storm thundered outside for hours. Xanthar paced and fretted. When the owl's voice came into the half-elf's mind at last, it was clear why.

I must summon help, Kai-lid. Tanis didn't bother to correct the owl. *I thought my strength would be sufficient, but you were right, Kai-lid. I should not have gone so far away.*

"Sufficient?"

The half-elf's voice seemed to jolt the owl back to reality. *Against Kai-lid's enemies, Tanis. But I am weakening fast. You will need help, and the Kernan will not be enough. Indeed, he may already be lost.*

"Kitiara will help. And Lida—Kai-lid."

What if they are dead?

Tanis leaned toward the owl. He laid a gentle hand on the bird's wing. "You said you would know if the lady mage was dead."

I am no longer certain of anything. I may have overestimated my own ability. Humility was never my strength. I fear . . .

"What?"

Nothing. Everything. I must summon help.

"Who?"

The giant bird didn't answer. Xanthar's feet scratched against the sandstone as he waddled away from the half-elf. The bird's breathing grew stertorous. Tanis felt the tickling in his mind that he'd felt before when the bird was speaking telepathically to

Lida but to no one else. Eventually the owl grew quiet, and Tanis realized that Xanthar had fallen asleep. The half-elf pulled his sword from his pack and stayed on guard. Although the den had been unoccupied, there was no telling if some former occupant might return. Tanis opened Kitiara's pack and forced back the false bottom. The ice jewels provided a cold violet light, offering some bare comfort.

Finally the storm abated. It was the silence, not Tanis, that awakened the giant owl.

It is over.

"Yes."

The owl shuffled toward the opening of the den. Sand and dust now spilled down the incline into their hiding place. *We must go now.*

"What about Caven?"

He knew the expedition would be dangerous. He could have ridden one of my children, but he insisted on staying with his horse. We must continue on. We have lost time.

"Caven may be lost in the plains. I don't think we should go on without him."

Xanthar sighed. *You have an oddly generous attitude toward your rival for Kitiara's affections. I suspect it is your elven upbringing; certain this philanthropy does not come from your human side.*

It took the two half an hour to dig themselves out of the den. As soon as they swept away some of the dun-colored sand, more spilled in. The sand was a variety of colors: tan, of course, but green and pink and gray as well. In any other circumstances, it would have been beautiful. But now dust and grit filled Tanis's mouth and nose and clouded his vision. The half-elf and giant owl were hacking and sneezing when they finally scrabbled into daylight.

Caven and his pony may be dead and buried under tons of this stuff, for all we know. We should go on, for Kai-lid's sake. And Kitiara's.

Tanis shook his head again. The owl squinted at him. When the bird spoke, he sounded more like the Xanthar of old. *An interesting situation. I will be nearly useless to Kai-lid in the Icereach without you, and you cannot travel far without me in this shifting ocean of grit. We could waste long hours, you and I, trying to sort this out.* Tanis didn't drop his gaze. *Very well, we will look for the oaf.*

The sky was as blue and cloudless as it had been when they'd entered the dusty plains. Tanis climbed on the bird's back and they set off, retracing their flight from the north. They'd traveled only an hour when Tanis shouted and pointed. On the horizon, looking like a beetle from their altitude, something black crawled at the center of the sea of sand. Within moments, they had landed near the struggling form.

It was Maleficent they had spotted. Caven clung to the horse's back. The animal, its hide streaked with sweat and lather, plunged and bucked, panicked by the sands that flowed around its hooves. Caven was hoarse from shouting. His hands were bloodied from sawing at the reins, his face lined with fatigue. Man and horse alike were encrusted with grime.

Tanis reached for Maleficent's bridle, fought with the mount for a moment, then soothed it. Within seconds, he was stroking the stallion's muzzle. The horse still breathed in bursts, but it stood still. Caven slid from the animal into the sand. His knees buckled, but he waved away Tanis's hand irritably. "I'm all right, damn it."

Xanthar snickered. *Certainly you are. Humans!*

Caven glared at the bird. "I see your parakeet friend

still speaks, half-elf." Bird and human exchanged nasty looks.

"Where did you wait out the storm?" Tanis asked.

Caven rose to his feet, dusted off his clothes, and brushed his hand through his beard. Sand fell from him like snow. "We found an outcropping of rock back there." He pointed to the north. "I thought we would be sheltered on the leeward side."

Xanthar snorted, an odd sound coming through a beak. Caven snapped at the owl. "All right, you overgrown canary, I was naive. I didn't know there wouldn't *be* a leeward side in a swirling mess like that." Caven narrowed his eyes, then turned again to Tanis. "I covered our heads so we could breathe. But the power of the sandstorm, by the gods! I can see why everything in this forsaken region is scoured to nothing. So would we have been if it had lasted much longer."

Tanis saw that the outsides of the mercenary's hands were as raw as his palms. Blood trickled from the wounds. Caven's gaze followed Tanis's. "I had to hold Maleficent. My hands were exposed." The half-elf's gaze returned to the horse; sand had blasted patches of hair from the creature's skin. "The question is," Caven said, "what do we do now?

Leave the pony behind. I will carry you both.

"You can't," Tanis said to Xanthar. "You're weakening even with one passenger, and you're losing your sight. You couldn't have carried two men at your peak. You certainly can't do it now."

I will if I have to. The bird pulled himself to his full height, towering over the two men. *Get on, both of you.*

Clearly Xanthar couldn't be dissuaded. They didn't have too many other choices. Tanis climbed aboard, but Caven Mackid stubbornly remained standing aside, one hand on his horse's bridle. "I'm not leaving Maleficent," he insisted.

"The stallion can make his own way out of the plains," Tanis said. "We've lost enough time." When Caven showed no sign of budging, Tanis added, "What's more important to you, Mackid, a horse or the fate of Kitiara and the lady mage?"

To say nothing of the horrors that the Valdane will unleash on Ansalon if he isn't stopped.

Caven glowered at both of them. "Unlike Kitiara, half-elf, Maleficent has never robbed me of my savings. And I don't owe this Lida woman anything. Anyway, owl, who's to say we'll be able to stop the mage and the Valdane, if it comes to that?"

The portent . . .

Caven snorted. "A veiled dream. And dreamed in Darken Wood, at that. Based on that weak logic, we're going to risk our lives?"

"We are continuing," Tanis said wearily. "Will you come with us, or are you going to stay here and die with your horse?"

They locked stares. Finally the Kernan looked down. "I will not ride the owl."

"Then stay here. Perhaps the sands will bear you like a magic carpet."

Tanis nodded to Xanthar. The giant owl took off into the sky once again. They were high above the Kernan when the half-elf finally looked down. Caven had remounted the stallion and was urging it forward through the sand. Maleficent fought against the shifting morass. "Will wonders never cease?" Tanis murmured to the giant owl. "Caven's heading south. Is the fool still trying to get to the Icereach?"

The sun was warm on his right cheek. Far ahead,

Tanis could see what appeared to be the edge of the sandy expanse. The sand glittered.

All of a sudden Tanis recalled a gnome named Speaker Sungear, back in Haven, and Speaker's use of a glowing purple jewel. He slapped his hand against Xanthar's shoulder, jarring a protest out of the tired owl. Tanis apologized, but he couldn't hide the excitement behind the words.

What is it?

Quickly Tanis sketched out his idea to the giant owl.

We need to act before sunset, then.

Xanthar wheeled and headed northwest, his wings beating powerfully; he seemed to have found new energy. Caven halted Maleficent and watched the pair, shading his eyes against the glare of the sun. Xanthar circled slowly just west of the stallion and rider as Tanis reopened Kitiara's knapsack.

Hurry. It will be sunset soon.

"I thought you didn't care if Caven died here?"

A pause. *No one deserves death. Especially for a good cause.*

"Xanthar," Tanis said, "you're becoming a sentimental old bird in your golden years."

Gray feathers rose on the back of Xanthar's head. *I would point out that, at a few seasons shy of a century, you're no spring chicken, yourself, half-elf.*

Tanis laughed. He displayed one of the ice jewels between thumb and forefinger. "I'm ready," he said. At a signal from Tanis, Xanthar faced into the south. The half-elf held the stone high above his head, watching to make sure it was aligned correctly. "The stone is growing warm," he shouted.

Didn't you say this Sungear fellow finally blew up the jewel he had?

The stone had become hot in Tanis's hand, but still no beam shot from the crystal. Even if the stone did work as the gnome's had, Tanis didn't know if he'd be able to continue holding the searing jewel. Finally, with a curse, he dropped the stone and it plummeted, glittering, to the sands below. The jewel disappeared into the shifting sand.

Xanthar turned north again while Tanis drew an arrow from his quiver. With his dagger, he split the arrow shaft lengthwise, leaving the two parts attached at one end to form a rude pair of tongs. He removed another jewel from the pack.

Try not to lose them all. I thought you had some idea of using them for ransom.

Tanis muttered and wedged the jewel between the prongs of the new implement. Then he held the whole apparatus above his head, trying a different approach.

Hurry. The sun . . .

"I know."

Again the jewel heated, but the makeshift tongs enabled Tanis to grasp it without difficulty. Even so, the stone seemed to grow only so hot, and then no more. "It's your wings," Tanis grumbled.

What?

"Your wings! The sun's dropping lower. Your wings keep shading the stone."

Would you rather I didn't use them?

"Don't be sarcastic."

Xanthar, shrugging, headed north again. Caven, meanwhile, had dismounted and was attempting to lead the stallion. This met with no greater success; the horse was floundering in the sand.

"I have another idea." Without pausing to consider the risk, Tanis loosened the harness that held him to the owl. Carefully he knelt on the back of the bird.

What are you doing? Half-elf, you're off balance—I won't be able to catch you if you fall!

Ignoring the bird, Tanis crouched on Xanthar's back. The owl's feathers were slippery beneath Tanis's moccasins. The half-elf rose to his full height, his left arm outstretched to the side for balance. Then, with his right arm, he stretched the tongs and the jewel high above his head. He tried not to think of the ground so far below him. Suddenly Kitiara's pack, with the remaining seven jewels, tumbled from the bird's back. Tanis lurched and slipped, landing on Xanthar's back with a cry. He was sprawled crosswise on the giant owl, his legs dangling on one side, his head jutting over the other. This gave him a fine view of the pack spinning end over end and smashing into the plain. Dust rose around the area of impact. Tanis scrambled to regain his seating. At least he hadn't dropped the tongs.

Again Xanthar turned north, then, after a short time, headed south once more. Soon Tanis was back in position, standing with one arm outstretched to the side, the other, with the jewel, high above his head. He dared not look up to see if the stone was in the correct alignment.

Half-elf . . .

The bird's telepathy was interrupted. Humming burst from above. Out of the corner of his eye, Tanis saw an amethyst-colored beam arrow toward the sand. "Is it working?" he cried. "Is the sand melting?"

From this angle, I cannot tell.

"Keep going."

They continued their slow passage southward, the stone thrumming all the way, until practically an hour had passed and Tanis's muscles screamed for relief.

Finally they reached the edge of the sand. Tanis slipped gratefully to his knees and clung to the owl as the creature glided to a landing. Then, just as the sun slipped below the horizon, they turned and looked back.

Trailing straight through the expanse of plain was a gleaming path of melted and hardened sand. And in the distance, inching cautiously down the strange trail, were Caven Mackid and a visibly limping Maleficent. Caven waved Kitiara's fallen pack triumphantly over his head.

* * * * *

They had stopped for the night. Xanthar napped. Meanwhile, Caven tended Maleficent, who had pulled a tendon struggling in the sand. The huge horse stood with one leg dangling. His breath rasped, and he refused food.

"There's nothing to do but let him rest," Tanis said.

The next morning, Maleficent was hot with fever and barely conscious. Caven stood looking down at his horse, saying nothing, hand on the hilt of his dagger. Tanis moved away, and the Kernan put the stallion out of his pain.

"What now?" Caven asked Tanis afterward. "We're at least a hundred miles from the Icereach. The owl can't carry us both."

Their gaze turned to Xanthar, still asleep on a rock overlooking camp. His exhausted snoring was audible a hundred feet away. As though the men's gaze had disturbed him, the owl awakened with a snuffle and looked around dimly.

"He won't be able to haul even me much longer," Tanis whispered. "He keeps calling me Kai-lid."

Caven's eyebrows rose, and Tanis explained. "Lida's Darken Wood name, the owl said."

The Kernan's confused look changed to one of expectation. "So what do we do now?"

Irritation rose in the half-elf. "Who elected me emperor of this expedition?" Caven waited. "Do?" the half-elf repeated. "I believe that what Xanthar should do is go back to Darken Wood; obviously he drew strength and powers from there, and he's losing both. And what you and I should do, Caven Mackid, is to continue on without him."

"How?" Caven demanded.

"How else? We'll walk."

Chapter 17

Kitiara and the Valdane

"Hurry, hurry! Valdane wait."

Both of the ettin's heads spoke at once as the beast looked down from the access hole high in the dungeon cell. The ettin's roar reverberated through the bare chamber, and Lida jumped. Kitiara took pleasure in goading the beast by taking her time in sauntering to the wall opposite the portal. The two-headed troll flung a rope through the opening and climbed down. He grasped at her with dirt-encrusted hands. "Hurry. Want now. Now, now, now." Kitiara caught the fetid odor of fish on his breath.

The thirteen-foot ettin dragged her over to the crude ladder. Lida attempted to follow, but Res-Lacua stopped her. "Just soldier lady."

"It's a private party," Kitiara said acerbically.

Res-Lacua cuffed her above her right ear, lifted her to his shoulder with one hand, and then sprang up the rope. "No touch ice," he chanted in a whisper. "No touch corpses. Not eat, not, not. No touch ice." He flung her through the hole, then drew up the rope and hung it on a peg on the wall.

The swordswoman ignored the cry of "Kitiara, don't cooperate with them!" that wafted through the portal. Instead, she took a swing at the ettin. "If I had my sword . . ." she threatened. The creature guffawed and towed her up a sloping hallway bathed in icy blue light, then through a maze of identical hallways.

Kitiara complained as she struggled to keep her footing. "The man abandons us for days . . . ignores us completely . . . doesn't even send us food . . . then all of a sudden he has to see me *right away?*"

The ettin skidded to a halt, crashing a fist into an oak door. When he thundered on the door again, Kitiara realized it was an ettin version of knocking.

"By Morgion, ettin!" the Valdane exploded, opening the portal. "Can't Janusz teach you any—"

His eyes widened when he saw Kitiara. Then his hand snaked out, caught the swordswoman by the shoulder, and propelled her into the room. The ruler slammed the door in Res-Lacua's faces.

The Valdane's quarters were as opulent as the dungeon had been spartan. Velvet tapestries in deep blues, greens, and purples covered most of the walls, with only a few sections of ice left exposed, probably to let in the blue light. A gilded throne stood in the center of the room. The ruler's huge bed was draped with brocade and silk embroidered in the colors of the Valdane's standard, purple and black. One wall boasted a window of sorts—undoubtedly magical, as they were hundreds of feet below the surface. As Kitiara watched, the scene shifted from a view of the Icereach to a springtime panorama of the Valdane's former holdings near Kernen.

Kit felt his breath on her shoulder, but she forced herself to meet his eyes. The Valdane had bathed, combed his red hair, and donned clean clothing—tight black leggings, knee-high boots of the same color, and a loose purple shirt laced loosely at the front. He looked only a few years older than she. He gazed at her, and she saw appreciation and hunger in his eyes.

He spoke softly and smiled, but the hard look in his eyes never varied. "The mage believes I should let him torture you, Captain, until you give him some information about the ice jewels. And then he wants to have the pleasure of killing you himself."

"The mage shouldn't be too optimistic about torture. I've been tortured before—by the best, or should I say worst?"

The Valdane nodded. "So I told him. But he feels he has a personal score to settle with you, Captain."

She grinned crookedly. "He shouldn't leave his belongings lying around where anyone can make off with them."

"I agree."

They sized up each other. Then the Valdane spoke offhandedly. "I submit it would be best for us all to cooperate." The Valdane lounged on his bed, stroking the silken coverlet. He beckoned to Kitiara. Kit came over and sat next to him, judging him a fool. "You have something we want, and we—or at least I—can provide something that Captain Kitiara Uth Matar desires above all else."

"And what is that, Valdane?" Kit asked coyly.

"Power."

"Indeed." She raised one eyebrow.

"And wealth."

"Really."

"You saw my troops. Could you command them in alliance with Toj?"

She barked out a laugh. "The soldiers haven't been born yet that I can't command."

"Then you will join us?"

"In exchange for . . . ?"

"The jewels, of course."

Kitiara leaned back lazily against the bed and smiled up at him. "I know where the stones are, and I know that once they've been mastered, they could provide all the power and wealth I need. Why should I cooperate with you or your mage?"

The Valdane's eyes danced with fury. He jabbed a finger toward the window. When Kitiara looked, she saw Janusz's face. The mage was chanting. Suddenly pain tore through her. She twisted and rolled off the bed and fell writhing to the floor, her hands clutching her abdomen. She bit her lip to keep from crying out and felt blood trickle down her chin. Through a haze of pain, she heard the Valdane rap out an order. The chanting stopped, and the agony vanished as suddenly as it had begun. Kitiara lay panting on the thick carpet. She fought the desire to retch.

The Valdane's boots swam into her vision. The toe of one boot nudged her chin until she was peering up at him.

"Why should you go along with me?" he repeated gently. "You forget the being growing within you, Kitiara. We can deal with it however we want, the mage and I. And don't mistake us; some of our tricks are quite painful. This was just a modest sample."

She spat at him. Spittle dripped down his left leg, but the Valdane didn't flinch. "Where are the ice jewels, Kitiara?" he asked quietly.

"Go to the Abyss."

"Where are they?" His voice rose.

"Didn't you hear me the first time, Valdane?" She rolled cautiously over and pulled herself to a crouch. Her head swam; she hadn't eaten in nearly a week, and being with child was yet another drain. "I don't *have* the damned stones anymore, Valdane."

"Yet you said your friends, coming so valiantly to rescue you, do."

"I said they had *information*. They'd hardly be so stupid as to haul the jewels straight to you." Hoping that last remark was true, she wiped the sweat from her face on the silk of his bed covers. Then she rose. "You need me more than I need you, Valdane. Who's going to lead your army? Toj? Those power-mad minotaurs? Do you think they'll stand by and let you hoard all the wealth? The walrus men? They'll serve as little more than dumb bulwark. And the ettins . . . there isn't an ettin on Krynn with an ounce of brains."

"Res-Lacua . . ."

"Res-Lacua is terrified of the mage, who drills him endlessly to coordinate his every move. Those ettin slaves can't think for themselves. Why, they can't even get their right and left heads to agree with each other."

"The mage . . ."

"The mage has exerted himself to his limit."

The Valdane looked thoughtful, but when he spoke, he oozed with sarcasm. "And Kitiara Uth Matar, about to become a proud mother, could you do anything about all that? Do you think I ought to plan my campaign around your confinement?" He affected a whine. " 'I'm sorry, Valdane . . . we can't take Tarsis now, Valdane . . . I think I'm having contractions today, Valdane.' "

Stung, Kitiara shot back, "Don't forget, Valdane, I know where the ice jewels are. They offer limitless power to the one who can unlock their secrets. And about that other 'problem' . . . your mage could help take care of that as part of the bargain."

"The baby?"

"The child need never be born," she snapped.

For a moment, neither spoke. The Valdane's thoughts lay masked behind an unfathomable stare. But in another of his mercurial shifts of mood, his next words were gentle. "It doesn't have to come to that, Kitiara. We don't have to be enemies, you and I. Once we fought on the same side."

Kitiara forced an implacable tone. "I remember that *I* fought. *You* stayed safely in your tent."

He put a hand on her arm. "Let's end this bickering for now. I'll have lunch brought here." He directed his words at the mage, behind Kitiara, where he awaited his master's command. Janusz murmured something that Kitiara didn't catch, but her stomach grumbled. No doubt about it, she was hungry. "You'll probably poison me, Valdane." She affected a lighthearted tone.

He smiled. "If I kill you, I'll never learn where the jewels are, will I? As you yourself have pointed out. We are in a most interesting predicament, you and I."

At that moment, the ettin thundered at the door. The creature ducked beneath the doorjamb, carrying an enormous tray covered with thin white canvas.

The ettin tossed the cloth on the floor and began pitching platters and bowls onto a corner table with such enthusiasm that a third of the crockery broke. "Dead fish here; dead bird here," the ettin chanted, and Kitiara heard a snort from the mage. "Bare plate, bare plate, fork, fork. Hoof jelly, spicy. Seaweed—cold, cold. Thanoi cheese, gray, chewy."

"I'll confess, Valdane," Kitiara said, "after a stint in your dungeon, any meal would sound wonderful." She smiled at the ruler and sat down. "But," she added sweetly, "I'll still let you taste everything first."

*   *   *   *   *

Afterward, their stomachs full, Kitiara and the Valdane, enshrouded in fur parkas, sped across the snowy landscape in a dire-wolf sledge. Res-Lacua bumbled behind, humming, until the Valdane thundered back to him to keep quiet.

Kitiara mulled over her mealtime discussion with the leader. She had no intention of turning the nine ice jewels over to the Valdane. Kitiara had her own plans for such valuable artifacts. But she had to stall the Valdane until help arrived.

"You're awfully quiet. Are you planning strategy?" the Valdane asked now.

Kitiara blinked. Strategy? Of course. They were off to lead the minotaurs and the rest of the Valdane's forces against another helpless Ice Folk village. Kitiara had agreed to lead the attack. She hoped the defeat and enslavement of the village would buy Caven and Tanis time to arrive. Kit had an idea that she could make the campaign last several days. The Valdane might enjoy the thought of toying with the Ice Folk for some time before closing in for the kill.

Kitiara let one side of her mouth rise in her characteristic crooked grin. "I'm *always* planning strategy," she answered.

The Valdane smiled back.

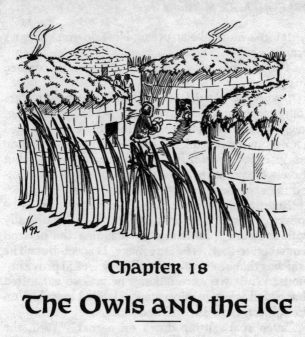

Chapter 18

The Owls and the Ice

Surprisingly, Xanthar had retreated north-
ward without demurral. Xanthar had merely dipped
his head, touched Tanis's sleeve with the tip of his
beak, flattened his ear tufts against the sides of his
head, and launched into the air.

"Not a word," Caven had said, marking Xanthar's
progress until the giant bird was just a dark gray spot
against the sky. "I expected an argument."

That had been days ago. Since then, the half-elf and
the mercenary had walked nearly ceaselessly—and almost wordlessly. Now they stood upon rocky heights
overlooking a vast sea a hundred feet below. "Ice
Mountain Bay," Tanis said.

"It looks more like an ocean. How do you know it's simply a bay?"

"The owl told me, days ago, that we would come to this place."

"I wish the blasted owl had told you how we are going to get across." Caven scowled at the seething, steel-blue water dotted with floes of ice. He edged back from the precipice. Beads of icy sweat shone on his forehead. Seabirds flew overhead, cawing, but there were no other signs of life. Copses of trees dotted the expanse of rocky soil behind them.

"Right after the sandstorm, Xanthar seemed to be speaking—or at least trying to speak—telepathically with someone," Tanis mused, scanning the horizon from west to east. "The lady mage, I expect. But all he said was that our way across the bay would prove obvious. While we were talking, he was so exhausted that he fell asleep in midsentence. I didn't press him on the subject. Now I wish I had."

Caven spat, sitting down on a rock. "Well, the way's not obvious to me," he said petulantly. "Unless the overgrown chicken thought we could swim through that frigid muck, or sprout wings and fly."

Tanis nodded absentmindedly. He leaned over, picked up a piece of driftwood, and regarded it thoughtfully.

Until now, each man had instinctively shied away from the real thing weighing on their minds. But shivering in the needle-sharp wind that angled north off the bay, Caven broached the subject.

"Do you think she really *is?*"

"Is what?" Tanis asked. He looked up from the piece of driftwood to Caven, who didn't meet his eyes. The half-elf tossed the branch behind him.

"*With child*, half-elf. Like the owl said."

Tanis considered. "I think so, yes," he said at last, as though he hadn't been thinking about the same thing incessantly ever since Xanthar had made the revelation.

They sat in silence for a while. Caven finally shrugged. "I can't see Kitiara getting married," the mercenary said. "Or basking in motherhood. Especially that."

Tanis ran his hand through his hair. "No," he said. He frowned and turned his back on the bay, facing north. The valley they'd just traversed sloped before him. The wind howled and pushed against his back.

"Maybe it was some other . . ."

All of a sudden, Tanis froze, holding up a hand in warning. Caven stopped in midsentence. The Kernan rose and drew his sword. Tanis unfastened his bow from his pack and checked his sword.

"What is it?" Caven whispered.

Tanis shook his head.

"Battle drums?" Caven ventured. "I've heard the dwarves of Thorbardin bang the hollow trunks of symphonia trees to scare their enemies, and Thorbardin is up that way. But I've never heard . . ." He paused to listen. "An attack from the north? It makes no sense. We've been all the way through the dust plains. I saw nothing to threaten us except miles of shifting sand."

Tanis strained his eyes, trying to see as far back as he could into the direction from where they had come. Except for a dark line in the sky, which looked like a low bank of storm clouds, there was nothing out of the ordinary.

Tanis pointed. "If you told me the Valdane knows we are carrying these magic jewels, I'd say that maybe we've become a target."

They looked at each other then. Hazel eyes met black. "He might have ways of knowing," Caven replied.

Seconds later, they were hiding among the trunks of the nearest trees. The pair bent some branches to improve their cover, then crouched, armed, behind their makeshift bulwark.

The drumming grew louder. The pounding racked Tanis's nerves. It sounded like battle drums, but slower—more like the beat that resounded when a prisoner marched to the gallows. Now Tanis thought he could hear smaller beats, sounding counterpoint to the loudest reverberations. Perhaps it wasn't one large creature at all, but many smaller ones. He said as much to Caven.

"In the name of Takhisis, could it be dragons?" the Kernan whispered.

"Dragons haven't been glimpsed on Krynn for thousands of years. If ever."

Caven and Tanis waited, motionless, as the black line drew closer, widened, and deepened. Then, with a roar of wings, they were there. Cream-colored underfeathers flashed as more than three hundred giant owls settled onto the rocks and trees of the shoreline. At the fore, dropping clumsily onto a needlelike protuberance of rock, was Xanthar. In a flash, Tanis and Caven were out of the trees and dashing toward him.

Tanis shouted the owl's name, expecting to hear the creature's sardonic tones buzz in his head. But there was no telepathic reply. Tanis looked alarmed, Caven surprised. They slowed to a halt before the giant owl.

"What's wrong with the old canary?" Caven muttered.

Tanis looked up into the bird's flat eyes, the color of mud, dimmed with pain. The bird's beak was partially open. He seemed to be panting. Up close, the half-elf barely recognized the once-sleek creature. The bird's proud carriage couldn't disguise that Xanthar had withered to little more than bones and feathers.

"He *can't* speak to us," Tanis told Caven. "He's been out of Darken Wood too long. The lady mage warned him." The bird nodded. "But he can understand whatever we say." Xanthar nodded again.

"What about the other birds?" Caven demanded. "Can we communicate with them?"

Tanis turned toward the chattering mass of giant owls, which stretched for some distance in both directions on the shore. Xanthar was shaking his head. "From what Kai-lid said, I'm guessing that only Xanthar had the rare ability to mind-speak outside his race," the half-elf said. Xanthar dipped his head again.

"Could he still speak to the mage?"

Xanthar cocked his head, and Tanis shrugged. "Maybe. He trained her. They have a special bond. But it doesn't matter, does it? She's not here."

Four somewhat smaller owls gathered around Xanthar. They appeared to be arguing with the old bird. Perched at the apexes of four dead oaks, the quartet broadcast their agitation with chittering, wing-flapping, and much whetting of beaks. Xanthar sat, apparently unmoved, at the tip of the stone, imperiously overlooking them all. The smaller birds chittered again; Xanthar dipped his beak in what Tanis interpreted as disagreement. The others cross-stepped back and forth on their branches, squawking some more. Xanthar appeared to consider, then dipped his beak again. The four other owls seemed to think a decision had been made. They leaped into the air with a rush of wind.

Xanthar didn't follow. Instead, he straightened and

called out to them, a screeching that rivaled the tempest of wind, ocean, and crackling ice floes.

Several owls took to the air and circled overhead, calling down to the giant owl. One seemed particularly disturbed, darting again and again at Xanthar, screeching raggedly.

"I think they want Xanthar to go back home," the half-elf said, watching as the huge owl raised his beak and uttered a deep trill, the sound of water over stones. At that, the four returned, but with a deflated air. This time, as they landed on the ground, they turned large eyes toward Tanis and Caven.

"I hate that stare," Caven whispered. "It makes me feel like lunch. *Their* lunch."

"I see that Xanthar rules his family still," Tanis said, ignoring his companion's remark. He raised a hand to the closest bird. The owl dipped its head slightly.

Caven raised an eyebrow. "Family?"

"Look at them." Tanis pointed at the four and to other owls on each side. "Xanthar's dark brown and gray, and they're lighter. Those two are golden, but some have the same patch of white he has over the eye. Look at their markings, at the way they stand. Do you doubt the evidence of your eyes?"

The Kernan gaped for a while, then shook his head.

"At least it's obvious how we're getting to the Icereach," Tanis commented. Xanthar nodded.

"Obvious?" Caven's eyes darted nervously from Tanis to Xanthar, then over to the pair of tawny owls waddling across the heights toward the half-elf and Caven. Looks of determination lit their round eyes, and panic flickered across the mercenary's face. "Oh, no!"

Tanis ignored him.

"I'd rather swim across the bay than fly on the back

of one of those creatures," Caven said, swallowing. He took a step backward. "I—I wasn't meant to fly like a bird, half-elf."

"You mean you're afraid of heights," Tanis said.

Caven bristled. "Afraid? Not me. I'd just rather . . . rather . . . walk."

"You'll *have* to fly, and that's that."

"I . . . can't."

"Not for Kitiara?"

"Not for anybody. I suffer from vertigo. . . . I'd fall off. Half-elf, no one can defeat me in hand-to-hand combat, or on horseback, but up in the air . . ." A shudder shivered through his frame. "By the gods, I don't dare!"

"We need you," Tanis replied. "You can use my harness. Strap yourself on; you won't fall off."

One of the birds, a blaze of white marking its tawny forehead, had reached Tanis and turned around, presenting its broad back. The half-elf dug the leather apparatus out of his pack and fastened it around the bird's wings and chest. The owl flexed its wings, testing the harness.

"Half-elf . . ." Caven said warningly.

The other bird, the same golden color as the first but without the blaze, came up on Caven's other side. It looked down on him solemnly, then plucked at his shirt with its beak, nudging the mercenary toward the waiting owl. "No!" Caven said. "Go away!" He put a hand on the hilt of his sword, looking wildly from side to side.

The two owls exchanged looks, then glanced at Tanis. The half-elf heard no voice of telepathy, but he understood the birds' intention. At that moment, the unharnessed owl raised its beak and screeched. The sound was enough to raise the hair on Tanis's neck, and Caven whirled, fumbling with his sword. At that, the half-elf leaped for the driftwood he'd thrown away moments before, hefted it in one hand, and as the mercenary began to swing back the blade, brought the piece of wood down on Caven Mackid's head with a crack. The Kernan went down like dead weight.

Moments later the owl with the blaze, the unconscious mercenary lashed to its back, plunged from the ridge into the dizzying space above the churning waters of Ice Mountain Bay. Tanis's owl followed suit, the half-elf clinging to its neck. Xanthar launched from his pinnacle and swooped into the lead. They circled once, then turned due south.

Behind them, spread across the blue-gray sky, hundreds of giant owls followed.

* * * * *

Kai-lid.
Curled on the floor of the icebound dungeon, Kai-lid lifted her head and pushed back her coverlet. Her head swam. She hadn't eaten for days, although the ettin had begun showing up regularly several days ago, right after Kitiara had been dragged from the prison, to lower a pail of water. The swordswoman hadn't returned, and the ettin wouldn't answer Kai-lid's entreaties about Kitiara's safety. Several times Janusz himself had showed up and renewed the offer he'd made in the Valdane's camp, that she join forces with him and continue the magical training he'd begun with Lida and Dreena years ago when they were teen-agers. Of course, he would add, it was assumed that she would don the black robes and become his lover. Each time Kai-lid turned her head away, and

when she looked back, Janusz would be gone, his scent of spices and dust lingering behind him. Her magic was useless in the face of the other mage's greater powers.

But surely she had just heard a summons. Was she hallucinating from lack of food?

Kai-lid Entenaka. Can you hear me? Have caution. I sense the presence of another, who watches. Do not speak aloud.

Kai-lid's trembling dropped away like the sloughed skin of a snake. She forced herself to concentrate, to look within, and to remain seemingly calm in the cold light from the walls, but her heart leaped.

Xanthar, is it you?

A pause. *Do you speak like this with anyone else?*

The lady mage practically sobbed with relief. She hid her emotions by rising and moving to the pail of water under the portal. She filled the dipper and drank deeply, all the while focusing her mind for telepathic speech.

Xanthar, my father has enslaved the Ice Folk. Kitiara has been gone for several days. I don't know if she's alive or dead. I fear she's cooperating with him. I am his prisoner, deep in some ice crevasse. Quickly returning to the parka and resuming her somnolent position under it, she mentally sketched in their trek over the Icereach in the dire-wolf sledge. *You are near, Xanthar?*

We are approaching the Icereach, my dear. I have brought my sons and daughters, and their sons and daughters, plus a few hundred cousins.

Anyone else? She let the parka's hood fall forward to cover her expression.

The half-elf and the Kernan. They will be there soon.

They? Not you, too?

A long pause ensued, until Kai-lid felt fear twist within her. *Xanthar, are you ill? I told you not to travel so far. . . .*

Don't be ridiculous. Even by telepathy, the giant owl's tone was gruff. *Of course I'm coming. And you must be ready to help us.*

I'm helpless! She explained the surroundings and Janusz's offer. *He—he feels responsible for my death—that is, for Dreena's death. Xanthar, Janusz says he hates Kitiara because she stole his ice jewels, but also because he blames her for Dreena's death. He says he loved Dreena. I swear I never knew, Xanthar. He taught both of us magic, Lida and me. He says the love of Dreena's maid would remind him of the happy times of the past.*

The owl pondered long before answering. *You must buy time, and you must get out of that dungeon and rebuild your strength. Comply with the mage, Kai-lid.*

Comply? Kai-lid couldn't hide her disgust. *I'd rather die.*

That appears to be your choice, Kai-lid. But this pride is self-indulgent. We need you. You must find out what the mage has learned from the ice jewels. If you have to suffer his advances in order to do that, then you must. I'm sorry.

But Janusz wants . . .

Suddenly she felt the owl's pain through the telepathic link. She interpreted it as empathy for her, and Xanthar did not correct her. *Say you are ill, Kai-lid, weak from lack of food. Put the mage off as best you can. We need a day or two to find the Ice Folk and plan an attack.* A note of forced humor entered his words. *I know you are absolutely unbelievable as a liar, Kai-lid, but he must believe you, so make a good pretense of going along with him.*

The lady mage sat up, agitated, stroking the seal-skin trim on the sleeves of her parka. Finally she nodded, forgetting that the owl couldn't see her.

Kai-lid?

I will try, Xanthar.

Then . . . The link faded, and Kai-lid sensed that the owl was struggling for words. *Farewell,* he finally said simply.

For now, she amended.

Of course, Xanthar said gruffly after another pause. *For now, my dear.*

Then the link dissipated. Kai-lid waited for a time, wondering if the giant owl were truly gone. Then she raised her voice, addressing the walls. "Janusz? Are you there? I have decided."

Moments later, the mage was at the portal, gazing down at her, hope dancing in his eyes. She let herself sway as she stood looking up at him. "I can stand the hunger no longer, Janusz. I am ill. I will . . . I will do as you ask, but I need time to recover."

As the mage surveyed her, Kai-lid felt a shiver of fear. The mage had been watching her, Xanthar had said. Could Janusz tell that she had been mind-speaking? He'd given no hint that telepathy was one of his skills. She forced her expression to remain blank, but her hands trembled. She toyed with the pouches of spell-casting material at her belt to hide her terror.

But Janusz's next words were neutral. "Very well," he said. He threw the rope down. "Climb up."

She tried, but the parka and her fear of touching the clinging ice hampered her. Finally Janusz spoke an incantation and drifted down beside her. He placed one hand on her shoulder and declaimed a second spell. They rose gracefully into the air, drew even with the portal, and drifted through. Once their feet touched the floor, Janusz helped her down the long hallways to his quarters. She forced herself to lean against him.

* * * * *

Xanthar almost missed the Ice Folk village. The native people covered their dwellings with white fur and snow, and the village blended in perfectly with the glacial setting. Xanthar was nearly blind by now, and the other night-seeing owls were experiencing difficulty in the glare. It was Tanis who spotted the spindle of smoke that trickled up from one of the dwellings. He shouted, and Xanthar angled down, followed by Tanis's owl, whom the half-elf had dubbed Golden Wing, and Caven's mount, whom Tanis had named Splotch, for the mark on his forehead.

At the last moment, instead of landing within the village, Xanthar swung to the south and brought the group down in an open field nearby. The field was outside a wall of gigantic rib bones, taller than a man, that formed a border around the community. The rest of the owl phalanx landed silently. Once again Tanis marveled at the discipline the birds showed. They could fly without a sound, as they had just now, or with a slight change in the way they used their wings, they could soar with the insistent booming that had so unnerved him before.

For a moment, nothing happened. Tanis untied Caven, who regained consciousness to complain about the cold and a splitting headache. Tanis glared him into silence. Neither man was dressed for the bitter wind, which blew right through their clothing.

Then a lone figure, swathed in furs, emerged from a chink in the rib fence. The figure carried a spear and a shiny weapon that seemed to be an ax made of ice. Soon a dozen other figures, similarly dressed and armed, joined the first. At a spoken command, they moved as one toward the giant owls. Tanis slid from Golden Wing and stepped forward. Caven slipped off Splotch, clinging to the owl for a moment, then hurrying unsteadily after the half-elf. Xanthar, a head taller than the other owls and imposing despite his infirmities, shuffled forward, too. Tanis didn't draw his sword, and when Caven moved to pull his weapon from his own scabbard, the half-elf waved for him to stop.

The two groups, one armed, the other staying their weapons, surveyed each other silently. Then one of the Ice Folk, a man of medium height with a dark, hatchetlike face, handed his spear to a companion and used his free hand to pull back his hood. His hair was dark brown, his face smeared with grease— protection against the cold and wind, Tanis guessed. The owls seemed unbothered by the cold, but he and Caven were shivering.

"You speak Common?" the man asked.

"He and I do." Tanis pointed to Caven Mackid and introduced the Kernan, then Xanthar, Golden Wing, Splotch, and himself. The eyes of the giant owls widened as the half-elf uttered their new human names, and Xanthar rubbed his beak with a claw, a movement that Tanis had long since realized signaled amusement. Golden Wing and Splotch merely looked at each other, blinking.

"I am Brittain of the White Bear clan. This is my village. What do you want here?" the leader asked.

Trained in the formalities of Qualinesti greeting rituals, Tanis matched the Ice Folk leader's ceremonial tone. "We have come to the rescue of two friends, kidnapped by an evil man and brought to the Icereach. We fear for their lives—and the lives of the Ice Folk—if he is not stopped."

His men murmured, but the leader didn't move. The wind ruffled the white fur at the edge of his hood. His glance flicked from half-elf to the Kernan, then to the owls. "I believe you are lying. I believe you are an emissary of this evil one of whom we have heard much. I believe that you and your followers seek to learn about yet another village of The People so that you can take this knowledge back to the evil one and his hordes of bull men, walrus men, and two-headed slaves." Brittain scowled. "You are our prisoners." He gestured, and a squad of armed Ice Folk strode forward, grabbing Tanis and Caven by the arms.

"Don't struggle," Tanis whispered to Caven. "We must convince them that we mean no harm. We don't have time to fight another battle."

Caven glared and set his feet in the snow. "I'm a man, half-elf. I will not be taken without a fight!"

Tanis sighed. For a moment, he locked gazes with Brittain. He was surprised to note humor creep into the leader's brown eyes. However, that hint of goodwill, unless he imagined it, was gone as quickly as it had come.

At that instant, Xanthar, Golden Wing, and Splotch stepped forward. Xanthar lifted his head and trilled, and the giant owls in the field beyond turned and massed into lines. As one, they dipped their heads in unmistakable greeting. Xanthar, Golden Wing, and Splotch leaned forward and plucked the hands of the Ice Folk captors from the arms of the half-elf and Kernan.

Brittain signaled to his followers. "These great birds are not of the Icereach . . ." he said tentatively.

"They are from the north, as are we. They desire only good, as do we."

Brittain smiled at last. "We shall see."

"They come at the behest of Xanthar, who is their elder and leader, not at the call of the evil one."

Brittain's smile broadened. "We shall see," he repeated. "You are hardly dressed for the Icereach. Indeed, the evil one would have more sense."

Xanthar trilled again, and Tanis, turning toward the owl, felt a familiar sensation within his mind. Could the bird still speak telepathically? Had he the strength? Caven's own expression was surprised. Brittain, too, seemed alert to some message.

"Grandfather owl," Brittain murmured respectfully. "The People revere the aged, and you appear to have much wisdom."

Xanthar's eyes were closed. His claws gripped the snow so tightly that it melted beneath him. He was concentrating with all his dwindling power, Tanis could see. The telepathy flickered in the half-elf's brain again.

"The . . . the . . ."

It faded and returned. Xanthar staggered with the effort as Golden Wing and Splotch hurried to his side.

"The lovers . . . three, the . . . spell-cast maid . . ." Xanthar took a shuddering breath and leaned against the two owls.

"Tanis!" Caven hissed. "The dream! What's he doing?"

"The winged one of loyal soul," the owl continued. He opened rheumy eyes for an instant. *That's me, half-elf.*

Tanis, too, recited. " 'The foul undead of Darken

Wood, The vision seen in scrying bowl. Evil loosed with diamond's flight.' "

Caven joined in on the second stanza. To Tanis's surprise, Brittain spoke in concert on the third.

> *"The lovers three, the spell-cast maid,*
> *The tie of filial love abased.*
> *Foul legions turned, the blood flows free,*
> *Frozen deaths in snow-locked waste.*
>   *Evil vanquished, gemstone's might."*

The last syllable faded, and the tickling in Tanis's mind ended. Xanthar swayed against Golden Wing for a moment, then he sighed and slumped to the snow. By the time Tanis and Caven had reached him, the giant owl was dead.

A cry of despair rose from Golden Wing, Splotch, and the other owls. Caven swore violently. Tanis was silent. Tears welled in his eyes as hundreds of owls trilled and keened behind him. He felt a hand on his arm and shook it off, thinking it was Caven's, but the hand returned and Tanis looked up. It was Brittain.

"I, too, had a dream," the Ice Folk leader whispered, "many weeks ago, before the evil one destroyed the first village. The Revered Cleric said the dream, sent to warn us, came from the great polar bear. Since then the evil one has taken many of The People." His brown eyes studied Tanis for a moment, the pressure of his hand increasing on Tanis's arm. "You cry real tears for your friend. I am convinced."

Brittain barked orders, and his followers hurried forward to raise Xanthar's body. Leaving the mourning owls on the icy plain, Tanis and Caven accompanied the Ice Folk into the village.

Women and men scurried right and left to accommodate the newcomers. Brittain's wife, Feledaal, gave orders to a crew of women and children who were concocting a vat of fish chowder.

"Prepare for the funeral of a great warrior," Brittain commanded a man in a robe decorated with beads of pebbles and bird bones. "Our Revered Cleric," Brittain indicated respectfully after the man had bowed and hurried off, his beads clicking. "He interprets our dreams and fashions our frostreavers, among other things. Although I am master of our glacier-bound life and the Revered Cleric pretends to follow my dictates, he controls all things spiritual. Thus I sometimes suspect our Revered Cleric has more real power than I do."

Tanis and Caven were speedily equipped with clothing for a glacial climate—fur parkas, sealskin boots lined with fur and sealed with walrus oil, and thick mittens. The travelers also received a strip of leather with slits cut in the front, and Brittain showed Tanis how to position the slits before his eyes and tie the ends behind his head. "To guard against snow blindness during the brightest part of the days," Brittain explained.

Brittain told Tanis he would take him on a tour of the village. Caven, on the other hand, surprised them both by gathering some of the village's warriors and heading back into the area south of the village. "I will show these Ansalon-bound rustics how trained soldiers can fly," he explained stoutly, tying his leather strip around his head.

Brittain pointed toward the largest construction in the village, a dwelling of packed snow and ice topped with white fur and snow. "We gather there for discussions that affect the future of The People," Brittain said. He motioned to two children who leaned against the side of the building and watched the activity with solemn eyes. The rest of the Ice Folk children wore their hair long, but these youngsters' brown locks had been shorn just below the ears. Their face bore smudges of gray and white ash. Neither child smiled. At Brittain's gesture, they came swiftly over, their gazes never leaving the half-elf.

"You must forgive their stares. We have heard of the pointed-eared people to the north, but we have not seen them in this village. Terve, Haudo," he said, his voice gentle, "this is Tanis Half-Elven. He has come to help us fight the evil one." The boy nodded; the girl said nothing. Brittain dismissed them, sending them to help with the food preparation.

"They are in mourning, as you can tell," he explained as soon as the children were out of earshot. "We received from them our first word of the evil one's rapacity. Their parents were killed, and the rest of their village, too."

Tanis turned back toward the children, but they had vanished into a hut. "What do you know of the size and nature of the Valdane's forces?" he asked. Then, at Brittain's quizzical expression, he explained that the Valdane was the name by which he knew the "evil one."

Brittain stood back to make room for two women who struggled past with a seal carcass. "For the evening's chowder," Brittain said. Then he returned to Tanis's question. "We hear reports and estimates from members of The People who have escaped when their villages were attacked, or who have fled the enemy camps and made their way back to us. Thanoi guards distract easily, apparently." He sketched in the latest intelligence of the size and makeup of the Valdane's troops, and where they had established their main camp. "There had been rumors, of course, that some-one of great power had come to the glacier, but the destruction of Haudo and Terve's village was the first proof we had that the power was of evil intent. Since then, reports of fresh atrocities have arrived nearly every day." Brittain turned aside and seemed to be struggling with great emotion. When he turned back, his face was composed but pale. "You will forgive me. Terve and Haudo's mother was my sister."

Brittain forced a dispassionate note into his deliv-ery. "We have heard that the evil one lives under the ice and that the entrance to his dwelling is nearly im-possible to spot. But our spies have located it, and they can pinpoint it on a map. Even better, they can lead us there. Look! One of them is practicing owl flight with your friend!"

As he spoke, four owls whooshed overhead, barely missing the tops of the Ice Folk dwellings. Four parka-clad men clenched the birds by the necks, shouting in a strange tongue. Caven, on Splotch, yelled direc-tions from the rear. The sight brought a faint grin to the Ice Folk leader's face. "They cry out in the tongue of our fathers for the protection of the polar bear," he explained. Then he grew solemn again.

"We have heard sickening rumors of this evil one, and they grow worse with each day," Brittain said, seating himself upon an ice bench next to a dwelling. He indicated the empty space next to him, and Tanis sat, too.

"Rumors?" the half-elf prompted.

Brittain nodded. "Of deadly ice that holds its vic-tims until they die—or are released magically. Our Revered Cleric has an ointment that he believes will offset the ice, but he admits that he has not had the opportunity to test it."

Tanis stored the information away, urging the leader to continue.

"We know that the evil . . . that this Valdane has a powerful mage who sometimes oversees the troops. We know the mage appears old and frail, and our Revered Cleric has posited that the mage's strength wears thin from the oppression of this Valdane. That gives us cause for hope. But the latest rumors have been the most troubling."

"And they are?"

"That the Valdane has found a new commander who has great practical skills and has led enemy troops, within the last days, into a deadly assault against a village of The People."

"What do you know of this new commander?" Tanis pressed.

"Only that it is a woman."

Tanis felt his face grow pale, but he said nothing as Caven and his Ice Folk students returned boisterously from their practice flights. Brittain ushered them all into the large central dwelling for supper—and a planning session.

Chapter 19

The Attack

Tanis knelt in the Ice Folk village, waiting for the Revered Cleric to begin Xanthar's funeral. Behind the half-elf were arrayed several hundred owls.

At this time of the year, the Icereach experienced its own version of spring, but the signs were sparse. The bitter temperatures of winter eased slightly. The wind-swept ranges saw increasing hours of daylight, and dusk lingered long into the night. Although the clatter of the Ice Folk had awakened Caven and Tanis in the middle of the night, it was still light enough to see without the aid of walrus-oil lamps.

Turning a deaf ear to Caven's grumbling, Tanis had slipped on his travel-worn leathers and covered them with a long parka of black sealskin. The half-elf had split the lower seams of the garment with his dagger, like Caven and the Ice Folk warriors, to be able to wear the warm coats comfortably while perched on the backs of the giant owls. The villagers had spent hours fashioning sealskin into harnesses like the one that Tanis now tucked into his pack, but theirs had a certain modification—a loop that would carry the Ice Folk warriors' frostreavers. Slipping the mask to prevent snow blindness into a pocket and putting on the lined boots that Brittain had lent him, Tanis headed for the doorway, bending over at the waist to step beneath the jamb. The Ice Folk kept their entrances as small as possible to conserve heat. Caven followed close on the half-elf's heels.

The sight of a mound of peat had greeted their eyes. The Ice Folk had erected a low bier of ice blocks, with a canvas sling across the top that held Xanthar's shrouded body. Peat, a valuable commodity among the Ice Folk, was piled at the base.

It had taken some negotiating, in the form of gestures and much acting out, to persuade the giant owls to allow the Ice Folk to cremate Xanthar's body. Beyond the trilling and crying that had immediately attended Xanthar's collapse the previous day, the giant owls practiced no formal rites after the death of a comrade. The concept of "funeral" seemed to confound Golden Wing and Splotch. Tanis had attempted to explain that consigning a body to smoke and fire was a great honor among the Ice Folk and that the ceremony, these villagers believed, would release Xanthar's essence to continue to soar across the sky in death as the great bird had in life.

Ultimately the owls seemed unpersuaded but resigned. Tanis was left suspecting that the giant owls believed these humans embraced the astounding view that poor Xanthar was merely frozen and thus would rise from the bier once he was warmed. Their acquiescence was more bemused than sorrowful.

Now the giant owls, no doubt driven as much by curiosity about the Ice Folk as by respect for Xanthar, stood in rows at the rear of the villagers. Silence fell over the crowd. The warriors, attired in sealskin parkas, were kneeling at the fore; others stood behind them, and the owls towered in the back. Tanis was jammed between Caven and Brittain. He sniffed the stench of the special unguent that the Revered Cleric had insisted he and Caven anoint themselves with to protect them from the clinging ice of the Valdane's warren.

The Revered Cleric stood and spoke to the crowd. Tanis realized that while the ordinary people of the village spoke Common, it was a courtesy to the newcomers and not their native language. He could follow little of the cleric's untranslated speech this morning, and he soon gave himself up to his own thoughts—first to musing about Xanthar, and then to wondering whether Kitiara had indeed allied herself with the Valdane.

He glanced over at Caven, his rival of the past few weeks. The Kernan's features were heavy, and Tanis saw exhaustion and sadness written in his eyes. Caught by the half-elf's stare, Caven turned toward him and nodded gravely. After a moment, Tanis inclined his own head, and then, feeling as though something had been settled between him and the Kernan, he turned back toward the Revered Cleric, who leaned toward the bier with a torch.

A sigh rose from the crowd as the flame touched and caught. The women and children began to sing in a minor key, high-pitched, with a walrus-bone flute for accompaniment. Then the warriors joined in, baritones and basses adding depth to the lament. The owls suddenly stood at attention, raised their beaks, and trilled a softer version of the previous day's mourning. All the while, the flames flickered stronger. Finally the canvas that wrapped Xanthar's body began to smolder just as the ice blocks of the bier melted. Almost magically, the owl's body sank into the roaring flames.

At that, the Ice Folk rose as one and filed silently from the central area of the village. The owls parted ranks to permit the humans' passage, then followed.

Soon the warriors were mounted, spiraling into the sky around the column of smoke from Xanthar's pyre, forming a line, and heading south. Two hundred owls flew without riders. Tanis watched from Golden Wing as the Ice Folk's chief scout, mounted on a gray owl, eased into the lead, trailed by three other scouts. Soon the four were out of sight, roaming far ahead.

Caven and Splotch flew at the rear, winging from warrior to warrior, offering advice and encouragement to the neophyte fliers. Brittain, atop a gray and white owl he'd dubbed Windslayer, was positioned next to Tanis. The wind was too strong to permit conversation at anything less than a bellow, so the half-elf and the Ice Folk leader communicated mainly by pointing.

An hour later, the scouts hove into view, darting toward the main group. "They're just over that rise!" Delged, the chief scout, shouted to Brittain and Tanis. "Behind a great wall of ice blocks."

"Describe the camp," the half-elf ordered.

"A thousand minotaurs, walrus men, and ettins," Delged replied, his face red with the wind, the cold, and the shouting. Tanis nudged Golden Wing closer to Windslayer.

"And our people?" Brittain persisted.

"A hundred captives." The scout pointed. "In pens to the east."

"Only a hundred?" Brittain demanded. "But far more than that were taken from the fallen villages!"

The scout looked away from the leader for a moment, then shouted back, "There are bodies of The People strewn across the glacier. Some . . . some appear to have been devoured."

The three were silent for a time. Finally, as the glittering tops of the ice blocks came into view, Tanis pulled Golden Wing into a wide spiral. The rest followed, then moved into the battle positions they'd devised.

Brittain's chief officer, who would free the captives, split off to the left with forty owls and warriors. Brittain and Windslayer would lead the main force, which swooped to the ground now, then rose heavily into the sky again, each owl hefting a jagged chunk of ice in its talons.

"Attack!" Brittain commanded as they passed over the ice blocks.

The mass of bull men, thanoi, and two-headed trolls looked overhead in dumb astonishment. At that moment, the owls altered their flying technique, their wings fighting the wind, booming with noise instead of slipping soundlessly through the air. The resulting roar split the morning air, further terrifying the amazed foe. The thanoi and ettins scattered to the edge of the force. Only the minotaurs remained, calmly preparing for battle. Windslayer, in the lead, dropped his ice chunk onto a minotaur, who toppled to the ground. A pool of blood widened on the snowy terrain. The felled enemy didn't move. The attacking force let out a cheer, and dozens more of the sharp, frozen projectiles hurtled toward the Valdane's forces.

"Where is the leader?" Tanis shouted.

Brittain surveyed the enemy below, but it was Delged, the scout, who provided the answer. "There!" He pointed to a heavyset figure dressed in a leather harness, wielding a battle-ax. "The minotaur! Toj, they call him."

"But what of the woman?" Brittain demanded. "Did you see the woman we've heard about?"

Delged shook his head.

"Only a rumor, maybe," Tanis said. Brittain gave him a look but said nothing. Then the Ice Folk leader nodded at the half-elf, touched the hood of his own parka, and guided Windslayer and the rest of the troops into another attack.

Already more than a hundred enemy soldiers lay motionless on the ground, and not one of Brittain's forces had been lost. Another cheer rose from the Ice Folk, echoed by the captives below. Tanis scanned the camp again and again. Caven pulled next to him on Splotch.

"See any sign of Kit?" Caven demanded.

"Nothing."

"The Valdane? Janusz?"

"Nor them."

"Good. We've taken them by surprise."

The minotaurs had obviously realized that massed forces were vulnerable to an air attack. They scattered and hauled catapults into play. The bull men drove the disorganized ettins before them, forcing the two-headed beasts into the battle despite themselves. Soon Brittain's force was dodging airborne boulders and the same ice blocks they'd hurled at the minotaurs. Tanis watched as a stone broke the wing of an owl, sending the bird and its Ice Folk warrior crashing, screaming, into the Valdane's camp. A second volley from the catapults killed three more owls and riders.

Another shout rose from below, to the east. Tanis saw a score of frostreaver-wielding warriors guide their owls close over thanoi guards, slashing this way and that with the ice weapons. Then more owls, outfitted with harnesses but no riders, flew low over the captives' pens, using their talons and beaks to tear at the walrus men. A third attack followed, and this time each riderless owl rose with an Ice Folk slave in its talons. Clutching the captives' clothing, the birds carried the people away from the camp, then landed and urged the newly freed slaves onto the birds' backs. The captives were weak, but the bravest of them gamely clambered back onto the giant owls. The attackers' forces swelled as more owls retrieved the rest of the captive Ice Folk.

At that moment, Splotch gave a cry; Caven echoed it. A jagged chunk of ice, launched by a catapult, whizzed toward the two. Splotch lurched desperately to the right while Golden Wing dived to the left. Accustomed now to the vagaries of owl riding, Tanis instinctively clenched the harness and ducked close to the tawny owl's back. But Caven teetered, both hands suddenly free. Splotch tried to correct his own movement just as Caven threw himself the other way. With a shout, the Kernan slipped off Splotch and hurtled toward the ground. Splotch dived after him.

Tanis rapped Golden Wing on the tip of his wing. "Help them!" the half-elf ordered. "I can hold on! Go!"

Without hesitation, the golden owl dropped after

Splotch. Tanis tightened his grip on the harness. His eyes watered from the speed of the descent; the icy wind roared in his ears. Golden Wing headed nearly straight down, wings plastered flat against his sides, pinning the half-elf's legs. Splotch was diving likewise.

Suddenly Splotch was next to the falling Caven, then below him. Tanis's mount arrowed toward the Kernan, mere feet beneath them. Then Golden Wing spread his wings with a snap; his feathered head shot up, his stub tail slammed downward, and his horned feet swung forward. The owl's talons grasped the back of Caven's black parka, held on—and then lost their grip.

The movement sent Golden Wing and Tanis spinning. But it slowed Caven's descent. The Kernan sprawled on Splotch's back, caught the harness, and held it. Both owls backpedaled frantically as the ground swirled up toward them. They managed to land in the snow, but Splotch tumbled to one side, sending Caven crashing into the ground, and Golden Wing rolled over twice. Tanis slid into the snow as the tawny owl spun.

"Death to humans!" The shout was deep and strangely accented. The half-elf struggled to his feet in the snow to meet the new threat, then froze when he realized the shout wasn't directed at him at all. Before a stunned Caven Mackid stood the minotaur that Delged had identified as Toj. A ring dangled from his nose, another ring from one ear. A double-edged ax dangled from a heavily muscled arm and hand. The creature roared a Mithas battle cry. The screams of battling and dying minotaurs, ettins, and thanoi resounded around them.

Caven, disoriented, struggled to his knees and

groped for his sword, but the weapon was gone, fallen into the snow. The minotaur's roar turned to a laugh; the sound echoed like a bray across the frozen terrain. Tanis reached for his own sword. The half-elf felt Golden Wing's presence at his side; the owl dropped Tanis's sword into the snow beside him. Roaring again, the minotaur raised the ax above Caven's head.

"Is this how Mithas minotaurs meet their enemies?" Tanis shouted at the beast. "By attacking them when they are weaponless?" The half-elf, sword ready, advanced on the minotaur. The creature towered head and bulging shoulders over him.

The minotaur lumbered toward the half-elf, growling, "Fierce words from a scrawny elf." Behind the minotaur, Caven stood and retrieved his sword. Then, with the minotaur distracted, the Kernan attacked the creature from the rear. Tanis leaped into the fray.

Toj deftly met the onslaught, driving back the human and half-elf and waving away thanoi and ettins who came to his aid. The other minotaurs offered no assistance; they merely nodded gravely to Toj and resumed their catapult attack on the airborne forces. Toj's double-bladed ax waved back and forth before Tanis and Caven. The bull man's left hand held a long whip.

"We can defeat him," Tanis said to Caven.

"I know," the Kernan said. There was no fear in the man now, Tanis could see; the mercenary itched to battle the minotaur. "Minotaurs have their weaknesses, too."

"Don't be too sure, human," came Toj's reply. "You and your elven friend would be better off surrendering now."

"Don't do it, half-elf," Caven said. "He'll kill you. Minotaurs take no prisoners."

What was this minotaur's weakness? Caven wondered. Gambling, perhaps? It's how Caven had won Maleficent, after all. He raised his voice, addressing the minotaur general. "Perhaps we are equally matched on the battlefield, bull man, the one of you against the two of us. Perhaps the three of us would be better off settling this with a game of bones."

"Bones?" Toj echoed. He slowed the ax for a moment, gazing full upon the Kernan. "You propose *games* on the battlefield?" Incredulity filled the minotaur's words. His hooves scraped agitatedly against the ice.

"Unless you fear you'd lose," Caven said offhandedly. "It's likely, you know. I've a fine hand at bones."

Toj snorted. "You bait me, human."

"Winner take all," Caven continued. "If you win, we are your prisoners. If we win, we get you." He whispered to Tanis, "Be ready to attack."

Toj stood stock-still. The minotaur still held his ax in his right hand, a long whip in his left. A crafty look settled on his bovine features. "It's worth a try," Toj said. Caven, still holding his sword, started toward the minotaur. Then the Kernan dived toward the creature, driving straight forward with his sword. "Now, Tanis!" he yelled.

But Tanis was already moving. He lunged toward Toj and twisted aside just in time to avoid the deadly blade of the ax. The half-elf whirled, nicking the minotaur's leather and mail harness. A trickle of blood oozed from Toj's side.

The creature went mad with bloodlust. Toj hurtled at Tanis, and Caven and Tanis drove the minotaur back with their swords. Toj's yell mingled with the din of battle. The whip snaked forward, wrapped around Tanis's left arm, and dragged the half-elf toward his foe.

Tanis managed to keep his head. His sword was in his right hand; he wasn't helpless yet. He allowed Toj to draw him forward. Caven swept down upon the minotaur with a battle cry, but Toj held him off with the ax. Meanwhile Tanis was drawn inexorably closer.

The half-elf pretended to fight the whip, feigning panic. Tanis saw satisfaction settle on the minotaur's furred face. When the half-elf was within reach of Toj's ax, he saw the weapon begin to hurtle toward him.

At that moment, Tanis stopped resisting the pull of the whip. Instead, he dove toward the minotaur, inside the arc of the ax.

Tanis drove his sword deep into the minotaur. Before Toj's companions had a chance to react, Tanis and Caven were racing toward the waiting Splotch and Golden Wing. Within minutes, the two men were circling high above the seething army again.

Delged, the scout, shouted to Tanis and Caven. "Hurry!" He and his owl darted to the south. The roar of the battle had receded behind them when Delged urged his owl into a descent. He pointed again. Tanis saw the slash of blue-gray in the seemingly endless snow, saw the shadow that Delged had said masked the entrance to the Valdane's castle. Golden Wing and Splotch landed, waiting until Tanis retrieved his pack, bow, and sword, and Caven his own weapon. Then the owls leaped into the air again and, with Delged, headed back toward the battle without so much as glancing back.

Tanis stepped cautiously to the edge of the crevasse. Caven followed and poked at the grayish snow with his toe. "I hope the scouts have the right crevasse," Caven muttered. Suddenly a chunk of snow broke away, followed by the entire slab that had hidden the glacial crack. The two gaped into the depths. The sides of the crevasse emitted weird blue light; they could see no bottom to the plunge.

"Just jump, Delged said," Caven muttered softly. "And to think I used to be afraid of heights."

Tanis smiled, his smile masking his own fear.

"Tell me again why I'm doing this," Caven continued, his face sweaty, his gaze unwaveringly set on the crevasse.

"The poem," Tanis replied. " 'Lovers three' . . . That's you and me and Kitiara. The 'spell-cast maid' is Lida."

"So you've said," Caven muttered. "But move ahead a bit to the part about 'frozen deaths in snow-locked waste.' Is that us, too?"

"I believe we all have to be together, with the ice jewels, for Lida's magic to be able to defeat the Valdane and his mage," Tanis said. "I hope it's *their* deaths that are mentioned in the verse. Anyway, it's too late to go back now."

"It's never too late," the Kernan said in a low voice. As Tanis was about to reply, Caven leaped into the crevasse. The half-elf bounded after him.

Soon they stood safely at the bottom, staring at the dungeon's walls and the corpses. "To starve in such a place," Caven whispered. "That's no way for a warrior to die." His hands clenched his sword so tightly that his knuckles turned white.

Tanis pointed to the portal some height above the floor. "If I stood on your shoulders, I could pull myself up through there and then haul you up."

"What about the ice wall?"

294

"Let's hope the cleric's ointment works."

"Cheerful thought," Caven said. The Kernan sighed, bent over, and interwove the fingers of his hands. Tanis placed a booted foot in Caven's hands, climbed onto his shoulders, and after the Kernan stood upright, gingerly placed an ointment-daubed finger on the edge of the portal. His finger didn't stick. The half-elf pulled himself through and tossed the rope that hung from a peg next to the portal down to Caven. Tanis felt edgy. "This is too easy," he muttered.

Caven heard him. "You're too suspicious, half-elf. Even if they knew we were coming, they probably thought we'd get caught in the dungeon or stuck to the walls like the rest."

Swords drawn, they stood quietly in the hallway. "Not a sound," Tanis observed.

"We're a long way underground," Caven added doubtfully.

"Aren't there any guards?"

The two men crept through the hall. The illumination from the ice was so even that it cast no shadows, but it cast both men in a ghostly mien. "Maybe it's a good sign that Kitiara and Lida weren't in the dungeon," Caven whispered. "Maybe the Valdane is treating them well."

"And maybe the women have gone over to his side," Tanis said.

"Kitiara, maybe. But not the lady mage."

They came to the end of the hallway. Other halls branched to the right and left. A short way down, each branched again. Caven swore. Tanis picked the far right one and headed down it. "It's as good as any," he explained to Caven.

Just then, Caven reached the end of the hall. As he hesitated, a hairy form lunged at him. A second form caught Tanis from behind. Three more ettins waited behind the first two.

The two men struggled, but they were woefully outnumbered. Soon the ettins had overpowered and disarmed them.

"Caught, caught," one ettin sang out. "Master right. Big dumb guys walk right in trap." He snickered and hopped up and down, cracking Caven's head against the wall twice in his enthusiasm.

"Big dumb . . . You idiot, Res-Lacua!" Caven spat out. "Stop that jumping!"

The ettin halted and gazed at the Kernan with both pairs of eyes. "You know Res?" the right head asked suspiciously.

"I fight for the Valdane, you dolt! Don't you remember me?" When the right head continued to look stupefied, Caven turned to Lacua. "Do *you* remember me?"

Lacua nodded slowly. "Long time ago. Not now."

"Let go of me," Caven ordered. "The Master would be furious."

Tanis held his tongue. Slowly the ettin loosened his hold on Caven Mackid. The Kernan straightened his clothing. "Now take me and my prisoner to Captain Kitiara."

Res-Lacua gazed from Caven to Tanis. "Prisoner?"

"Yes. A . . . a gift for Captain Kitiara."

Two sets of eyebrows furrowed. "Not captain."

"Yes, the Captain."

"General."

Caven barely suppressed a double-take. "Yes . . . Well, take me to *General* Kitiara." He drew himself erect. "Now!" he added. The ettin's four eyes turned toward Tanis, who slumped and tried to look as much like a prisoner as possible. The other ettins mumbled, but in no language that the half-elf understood.

"Master said to bring to him," Res-Lacua insisted.

"To General Kitiara. He meant to say General Kitiara," Caven insisted. "He told me so. After you left him—ah, just now. I just came from him."

Two pairs of pig eyes squinted. Res-Lacua frowned. "Take to Master," Lacua said stubbornly. "Yes, yes," added Res. Just as Caven appeared about to insist once more, the ettin's left face brightened. "But," Lacua said happily, "General *with* Master!"

"Marvelous," Tanis hissed to Caven as the two were escorted down one hallway, then another, then a third. "Pay attention to the route," Tanis added. "We may need to leave in a hurry."

"Up through the crevasse? How?" Caven attempted to pause to talk to the half-elf, but Res-Lacua hauled him down the corridor.

"Don't forget—with luck, we'll have a mage with us," Tanis reminded him.

Several twists and turns later, Tanis and Caven stood before the Valdane in his chambers. The Valdane lounged on a gilded throne, his red hair bright against the purples and blues of his loose silk shirt. Behind him, Janusz worked over a wide bowl on a table set before what looked like a window. Lida assisted him, handing him salvers holding what appeared to be herbs. She didn't meet the captives' eyes. Kitiara, dressed in polished black leather leggings, a tight bodice under chain mail, and a sealskin cape trimmed with thick white fur, had no such reservations. Her stare was cold. She stood motionless at the side of the Valdane's throne.

The view in the window shifted, and suddenly Tanis was gazing at the battleground he'd just left. But it was different now. Puffy white clouds, looking almost friendly, floated above the attacking army, where before the sky had been clear. The Valdane's troops were edging out from under the clouds, but the attacking army seemed not to have noticed.

"By the gods!" Caven murmured. "Magefire?"

"I see you remember the Meiri, Mackid," the Valdane said. "But, no, not magefire. Something much better. Something the ice jewels taught the mage. Magesnow, I imagine you'd call it. They, of course"—and he indicated the window—"will think it the agony of the Abyss."

"*Aventi olivier,*" Janusz chanted, and all of the ettins but Res-Lacua vanished from the Valdane's quarters. Tanis saw the other four appear among the troops in the window.

Janusz dusted the surface of the bowl with orange powder. "*Sedaunti avaunt, rosenn.*" Lida's features grew more tense with each word, as though she were concentrating hard on something deep within her. She still didn't look up at the newcomers.

A scream pealed from the window. The roar came from the warriors atop the attacking owls. Snow had drifted down upon them from the clouds. But this snow twinkled, and when it touched Brittain's flying corps, it burned. Several warriors lost their holds on their harnesses and pitched to the ground below. A few owls gyrated from the pain of the magesnow, unseating their riders and darting this way and that in a frenzy. Thunder rumbled. The minotaurs and the enemy had taken cover under tarpaulins.

Tanis caught sight of Brittain atop Windslayer, gesturing with his frostreaver and issuing orders as though the magesnow were but an irritant, as though he'd fought many a battle from several hundred feet above the ground.

"Stop it, Janusz!" Lida suddenly begged. "Stop, at least for now. I can't stand it. Dreena's death . . ." She clutched his black robe with a brown hand.

Tanis saw a look of regret pass over the evil mage's features. "I can't, Lida," he said softly. "This is war, and I must do my part. It will be over quickly."

Then the screams ended, as though Janusz's prediction had come true. But Tanis could see that the mage was as surprised as he was.

"What is it?" the Valdane demanded. "Is it over already?" He sounded disappointed.

"They've gone above the clouds," Janusz said wonderingly. "By Morgion, they flew right into the clouds and through them! The pain . . ."

"But they're safe now?" Lida asked.

"For the moment."

Lida sighed.

"Raise the clouds, you idiot," the Valdane snapped. "There must be a spell for that."

"Valdane," the elder mage said with a sigh, "despite what you may think, there is more to magic than reciting a few words. Much study is involved. And . . ."

"And?"

". . . and I am not yet fully adept in controlling the magesnow clouds. It requires a great deal of study from my books and conferring, practicing, with the ice jewels."

"Well, then, study!"

With another sigh, Janusz indicated a blue-bound book upon the table. Lida brought it to him and bent her head with his over the tome.

The Valdane pulled himself erect and gripped the arms of his throne. "Now," he said to the half-elf, "about the ice jewels . . ."

"We don't have them," Tanis said.

"Yet you know what they are."

Caven broke in. "We traveled with Kitiara, after all."

The Valdane smiled, but the movement was devoid of humor. His blue eyes glinted. "Where have you hidden them?"

Kitiara put a gloved hand on the Valdane's shoulder. "They haven't hidden them," she said to the leader. "They have them now." Janusz and Lida looked up from their work.

Nausea rose in Tanis. Brittain was right; Kitiara had joined the Valdane. He and Caven had ventured across Ansalon only to meet their deaths at her whim. "I left the pack in Darken Wood," the half-elf said sullenly. Janusz laughed, but Lida made no sound.

"Yes," Caven echoed. "In Darken Wood."

"No," Kitiara corrected them. "You brought my pack with you." She pointed to the pack in Tanis's hand.

The Valdane turned in his throne and stared hard at Kitiara. She met his gaze. "I told you you could trust me, Valdane," she said softly, smiling provocatively. "We'll make a great pair. I've proved that, haven't I?"

"Astounding," he murmured.

"Tanis," Kitiara declared, "cooperate with the Valdane. Join our cause. It will be well worth your while."

"I forget where I hid the ice jewels," Tanis said. He let his eyelids drop and glanced to the side, marking where Res-Lacua stood, holding his and Caven's swords. Neither man would die without fighting, that was certain.

Kitiara stepped down from the dais that held the throne and moved toward the table where the two mages sat. "Tanis, Caven," she said. "Don't be fools!"

"This is ridiculous," the Valdane snapped. "Ettin, ake the pack from the half-elf."

"Wait!" Kitiara commanded. Surprisingly, the lead-r held up a hand. "Bring the jewels to Janusz, half-elf. Ie's the only one who can use them, anyway."

"He'll kill everyone who stands in his way," Tanis aid. "Including you, Kitiara."

"But, Tanis," she rejoined smoothly, "I have no in-ention of standing in the mage's way, or the Valdane's." Her brown eyes stared straight into his tilt-d hazel ones. "Come here, Tanis. *Come stand by me nd Lida*, both of you, and bring out the ice jewels vhere we all can admire them."

Res-Lacua, clenching the captives' swords in one and, stood between Tanis and Kitiara, and Tanis un-lerstood then.

"Tanis, don't!" Caven shouted as Tanis stepped for-vard with the pack. An arm's length from Lida, the alf-elf opened the false bottom as the Kernan leaped orward. Violet light from the jewels spilled into the oom, and the Valdane gave a moan. Janusz's eyes lowed, while Lida's filled with tears.

Then suddenly Kitiara was at their side, their words in her hands. The ettin gaped witlessly. The Valdane swore and drew his dagger.

"Tanis!" Kitiara shouted. "Give Lida the jewels!"

The swordswoman whirled toward the female pell-caster and ordered, "You, mage, you've been tudying with Janusz. Use the jewels to get us out of ere. Now!"

Lida closed her eyes and began to chant. She held ut her hands, and Tanis leaped to place the eight re-naining stones on her palms. A spasm of pain cross er face, but she continued to speak the words of nagic. "*Teleca nexit. Apprasi-na cas. Teleca nexit.*

Apprasi-na cas." Over and over she chanted the strange words, until they wove in among themselves like fine needlework, one word indistinguishable from the next. "*Teleca nexit. Apprasi-na cas. Teleca-nexitapprasinacas.*"

Janusz raised a hand to strike Lida, but Caven jumped forward, sword at the ready. The Valdane hurtled toward Kitiara with fury, and Tanis whirled to shield the swordswoman.

Res-Lacua blinked stupidly at the humans. Then he saw the sword of the bearded, black-haired merce-nary slash the hand of the Master. As Janusz cried out and flung himself back against the wall, clutching his hand, the ettin came to life. "Master!" he roared, grabbing Caven around the midsection. He hurled the Kernan against the opposite wall and laughed at the sound of Caven Mackid's neck breaking.

Kitiara lunged at the ettin, her sword piercing the two-headed creature through his one heart. With his last vestige of strength, Res-Lacua tossed her against the Valdane's throne. Kitiara slid, unconscious, to the floor.

Lida's voice cut through the furor. "Tanis!" she cried. "I can't use them! The jewels . . . they're too powerful." She moaned, then collapsed, sobbing, against the table, the glowing stones spilling from her lap across the floor.

Tanis had no time for the lady mage. Caven was dead. Kitiara lay senseless on the floor, perhaps dying. That left the half-elf alone against the Valdane and the mage. Tanis plunged toward Janusz. Even as the half-elf flew toward the wizened spell-caster, Janusz spoke new words of magic, and Tanis slammed into an invisible wall. The mage grinned at the half-elf. "A protection spell," the wizard noted.

But Tanis's attention was riveted. The Valdane's fingers were bloodied, even though neither Tanis nor Caven had touched the leader. "The bloodlink," the half-elf rasped. "Wode was right. What hurts one, hurts the other. . . . Maybe what *kills* one will also *kill* the other," he added in a louder voice.

The mage's smile never wavered. "The force field protects us both," he said. "And you won't survive much longer in any case. I can magically summon minions at any moment."

Lida raised her head. "No, Janusz," she whispered. "You can't cast magic through such a protection spell. You would have to lift the first spell in order to do that."

Tanis waited at the periphery of the zone of protection, his sword in one hand, his dagger in the other. "And as soon as you lift it, I will kill you," he said.

Tanis beckoned the lady mage to his side with a gesture. Kicking the spilled jewels aside, Lida hurried to Tanis.

"The poem," he said softly. She raised her brows in question. "The portent, I believe, was sent by your mother from wherever she is, either dead . . ."

". . . or escaped to Darken Wood," Lida broke in. "As I believe."

Tanis went on, his voice a low whisper. "The poem called for you and Kitiara and Caven and I to be together with the jewels, for you to work the magic to end all this." Janusz's gaze never left them. The Valdane was curiously still, his eyes alert. Tanis continued. "But Caven is dead, and Kitiara is unconscious. There's only we two, Lida . . . Kai-lid."

Lida's mouth opened slightly. Tanis saw her lips move, and he realized she was reciting the poem of portent to herself. Her focus shifted; she turned inward, and her eyes, her face, went blank for a moment. Then she spoke. "Xanthar isn't at the battle, is he? He is dead." It wasn't really a question. Tanis nodded.

Lida swallowed hard and dipped her head. When she looked up, there was new resolution in her eyes. She faced Janusz. A flicker of puzzlement showed in the older mage's face. She addressed the Valdane, who noted her movements warily. "You knew my mother long ago," she said. "You tormented her ceaselessly, until she called on those who would succor her, and escaped. It was to her eternal sorrow, I believe, that she couldn't take her young daughter with her, but the rules of Darken Wood are strange and often unfathomable . . . as I well know."

Lida drew another breath; her voice grew stronger. "When the time came, she appeared to help me." Lida clasped her hands and recited,

> *"The lovers three, the spell-cast maid,*
> *The tie of filial love abased,*
> *Foul legions turned, the blood flows free,*
> *Frozen deaths in snow-locked waste.*
> *Evil vanquished, gemstone's might.*

"Two of the three lovers appear to be gone, Valdane," Lida went on. "But I am three, too. I am Lida Tenaka, handmaiden to the Valdane's daughter," she said. "Or so I appear to you." Her hands untied a pouch at her waist, took out a pinch of herb dust, then opened another sack with the same fluid movement.

"I am also Kai-lid Entenaka of Darken Wood, friend and student of the mentor, Xanthar," she went on.

She tossed the herbs into the air; red and blue dust caught in her sleek black hair.

"*Temporus vivier*," she whispered. "*Reveal, reveal.*"

At that instant, Lida's hair gleamed ash-blond, not black. The Valdane uttered a cry. The woman's azure gaze, so like her father's, skewered the Valdane.

"And finally I am Dreena ten Valdane," she concluded, "saved from death by magefire through the love of my servant."

Janusz moaned deeply and spoke a word of magic. At that moment, Tanis was able to push forward; the spell of protection had dissipated. The half-elf flung Dreena aside, even as the Valdane dove for her. Tanis hurtled toward Janusz and drove his sword deep into the wizened mage's breast.

The older mage collapsed without another word. At the same time, the Valdane screamed in agony, crashing to the floor at Dreena's feet. Blood spurted from the leader's chest, not from Janusz's, although the sword stuck in Janusz's breast.

The sound of chanting rose behind Tanis. Dreena was twirling around slowly, hands outstretched, an ice jewel in each cupped palm. "*Terminada a ello. Enondre du shirat.*" She swirled faster, her slippered feet a blur at the hem of her robe. "*Terminada a ello. Enondre du shirat.*" Tanis heard a groan come from the walls around him. At that, Dreena slowed and halted. She shook her head, tears in her eyes, and spoke. "Janusz's death will bring destruction. I have done what I could to give us some time to escape. But we must leave now, quickly."

"And the jewels?" Tanis asked, hurrying to the unconscious Kitiara and gathering her in his arms.

Without a word, Dreena flung the stones from her with a spasm of disgust.

Beads of water appeared on the ice wall. The dying Valdane tried to reach for an ice jewel, but Tanis kicked the stone out of his reach. Suddenly, as the room grew warmer, the floor turned damp and slick. Tanis and Dreena made their way carefully to the door. They paused at Caven's body. "We'll have to leave him," Dreena murmured.

"I know." Tanis offered a silent farewell to the Kernan. The ice blocks were gradually giving way. At the doorway, Dreena hesitated, looking back at the mage who had loved her, and her father who had betrayed her, but Tanis forced her out into the corridor.

The mage had slumped to the dais. The Valdane tried to crawl after the trio, but he collapsed after a few feet.

Snow sifted from the ceiling, a gray-white veil drawing a curtain on the room of the dead and the dying.

"Tanis! Hurry!"

Tanis ran down the corridor after Dreena. Suddenly the ice walls lost their illumination, plunging them into total darkness.

"Janusz is dead. Thus so is my father," Dreena said flatly. "*Shirak.*"

Magelight glowed around them, lighting their way. Dreena halted in confusion in the maze of corridors. "This way," shouted the half-elf, and guided by the magelight, he sped down one corridor, Kitiara a heavy weight across his shoulder. Soon Tanis saw the rope coiled at the portal above the dungeon. He slid to a halt at the opening. "Can you levitate us up through the crevasse?" he asked the mage.

"I don't know," she replied. "I can tr—"

A roar interrupted her words. The two of them leaped back as tons of snow crashed down from above the dungeon.

"The crevasse," Dreena said weakly, her face paling to porcelain in the magelight.

"Is there another way out?" Tanis demanded.

"Not that I know of." At that instant, Dreena grabbed the half-elf's arm and towed him back up the corridor. "Janusz's quarters!" she shouted back. "His books!"

Many of the corridors had collapsed inward by now. Tanis, burdened by Kitiara, stepped carefully over the ice shards and drifted snow that impeded their path. He saw the luminous circle of magelight disappear through a door, and followed.

Then ensued a supreme test of the half-elf's patience. As the ice palace crumbled around them, he had to wait while Dreena riffled through the mage's parchments and books, then, when she crowed with joy and burrowed into one bound sheaf of parchment, he had to wait minutes longer while she studied and memorized the appropriate spell.

One wall of Janusz's spartan quarters had collapsed into slush. The melting ice made groaning noises. Tanis practically had to shout to be heard. "Can't you just read the spell?"

Dreena's long blond hair waved as she shook her head. "A mage must memorize the spell in order to use it properly. Now be still." She closed the book and shut her eyes. Her lips moved, but no sound issued. Then she began to chant, "*Collepdas tirek. Sanjarinum vominai. Portali, vendris.*" Nothing happened. Dreena cast around her as Tanis shifted his weight from foot to foot. Kitiara moaned, draped over one of his shoulders. Then Dreena reached for a box, a rosewood box with intricate carvings of bull men and thanoi. She opened it, and violet light bathed her face. She cradled the lone stone. *"Collep-das tirek. Sanjarinum vominai. Portali, vendris."* Her hands danced.

Just as the three vanished from Janusz's quarters, the Valdane's stronghold buckled with a crash. Suddenly Dreena and Tanis, still carrying Kitiara, were treading water in a frigid lake teeming with minotaurs, walrus men, and ettins.

Tanis held Kitiara's head above the water, searching for Dreena. She was bobbing nearby, swimming capably but shivering almost uncontrollably.

A vast section of the Icereach had imploded, melted, and turned into frigid sea. The bodies of slain Ice Folk and owls floated on every side. Tanis saw thanoi swim through the water, seeking safety, mindless of the cold and heedless of the presence of the half-elf, Kitiara, and Dreena. Minotaurs, tangled in pounds of metal weaponry, struggled in the waves. Ettins perished as each creature's heads argued whether solid ground lay on one side or another.

Golden Wing and Splotch, crisscrossing the waters just above reach of the struggling army, plucked Tanis, Dreena, and Kitiara from the icy waters. They rejoined the attacking force, which was safe on the backs of owls, high above the swirling lake. Kitiara awakened to find herself pinned in front of the shivering half-elf on the back of Golden Wing and gazing, not at Lida, but at Dreena.

"Who . . . ?"

Then Kitiara's mouth gaped in horror as Dreena ten Valdane tossed the last ice jewel, the one she had taken from Janusz's quarters, into the lake far below.

"What are you doing?" the swordswoman screamed at the mage. The glowing stone hit the water and vanished beneath the surface—and at that moment the lake refroze, trapping the remains of the Valdane's army. Even as Tanis watched, snow began to drift across the ice, packed with grotesque figures frozen in death.

Only a third of the attacking force had survived. Brittain saluted Tanis from the back of Windslayer, but there was no sign of his scouts or his chief officer. The victorious army spiraled higher, then swooped north across the snowy range. Tanis sat up, ignoring the bitter wind and Kitiara's complaining, and looked homeward.

The snow fell with a fury. Except for a slight depression on the ground, there was no sign they'd been there at all.

Epilogue

*After leaving the Ice Folk, the giant owls head-*ed north with Tanis, Kitiara, and Dreena. The mage had resumed her Darken Wood guise and answered only to the name of Kai-lid, insisting that now, truly, Dreena was dead. The birds deposited Kitiara and Tanis on the road outside Solace. Kai-lid and the giant owls flew south toward Darken Wood, and the half-elf and swordswoman turned toward Solace.

After a while, Tanis gave up quizzing Kitiara about her pregnancy and about her role in the attack on the Ice Folk. She contended stubbornly that she'd been merely pretending to be an advisor to the Valdane in order to stall for time until Tanis and Caven showed up. About the pregnancy, she was adamant.

"Xanthar was wrong," she snapped. "The only thing that owl was good for was transportation. Although the concept of a mounted army flying high above the enemy does intrigue me, half-elf. Perhaps the owls would be interested in the mercenary life."

"You're changing the subject."

Kitiara swiveled around and swore. "Half-elf, let it go. If I were with child, I'd know it, wouldn't I? And why would I hide that from you, of all people?"

Tanis just looked at her. After a time, she reddened and looked away. "The owl was wrong," she repeated, running her hand through her curls.

"Was Kai-lid wrong, too?"

She didn't answer. They walked on in silence. Soon they halted on the stone path outside Flint Fireforge's home in Solace. In a moment, Tanis would rejoin the dwarf and Kitiara would seek out her twin brothers.

"Kitiara," Tanis said, rallying, then paused and frowned. "I . . ."

"Don't, half-elf. You'd expect too much of me. I'd disappoint you, and then you'd end up hating me for being the woman I am." She looked down at her hand, resting on the hilt of her sword.

* * * * *

A few months later, the swordswoman disappeared. She reappeared several months after that, claiming disappointment at not having found the purple stone that had been lost in the Plains of Dust. But Kitiara seemed curiously at peace for the first time in months.

Tanis was left wondering.

DragonLance® Saga

Meetings Sextet
The Adventures Continue

The Companions: Vol. Six
Tina Daniell
Caramon, Sturm, and Tasslehoff are transported by a magical windstorm to the eastern Bloodsea, and Raistlin convinces Flint and Tanis to journey with him to rescue them. Once in Mithas, however, the companions must battle the Nightmaster of the minotaurs, who plans to conquer Krynn. On sale January 1993.

Kindred Spirits: Vol. One—Flint Fireforge travels to Qualinesti, where he meets the half-elf Tanis and becomes embroiled in political intrigue and betrayal.

Wanderlust: Vol. Two—Tasslehoff Burrfoot accidentally pockets one of Flint's bracelets, triggering a dangerous adventure for Flint, Tanis, and the kender.

Dark Heart: Vol. Three—The story of beautiful, dark-hearted Kitiara's fascination with evil, and of the birth of her twin brothers, Raistlin and Caramon.

The Oath and the Measure: Volume Four—Sturm leaves his friends Raistlin and Caramon to seek a place with the Knights of Solamnia. In searching for the truth about his father, he discovers an old enemy and a new friend, both of whom hide their true intent.

DragonLance Saga

Tales II Trilogy

The Reign of Istar
& *The Cataclysm*
On sale now
The War of the Lance
On sale November 1992

Margaret Weis and Tracy Hickman,
Michael Williams,
and Richard A. Knaak,
among others,
return to the DRAGONLANCE® World
in this trilogy of anthologies.